Praise for

A Place to Call Home

"A gracefully written and absorbing tale . . . seductive . . . a page-turner."—*Publishers Weekly*

"Laughter, wonderment, unrequited love! Meddling old biddies, warring families, lovers reunited. What more could you want?"—Rita Mae Brown

"These characters leap off the pages. A moving story that holds you to the end and has all the warmth and tenderness of LaVyrle Spenser at her best." —Iris Johansen

"A must-read . . . sweet, salty, passionate and wise."
– *Woman's Own*

"This incredibly magical book will bring a tear to your eye and a smile to your heart. Storytelling at its VERY best!"
– *Romantic Times*

"Clear the decks when you read this book because you're not going to be able to to put it aside until you've finished the last delicious page."—Janet Evanovich

"An engrossing read. The reader's sense is that these two could only belong to one another, and no one else. I also loved the rich detail of family life, especially the uniquely Southern aspects." —Eileen Goudge

BY DEBORAH SMITH

from bantam books

When Venus Fell

A Place to Call Home

Silk and Stone

Blue Willow

When Venus Fell

DEBORAH SMITH

Bantam Books

NEW YORK TORONTO LONDON SYDNEY AUCKLAND

This edition contains the complete text
of the original hardcover edition.
NOT ONE WORD HAS BEEN OMITTED.

When Venus Fell

A Bantam Book

PUBLISHING HISTORY
Bantam hardcover edition published July 1998
Bantam mass market edition / October 1999

ISBN: 0-553-56279-7

Published simultaneously in the United States and Canada

Bantam Books are published by Bantam Books, a division of Random House,
Inc. Its trademark, consisting of the words "Bantam Books" and the portrayal
of a rooster, is Registered in U.S. Patent and Trademark Office and in other
countries. Marca Registrada. Bantam Books, 1540 Broadway, New York, New
York 10036.

PRINTED IN THE UNITED STATES OF AMERICA

OPM   10 9 8 7 6 5 4 3 2 1

Dedication

Well into her elderly years my paternal grandmother regularly tucked her sawed-off shotgun into the crook of her arm, set her straw sunhat firmly on her head, and set out to walk the boundaries of our farm. She never found any trespassers worth shooting, and I was never quite certain who or what she feared might threaten us, but her message was clear and strong.

Protecting our family's land was a sacred duty.

That isn't an uncommon idea among farm-born southerners of an older generation. As suburban subdivisions and malls creep across the farmland there are still stories of old men and old women who turn down millions of dollars in order to leave their homesteads to their children and grandchildren. To own even a small piece of land is to have roots, to have a home, to never turn your face away from who and what and where you are.

And so it's natural for me to write about the Camerons, a family of southerners who will go to any lengths to preserve their isolated mountain valley and historic house. The allure of old homes, whether grand or simple, is as powerful as the love for the land. An old home breathes with memories; its walls can talk if you listen hard enough.

When my family finally had no choice except to sell our farm and move on, the new owner cut the old house in two, carted half of it away, and bulldozed the rest. I collected a wheelbarrow full of faded, red, handmade bricks from the foundation, and hundred-pound granite rocks that lined my grandmother's side yard.

These solid pieces are part of my homeplace, now. Part

of my land, which I walk with pride and defense and love, as my grandmother did.

And so this book is for her, my father's mother, my grandmother Rachel Bennett Brown. And as always, for my husband, Hank, and for my mother, who walk with me.

Let the music swell the breeze,
And ring from all the trees
Sweet freedom's song,
Let mortal tongues awake;
Let all that breathe partake;
Let rocks their silence break,
the sound prolong.

"My Country 'Tis of Thee"

—THE SECOND VERSE, WHICH NO ONE SINGS

When Venus Fell

Prologue

By the time Gib Cameron found us, my sister and I were failed southern belles who could no longer count on the kindness of strangers. We lived like gypsies. Home was a forgotten memory. Like lost birds, we had migrated to a cold climate. Our distant connection to Gib and his family was all we had left of an innocent and proud past.

"Pride and self-respect are earned, not given by birth," Pop always told us when we were growing up amid the gothic gentility of New Orleans. "Nothing else matters." He had had more pride beaten into him than any man deserved, and it nearly destroyed us.

Ella had developed a chronic case of what would have been called the fancies in more polite eras, and I was well on my way to becoming what would have been deemed a pinched-heart hellion. In more polite eras, of course.

Purists might insist my sister and I were never southern belles to begin with. Pedigree alone should have disqualified us. Our steel-magnolia family tree included one Japanese grandmother and one grandmother of Swedish extraction, who was a truck-stop floozy. Our father was a California-bred Italian-Asian American, not to mention a Communist.

He spent his childhood in a California internment camp during World War II. His Japanese mother—my grandmother Akiko—died there, and Pop swore he'd hate the United States government for the rest of his life.

So maybe my sister and I were doomed from the start.

When I was a child my piano tutors told stories about the Phantom Alligator Lady of Bayou Caveaux. Rumor had it she was a failed concert pianist, though when I was a little girl none of my tutors would admit she existed except in self-serving piano-tutor mythology.

They claimed folks glimpsed her around one of the concrete-walled, rusty-roofed little houses off a swampy back road a few miles outside New Orleans. She had doomed her career, her youth, her very soul because she let worldly distractions steal her art. Thus she turned into a crazy, bitter old failure who lured children into her home and forced them to play an untuned upright until they died, mind you—and then she carried their bodies outside and fed them to her alligators. I guess you could say she was the ultimate music critic.

I not only believed in the Alligator Lady, I carried the fear of her into adulthood. I heard her whispering encouragement in the back of my mind like a ten-cent harmonica gone sharp.

I pictured myself growing old and mean, peering spitefully out my windows at strangers while I eked out a living, teaching piano lessons to nose-picking ten-year-olds who deserved no better audience than my asthmatic pet toy poodle—which I would name Dog, or Poodle, because my mind would be gone by then. And while my students practiced I'd drink iced tea mixed with gin as I apathetically watched the poodle hoist his tiny hind leg and pee on dusty scrapbooks filled with clippings that proved I'd been a child piano prodigy, once upon a time.

And those clippings might have been all that was worth telling about Venus Arinelli. Or about any Arinelli, I guess. We were culturally jumbled but southern clear through by the grace of a god who obviously knows where odd people will best fit in. Yet everyone is made up of parts and pieces of their family's music. The saddest thing is to forget where our songs end and our parents' begin, because each of us plays the next note for them.

Before Gib Cameron found me, I was sinking into silence.

One

When the Oklahoma City federal building blew up, Ella and I had just signed a six-month contract to perform in the piano lounge of a hotel in New York. It was the best job we'd had in years.

"You and your sister are fired," the manager announced. "Pack up your equipment and get out. I won't have people like you working in my club."

The TV sets above the club's bar were turned to CNN, where a tape replay showed rescue workers carrying dead and injured children from the rubble in Oklahoma City. Ella had been pale and hollow-eyed for two days. I was scared and on alert, expecting trouble.

"We have a contract," I reminded the manager, a burly man whose suits cost more than he paid us in a month. "And we haven't done anything wrong."

"I know about your old man," he replied, jerking his head toward the TV, his face as red as the rare prime rib served in the bar's dining room. "A couple of federal agents are in my office. They want to ask you and your sister some questions. They say you've got connections to antigovernment groups."

"They always do. If a kid throws a rock at a government

building, these guys show up wherever we are and ask us if we know who did it. But we have nothing to do with that. We never had anything to do with it. We just want to be left alone to earn a living."

"Government agents don't ask questions unless they think you know something. I was in the Army. I believe in this country. I don't want my business associated with a group of immoral fanatics."

"Neither do I, but they show up more often than a government holiday."

"What are you talking about?"

"The FBI. Government men. It was a joke."

"You think our government is a joke?"

"Not at the moment. Look, my sister and I need this job, but I won't apologize for my father. He wasn't a monster."

"That's enough! Get out of my club. You're trouble."

This wasn't the first time Ella and I had been fired because the Feds dropped by to tell our boss we were Max Arinelli's daughters. I dragged myself back to our dressing room. Ella was watching CNN on a portable TV and crying softly.

"We're outta here, Sis." I grabbed a piece of our gear and hoisted it to one shoulder. She turned to stare at me. Behind her, on TV, a paramedic bent over a bloody, limp little boy. "Oh, no," she said brokenly. "Oh, *Vee*. How could *anyone* think we'd know anything about the person or the group who committed a horror like this."

I forced myself to look at the unconscious child on TV. We had to share the blame for all the brutal crimes of all the vicious lunatics of the world, because to the world our own father would always be no better than the cold-blooded psychos who maim and kill the innocence in all of us.

And so we left.

We were always running from crimes we didn't commit.

.   .   .

After that I perfected the art of disguise and outright evasion. For several years the plan worked fairly well. Until Chicago.

The marquee poster in the lobby of Hers Truly, the city's priciest women-only nightclub, proclaimed Ella and me the Nelson Sisters. When I chose the name, I hoped the government would have a helluva hard time keeping track of two Nelsons, particularly two Nelsons named Ann and Jane. You couldn't get more all-American ordinary than that.

The Hers Truly was a fern-draped art-deco show bar filled with women wearing formal gowns and tuxedos. On a small stage in one corner of the main room I played electronic piano keyboard in duet with my sister's electric violin. We competed with the clink of bar glasses and the soft conversation of women seducing women. In that nightclub packed with women celebrating their true identities, we were the only ones hiding behind a lie.

I was Ann. Ella was Jane. "Next year we'll switch and I get to be Jane," I had joked when we split a lobster tail and champagne on my twenty-ninth birthday. Ella was three years younger. I'd been brooding about growing old. About dead ends and hopeless wanderings.

Ella and I kept a low profile by playing the kinds of hotel lounges and nightclubs where admirers don't stuff the tip jars with ten-dollar bills because they love Rachmaninoff. You gotta have a gimmick. I added a three-foot-long synthetic weave to my hair and kept it in a mass of tiny cornrows and braids dyed eye-popping golden-blond. I wore so many rings and studs in my earlobes I could have picked up signals like the Hubble telescope.

I'd pierced my navel and decorated it with the glitteriest belly-button jewelry I could find at the flea markets and junk shops where Ella and I did most of our shopping. I had to be skanky enough for both of us, since Ella looked ridiculous in anything skankier than slim black trousers and sequined black tops. She kept her black hair dyed a demure honey color.

Our efforts were amateurish, but they helped. We were professional, dependable, and honest, but reclusive to the point of oddity. We were the daughters of Max Arinelli, and even though Pop was dead we remained under scrutiny. So we kept to ourselves and moved on quickly each time government agents found us.

Which was often enough.

The stranger caught my attention like a trumpet player blowing a high C in the middle of a harp solo.

I always drew up in a knot when a certain type of man watched Ella and me in public. Over the years I'd developed a knack for pinpointing the kind who considered himself the guardian of truth, justice, and the American way. But this one stood out more than usual, particularly in the Hers Truly. After all, he was the only genuinely masculine patron I'd ever seen in the audience. In fact he looked like the kind of man who'd been born with a more than ordinary share of testosterone.

I blinked, then stared again through the haze of stage lights and cigarette smoke. Holy freakin' moly, as we used to say at St. Cecilia's, when the nuns weren't listening.

He was tall, dark, and yes, bluntly handsome. But badly worn around the edges. His face was gaunt, his skin was pale enough to show a beard shadow even in dim light, his mouth was appealing but too tight. He was watching me as if I were doing a striptease and he were an off-duty vice cop.

He kept his hands in the pockets of khaki trousers. His shirtsleeves were rolled up. The throat of his collarless gray shirt was unbuttoned. I saw a hint of dark chest hair. The crowd at tables nearest the stage suddenly sensed manly pheromones, like the aroma off a toxic-waste dump, and turned to scowl at him as if he were about to ask the waitresses to fetch him a pitcher of beer and start the wet T-shirt contest.

"Hey," a beefy redhead in leather shouted at him. "What d'ya think this is? A peep show?" He smiled thinly and nodded without taking his eyes off me. A dozen women began gesturing for the manager.

Ella and I were playing a k.d. lang medley. She pivoted and looked at me frantically, her violin quivering against the ashen curve of her chin, her short blond hair dancing as she sawed the bow across the strings. She'd spotted the stranger, too. *Trouble,* she mouthed like a plea. I nodded. We always had an escape plan.

I leaped up, grabbed her by one arm, and hustled her from the stage. As we hurried down a back hall the manager approached us. "What's wrong?" she demanded. "The set's not half over."

"Migraine." I nodded toward Ella. "Jane's about to pass out." Ella clasped the left side of her head and moaned. She had no trouble faking the vicious headaches because she suffered real ones so often. She was, by nature, a bad actress but an elaborate fainter.

"Oh, dear, I see halos and sparkles." She moaned again. Levering an arm under her shoulder blades, I guided her over pockmarked floor tiles that caught on my stiletto heels and caused her smooth-soled flats to slip. I was strong and alleycat lean; she was shorter and softer. "Try to breathe, hon. I'll get you outside in the fresh air. Well, *night* air, anyhow. Can't promise it won't smell like a—"

"Fainting," she mumbled. And then she went limp.

I caught her as she collapsed. I'd had a lot of practice catching my sister over the years, and more than average in the last couple. A failed romance with a smooth-talking Detroit nightclub owner had nearly destroyed her. It was why we had left Detroit for Chicago. Her health—physical as well as mental—had improved slowly. She'd only recently begun to smile like her old self.

We sank to the hall's floor. Her eyelashes flickered. "Get me a damp cloth and a glass of water," I called to the manager, a small crew-cut brunette in crisply tailored slacks and a man's dress shirt, who hovered over us sympathetically.

"Be right back," she said, then hustled toward the kitchen. I gently slapped Ella's cheeks and rubbed her hands. She opened one eye, then whispered, "Do you see him heading backstage?"

"Not yet. We'll hide here a minute and then we'll run for the back exit."

She sighed. "The other day when I really *was* sick I saw the most beautiful kaleidoscope aura before the pain started. I wanted to float away. I wish that rainbow place existed. You and I could go there and take every lonely, needy, homeless person in the world with us."

That afternoon I'd caught her giving fifty bucks to a bum outside our camper. Ella didn't give a dollar, or even five dollars, the way I did sometimes. No, she gave lifetime endowments, even when we could barely pay our own rent. I yelled, "Give me that money back, you parasite," then wrestled the fifty out of his hands. Ella turned white as a sheet. "He said he needed it for his baby," she moaned.

I should have known. The nightclub owner in Detroit had proposed to my sister, given her a huge diamond ring, then skipped town with the IRS hot on his heels. The ring, as it turned out, had belonged to a former fiancée of his. That last bit of news made my sister scream and double over with cramps. I rushed her to the hospital. She lay on a gurney in the emergency room with blood and clotted tissue seeping between her legs.

She had miscarried a month-old fetus before she even realized she was pregnant. A loss that might have seemed like a practical blessing to some women was devastating to my sister. She'd grieved for that baby ever since.

"Rainbows," she repeated now. This was a typical Ella reaction to stress—she went window-shopping for ethereal visions. "Just stay here on Earth," I ordered wearily, then cradled her head on my shoulder. I smoothed her hair and rocked her as if she were a child. "Maybe the man out front just likes alternative nightclubs," she murmured. "I hope we don't have to pack up and leave. I like this job. Lesbians are so polite."

I heard heavy footsteps striding along the tile floor in our direction. My stomach churned. I felt as if I'd lost the energy to get up again. I bent my head and whispered into Ella's ear, "Let me do the talking." She shivered inside my arms. Tears squeezed from under her closed lids.

"Let me help you with her," a deep male voice said. It'd been years since I'd heard a southern drawl thicker than our own. The voice belonged to him, of course—the watcher. I glared at him but a knot of fear formed in my chest as he dropped to his heels beside us. "She has a lot of these nasty headaches, doesn't she?" he asked.

I went straight into my cornered-junkyard-dog-with-pups attitude. "You're freakin' brilliant. Let a woman faint in front of you and you deduce she's sick. Great work, Sherlock. Get stuffed."

The worry lines deepened across his high, pale forehead. I noticed a slip of gray in a forelock of his dark brown hair. He didn't look old enough for the gray or the lines. He clucked his tongue at me. "You were raised to behave better than this. You could at least tell me to get stuffed in French or Italian. You speak both."

He continued absurdly, "Or you could at least make a curtsy when you tell me to get stuffed. Your dad taught you when he put you onstage. You weren't more than four years old. Barely out of diapers. You could play Mozart and you could curtsy. Now all you can do is bang out mediocre pop songs in an all-girls club and tell people to get stuffed."

"Okay, you sonuvabitch. What are you? FBI? Justice Department? Is there ever going to be a day when you people stop dropping into our lives for these little chats? It must be a slow day in the goon-squad headquarters. I'd think my sister and I would rank below your *fun* cases—like harassing old dopers and trying to catch congressmen taking bribes."

"I was in the Boy Scouts once," he said sarcastically. "Does that count as a fascist arm of the government, too?"

"It's a paramilitary organization designed to indoctrinate children, so yes, it counts."

Ella moved weakly in my grasp. "Who?" she moaned. I smoothed a hand over her forehead. "Sssh."

He nodded toward Ella, frowning. "She needs help. I can carry her out to your car. It's running today, isn't it?" He arched a dark brow. "You know, I never thought a car that old could start without a crank on the front."

He even knew about the ancient, undependable hatchback. My mouth went dry. "I don't need your help. Or your bullshit. Just go back and report that as usual, we're minding our own business and trying to get along. We pay our bills, we pay our taxes. Believe it or not we are *still* not consorting with the type of people you government SOBs assume we might consort with So leave us alone."

"I wish to hell I *could* leave you alone, but it took me months to find you. I give you credit—you're an expert at keeping out of sight. You were a challenge, even for me. And I have sources most people don't have."

The implication made me stare at him in genuine fear. The manager ran back with a washcloth and a cup of water. I helped Ella sit up and wiped her face, then forced myself to speak calmly. "It's okay, El. Relax. I'll get your pills."

She sipped from the cup, then coughed and gagged. I guided her head off my shoulder, then gave him a frigid stare. "I know you guys get your jollies bullying innocent citizens, but would you mind coming back when my sister feels better?"

"I want to get this over with. I have to leave town tonight."

"Too bad. You can talk to me when hell freezes over." Ella groaned, leaned her head back on my shoulder, then shut her eyes. I dabbed her forehead. He waited patiently through all this, and I noticed he had the good grace to avoid looking at her. I could have done without his narrow-eyed scrutiny on me, however. "You know," he said evenly, "it's not that much fun tormenting somebody who's already got so much trouble on her hands. Even if you do fight back pretty well."

"What a compliment."

"Look, let's stop this. I'm not what you think I am. I'm not a friend, but I'm not an enemy, either."

"Oh, really. How mysterious. Look—either tell me what you want or get out of here."

Frowning, he pulled a dog-eared black-and-white photo from his shirt pocket and held it out. For the first time I noticed his right hand. I froze. Whoever he was, something awful had happened to him.

His ring finger and little finger were gone, as well as a deep section at their base. His middle finger was scarred and knotty. Lines of pink scar tissue and deep, puckered gouges snaked up his right forearm. Grotesque and awkward, the hand looked like a deformed claw.

Suddenly I was aware of my own fingers, flexing them, grateful they were all in place. He wasn't an invincible threat. He was very human, and more than a little damaged.

"Enjoying the view?" he asked tersely. I jerked my gaze to his face. Ruddy blotches of anger and embarrassment colored his cheeks. He quickly transferred the photo to his undamaged left hand and dropped the right hand into the shadows between his knees. "Have you ever seen a copy of this picture before?"

I took a deep breath and looked at the photo. A solemn, handsome young boy gazed back at me from my parents' wedding picture. There was only one copy of the picture, I thought, and I still had it. "Where did you get that?"

"It's been in my family."

"Who? What family?"

"The Camerons."

I leaned toward him. "Who are you?"

He pointed to the boy. "Gib Cameron," he said. "Does that mean anything to you?"

My head reeled. When I was a child I'd decided I'd never meet Gib Cameron in person but I would love him forever. That childhood memory had become a shrine to all the lost innocence in my life.

But now the shrine was real. *He* was real. "I remember your name," I said with a shrug.

"I remember yours," he said flatly. "And it's not Ann Nelson."

"Why are you here?"

He smiled with no humor. "I'm going to make you an offer you can't refuse."

It was appropriate that Gib Cameron knew who I really was. After all, he'd helped my mother name me before I was born.

Two

As long as I could remember, I knew we Arinellis of low-country Louisiana had a special bond with the Camerons of high-country Tennessee. I put a voodoo love spell on Gib Cameron the year Mom retired from her singing career and our family settled in New Orleans. I was six years old. Mom wanted to stay home with us and be the kind of Donna Reed–type mother she had wished for hopelessly when she was a girl.

Pop would have given her the moon if she had asked. New Orleans and Donna Reed were easy then. I believed my father could accomplish anything. He was a very successful composer and all-around brilliant jazz man. Although he was half-Japanese, with black hair and golden skin, he stood over six feet tall and his eyes were gray. As a kid I watched as restaurant maître d's called for Max Arinelli then did double takes when Pop stepped forward. He was raised Catholic but he had no god he would speak of. He brought up Ella and me in the Church only because Mom wanted it that way.

Mom was the blond daughter of a hard-drinking Louisiana truck-stop guitar player named Big Jane Kirkel-son. Big Jane died young and my mother, a southern nobody with the strangely redneck-Nordic name of Sherry Ann Kirkelson, was taken in by a Catholic foster home, which turned her loose at eighteen, a loving, morally determined girl with a pretty singing voice and ambitions. She got a job with an early-sixties ditty-bop girls band then moved to New York, where she managed to earn a respectable career as a backup singer by the time she met Pop. By then, Sherry Kirkelson had become Shari Kirk.

We had plenty of money when we moved back to Mom's home state. Pop bought a nightclub in the French Quarter and began remodeling it. He created elegant dining rooms and fine jazz music, champagne brunches and smooth blues. I think his combined devotion to Mom, Ella, me, and the night-club would have been enough to protect him from his demons for the rest of his life.

Ella and I had Pop's soft black hair and slightly hooded eyes, but the color was green, like Mom's. People might imagine our Asian grandmother peeking out through our eyes if they tried hard, but my sister and I were more mysterious than exotic. We felt perfectly secure among the heat-steamed blossoms of New Orleans nightclub society, where our mixed-race father fit in easily with the Cajuns and Creoles and Africans and other varieties and mixtures of humanity that made that world so exciting.

Our house in the old-money Garden District was filled with luxuries I took for granted, with joy and passionate music that was as much a part of me and my family as the blood in our veins, and with fervent left-wing political meetings that would have gotten Pop blacklisted for life during the McCarthy era.

Pop's fire-breathing friends would have been stunned to know about Mom's long friendship and correspondence with Gib Cameron's family. Even Pop cherished that bond, deep down, though he never admitted it. He couldn't bring himself to say he respected and admired a family so all-American they must bleed red, white, and blue.

I think he feared we would always be measured against

standards the Camerons epitomized. Compared to them and their two centuries of pioneer Scottish American history we barely deserved to pledge allegiance to the flag. Cameron ancestors had settled the colonial wilderness of Tennessee's mountains, built themselves an estate of enduring grandeur, and were the centerpiece of social and civic life in the southern heartlands. We homegrown Arinellis were a twentieth-century creation, scraping for acceptance, only one generation removed from all things foreign and exotic and therefore vaguely notorious.

When I was a child Mom happily told and retold the story of her and Pop's wedding at Cameron Hall. In 1968 my parents were on tour in Nashville, Tennessee, with a Top 40 show called *Dance Parade*, which was sponsored by Decca Records. Mom and Pop heard about an inn that had just opened high in the mountains east of Nashville—wild, beautiful, difficult territory that the lowland world still regarded with awe and, occasionally, fear.

Mom didn't confess that she and Pop weren't married when she called to reserve a room, and Gib's family never thought to ask. Those years in the late sixties were the last gasp of social innocence—or at least the pretense of innocence.

The Camerons took my parents in as if they were kinfolk, a welcome my mother never forgot, because she had no family, and neither did Pop. Pop proposed to her there, and the Camerons organized a quick wedding in their own family chapel.

It was amazing that Mom and Pop married at all; Pop always said he wouldn't let the government sanctify *any* part of his life, and he considered marriage certificates one more way the government sought to regulate people. Yet he married Mom and loved her dearly, just as he loved my sister and me. I've never doubted that.

Mom and Pop wrote a song on their wedding day titled "Evening Star," which hinted, of course, at my name. Venus. The song was the only top-ten single Mom ever recorded.

I was born not quite nine months after the wedding.

So I was probably conceived at Cameron Hall.

That was the closest any Arinelli had come to being a pioneer.

I started picking out songs on the piano when I was two. By the time I turned three I could—with Pop's excited coaching—struggle through one or two simple little concertos. I couldn't recall a time when I didn't play the piano. Pop never forced music on me, though. I was addicted to it, and when I was alone in our music room I practiced at my gleaming black Steinway and chatted happily with Gib, who posed in Mom and Pop's wedding photo atop the baby grand in a silver frame.

I practiced piano for several hours each day and had lessons three times a week with the famous concert pianist Madame Le Ong; it was an enormous honor for her to accept me as a student. She called the wedding photograph a distraction but Pop let me keep it on the piano anyway.

In it Gib was a handsome, solemn, dark-haired boy, about five years old. He perched at the top of stone steps that led up to the Cameron chapel. The chapel sat atop a small hill covered in grass. Ivy graced its stone walls and flowers vined across the carved beams of its porch. Sunlight gleamed on the copper bell cupola. Enormous round mountains jutted up in the background.

His family—a much older brother and the brother's wife, two baby sisters, and two peculiar-looking middle-aged aunts—posed around him. But Mom and Pop stood in the center of the small group in front of the chapel's doors.

Mom wore a pale minidress and carried a bouquet of wildflowers; her hair was set in its perfect flipped-up style. Pop was the handsomest man in the world, tall and straight, his black hair gleaming.

In his dress shirt and crisp dark trousers, Gib looked equally handsome. He had one arm draped over a big, light-eyed dog with a large, jaunty bow tied around its neck. Since the picture was in black and white, I had no idea of Gib's hair or eye color, or the color of the dog. I wondered endlessly what Gib thought of Shari Kirk and Max Arinelli, a perky pop-song singer and her exotic-looking bandleader, who had suddenly decided to marry when they visited his home.

"Someday, when I take you to meet the Camerons, you'll see how pretty their valley in the mountains is," Mom told me every time she recited the wedding story. "It's the most beautiful place in the world. It's magical. It worked magic on your daddy. And on me. And the magic created *you*. An angel put you under my heart the very first night. Right there in the middle of the Tennessee mountains. She followed the light of the evening star and glided right down into the Camerons' big house and gave you to your dad and me."

"With a whole bunch of Camerons watching?" I'd always ask, because it made Mom laugh, and nod.

"I want you to have something very special," Mom said on my sixth birthday. "Gib Cameron gave it to me when your daddy and I got married. It's a piece of a star. It's your namesake. It fell into a beautiful pond of magic water, and Gib found it there."

She handed me a walnut-sized chunk of white quartz from her jewelry box. "He told me I could wish on the evening star and it would hear me, because I was taking care of one of its babies." She held out the rock. "I wished for a baby of my own, and I got you."

"How'd he know that would happen?" I blurted.

"I think he knew you'd be his friend," Mom said solemnly. "I have to tell you something sad about him now that you're old enough to understand. Not long before your dad and I went to Gib's home and got married, Gib's parents passed away."

"He's got no mom and pop?"

"That's right, sweetie. They passed away."

I was given to Pop's pragmatism, even at six. In Mom's

gentle world people *passed away*. In Pop's brutally realistic world they *died*, usually in some gruesome way that Pop blamed on The System. "Did the gov'ment kill Gib's mom and pop, *too*?" I asked urgently.

"Oh, no, sweetie, where'd you get that idea . . . No, I promise you the government does not make people pass away on purpose."

"But Pop says the gov'ment killed Grandmother Akiko. He said her heart was broke by gov'ment bastards."

"Don't say 'bastards,' sweetie. I know you got that from your daddy, but he's allowed to say bad words. He's grown up. He learned to speak that way before he was old enough to know better."

"But what happened to Gib's mom and pop? I have to know. I just have to. I bet Pop knows."

Which meant I'd ask him if she didn't tell me. She knew I would. Mom sighed. "They didn't pass away near here. They passed away in a hotel in England. All the way across an ocean. Far, far away. When Gib was only about five years old."

"I used to be five!"

"It has nothing to do with being five," Mom said frantically. I made strange leaps of logic, much like Pop when he talked politics. "It had to do with England, so you don't have a thing to worry about."

Mom always assumed I wouldn't fear anything if she said it only happened to people outside our own geographic boundaries. Boogeymen, closet monsters, and other assorted childhood devils all lived in Russia, for example. She was a child of the Cold War, afraid of Russians like everyone else back then. I'm sure Pop's leftist political leanings scared her, too. I expect she worried that some fanatical ideology might slither across the Ukraine in Pop's vulnerable direction.

"England," she repeated soothingly.

"What killed Gib's parents in England?" I persisted.

She gave up on diplomacy, at that point. "Some bad men set a bomb in a hotel where Gib's parents were staying. They happened to be in the hotel when the bomb blew up."

"And they got blowed up, too? In big pieces?"

Even now I vividly recall Mom's amazed expression. "You'll have scary dreams if you think like that, sweetie. Little girls don't want to hear about people getting, uhmmm, passing away."

"Pop says—"

"Yes, all right, they were blown up. But the bad men who did it won't ever come here and blow up anyone we know."

"The bad men live in Russia?"

"No. They live in Ireland."

"Did the police arrest 'em?"

"No, the police never found the bad men. But the bad men live in Ireland and don't like to travel. I promise."

"I bet Gib will go find 'em. And kill 'em. I bet he will."

"No, he was only your age when his mommie and daddy passed away—"

"Got blowed all up."

"Went to England."

"He'll get 'em. The bad men. I bet."

She heaved an exhausted sigh. "My whole point is that now you understand why Gib is lonely, and why he needs a friend like you. And I hope you'll always be friends with him. We're going to visit him someday, as soon as your dad has time for a vacation."

I was hooked. He'd given my mother a magic rock that brought me into the world. He'd even given her the idea for my odd name.

My sympathy for his orphanhood, my romantic imagination, and my little-girl conviction that every little boy is secretly enamored of her combined to convince me that he belonged to me.

It helped that from the time I was born he'd sent me birthday cards and Christmas cards. He actually addressed them and signed them, in what could only have been his boyish, thick scrawl.

Mom addressed birthday cards and Christmas cards to Gib for me in return, and I signed them as carefully as he signed his name for me. "VENUS LIKE THE STAR," I always wrote in large, merry letters. Mom would write out what I wanted to say, and I would copy it. One year I added a tender, heartfelt postscript.

"THE BAD MEN CAN'T GET US IF WE STAY PUT."

The world was a very cruel and unfair place, Pop said. We Arinellis truly were odd fruit, and we were also forgotten fruit. We'd flowered on vines that were never meant to entwine. Music was the one thing that linked us to every branch of our strange ancestry. Every one of my four long-dead grandparents had been a musician of some sort.

Our paternal grandfather, Paolo Arinelli, had arrived in New York from Italy as an orphan sometime around 1910. He became a pianist and orchestra leader. An inborn talent for music was all he could afford to take with him from the old country.

From his handsome pictures and Pop's proud memories of him, my grandfather leaped out, larger than life, always in formal attire with his black hair slicked back perfectly, a music baton in his hand and a rakish smile on his lips, chasing women, drinking illegal liquor, making glorious music for glorious people.

He met our grandmother in New York at a performance of a Japanese cultural troupe sponsored by the Japanese embassy.

Akiko Nakado was the daughter of a prominent and very traditional Tokyo clan descended from a samurai. Dressed in an elaborate kimono, she knelt in front of a long, stringed koto, playing the traditional instrument with filmy finger picks, the music sounding like raindrops on a timpani; judging by her pictures she was as lovely as a silk-screen painting and as perfect as a haiku. She was only sixteen years old, and Paolo was thirty-five.

When she ran away with him to California her family in Tokyo held a ritual ceremony. They declared her dead.

Pop was born in Los Angeles in 1932. His life was charmed when he was small; Grandfather Paolo had become a successful composer and arranger for one of the major movie studios, listed in the credits of dozens of films under the name Paul Aaron. The name change wasn't a choice forced on him by the studio. Grandpop was proud to be an American citizen. Grandmother Akiko devoted herself to the same holy grail. Pop remembered how she worked to perfect her English, studying American history even after she passed her citizenship exam.

One of Pop's dearest possessions was a photograph of himself as a boy posed with his parents at the rim of the Grand Canyon. The three of them had dressed in dungarees and matching checkered shirts, and all of them wore Angels baseball caps. Pop loved baseball and played third base like a charm.

He was only ten years old when Grandfather Paolo was killed in World War II.

Paolo had been too old to fight but not too old to tour with the USO. His plane went down en route to New York, where he was to perform for soldiers headed overseas.

Pop and Grandmother Akiko were rounded up in Los Angeles with thousands of other Asian Americans and placed in an internment camp. They lost everything they owned; Pop suddenly stopped being an all-American baseball-playing kid and became an outsider. He never forgot the shock of being locked behind a fence for no good reason and no crime.

Grandmother Akiko died of pneumonia the next year. *That goddamned American gulag killed her,* Pop always said.

When the camps were opened, he had nowhere to go among millions of patriotic homefolk waiting to torment

him. After all, he was half-Japanese, with black hair and al-
mond eyes and skin the color of pale honey. It didn't take long
for him to learn to fight like a trapped dog in the back alleys
of L.A.

And he never stopped hating the government.

When he was fifteen he lied about his age and got a job
playing saxophone in a burlesque band. By the time he met
Mom in 1962 he was a conductor and arranger for a record
label. He'd played sax and piano for most of the big names in
pop music, including Sinatra, who introduced him to pretty
blond Shari Kirk when she sang backup on a Tony Bennett
album.

"This chick's a sweet kid," Sinatra said to Pop. "She's got
class. A guy like you needs a chick like her. Raises your level
of expectations."

Pop took that advice to heart. He developed what Mom
called dreams but strangers called pretensions. I heard people
whisper it when I was small. I thought pretensions might be
like chicken pox. You scratch and people notice it, but the
wounds heal eventually. I was too embarrassed to ask Pop for
an explanation of his disease. He looked fine to me, and I
adored him.

Together, Mom and Pop headed for the top. By the time I
was born she'd become a two-hit girl singer—the last of the
Doris Day clones, with flipped-up blond hair and a wholesome smile. She made a career singing sweet ballads about
true love. Pop managed her career and wrote her music.

They were good together, my parents.

They deserved a happy ending.

"My mom's going to have an operation," I told our next-door
neighbor. "I need some voodoo advice."

Mrs. Duvelle was a rich divorced woman, I had heard
Mom say, very heavyset but very pretty. Mom rarely let me

talk to her, even through the stone fence covered in jasmine, which separated our backyards. There were rumors about the men who visited her.

But Mrs. Duvelle taught me voodoo, just enough to get by, she said, because I was special and would need all the help I could get. She swore it was all right for a Catholic girl to do it, but I decided to be on the safe side and not mention it to the nuns at school.

I had already put the voodoo to the test with a sour-faced babysitter called Nanny Robicheaux, who slapped Ella on the head when Pop wasn't in the house. Maybe it was the mix of chicken's foot (stolen from the market) and red paint (for blood) that scared her off, or maybe she got tired of my smart mouth, but she abruptly gave notice on the very day I'd flung the bloody-looking mess on the patio where she was enjoying a cigarette break.

Sister Mary Catherine, a lemon-faced, strict old head nun, warned Pop that his religious and political anarchy would ruin me and Ella. Children raised to revere the church but also the godless activities of a lapsed parent will lose their way in the wilderness, Sister Mary Catherine said. Pop told her God was music and music was the church, as far as he was concerned, and that's why he'd agreed with Mom to choose Catholic school for Ella and me, because Catholics have the best music. He said his daughters would always find their way.

I had also used voodoo on Gib.

I made a love charm from a piece of my straight black hair and a speck of congealed bacon grease, and I smeared the hairy goo on the back of the photo, above his face.

Considering my successes with Nanny Robicheaux and Gib, I confidently set up a protective shrine for Mom. It included a piece of her hair, some of Pop's whisker shavings, and my quartz rock. I hid it in my closet.

"Take care of Pop and Ella for me until I get back home

from the hospital," she said cheerfully, and I promised. It was a heavy load for a first grader, even one deemed a child prodigy. "We are a very special family," she said. "We don't have grandparents, or aunts and uncles or cousins, like most other people. So we have to take care of each other especially well. You and Pop and Ella and me."

"I know. Stick like glue and shake our fists at Uncle Sam."

I remember her rubbing her forehead as she considered that. I had gotten the words from overhearing Pop discuss the government. "It's not polite to shake your fist," she countered. "Just give Ella and Pop lots of hugs while I'm gone."

"I promise. But you'll be back right away—Pop says so. I just wish he weren't going off to the hospital all the time, too. I don't want Sister Mary Catherine to come here. She only watches Lawrence Welk on TV. If I could just go sit at the hospital I'd be real quiet and nobody'd even know I was waiting for you."

I'm sure Mom realized how frightened I was. "If you need to talk to someone you can talk to Gib in the wedding picture," Mom said gently. "I've always known you like to share things with him. I mean, just in case you feel like you need to talk to someone until I come back home. He'll always be there. Promise me you'll talk to him?"

"I promise. And I promise I'll take the best care of Ella and Pop."

Mom hugged me. "Then I won't worry about a thing," she whispered. I latched my arms around her neck. She held me so long I fell asleep, and so my last memory of her is warmth, and peaceful dreams, and the scent of her perfume against my cheek.

She died the next day, during what was supposed to be a routine hysterectomy; her congenitally weak heart couldn't tolerate the anesthesia. I remember Pop sitting on my bed that night and holding on to me for dear life, and I remember crying until I was sick—the first of many times like that. I remember patting his head in sympathy. I remember him crying against my hair. It was the only time I ever knew he was capable of tears.

I was suddenly the lady of our house. I became the self-appointed helpmate of a brilliant but embittered father and a sweet, delicate baby sister who chirped like a bird when she was upset. Pop treated me like a small adult. Immediately he took Ella and me to a salon to have our black hair dyed blond, and he insisted we keep it that way; he was trying to erase even the smallest evidence of our ethnic background. He'd never forgotten the prejudice and abuse heaped on him as a child.

I sensed he had changed in some hopeless ways I couldn't understand yet. But he had big dreams for me and Ella, especially for me, and I knew I'd never let him down. Still, I was desperate for comfort and advice. I talked to Gib's picture constantly.

When I was older I understood that Pop began to withdraw from the light after he lost Mom. That he immediately started tightening the circle of people in our lives that he trusted. But when I was little I obeyed his strange whims blindly, with wild, devoted, miserable confusion.

For a while I continued to believe I'd meet Gib someday. I needed to share my miseries with him face-to-face. I needed to tell him that, like him, I didn't have a mother now. I asked Pop several times when we could go to Tennessee. Mom had promised. I was worried. I hadn't gotten a card from Gib in a long time.

We had already become a house that the postman passed by. Pop channeled all the household mail through the club. And we had an unlisted phone number. It was the beginning of his secrecies, when his anger at the world began to grow around us like thorny vines. Sentimental ideas, Pop finally explained, had no place in a disciplined person's life.

"We have to take care of ourselves. Every day has only a precious amount of time, not something to waste on people we barely know," Pop told me. "Gib and his family aren't like us. They don't understand what we're all about. You don't want Gib to grow up expecting you to be a type of person that you're not. You're going to be a very special and important person. You don't ever want to be helpless, do you? Being too friendly with other people makes you dependent, and then people take advantage of you."

"I don't want to be helpless, Pop," I recited fervently. But I was heartbroken and bewildered. Pop had turned me into a silent soldier in his one-man war on ideological crimes committed against our family.

My duty—as Pop directed me—was to perform brilliantly on concert stages. In that arena I'd rise to a rank so high that no one in the world would dare harm me or anyone else Pop loved.

I missed Gib for years.

Three

I was nineteen years old when Pop's bitter choices caught up with him. I thought he had cloistered us from a world that lurked outside our door with the threat of eternal evil, but that year, 1988, our protected lives began to unravel.

Federal court judge Lytel Billings, his wife, and their three teenage sons burned to death in an arson fire at their upstate New York house. The story was plastered all over TV and the newspapers for weeks. Billings had been on the Reagan administration's shortlist of Supreme Court candidates. His fans loved his merciless, hard-line record on immigration law. I knew all about Judge Billings because Pop hated his guts.

"If Billings had his way my daughters would be labeled as second-generation Jap-Wop on every document from their birth certificates to their driver's licenses," I'd heard Pop say more than once. "Hell, he'd probably have ethnic code numbers tattooed on their arms like the goddamned Nazis."

But then Pop despised a lot of prominent judges and politicians; our house had always been littered with left-wing newsletters and magazines that stopped just short of calling for all-out anarchy.

Pop taught us to distrust and scrutinize all government

programs and authority—I could sniff out a potential conspiracy or official corruption, real or imagined, a mile away.
But that had all been a game to me, growing up in a safe, tree-
lined, moss-draped, expensive New Orleans neighborhood
where the local police officers knew Ella and me by name.

The Louisiana state attorney general, for God's sake, was
a regular visitor to Pop's nightclub. The *governor* had once sat
in on drums with a clarinet man named Blues Joe, and Pop let
me play keyboard with them. The government was made up
of friendly, familiar faces, and We the People included Venus
and Ella Arinelli.

I had never taken Pop's rants seriously. Ella and I had
been weaned on his extravagant rhetoric—the political meetings he attended, the passionate activists' groups he hosted,
and the frequent dinners at our house where the guests were
old-style radicals from the music world. They scared Ella,
who refused to listen, but I hid at the top of the stairs, grinning as aging musicians shouted opinions at Pop and each
other before adjourning to the music room to hold ad-lib jazz
sessions. When I thought about Pop's leftist politics I imagined them underscored by jazz rifts and scented with the mellow, sweet-musky smell of marijuana. They seemed quaint.

So even though the murders of Judge Billings and his
family meant more in our household than to most Americans, it
was only because we were already familiar with a whole gallery
full of Pop's ideological dragons. I couldn't imagine it meant
more than that. Whatever dark childhood fears I'd had about his
eccentric and controversial ideas, I lived a pampered life.

I dressed like a poster girl for upper-class preppies—a lot
of plaid, a lot of khaki, and my hair straight, shoulder-length,
and still a soft honey shade, like Mom's. When I was a teenager I rolled my eyes at Pop's outdated ideas about prejudice
against Asian Americans, but did as he told me to do. I looked
in the mirror and saw a green-eyed blond with large, slightly
hooded eyes. I was exactly who and what Pop told me to be.

Safe behind his wall of hate.

.   .   .

Pop watched proudly as I won the most prestigious classical pianist competition in the Southeast, the preliminary auditions for the Van Cliburn International competition. I was moving swiftly into the kind of adult acclaim given to only a few pianists in the world.

I'd travel to Texas to compete in the finals with about thirty of the best young pianists in the world. I was the first female finalist in the history of the Van Cliburn—if I won or even placed at the silver or bronze level I'd be guaranteed concert tours, recording contracts, international recognition. Pop was convinced I'd take the gold medal. So was I. Confidence ran deep in our family then.

Until the day of the finals. When I glanced into the wings as I bowed to applause, I saw my sister sobbing hysterically in the matronly, peach-clad arms of the public-relations woman, while the competition's program director motioned wildly for me to hurry.

I bolted from the stage as gracefully as possible in a billowing satin gown. Ella fell into my outstretched hands. She was a daisy-like sixteen-year-old who looked much younger. "Pop's in some kind of trouble," she cried. "The police took him away! It has something to do with the murder of that judge!"

"It's a mistake," I said loudly, but my heart pounded violently. Not the police, I learned a few minutes later. Federal agents. FBI. Men in crisp dark suits walked up to Ella and me, and flashed their badges, and said a lot of soothing, fatherly things to us—at least for the first few hours. That was before they had charged Pop with a long list of federal crimes that included conspiracy to murder a federal judge.

When I finally saw him the next day, his high-priced, long-haired, mob-connected defense lawyer shadowed him at a court hearing. Pop searched me out and I saw something

in his eyes that was tragic apology but also something that
was rage.

"I swear to you on your mother's grave," he said to me
when we were allowed to meet in an interview room, "I had
nothing to do with the Billings arson."

"I never thought you did," I said. It was that simple. I
don't know if I believed my own words or not, but I never
considered saying anything else.

"I'm going to fight this. I'll clear my name. I swear to
you."

"I know, Pop." I didn't cry; it was as if we'd both always
known I was tough like him, that I'd absorbed his nature.

"Dear God," he murmured, his eyes vacant, searching.
"What have I done to you and your sister?"

It was the closest I ever heard him come to uttering a
prayer. The lapse of pure control terrified me. I think he knew
that what he'd dreamed for us—for me, in particular—was
ruined already, and he'd betrayed the faith our mother had put
in him before she died. He'd broken our hearts and his own.

The last time I saw him he was in handcuffs. I couldn't
even get close enough to touch him when he was taken out of
the courtroom. I remember Ella sobbing.

He died that week of a heart attack, in a jail cell, alone.

My father came full circle in a system that betrayed him,
dying in government custody. I went to the morgue and took
his elegant, golden hands in mine, and my mind was open and
blank as an empty song sheet.

I absorbed his rage and sorrow from his cold skin. I for-
gave his mistakes and believed him innocent of murder if not
of revenge, and I swore to him I'd never forget the betrayals
that made him the way he was.

After Pop's death, friends of his were scared to help us, talk to
us, or even admit they knew us. Ella, who had always been

dreamy and excitable—a lot like Mom, Pop always said—fell apart when the FBI agents began interrogating us about every detail of Pop's life. Her terror made her almost incoherent; there were times when she hid in an upstairs closet, trembling violently, sweating, trapped in episodes of blind panic or hysterical sobbing she couldn't control.

The doctors put my sister in the psychiatric ward. I went back to the house alone. When cronies of Pop's showed up and told me they needed files he stored in his bedroom closet, I let them take everything. I was so stupid. So scared and naive and desperate to protect my dead father and damaged sister. I had no idea what the files contained, but I assumed the information could hurt Pop. I gathered all of his office papers at home, carried them into the backyard, and burned them.

The Government arrived an hour later. It arrived in the form of dull-colored sedans and men—all men, no women—in dark suits, wearing shoulder pistols and flashing badges, and carrying notepads, tape recorders, and search warrants. Then came the men with equipment to test for fingerprints and other evidence.

To put our lives under a microscope.

"What did you do with the files upstairs?" they asked me. "What did you burn in the backyard?"

I never admitted anything. "You're in trouble," they said.

The next morning Pop was national news—the widower of sixties pop singer Shari Kirk, who was by then only an answer in Trivial Pursuit and whose quaint old ballad, "Evening Star," had become a standard on the oldies radio stations. The father of Van Cliburn finalist Venus Arinelli.

Max Arinelli, the embittered son of immigrants. That's what he was called in the news.

For twenty years he'd laundered dirty money through his club. Drug money, gun money, foreign money, all of it headed for an umbrella group of activists doing God alone knew what. Some of it was about funding legal defense for ne'er-do-well federal prisoners considered to be political victims. Some of the money went to rabble-rousing left-wing newspapers and underground newsletters, and some went to support candidates for public office.

And some of it went to a group who sent an assassin into the basement of Judge Billings's big colonial home and set the timer on a sophisticated device that exploded in white-hot flames a few minutes later.

Whether he'd meant to be or not, Pop was the money man for killers.

I was convinced—for a while, at least—that he was being framed. I wasn't going to list the names of harmless friends and old-timer musicians who ranted about politics over dinner at Pop's club. I wasn't going to strip our lives naked of the dignity Pop had cocooned around us. We were innocent, he and Ella and I, but these government men wanted information of any kind, and they hounded me for it.

And I didn't give in.

Which upset them, the government men. They get very testy when teenage girls refuse to back down about basic constitutional protections, when teenage girls quote the Bill of Rights to them.

And when they get testy they break things. They jerk drawers out of the dining-room sideboard and spill sterling-silver flatware on the floor, and then they accidentally crush the filigreed iced-tea spoons under their shoes. They bump your mother's imported demitasse cups while rummaging through the china cupboard. They shatter the crystal flower vases.

They drop jewelry into their coat pockets. "Don't you dare take my mother's pearls," I said as a government agent flipped the necklace into a bulging canvas bag. I lunged for the bag and he pinned me against a wall. "They're evidence now," he said.

They scatter your panties and bras across your bed. "You like pink," an agent said. "Tell me why pink turns you on." A grown man saying that to a teenage girl. I never forgot the look in his eyes.

They strew clothing, rip out wallpaper, search beneath floorboards, snatch photographs from albums. "Who are these people?" they demand. When I visited Ella in the hospital she could only clutch my hand and stare at the ceiling, hollow-eyed and speechless.

I was terrified that she had left me forever, too.

I hid Mom and Pop's wedding photo inside my blouse before the agents got to the music room. They snatched up the rest of the photos on the piano. The picture was the only belonging I took when my sister and I disappeared onto the long, anonymous roads stretching in endless loneliness across the years.

There were no simple answers anymore. Ella and I were outcasts. I promised myself we'd survive. I was still keeping that vow ten years later, when Gib Cameron, the childhood sweetheart I'd never met, tracked me down in Chicago.

I'm going to make you an offer you can't refuse. Gib's untapped threat—or promise—rang in my ears.

When we arrived at a dingy RV campground on the edge of a high-rise Chicago neighborhood, I watched him surreptitiously. I had a bad feeling he'd already checked out our temporary home in the lovely Trailer and RV Paradise, an acre lot trapped like an armpit between an apartment building and an all-night convenience store. The silhouette of Chicago towered behind him in the midnight sky. Mountains. I'd always thought of Gib Cameron among mountains, and there he was.

"Home sweet home," I said dryly. "Like it?"

He perused the trailer park with obvious disapproval. "It reminds me of a bad truck-stop motel."

"You speaking from personal experience, hillbilly, or from just peeking in motel windows?"

"Now don't go and make fun of my hobbies. I'll have to

throw you in that cement pond over there." He nodded at the decrepit concrete fountain at the trailer park's center, then gazed at me steadily. "You could use a good soak. I expect you're pretty under all that stage makeup."

I slammed my car door and said no more as I strode around to the passenger side. I knew how I must look to him. Like punk trash or a street hooker. My low-cut two-piece black minidress bared enough cleavage and midriff to qualify as a bikini. The trusting little girl who resorted to voodoo spells had turned into a cynical woman who might have been mistaken for a blond voodoo queen. I could tell him it was all part of my act, but he'd never believe me.

I opened the hatchback's passenger door and bent to take Ella's black vinyl tote from her fumbling hands. "Sorry," she whispered. "Now I really am sick. My head's killing me." The scent of vomit wafted from the towel in the floor between her feet. "Just give me a minute to clean up."

"No problem. I'll ward off Dudley Dooright with my wicked urban wit."

I shut the door and busied myself straightening the contents of her purse. Gib walked over from his own vehicle, an old jeep, one of those hulking models that had led a hard, true-jeep life. Next to the jeep our faded little hatchback had the personality of a pigeon. "Can I help with your sister?" he asked.

"You can help by stopping where you are and not embarrassing her while she does a little impromptu freshening up."

He inclined his head in a sardonic acceptance, but halted a few yards out, gallantly facing away from Ella. I strolled over to him, eyeing the jeep. "That's a lousy rental car."

"It's mine. World War Two vintage. My father's older brother was killed in England during an air raid. He was a driver for General Eisenhower. The general sent the jeep to my family as a gift, after the war."

I stared at the vehicle. The Cameron family had an even more patriotic history than I'd realized. I took a deep breath.

"Don't tell me you drove a fifty-year-old Army jeep all the way from Tennessee."

"I like to drive." He fished the remnant of a cigar from his shirt pocket, using his maimed hand awkwardly. When he saw me watching his hand he dropped the cold cigar butt into an overflowing trash can by the trailer park's communal picnic tables, which were each chained to steel eyelets set in the concrete pads beneath them. He scowled at the chained tables and the garbage can, then rubbed his eyes tiredly. "I haven't been able to get out and do much until the last month or so. I couldn't maneuver a steering wheel or a gearshift."

I avoided glancing at his hand again. "You must like being isolated up there in the mountains," I offered, by way of changing the subject. "You must stay busy."

He smiled a little. "Sure. Breeding with my first cousins and making moonshine takes all my time."

So much for my sympathy. He didn't want it. "First cousins? Why, I'm impressed you swam that far out in the family gene pool."

"Vee!" Ella whispered weakly through the hatchback's open window.

I opened the door again and bent over her. "Ready?"

"Yes. I think. I'm a little woozy. And I smell horrible."

"You don't smell worse than anything else around here." In the concrete fountain a few live goldfish swam anemically among more than a few dead ones. When we'd leased an RV berth Ella said the fountain smelled like the Louisiana bayous in summer. That the odor made her homesick. I said it just made me sick, period. Home, to me, smelled like jasmine and bougainvillea. The scent of the past could break my heart if I thought about it too much. I helped Ella from our car.

"Nice rolling motel," Gib said, looking at our ancient blue-and-white RV.

Ella leaned against the hatchback's hood and managed a weak smile at Gib, holding out one hand with delicate gentility, as if we were at the country club. "Vee told me our mother's stories about your home and your family when we were children," she said. "Our parents' wedding at Cameron Hall—and how Vee got her name—why, those were Vee's favorite stories. A real-life fairy tale. It really is nice to meet you."

I groaned inwardly at her openness. Gib shot a surprised glance my way as he clasped her fingers with his good hand. No one could resist Ella. "I heard a lot about your family, too," he answered.

Ella faltered. "Oh." She touched her forehead shakily. "I'm sorry."

I took her by one arm. "I'll be right back. Make yourself at home. Have a seat on any of the fine picnic tables over there." He responded with a slight bow. I quickly helped Ella inside our creaky RV.

"Get out the good wineglasses," she urged weakly. I guided her to the built-in bed behind a partition. "He's a friend, Vee."

"No, he's not. He wants something from us. I just haven't found out what yet. And Ella? Don't ever apologize for our family."

"I didn't mean to sound as if I were."

"All right. Just don't do it again."

"Gib went to a lot of trouble to look for us and to find us, Vee. His family remembers Mom and Pop just as vividly as we remember Mom's stories about the Camerons. The Camerons were special to us and we're still special to them. After all these years, that's amazing. It's profound."

"It's *peculiar.* Get some sleep," I whispered. My twin bed was bolted on the RV wall crossways of Ella's twin, but her side was all gauzy white netting and lacy white pillows, while mine was jumbled with everything from African kente-cloth blankets to a ten-dollar purple afghan I'd bought at a salvage shop—and the covers were usually scattered with composition sheets where I'd scribbled new duet arrangements for us.

Ella lay down gratefully and I pulled off her black pumps

and her demure black leggings, then rubbed her feet for a second. My sister had too many soft spots and I had too many hard ones. I adored her, despite everything. She would say the same about me.

Ella sighed. As I turned away she whispered, "Don't be too hard on him. I saw a feather this morning. It means something. I think he's somebody we can trust." Her eyes filled with tears. Her pale, champagne-fine complexion was quickly streaked with them. "I still want to trust people," she said. "I'm sorry. I can't help it."

Ella believed angels, or our parents, or, for all I knew, space Wookiees, watched over us. She was convinced the occasional bird feathers were good tidings from them.

I glanced at Gib out a window lined with Ella's feathers taped to the camper's fake wood paneling. Playbills, newspaper reviews, ticket stubs, and publicity photos of us were taped nearby. Mom and Pop's wedding photo hung in a small gold frame. "I saw a feather," Ella repeated. "It's a sign. Tell him about the feather." She turned uneasily on her pillow.

"It means a pigeon died," I said under my breath.

When I stepped out of the camper Gib was leaning against one of the trailer park's metal picnic tables with his hands in his pockets. He didn't look pleased as he surveyed the lines of campers squatting on gravel lots under yellow security lights. When he swiveled his attention to me I gave a small curtsy. "Is this more acceptable to your meat-and-potatoes idea of how a decent woman should dress?" I gestured toward my T-shirt, baggy shorts, and sandals. I'd pulled my hair back. The mass of tight cornrows was heavy enough to keep my head tilted back, a decidedly superior posture. I carried a half bottle of wine and a pair of plastic wineglasses.

"I miss the belly jewelry," he said.

"You've seen more than your share, I expect."

"How do you get past airport metal detectors?"

"I distract the guards with my tattoos."

"Which one do they like better? The burning flag or the hammer and sickle?"

I bristled like a cat. "It's the smiley face on my ass that really gets their attention." I sat down at the picnic table and unceremoniously removed the wine bottle's screw top. "Hope you like discount chardonnay." He eyed the plastic goblets just as he seemed to study every other detail of my world. He made me feel defensive without uttering another word.

I poured wine. He neither took a glass nor said anything. His scrutiny focused suddenly on my bright yellow cornrows and braids. "I can't figure out what kind of fashion statement you're trying to make."

"I'm sure you're used to women whose idea of a fashion statement is the bill they pay for a tease job at Lula Ethel's House of Beauty every month."

"I like women with big hair. I admit it." He sat down across from me slowly, gracefully, all long legs and broad shoulders, his knees brushing mine under the table before I twisted my legs aside. From his shirt pocket he pulled a folded sheet of notepaper and a yellowed envelope with a stamp so old it was peeling off. "Read this first," he said, handing me the note.

I frowned at the mystery as I unfolded the paper. The handwriting was spidery but strong.

Venus—
Gib found you for me. I've been waiting a long time to meet you. I believe your family's friendship is a treasure we lost and have to recover. You and your sister are our compatriot survivors of life's cruel fates. Now we've found you and you'll prove me right. I also believe your family shares my family's faith and hope. I believe that with all my heart.

It was signed "Olivia Cameron." Next, Gib laid the old, fragile envelope in front of me. "My great-aunt Olivia kept this. She asked me to give it to you along with her note. Your mother sent it to her."

I plucked out a color snapshot of Mom, Pop, me at about five, and Ella in Mom's arms. Little, dark-haired, innocent girls. A lump formed in my throat. "Read the inscription on the back," Gib said. My hands trembling, I turned the photo over and read in Mom's handwriting: *Dear Olivia, I'm going to bring my girls to meet you and yours as soon as I can coax Max away from his nightclub. Venus always asks me when she can meet "her" Gib. I promise we'll visit someday. You have blessed us with a friendship we cherish. I think of your family as our own special angels.*

Gib cleared his throat. "My aunt says it's time you made good on your mother's promise to visit."

I didn't know what to say. Suddenly I heard the muffled sounds of angry men arguing inside a trailer across the lot. Grateful for the distraction, I pulled a small can of pepper spray from my shorts pocket and set it on the table. Gib's dark gaze shifted to the trailer. The look in his eyes transformed his expression to one of deadly calm. Chilled, I sat there studying him. "Cheers," I said finally, and gulped a deep swallow of wine.

He didn't stop watching the trailer until the noise faded away. Then he exhaled, blinked, and returned his attention to me. "The pepper spray won't do you much good," he said, "unless you're about to cook dinner for me." He frowned at my ridiculous lipstick-sized canister.

"It works well enough. If you spot a biker with a purple ponytail coming this way, let me know. He has a drug habit, and he's a little too obnoxious when he's wasted."

He craned his head, staring past me suddenly. He was like a hawk. He didn't miss a sound, a movement. The soft hum of the RV's electrical system serenaded us. A long cord ran from the air conditioner to a post in the ground. "What's that light in the window?" he asked. "Did you light a candle?"

I swiveled to look, then faced him again. "My sister did it. She likes candles. Aromatherapy. She says the scent helps her headaches. I say they make our camper smell like soap."

He didn't laugh. I studied his straight-backed posture with a sinking heart. "Look, Mr. Cameron, you've come a long way to see my sister and me. What do you and your aunt really want from us? What's this offer I can't refuse? You and I have never even met before. You only met my parents once, and you were just a little boy then."

"If it's that simple, and you don't give a damn, then why did you remember me so quickly? No matter what your father told you, you can't deny that you didn't forget us."

"My father wasn't hostile toward your family. It was just that after my mother died, he felt we had nothing in common with you. He didn't believe in cultivating relationships that had no room to grow. His and Mom's wedding at Cameron Hall was just a sentimental memory to him."

"I see. Then why didn't you listen to him and forget all about me?"

We spent several long seconds studying each other in strained silence. I spread my hands awkwardly on the table, then curled them into my lap. "I'm twenty-nine years old and you're, what? Thirty-five? We're not childhood pen pals anymore. You wouldn't have gone to the trouble to find me if it wouldn't benefit you to do it."

The insult tightened his face and brought out a look of flat, cold-blooded scrutiny. It was a mask I'd seen on the faces of government agents. "There was a time when I believed in you," Gib said in a low voice. "It sounds stupid now. I was the kind of kid who took things seriously. I'd lost my parents. I hated the world outside my mountains. You were the only part of that outside world that I wanted to know. But after your mother died I never got another card from you. I was afraid you'd died, too. Even though I knew you hadn't, I decided to forget you."

"Wait a minute. *You* stopped writing to *me*." I didn't add that I'd grieved desperately over his silence, long after Pop told me Camerons had no place in our lives.

He shook his head. "I sent you letters for years."

I stared at him. "That's not possible. I would have gotten them. I—" My voice trailed off as I realized what had happened. Pop had intervened. I felt weighted down. "My father didn't believe in sentiment," I repeated wearily. "He must have thrown your cards away."

Gib and I shared a look of troubled understanding. "Thank you for telling me the truth," he said finally. "Even though it gives me one more reason to dislike your father."

"He wouldn't have judged *you* so superficially."

"Oh? If your father were sitting here right now, I expect he'd despise me." He held out his good hand. He wore a heavy insignia ring on his third finger. "Recognize this?" he asked.

"A college ring. So?"

"Not just any college. The Citadel."

The Citadel. Southern bastion of military machismo, graduating generations of ultraconservative traditional males and shouting huzzahs to all-American manhood. My throat clotted on years of fantasy and the cold reality of disappointment. "No wonder you looked out of place in a lesbian bar," I said. "You're John Wayne."

"There's more. I joined the Marines right after graduation."

"Do you want me to salute?"

"I'm everything you were raised to hate."

Silence. We both looked away. I finally offered, "My father never said a bad word against the Camerons. He knew how it felt to be hated without good reason. No one deserves it. That was the code he lived by." I paused. "And I certainly don't hate you. All I ask is fairness. I give fairness in return."

"All right."

"So you were a career Marine until . . . ?"

He shook his head. "I did what I was best suited for. What I'd always wanted to do since my parents were killed. I loved feeling that I was standing between an innocent person and danger. I loved feeling like I was out there"—he waved his good hand at the world beyond—"keeping everything safe for what I loved. Can you sympathize with that, now that you know me a little?"

"Of course. And I don't need to hear—" I halted. "What *kind* of career did you go into after college and a stint in the Marines?"

"I went to work for the U.S. Treasury Department."

The Treasury Department? "You were an agent for the Treasury Department," I echoed blankly, scrutinizing him. Some unfound piece of this puzzle floated in my mind disturbingly, but I couldn't place it.

"I transferred around the country a lot, tracking counterfeiters, working on cases involving credit-card fraud, that kind of thing. But I finally got transferred to the division I'd wanted all along. Worked like a dog to win that honor. It was the proudest day of my life. The proudest day for my family."

The implications were spinning into place. Only my obsessive backtracking over other details kept me from making the connection. "I've worked all over the world," he continued. "I've been privy to conversations with kings and queens and prime ministers. I've slept in the finest hotels, eaten the finest food, danced with the prettiest women, and traveled first-class. In fact, better than first-class."

"So you were some kind of corrupt bureaucrat in the Treasury Department." I uttered a sharp laugh. "Not that there's any such thing as an honest bureaucrat."

"My lifestyle wasn't exactly glamorous," he went on in a flat voice. "I've been spit on in public, and kicked, and hit, and shot at, and stabbed with a letter opener once, by a little old lady in Iowa who thought I was keeping her from the private meeting some tiny green Martians promised to set up for her. I was sworn to take whatever the world threw at me. Sworn to give up my life if need be to protect the symbol of everything your dad wanted to tear down."

Suddenly I understood. Shock washed over me. I pivoted toward him. Government agents were no better than Nazis to me, and he'd just told me he had belonged to their most elite group. "You were a Secret Service agent." I almost choked on the words.

He nodded.

I had good reason to hate him now.

Four

"I'm with the United States Treasury Department," the man in the dark gray suit repeated, unsmilingly, after I insisted he hold up his badge and his driver's license.

It was only a few days after Pop's death. We hadn't even buried him yet. It had been a week of constant interrogations, of men tearing our house apart and pushing me into corners. "You're from around here," I said to the man, as I inspected his credentials. Even his photo had the crisp look of a mortician. His chin was shaved so closely I could see a blue vein beside his mouth. "I thought the Secret Service was in Washington."

"I'm from the New Orleans office," he explained. "We have field offices everywhere." He looked at me as if he had daughters but they didn't talk back; he looked impatient. He stepped past me, latching a hand on the smooth, polished door framed by purple clematis. He didn't say another word as he walked into the front hall and onward to the living room.

He placed a tape recorder on the coffee table, removed a large notepad from his jacket, then sat down on the couch among the stacks of linen tablecloths I'd been folding. "Pull up that ottoman and have a seat across from the tape recorder here, Venus," he ordered casually, "and answer some questions for me."

I was ragged in grimy jeans and a T-shirt. I'd slept only a couple of hours a night. Each morning I presided over the dumped-out contents of every drawer in the house. The chaos had reduced me to small, obsessive efforts to fix, to replace, to restore order that was lost forever. "I don't understand."

"Sit," the man barked.

I continued to stand, swaying. My head felt like a balloon. "My father didn't kill anybody. And he certainly didn't threaten the President."

"That's not my problem. How he manipulated money is my area of interest. Credit cards, illegal transfers, fraudulent accounts, interstate financial shenanigans."

"I don't know anything. He never discussed any of it with my sister and me. I've told so many people already."

"He discussed it enough to make you understand which files needed to be gotten rid of once he was in trouble."

"I've told everybody. A friend said he needed the files. I thought my father wanted him to have them."

"Sit down, please."

"I don't think I should talk to you. I thought the Secret Service protected the President and other VIPs."

"That's part of what we do. Now, you don't have any idea whether your dad messed with funny money, do you?"

"I don't have to talk to you without our lawyer here. Why don't you leave, please?"

He stood. He took two long steps around the coffee table, nothing urgent about him, then suddenly he snatched me by the shoulders and shoved me onto the ottoman. He bent over me, his face beet-red and his eyes furious. "You self-righteous young woman," he yelled. "You're gonna end up in jail just like your old Commie-lovin' dad. You've got nothing and nobody to cover for your pampered little behind anymore. This is not a piano contest. Your dad raised you and your sister in a sewer of filthy money. Everything in this fancy house reeks with the stink. From the clothes you wear"—he tugged at the sleeve of my T-shirt—"to the food in your kitchen, you have not got one thing to your name that can't be taken away under the law. Because there's not a damned dollar of your father's money or his business or his belongings that isn't tinged with the dirty red color of death and crime."

"Nobody can claim our house and take away everything."

"Watch us do it," he said. "I hope you and your sister have friends who can help you out. Because we're about to confiscate every penny of your dad's money and every square inch of his belongings."

And they did.

That was my encounter with the Secret Service. Guardians of the world's leaders. Protectors of the true-blue currency.

Who sent moving vans and carted away every piece of furniture, every china setting and lamp and couch and chair, beds, pillows, paintings, and even the linens I had folded time and again. Our diaries, our school yearbooks, letters and birthday cards we'd saved, poetry we'd written.

And Ella's violin. And my piano.

Our music.

Our innocence. Our life.

As my shock over Gib's past career settled into leaden acceptance, I walked a few feet away, took a deep breath, then demanded in a low voice, "Did you ever harass women and girls? Did you ever bully innocent people and confiscate everything they owned?"

"No," he answered quietly. "I know you dealt with Treasury Department agents after your father died, and I'm sure it wasn't pleasant, but the men and women I've worked with would die to protect your rights."

"Then you didn't work with the ones who came to see my sister and me."

I'm sure he saw the disgust I felt. He had no nervous

mannerisms except for subtle efforts to keep his disfigured hand out of sight, and now he planted the other broad, handsome hand on his left knee, as if showing me it was safely anchored there. "Be fair," he said. "Don't despise me on principle alone. At least let me give you good reason to despise me. Do you know what the first week in September is?"

"It's my parents' thirtieth wedding anniversary." I watched him like an angry cat.

"That means it's the inn's anniversary, too. Thirty years ago your parents were our first guests."

"I know that."

"I don't want to sentimentalize that history any more than you do. Your life's been hard in the past ten years. I can see that. You've learned some ugly lessons. You've survived some bad treatment. You have a right to be suspicious of anyone who pokes around in your business. But there's no excuse for your outright distrust when I haven't given you any reason to distrust me." He paused. "Unless you're trying to prove you're as paranoid as your father was."

I leaned toward him furiously. He just couldn't resist the subject of Pop. "I know your type. I don't like you because you remind me of all the smug, patronizing, holier-than-thou minions of Uncle Sam who've deliberately made our lives miserable. You don't give a damn about my wishes or my opinion. Go back to Tennessee and leave me alone."

"I can't fault you for defending your own daddy, but you could have honorably cooperated with the investigations, and you didn't. You sacrificed any chance you had of going on with your classical career. You dragged your sister along on this odyssey to see how much punishment you could take while you thumbed your nose at the rest of the world."

"How dare you judge me! You don't know—"

"Isn't it time to stop before your sister ends up back in a mental hospital for another round of treatment?" He paused, his eyes merciless on mine. "Yes. I'm talking about Detroit."

I had a hard spine but a soft underside, and he kicked me where it hurt. I balled my hands into fists. He'd gotten Ella's medical files.

"Go ahead. Hit me," he urged in a soft tone. "You want to fight with the *Man*? The System? All right, I'll take the rap. Let me have it. I won't hit you back. I'm not the one who ruined your prospects. I'm not here to hurt you—or Ella."

"Tell me what you want."

He was silent for a few seconds, searching my eyes as if he needed to see my soul—to prove I had one. Then, in a quiet voice, he said, "Your father left you a hundred thousand dollars. I've got it."

I opened my mouth, shut it, tried to think, to absorb that unbelievable claim. Finally I simply pivoted and made my way to the concrete water fountain. I tracked the sluggish goldfish as if they were my own dizzy thoughts. Gib walked over and stood beside me, staring down into the algae-crusted water. "Surprise," he said.

"This is a bad joke."

"No. Ten years ago a stranger walked up to my older brother outside a building at the University of Tennessee in Knoxville. My brother was there to accept an award from the College of Business. My brother—Simon. This man—this stranger—had obviously been following him, waiting for an opportunity. It was the same week your father died, after he was arrested. The stranger walked up to Simon and shoved a small briefcase into his hands. He said, 'Max Arinelli begs you on his wife's soul to keep this for his daughters. Just keep it until they come for it.' The man turned and ran. My brother opened the briefcase. It was full of hundred-dollar bills."

My head swam. "I've never known *anything* about money being sent to your brother. Nothing. If you don't believe me—"

"Since you never showed up to claim it, I think you're telling the truth."

He studied me with a troubled expression. I shook my head. "I don't understand. Everything my father owned was confiscated or—"

"Obviously he had money hidden for an emergency. When he was arrested he got word to somebody he trusted. Somebody willing to go to Tennessee and deliver the money to my brother." Gib leaned toward me, a muscle popping in his jaw. "I don't understand why your father did that, but I'll give him the benefit of the doubt and say he never forgot how he and your mother were treated by my family. No matter how much he rejected us—the same way he rejected all his old friends after your mother died—I guess when push came to shove he still thought he could count on my family for help."

"You don't know what this means to me," I whispered.

"Here's what it means to me: My brother agonized over that money. He knew he should turn it in to the authorities, but he couldn't bring himself to do that. He stuck the money in his office safe and waited for you and your sister to come for it. When you didn't, he never touched it again and he never told a soul. My brother wasn't the kind of man who kept secrets from his family. I don't doubt the deception worried him for years."

"I'm sorry, but I'm still waiting for you to laugh and tell me you made this up."

His face darkened. "My brother's honesty and sense of duty isn't a joke."

"I didn't mean—"

"I wish it were that simple. The money's dirty. Drug money. Gun money. From all that money your father laundered to serve his cause. That fact weighed on Simon's conscience—but not as much as his compassion did. He was a father himself, and he understood what your father was trying to do. He left a letter in his safe-deposit box saying he felt like a coward for not finding you and Ella and handing you the money. He'd been afraid that somehow it could hurt our own family to be associated with Max Arinelli's hidden money. But he said in his letter he'd been wrong. That only God could judge your father's legacy to you."

"Your brother," I said numbly. "Simon. What happened to him?"

Gib was silent for a moment. His throat worked. "He died a little over a year ago."

My mind whirled again. "Died? You found the letter—"

"A few months later. In his papers. Now my sisters and my great-aunt know about it, too. And Simon's wife knows. We all know. We're trying to do what he wanted done. He wanted you and Ella to have that money."

One hundred thousand dollars. It could be the down payment on a small music club somewhere. Or on a house. Or the start of a retirement fund that would ensure that neither Ella nor I ended up on the street playing for tips and eating out of garbage cans. I had promised Ella for years that someday we'd have the money to settle down.

"The money's yours," Gib insisted. "No strings attached."

My daydreams cooled. "There are always strings."

"Well, nothing you can't handle."

I stared at him. "I swear to you I didn't know about the money before."

"I can only assume your father intended to tell you."

"He didn't live long enough to tell me anything."

"He lived long enough to pull my brother into a dicey situation."

"I see. Anything associated with my father is automatically tainted. Including me. Including Ella."

"Look, I'm here to fulfill my brother's wishes. My whole family's wishes. I've found you and Ella for them. The money's waiting for you at Cameron Hall. As far as I'm concerned it doesn't exist. If you don't come to the Hall and carry it away with your own hands I swear to God I'll burn it."

I turned without another word, walked back to the picnic table, and sat on the tabletop staring blindly at the plastic wineglass I cupped in my hands. I clutched it so hard the bowl cracked. I was dimly aware when Gib sat down beside me. He took the ruined glass out of my hand and tossed it neatly into the trash can. "The money's yours, either way," he said.

I gritted my teeth. "I learned a long time ago that no one gives a damn about my sister and me. If I didn't want the money for Ella, I wouldn't humble myself to sneak into your ancestral home like a whore."

"Interesting choice of words. Unfortunately, your plan won't work."

"What do you mean?"

He rubbed at lines of fatigue and tension in his forehead. He blew out a long, disgusted-sounding breath. "You've been imbued," he said, "with an importance far greater than you want to imagine."

"I don't like the sound of that."

"You read my great-aunt's note. You and your sis are invited to the Hall," he repeated quietly. "That's what we call it—Cameron Hall. We've been closed for a year. I don't know when or even if we're going to reopen the inn. So you'll be our only guests."

The estate had been closed for a year? Before I could catch myself, I glanced meaningfully at his hand. "I don't want to be anyone's symbolic totem," I finally said.

For a second he shut his eyes, then opened them and scanned the distant skyscrapers as if searching for an escape. "Too late. You represent the triumph of old hospitality come home to roost. And of course the rest of the family sees welcoming you and Ella as the fulfillment of my brother's wishes."

"What do you see us as?"

He hesitated. "A gamble," he said.

I quickly looked away to hide my disappointment. "You're telling me that if I want that money I have to perform. What kind of act do you want?"

"You have to visit. That's all. Come set a spell. Kick your

shoes off. Allow yourself and Ella to be pampered. You've been designated as Company."

This was no small thing, in the southern sense of that word. If a person visited a home in the South for any length of time, whether for a mere one-night stay or weeks, months, even years of habitation, that visitor achieved the status of Company, meaning he or she received deluxe treatment.

"How long is your definition of a spell?" I asked, stunned. "How long does your great-aunt expect us to stay?"

"That's up to you. I'd say anything less than a week wouldn't even register on her Company scale. You have to understand. Our cousin Bea came to visit when I was a little boy. She's still there. Another cousin moved in two years ago. In your case, two weeks ought to do it."

"Two *weeks*? That's impossible."

"I'm not any more comfortable with this than you are."

"I don't need your charity. Or your self-righteous judgments."

"Maybe my family's a little crazy right now. Looking for answers to make the world feel safe again." He actually smiled a little. "Come and be crazy with them. I've spent most of the past year with my arm in a sling and my hand taped up like a baseball glove. All I could manage to do was type one-handed on a little laptop computer. That's when I started hunting for you through the Internet. On days when I thought I'd lose my mind I made myself focus on that. On finding information that would lead me to you."

His eyes were a light shade of brown, maybe hazel, flecked with gold I could see even in the shadowy light. Unrelenting. Goosebumps ran up my spine. I couldn't escape this man any more than I could escape the past. The days that followed Pop's arrest and death were burned in my memory forever. He'd used the Camerons to reach me with a gift of love. The money was now a bond between us all.

I didn't know what to say.

"Wait here." I stumbled to the RV then past Ella, sound

asleep and angelic in her bunk. I searched through a cigar box where I hid mementos and what little decent jewelry I had. When I walked back outside and held out my hand, palm up, a small, smooth quartz rock gleamed dully under the yellow streetlights. "You gave this to my mother. She named me Venus because of the story you told her about this. How it was a piece of the evening star. She loved that story. She recited it to me every night."

Astonishment showed in his gaunt face. I thrust my hand closer to him. I dared him to touch me, but he didn't move a muscle. My hand trembled, then sank. Holding on to my dignity was hopeless. "After my mother died I wanted to believe you'd always be special, just as she said you were. Maybe you're not special and neither am I. We don't have to care about each other. Just tell me if you really believe any good will come of me and my sister going to visit your family in Tennessee." And then I waited.

"I don't know," he said finally, searching my eyes. "I'm not an optimist by nature. But I promise you this much. You don't have to like me, but you can trust me. That's more than you can say about any other 'government man' you've known." After another awkward silence he frowned deeply and started toward his jeep. Just before he reached for the door he turned and looked at me one more time. "I like the way you take care of your sister," he said. "Family loyalty. I respect that. I hope you'll respect mine."

Tears stung behind my eyes. I fought any sign of weakness. I would honor Simon Cameron's kindness and Gib's devotion to him.

"I'll come and get my money," I said without a shred of emotion.

"Good."

He left. I strained my neck watching him drive away, even walking to the edge of the street to catch one last glimpse before he disappeared into the Chicago night.

Every note of music and every musical sound in life radiates outward. The vibrations become infinitely small, but they never quite fade. They can still reach you, when you're suddenly quiet enough and empty enough to catch the echoes inside you.

Promises and betrayals are the same way.

Five

"I don't know if I can do this," I told Ella the next morning. "I can't believe what's happening to us."

Ella looked at me with her strong, graceful hands clasped gently to her lips. "We have to go," she whispered. "I don't care about the money. I don't think it's a betrayal of Pop's ideals to visit Gib and his family. Gib seems to be a very honorable man who held a very honorable and important job. We have to be fair to him. Pop would agree with that. He preached fairness all his life."

"There's still no rational reason to drive hundreds of miles to spend two weeks with strangers. For all we know these people eat barbecued possum and really do marry their cousins."

Ella laughed. "Not at all like us decent folk from Louisiana, where our culture includes sex shows, gambling, and enough government corruption to sink a third-world dictatorship."

"But at least we don't eat possums."

"It would be nice to be wanted, for once," Ella said wistfully. "And I wouldn't mind taking the money." She looked at me in utter seriousness. "We could give half of it to a homeless shelter."

I sighed. Where did honor end? "The IRA killed Gib's parents when he was a little boy," I reminded Ella. "Don't imagine he and his family regard Pop as anything other than a fanatic and a terrorist, just like the Irish who did that to them."

"You don't know how they really feel. You always assume the worst." Ella linked her cool, trembling fingers through mine. "Everyone condemns Pop, except us." I looked at her angrily, but she was right. "We have to go there and represent Pop's good side to them. And Mom's. And not be ashamed."

"I am not ashamed."

"Good. Then we'll go."

Exhausted and shaky with emotion, I made a shooing motion at the bum who tapped on the RV's locked door that afternoon. He responded by holding up a Chicago Police Department badge.

I thought, *What fresh hell is this?* and formed my best Dorothy Parker smirk of sarcasm as I opened a side window vent. "You couldn't possibly have any business here." I had a problem with authority figures, even cops apparently working undercover in dirty jeans and a three-day beard.

"Chill out, ma'am," he said politely. "I just wanted to let you know I'll be working around here at night. You and your sister can sit out at the picnic table and none of the creeps'll bother you anymore."

I managed a garbled thank-you, then asked bluntly, "Did Gib Cameron use his connections to get this protection for us?"

"Maybe. He's got friends in the right places. Have a nice day." After he walked away I stood in confused silence.

I knew no other man who would have done this for me. I wasn't at all sure why Gib had. Ella and I seemed to be under the umbrella of Cameron noblesse oblige already, and we weren't even in Tennessee yet.

It was a strange sensation. For years I'd either shoved people away or ignored them. I couldn't take chances. I'd fought for decent bookings in the early years right after Ella and I disappeared into the boonies. I'd lied about her age to get us into nightclubs, then battled men who tried to hit on her. I'd begged or pilfered meals from the club chefs, even shoplifted petty necessities like shampoo and underwear. Whatever it took to keep Ella and me together, keep us working toward the day when we didn't have to ask anyone for anything, I'd do it.

I sat down in the RV's driver's seat. The white quartz rock lay on the dash. I scooped it into my hand. The lure of childhood fantasies was proud and seductive and probably disastrous.

Ella and I finished our contract with the Hers Truly club and turned down the manager's offer to extend our stay for better money.

"We're leaving early," I announced to Ella. "I want to check out the situation in advance. I think we should go on to Nashville after our visit. I've got some feelers out. We could find work there. For one thing, Opryland is hiring for a piano bar in one of its restaurants. We'll have to come up with some discreet ways to invest our money. We can't just plop it in the bank as if a customer suddenly gave us a huge tip. The IRS could be watching."

Ella stared at me over an issue of her Martha Stewart magazine. "If this were a song," she said gently, "I'd have to say it has no coherent melody."

"I'm just saying we should get a head start in case we end up ditching the whole visit to Cameron Hall."

I decided we'd come back for the RV if we found long-term work down south. I left it in a tract-house suburb south of Chicago, at the three-bedroom ranch where an old friend of our grandfather Paolo's lived with his granddaughter. Fifty years ago the friend had been a young trumpet player in Grandfather's studio orchestra.

And so, in the last week of August, sticky with heat, fanning ourselves in our tank tops and thin cotton skirts and flip-flops, a blues CD blasting on the car's high-tech player—all right, we spent money where it counted—Ella and I drove south out of the Windy City, me eating a Polish sausage and Ella sipping mineral water. "If we keep our expectations low we'll probably have a decent enough visit," I said, to which my sister replied, with her eyes shut dreamily, "My expectations have been growing wings for so long, I want to fly." She stroked a white goose feather she'd attached to the rearview mirror.

I didn't tell her I thought her expectations had molted pretty badly over the past ten years. On a map Gib Cameron had sent, I set course for an area that appeared to be no more than a handful of remote roads crisscrossing the green splash of the Great Smoky Mountains of eastern Tennessee.

Tennessee. Land of riverboats and mountain lions, Elvis, Davy Crockett, blues, bluegrass, hillbillies, honky-tonks, antebellum mansions, log cabins, moonshine liquor, fine bourbon, and a huge share of the music business.

And Camerons.

Ella ceremoniously placed Gib's driving directions on a clipboard I'd super-glued to the car's fading vinyl dashboard. She arranged several of her prize feathers around it. We looked at the bizarre little shrine fixedly.

Thirty years earlier, almost to the day, our parents had visited an inn that had just opened in the mountains. Cameron Hall. They'd married there, written "Evening Star" there, and, on a whim, selected a name for their first child there. Me.

Now Ella and I were going there to represent what was left of our family's pride. I put on dark rhinestone-outlined sunglasses and tried not to hope for the best.

·   ·   ·

Around noon the next day we crested a ridge on a nearly deserted two-lane road, passed a sign that welcomed us to Tennessee, the Volunteer State, and gasped in unison.

The low-country bayou gals had arrived at the top of the world. "Toto," I said in a small voice, "we're not in Kansas anymore."

Ella gave a soft, stunned sigh. "This has to be the Emerald City."

They are ancient and awesome, those Appalachian Mountains. Round and lush and green. From our vantage point looking out over them, the view startled and mesmerized me, too, because it was like suddenly flying over a cliff into sheer space. My hands trembled. I pulled off to one side of the road and got out of the car. Ella came to stand beside me.

The wind was warm but fast; the scent was green earth, blue sky, and waterways hidden in deep valleys we couldn't see. There were hawks and songbirds in the blue sky, and an unending, amazing, unsettling symphony of majestic wilderness. Somewhere down in one of those wild, secluded places was the chapel where Mom and Pop had married, and the room in the Cameron mansion where they had slept and made love on their first night of sanctified intimacy, and where I had come into being, no matter how small and casually biological. I had come to exist in these mountains.

"Can you imagine?" Ella whispered respectfully, "how the first settlers must have felt when they crossed this spot and saw the view?"

Oh, yes.

"Vee?" Ella said softly. She was crying. "Mom suspected she wouldn't live to be old! She knew it and she tried to find friends for us! Even before we were born she tried to make sure we'd always have someone besides Pop! She must have been so afraid he'd lose his way if she wasn't beside him! Oh, don't say it, don't say I'm imagining things! And I think Pop couldn't bring himself to completely forget what the Camerons meant to Mom. That's why he trusted Simon Cameron with our money. Oh, Vee, we were right to come here! It was meant to be!"

She cried with the lilting joy of relief and celebration. I took deep breaths, not wanting to stomp on her hopes. I wouldn't shout Praise Mary and rouse the saints. I was a lapsed Catholic and nobody's fool. Ella hurried along the roadside, bending down. "A wild turkey carcass!" she called happily. When she straightened she shook a ratty brown feather at me happily. "We were right to come! Our lives are on the right path!"

"I don't know," I said dryly. "It wasn't such a good path for that turkey."

I'd never openly admit that Mom had dreamed of this day coming to pass and later Pop, in his desperation, had guaranteed it.

New Inverness, the sign proclaimed. Unincorporated. Est. 1895. Population 25. Speed Limit 35.

We had arrived at the meeting point of two equally obscure little state roads, one of which we'd been following through the middle of nowhere for the past hour. New Inverness was the landmark Gib had mentioned in his printed directions. It wasn't even a town. It was barely a wide spot in the road.

I stopped the car. There was no traffic in any direction, so I could simply let the car idle in the middle of the intersection. I studied a bevy of sun-faded road signs, most of them pockmarked with bullet holes. Hightower 10 miles. Attenborough 18 miles. Knoxville 102 miles. Watch Out for Falling Rocks. Steep Grades Ahead.

"Now I know what Nowhere looks like," I said.

Ella craned her head. "It's just the way Gib described it in his driving directions."

"Small." But on one corner of the crossroads sat a large, handsome stone house among vegetable gardens, roses, and outbuildings that sheltered tractors, trucks, a school bus, and an ambulance. The opposite corner was home to a hodge-podge of buildings. On closer inspection they made up one single low structure with additions of various concoctions. Numerous doors and windows led to God alone knew where, but the main entrance was a double-screen door set under a big porch across the front, where farm equipment, animal traps, and decrepit lawn chairs argued for space. A fat black Labrador waddled a few yards toward our car, then lay down in the road and wagged its tail.

I snorted. "Must be the welcoming committee." I drove in and parked on a cracked concrete lot. In front of the main building was a parade of aged and dented gas, diesel, and kerosene pumps under a high tin awning. A huge, hook-necked, enormously ugly black bird perched menacingly on the awning's peak. "I think that's something prehistoric."

"It must be a buzzard," Ella said incredulously.

"I wonder what kind of meal it's hoping for in this park-ing lot. When we get out of the car, keep moving. And don't mention your feather collection."

We crossed the lot, giving the buzzard wary glances. The building before us bore a collection of fading gasoline signs and logos for companies that had been defunct for years, a weathered carved sign that said Sophia's Restaurant and Gift Shop, a rusting metal sign that proclaimed one end of the conglomerate Hoss's General Store, and beneath that sign a smaller one, very official in metallic green and white, that listed all of the New Inverness community services, includ-ing the post office, which were located inside.

We stepped into a general store with creaking wooden floors, clutter, video rentals, hardware, groceries, a pot-bellied stove, an espresso machine, and every curio known to mountain men. "Look at that stuffed turtle," Ella whispered, gesturing toward a wall covered in the musty heads and car-casses of wildlife, including rabbits, foxes, possums, and a *hamster*.

"I'm not sure he's stuffed," I whispered back. "I think he might just be scared to move. What kind of people stuff hamsters?"

A stocky older man with thick white hair and a face like a bulldog poked his head up from behind the cash register of a long counter crammed with displays and dusty knickknacks. "I loved that hamster," he said. "My youngest daughter named him after me."

We jumped. Grinning, he tucked reading glasses in the pocket of a Hawaiian shirt and got up from a recliner. His eyes narrowed into twinkling curiosity as he studied my mop of braids tied back with a fringed black scarf.

"Hold the fort," he said. "Where'd you get that yellow crown of fancy hair?" And in the same breath, "What can I do for you fine girls?"

I touched Gib's folded driving directions in a pocket of my skirt. "I need directions from here to Cameron Hall, please. I was told to stop at the store here and ask. And I understand you have some cabins to rent nearby. We're going to need a cabin for tonight if you have one available. I'm Ann Nelson and this is my sister, Jane. We're visiting—"

"We got cabins so darned modern the plumbing's inside." He waved his hands dramatically. "Why, you should see the way the outhouse works!"

Either he was practicing to audition for a remake of *The Beverly Hillbillies*, or he was making fun of us. "We'll take the nonsmoking and nonbuzzard cabin, please."

He roared. "You don't know whether to grin or skedaddle, do you? I own this store, and I'm just a bored old man who enjoys pulling your leg!"

Ella gushed, "You must be Colonel Cameron," blowing all hopes I'd had of quietly assessing these people before they learned who we were. "In his directions Gib said you were his cousin and that you run this store."

"Yes, ma'am! I'm Gib's father's first cousin's oldest son. Retired Air Force. Colonel Cameron. You can call me Hoss."

"Oh, sir, we are so *glad* to meet you. I'm Ella Arinelli and this is my sister, Venus. It's a pleasure to meet you." She reverted to southernness with an ease I'd never expected, introducing us as naturally as a bird sings to identify other birds.

The old man's eyes widened. A grin slowly spread the folds of his jowls. "You're a day early!" He gazed at me in awe. "Venus! No need to be shy about it!" He bowled around the end of the counter, narrowly missing a small table and chairs set up for a chess game. He grinned and waved his arms and bore down on us like an old freight train. I began to back up but Ella laughed and held out her hands. He grabbed her hands then turned and bellowed, "Sophia! Sophia, the Arinelli girls are here a day early! *And they are a sight!*"

"What?" a woman shrieked from a back room. We heard thumping and rustling sounds. A big-haired grandmotherly woman dressed in jeans and a T-shirt, her fingers glittering with diamond rings, hurried on short, plump legs through the narrow aisles of food and hardware and fishing tackle, spreading her Rubenesque arms to us. "Bless your hearts, little Arinellis," she said, with a heavy Italian accent. "My mother was a Campacho from Milan! *Sono molto lieto di fare la sua conoscenza!*"

Ella cried, "It's very nice to meet you, too! *Grazie!* You must be Sophia!" That was all the bonding ritual required to win over Sophia Campacho Cameron, of Tennessee by way of Italy. She grabbed me and Hoss grabbed Ella as if we were long-lost kin.

We were hugged and hugged again, patted on the backs, praised for our good looks, glowed at, offered wine, told we were godsends. It was like water falling on parched ground, to be welcomed that way by people who knew our family history. But they were ecstatic to see us. Or so they said.

"We prayed Gib would find the Arinelli sisters," Sophia sighed. "And that you would understand and come here. Now there is reason to celebrate."

"Understand what?" I asked warily.

"You're here for the thirty-year anniversary! We're all convinced this means Gib will take his brother's place and open the Hall again. You're a sign that the past has brought the Hall a future!"

I took a step back. I wasn't going to be sucked into this sentimental nonsense. I didn't like being an icon of Cameron hospitality. I was there to collect an inheritance and leave as soon as Gib deigned to hand it over, and I wanted to say so, flat out. But Ella's eyes were glazed with appreciation and acceptance. "I can't wait to see where our parents were married," she crooned. She radiated joy like a polished charm.

"Oh, but y'all can't go to the Hall, yet," Hoss announced. "Everybody's gone to Knoxville for the day."

"We weren't intending to stay there tonight—" I began patiently.

"But as soon as Gib hears, he'll come for y'all! We'll put you up in our house for the afternoon, and—"

"No, no, thank you. We really insist on renting a cabin. My sister's coming down with a headache, I'm afraid"—Ella stared at me with her mouth open in dismay at the lie—"and she needs absolute quiet. Really. So we really will rent a cabin."

"No way, no how will I put Venus and Ella Arinelli in a little bitty cabin like y'all are just tourists!" Hoss proclaimed. "Why, my cousin Olivia would skin my hide!"

"But dear Ella needs a house, not a cabin," Sophia crooned, reaching up to lay a hand against Ella's cheek. "I have the perfect bedroom for you in our home. You will rest and feel so much better."

"Why, thank you, and we accept most gratefully," Ella said, cutting her gaze at me.

"Here," Hoss said, snatching a pamphlet from beneath the counter. "It's a little map to the Hall. Tells you about the place, too."

Ella smiled. "Oh, we've been dying to know more about the Hall's history—"

"Thank you," I cut in, and took the pamphlet. On the cover a sketch of a vine-covered, tree-shaded old mansion was superimposed over a Scottish crest on a field of red plaid. "We'll just call Gib in the morning and tell him we're here," I said. "He's not expecting us until late tomorrow."

Hoss shook his head. "Gib and the family'll be back by then. But if they don't make it by dinnertime we'll set you up at the family table over yonder"—he pointed to the building next door, where lace curtains fluttered in open windows— "at the restaurant. We offer good homegrown chow to hikers and bikers and campers and general sightseers passin' through here"—he nodded toward a hall that led to the restaurant—"so we'll save you a two-seater tonight, all righty?"

"All righty," Ella chirped.

Cornered by the unnerving hospitality, I fumbled a hand across a small display of snuff cans and paper pouches of Tennessee Chaw chewing tobacco, which scattered over the counter. "I'm sorry," I mumbled, and began scooping them up.

"No problem, no problem, they're not fragile," Sophia said, laughing. "Nothing up here in the mountains will break that easily." As we stacked tobacco packets I saw a yellowed photograph under the scratched Plexiglas that aproned the counter around the cash register.

And I stopped cold, mesmerized. A Citadel-age version of Gib looked up at me with smiling hazel eyes, his body posture confident, handsome, and straight-backed, his right hand whole and strong. His dark hair was shaved to a military nub. But he was dressed in a flannel shirt, old jeans, and hiking boots.

He stood with his arm draped around another man's shoulders. They held a string of trout between them. The other man resembled Gib but was obviously a good deal older and less crisp. He had a comfortable look about his face, already wise and settled, maybe. He was dressed in a camouflage jacket and baggy trousers.

"Is this Gib's older brother?" I asked, pointing. Ella quickly huddled over the counter, too, her hands clasped together.

Tears rose in Hoss's eyes, to my embarrassment. "I can't do it. I can't talk to you about Simon," he said hoarsely. I straightened quickly and so did Ella. She and I traded strained looks.

"I'm sorry," Hoss said, wiping his face. "Can't help myself. Dear Lord." Sophia patted his shoulder, then began wiping her own eyes.

"We can talk about Simon later, if you want to know," she said. "Come along. You can settle in our daughter's old bedroom. Oh, Ella, you do look pale."

At that moment a small, wiry woman burst into the store, peering at us over purple-rimmed sunglasses. She wore thick-heeled granny clompers, tan Bermuda shorts with a crisply pressed blue blouse, and large earrings made of, I swear, it looked like small animal teeth. Little fangs were glued in a starburst pattern. Her hair was long, curly, blond-streaked brown with a poof of stiff-sprayed bangs on the front, surely half a foot tall.

She waved hands done in bright red inch-long nails decorated with pink stripes across the tips. "The Nellies?" she said breathlessly, pointing at us but gazing expectantly at Hoss and Sophia. "Johnny Mac called me on the CB and said he bet it was the Nellies in the parking lot."

"It's them," Hoss confirmed.

The woman raised her hands, then looked heavenward, whether in thanks or supplication I wasn't sure. She turned and ran out the door. I watched through the screen as she threw herself into a bright blue Camaro. The tires squealed as she drove off.

"Who was that?" I asked flatly. "And how does she get her hair to stand up that high?"

Sophia smiled. "That's Ebb Hodger. She and her sister and their mother have worked at the Hall for . . . oh, many years! Their grandparents before them. And their great-grandparents.

Now they have proof that all is not ended! The Nellies are here just as Nellies were here many years ago, and brought good luck! And Nellies will bring good luck again! The Hall will be open for business again! We are all convinced!"

No one could make me believe that nonsense. Ella and I had walked into a surreal world where people praised us, welcomed us, and waited to give us money. Well, I'd take the money and ignore the rest. I looked warily at all the animals parading in eternal performances along the walls.

We were not going to end up the same way.

Six

Sophia escorted us into her and Hoss's friendly old stone house, which was filled with European antiques, crystal, fine silver, and military memorabilia, including—out the window of our bedroom suite—a large American flag fluttering grandly on a flagpole set in a petunia garden. Hoss and Sophia had lived in Europe for many years during his Air Force career.

Now we were left to rest among their museumlike collection of keepsakes. Sophia brought us a pitcher of iced tea and pimento cheese sandwiches on a silver platter. Ella curled up on a lace-trimmed antique oak trundle bed with the hum of a tiny window air conditioner next to her and her face buried in the Cameron pamphlet. "You're going to read?" I asked in exasperation.

Ella sighed, "Hmmm-huh."

I heard a phone ringing somewhere downstairs. I suspected Sophia was telling the whole county that we'd arrived. "Don't you think it's peculiar that these people take in strangers like us?" I said.

"They know our family."

"Excuse me? They met our parents *once*. For a weekend."

"Then Mom and Pop made a huge impression. Relax."

"And that big-haired chick. What was *that* all about? I don't want anybody gaping at us that way. What does she expect?"

"We're honored guests. The Camerons haven't had many visitors in the past year. She was excited."

"I want to find out what happened to Simon Cameron."

"Don't pry. It's not polite. And it's probably a story that will just make us feel bad. Listen to this!" Ella waved the pamphlet at me. "The road between here and the Hall follows an old Cherokee trail. And you won't believe how the Camerons got started here." She got up and pressed the booklet into my hand. "Read this. You have to read this *right now*. Olivia Cameron wrote it. Gib's great-aunt. It's fascinating."

"All right, all right." I went over to a window and sat on the edge of a hard chair, very impatient and not intending to get sucked in by history. But then I read:

The first Cameron didn't exactly come to these mountains peacefully or willingly. But he found what has drawn people here through the ages. Sanctuary.

And I couldn't stop.

Even the Cherokees were looking for sanctuary when they came here centuries ago. Most of the southern Appalachians were settled by people seeking safety and freedom for one reason or another. A thousand years ago the Cherokees were pushed south by the Iroquois. The English came to get away from the king. The Scottish came to get away from the English. So did the Irish.

All looking for sanctuary.

But the first Cameron to set foot in our valley wasn't the first Scotsman there. Our family goes back one step farther to a MacIntosh. Tavis MacIntosh. Tavis explored the Cherokee lands in the early 1700s. In the old maps and books the territory was labeled with its Cherokee name, which was pronounced more or less like *Tennessee* though the spelling was *T-e-n-a-s-i*.

I expect Tavis just spelled it Eden. Paradise. That's what it must have seemed to him. Herds of buffalo, passenger pigeons by the millions, deer, bear, beaver. Rivers full of fish. Valleys so rich the Cherokee had farmed them for generations. Thousands of Cherokees lived in permanent towns with huts and sweat lodges and ceremonial council houses and farmlands. They were the most powerful tribe in the southern mountains then.

Tavis probably followed the east Tenasi trace, an ancient hunting trail and warpath, up from the coast into the Appalachians, until he finally came to a magnificent valley. There he found one of the largest villages in the Cherokee Nation. A peace town, they called it. Neutral territory—whether it was about Cherokees fighting other tribes, or white settlers, or each other—the valley town was a sanctuary.

The valley itself had been a sacred place for centuries before the Cherokee separated from their Iroquois alliances and came south. That's what Cherokee legends say, and that's what the archaeologists have told us. Tavis must have marveled at the fifty-foot-tall, hundred-foot-wide ceremonial mound at the valley's center. It predates even the Cherokee. Scientists have found arrowheads and pottery pieces in the vicinity that go back a thousand years.

Tavis built a cabin on the edge of the valley and set up a trading post. He married a prominent Cherokee woman named Two Doe and they raised a family. Tavis became an important trader in Cherokee, as well as white, society. In those early times the Scotsmen who explored in the mountains settled easily among the Cherokees. The Highland Scotsmen, being tribal folk accustomed to a clan system not unlike the Cherokees', felt at home.

In the mid-1700s, Two Doe died and Tavis became

fatally ill himself. He wished that their youngest children might be educated in Scottish ways and Christianity after his death. So he sent his grown daughter on the long, hard journey to the coast to fetch back a Scotsman. Her name was Soquena among the Cherokees, but Susan MacIntosh to the white settlers. She intended to hire a Scotsman to tutor her younger brothers and build a chapel for the family.

But when she and her entourage of Cherokee women friends and warriors arrived on the Carolina coast, the best she could find was a half-dead Highlander fresh off an English Navy ship and still in chains.

His name was Gilbert Cameron. He'd been rounded up by the English in the purges after the last Scottish rebellion. The English shipped many of the Highland clan leaders to the colonies in the West Indies and sold them into servitude on the plantations there.

Gilbert Cameron was lucky to end up on the coast of the Carolinas instead, though he was nearly starved and beaten to death during the voyage. Perhaps Susan took pity on him, or perhaps she had no choice; she purchased Gilbert Cameron from the English as an indentured servant. She believed she was buying an educated and obedient man and had little idea that he was in fact a Highland warrior intent on freedom.

Susan was as strong-willed as he, however. She marched him into the mountains, threatened him with torture when he attempted escapes, and, in short, fought a battle of control that has become a legendary frontier story. Before Gilbert Cameron and Susan MacIntosh made peace with each other she sliced off the tip of his right ear. Years later, one of their children wrote that "Papa never seemed bothered by the disfigurement much, and Mother never showed a great deal of remorse for the attack."

Gilbert did, in fact, build a chapel for her atop the ancient ceremonial mound, and together they raised six children, established the Cameron family in Hightower

County, Tennessee, survived Indian wars, smallpox epidemics, and the American Revolution.

Surely no two people better represented the collision of cultures and faiths in that era, or the loving alliances that have kept Camerons and MacIntoshes at their ancestral home for all the generations since.

"Sounds like a lot of melodrama and exaggerated history to me," I said, when I finished. "If this is an example of how the Cameron family conducts itself, we'll probably be locked in a room and *forced* to wait for our money." Secretly I'd found the story enthralling, but the family history of high-handedness did raise my hackles.

Ella huffed in exasperation. "I believe every word of it. We can look right out the window here and imagine how Susan marched her captive Cameron, along the very same path that the modern road follows! It gives me goosebumps! They followed the same path we're going to follow down the mountainside and into the Cameron valley. We are *part* of Cameron history now—just like Mom and Pop were when they came here. I feel connected. The same feeling I get when I think about Grandmother Akiko's ancestors being descended from a samurai. We are connected to the spirits of *our* ancestors here, Vee."

"And the spirits of our Japanese kin are probably toasting our mutt pedigree over a hibachi somewhere in the Buddhist hereafter. Because they sure don't give a damn about us." I arranged my braids in long, ropy masses front and back, buttoned a denim vest over my thin T-shirt, brushed cracker crumbs from a purplish cotton skirt, and put on some crimson lipstick. My sandaled feet were dirty. I washed them in a china-cup beautiful bathroom and dried them with towels embroidered with a Cameron crest.

I wiped my lipstick off. Who was I trying to impress? "Hold the fort," I told Ella, "and fend off any large birds of prey. I'm going to do a drive-by look-see at the Hall. I'll be back in thirty minutes, tops." I checked my purse for the pepper spray. Ella sighed.

"This is not a job, Vee. You don't have to scope out the sound system or determine whether the manager is a lecherous pervert. You don't have to be overprotective of me here."

"I can't change my obsessive habits. Why, without my obsessions I'd have no personality at all."

"I feel secure in these Cameron Mountains. I feel peaceful. I wish you did, too."

"I'll feel better after I figure out more about these people. Not glorious tales in self-serving pamphlets. No babbling about mythic anniversaries. The facts." I slipped downstairs and out a back door, then scurried to our car in the backyard.

I drove out of the yard and turned slowly up a twisting, narrow road hooded by steep hills, overgrown trees, and huge rhododendrons. I watched uneasily as New Inverness disappeared in my rearview mirror. Indian trail. Wilderness. The first Gilbert Cameron had been bought and paid for and unwillingly marched into this extravagantly Edenlike new territory. The latest Gib Cameron wanted me to believe Ella and I were welcome guests in a family as different from ours as Susan MacIntosh's had been from Gib's ancestor.

Nobody was taking a piece of my hide that easily.

I might just as well have driven off the edge of the earth. The map failed to do justice to the jumble of Tennessee mountains with hairpin turns and spots where the tiny, two-lane road clung to overlooks that might launch my old hatchback car into the stratosphere.

The brake pedal began to give as the car careened down another steep descent. I managed to turn onto a fingerlet of paved road fronted by a staunch brass sign that said HISTORIC CAMERON HALL 2 MILES. I drove in low gear and prayed to Saint Christopher, even slipping his medal off the collection dangling from the rearview mirror and clutching it in one hand.

Saint Chris, I only ask that the brakes and transmission hold out.

I would have pulled over except that there was no shoulder on either side of the road; to the right was a perpendicular slab of mountain rock dripping misty water and lichen, and on the left was a wooded gully that dropped fifty feet into creek bottoms filled with ferns among huge gray boulders.

I swooped down the last half mile of road in breathtaking free-form. I'm sure the car never moved faster than thirty miles an hour, but steering it on a road that doubled back every hundred feet was an exercise in terror.

Suddenly I entered an enormous cove in the lap of queenly mountains. I stamped the brake one more time and the car skidded into a shallow ditch. The front bumper stopped inches from a tall, majestic, moss-speckled stone pillar. Its twin stood on the other side of a handsome gravel road bordered by wildflowers and a few white morning glories steadfastly blooming in the mountains' afternoon shadows.

I gasped. I'd been dropped neatly at the entrance to the Cameron Valley. The entrance to Cameron Hall.

Taking deep breaths and wiping cold sweat from my eyes, I staggered out of the car. Everything was so quiet. I gazed around me at the cloud-shadowed, humpbacked old mountains. I inhaled the smell of lush forest. The only sounds I heard were the wind and distant water trickling down a small outcropping of rock.

I walked to the stone posts. Carved in a smooth stone plate on the front of one were the weathered words WEL-COME, FRIEND. On the other post, greetings of some sort were carved in symbols I couldn't decipher. Cherokee, maybe?

But elaborate and forbidding wrought-iron gates closed the road to me. They were padlocked at the center. "Some welcome," I accused loudly. The words echoed back at me and I shrank a little, as if I'd shouted during mass. Suddenly nervous, I wandered across an area of mown grass. Four large brass historical placards stood like proud sentinels in a glen. I made myself breathe calmly and concentrate on the inscriptions. The first one began:

> Gilbert Cameron arrived in this valley, 1746, expelled by the British from his native Scottish Highlands and sold into servitude.

The second sign began:

> Site of the sacred Cherokee town of Hightower and the Tavern of Scottish trader Tavis MacIntosh. Soquena "Susan" MacIntosh, daughter of Tavis MacIntosh and Cherokee princess Two Doe, purchased Gilbert Cameron and brought him to this Hightower Valley to build a chapel in honor of her deceased Scotsman father.

The third began:

> Through this ancient valley trail passed many legends of the American southern frontier, as guests at the MacIntosh/ Cameron Tavern prior to the construction of Cameron Hall in 1805 by wealthy merchant William Cameron, son of Gilbert and Soquena.

The fourth marker related the Cameron clan's local heroics in the Revolutionary War and the Civil War. Apparently, Camerons collected historical markers the way old people in New Orleans collected Virgin Mary statues and pink yard-flamingos. I tilted my head back and gazed around at the wild, green bowl of the valley, most of it hidden behind tantalizing forest. If a kilt-wearing Scotsman and a buckskinned half-Cherokee woman had stepped out of the woods, or a stagecoach had rumbled around the bend behind me, I would have curtsied and felt at home.

At home. What a useless thing to imagine. "George Washington probably slept here," I muttered wearily. I sidestepped the gate, stumbling over a low, crude wall of field stones. And now I, Venus Arinelli, the mingled essence of Asian aristocrats, Mediterranean troubadours, and Nordic ne'er-do-wells, former pampered Catholic schoolgirl piano prodigy, a grown woman fallen from grace as the daughter of a man the founding fathers would have hanged from the nearest tree, I dared to traipse where Washington had slept.

I raised my chin and went to a spring near the foundation I'd tripped over. The spring was crystal clear but warm, so warm it steamed on a hot late-summer day.

Suddenly I realized where I was.

The spring. This was the hot spring Mom told me about. This was where my quartz rock came from. This was the "magic pond" Mom always mentioned in her story. Where the evening star made promises come true.

I sat down slowly. Trembling, I pressed the water to my face. The earth gave off gentle heat. No wonder the valley was considered sacred. Its veins pulsed understanding and comfort. No one could take my parents' best memories from me here.

"I am losing my mind," I told myself sternly as I walked up the entrance road, trespassing. The car belched smoke from underneath and wouldn't crank. The cellular phone I stored under the front seat couldn't locate a carrier signal. I didn't have much choice.

My own pride had trapped me. Gib Cameron would come home and find me sitting on the Hall's doorstep like a fool. I dragged a sweaty forearm across my eyes, then strode up the curving lane between shadowy woods.

A minute later I entered a vast open area of pastures on either side. There the road was lined with magnificent crape myrtles; each tall shrub was still bursting with clusters of white, late-summer blooms. Crowded along the fences were lingering cleome, the long green stems nodding their top-knots of tiny blue-purple flowers in a warm breeze.

The pastures were dotted with giant rolls of baled hay and backed by towering, mist-draped mountains. I stared as a dozen wild deer raised their heads to watch me from the pasture. Some of the does had spotted fawns beside them. None even bothered to run from me. Grazing nearby was a mingled herd of horses, ponies, several mules, black cattle, and shaggy buffalo.

Buffalo.

Not wild. I hoped.

"Hello, cows," I called out with as much humor as I could muster. And to the buffalo, because I felt giddy, "Hello, cows with fur."

I walked past pastures for what seemed like a mile, my head throbbing and my knees weak. The woods closed in again. I began to think about being out there alone, with Ella not knowing I was stranded, and no one home at Cameron Hall. There were still plenty of bears in these mountains. I hurried up the next knoll.

The quality of light seemed to sharpen; I blinked slowly, in wonder, aware of some clarity I couldn't pinpoint, a sense of destiny that raised goosebumps on my arms and set a warm tingle in my stomach. It was the feeling you get walking into a place of spectacular, profound beauty or a place that pro-vokes instant memories. That you've been there before, or wish you had. It speaks to some memory or desire deeper than your conscious mind.

At the top of the knoll I looked across endless pasture-land stretching over rolling terrain. In the distance sat a broad stone mansion with long wings on either side, glistening in the sunshine with rows of tall, white-shuttered windows, fronted by a circular carriage drive, and topped by stately brick chimneys.

Cameron Hall. Surrounded by flower gardens, grand without being pretentious, shaded by enormous, gnarled oaks, the manor house and its lawns had a charm unlike any place I'd seen. Nearby were handsome gray-weathered barns and outbuildings. A split-rail fence wound across the lower front yard. A distant field was lush and green with late-summer corn. The shallow channel of a small river curled below the front lawns. A small stone bridge crossed it. The scene reminded me of a softly mystical, ethereal eighteenth-century painting—a Gainsborough, maybe.

Suddenly I heard rustling noises and a chorus of low growls. I froze, looked around frantically, then started for the nearest low tree limb. A dozen dogs surrounded me, some barking and wagging their tails madly, a couple growling; two shaggy, large, calico-colored dogs with china-blue eyes stared at me as intensely as judges.

I eased one hand into my skirt pocket and retrieved my pepper spray. I slipped forward on the balls of my feet, twisting from side to side in slow arcs, my arm extended stiffly with the pepper spray ready. "Let's all chill out," I warned in a low voice. I stared at the blue-eyed dogs. They looked like the dog in my parents' wedding picture. "Hello, China Eyes," I said tentatively. "Your pop or grandpop played best dog at my parents' nuptials."

One of the dogs wagged his tail. Then the other joined in. Of course they were only responding to my tone of voice. Ridiculous tears rose in my eyes, regardless. "You know I'm a friend," I said. The first dog wagged harder. I caught myself smiling at him. The blue-eyed dogs padded along with their eerie, ice-blue gazes on me, but they were wagging their tails.

As I hurried up the lane, the house disappeared as forest surrounded me again. Sweat trickled down my throat. I was tuned in to every crunch of my sandals on the gravel, to every flicker of canine eyes. But suddenly the dogs deserted me and bounded into the woods on my left, and even the blue-eyed dogs, as if more dignified, gave me dismissive glances as they, too, turned their backs and trotted lazily into the forest.

Wavering in the middle of the lane, sucking down deep, relieved breaths, I peered into the woods.

And saw the chapel.

It rose among the trees in a sunlit grassy clearing maybe a hundred yards from where I stood. The front faced away from me; I was looking at one ivy-covered stone wall along the side, but I could see the peaked, shingled roof and the delicate copper cupola, weathered green, above the trees.

The chapel sat about fifty feet higher than the clearing, built on the flat-topped mound, that man-made pedestal of earth and native sacraments. The sides of the mound were covered in soft, shaggy grass. The chapel's steeple prodded gently into the blue sky above the trees.

An old cemetery spread out around the base of the mound. Weathered, old-fashioned tombstones mingled with modern ones. Some of the older graves were covered in large stone crypts. Others were marked only by slabs no larger than a writing tablet. The cemetery was neatly mowed and scattered with handsome shrubs. The remnants of sawed-off stumps showed where older generations of plantings had grown large and died and been removed. I didn't want to look too closely. I might spot the graves of Gilbert and Susan. Or the grave of the beloved, mysteriously tragic Simon.

The Camerons were obviously a family who honored their dead—or couldn't bear to ignore their ghosts. I understood that sentiment all too well. The elaborate cemeteries in New Orleans had frightened and fascinated me after Mom died.

I glimpsed a winding path that linked the chapel to the gravel lane. Every other thought faded. I had come on a mission of pride—for all that we Arinellis had been and for all that my father had desperately wanted us to become.

Mom. Pop. I want to see where you were married. I want

to see where you were happy together. I hope you know I'm here. I hope you know I came.

I ran forward.

I rounded the lip of the path and halted, feet spread, lips parted—open and vulnerable and awed. My gaze rose up stone steps—the steps from the photograph, *exactly* as I knew them, only in living color finally, speckled with moss and the tiniest blue wildflowers that grew from cracks in the stones.

Up. Up, in slow, hypnotized motion, my childhood fantasy becoming as true as it ever could, and I knew exactly where Gib had sat on the top step, because I had memorized every detail over the years.

And there he was.

Seven

He was sprawled in a thronelike chair on the chapel's small, whitewashed porch. Piles of shabby planks were strewn on the narrow apron of earth around the porch, and I noticed a toolbelt lying haphazardly at his feet. He needed a good shave. He was dressed in a white ribbed tank top, dirty khaki trousers, laced muddy boots, and suspenders. He balanced a half-empty bottle of bourbon on one updrawn knee.

He didn't move, he didn't speak. His face was shadowed by a battered brown fedora; I couldn't see his eyes or read his expression, but from the tilt of his head there was no doubt in my mind he was looking straight down at me. Given the clothes and the fedora, he presented a picture straight out of every bad Hollywood version of southern manhood. Central casting, circa 1950. Sex, sweat, liquor, and attitude.

He touched the forefinger of his good hand to the hat's brim in greeting, then propped his chin on the hand. His slightest movements made sawdust drift from the chair's plush red upholstery. A golden tabby cat sat beside his chair. It reared on its hind legs, then rubbed its jowls on armrests that knuckled under into exquisitely detailed ram's heads.

Then the cat curled along Gib's lower leg and nuzzled his knee. A large butterfly landed on his bare shoulder.

A man couldn't look too sinister with a cat nuzzling him and a butterfly poised on his arm. I began to notice other details. His shoulders were rusty with dirt and fresh sunburn. His face was more haggard than I remembered in Chicago. The gouged scars on his forearm, laced with pinpoint white suture marks, were uglier in the sun.

I walked to the bottom of the steps. "I thought—" I stopped, cleared my throat, and started again, loudly and firmly. "I heard your family had all gone to Knoxville today. Why aren't you with them?"

"I had something to do," he said. "Privately."

I climbed the steps, keeping an eye on him. He slowly raised the liquor to his mouth and drank deeply. The bottle wobbled in the incomplete grip of his mangled hand. He perched it on his thigh again. "Couldn't resist your favorite government SOB, hmmm?"

"I've been insulted by meaner drunks than *you*." I frowned at the bottle.

"You're not a bourbon drinker," he said.

"I prefer blood." The truth was, drunkenness and other out-of-control behavior frightened me. Discipline was security.

I walked past him without another word. The chapel was as delicate as the inside of a Fabergé egg. The interior posts and beams were elaborately carved light wood, and the arched windows on either side were stained glass. The plank walls were painted in intricate, lovely but unsettling murals. I gaped at them as I realized what made them odd.

Saints. This was a Catholic chapel.

The oh-so-familiar saints were going about their instantly recognizable business here in the middle of the mostly Protestant mountains of Tennessee. Some of them were bearded mountain men draped in buckskin robes, and there was Saint Agnes in calico with a sunbonnet, and Saint Francis was

distinctly Indian—Cherokee, I assumed—bare-chested and
wearing a colorful blanket, a loincloth, leggings, and moc-
casins, with his hair plucked to a single long black lock at
the crown of his head, and a raccoon and a possum sitting at
his feet.

As I continued to wander around I saw the chapel was in
disarray. Its heavy, carved pews were stacked in precarious
formations at the back of the chapel, and long, rotten-edged
sections of the plank flooring were jumbled in dusty piles
along the walls. The floor had been patched with large sheets
of bare plywood that sagged and creaked as I walked across
them. A small but intricately carved altar—it looked out of
place, it was so formal and European—fronted a tiny choir
alcove where a small, simple, obviously antique organ called
me with the siren promise of music. I sighed and touched a
reverent hand to the organ's enameled backstop and yellowed
ivory keys.

"You're disturbing the ghosts," Gib said behind me, and I
pivoted sharply. The floor creaked and sent goosebumps
down my spine. Gib staggered to a stack of rotten boards and
put down the bourbon bottle. He lifted a plank and carried it
to me like a baby held gently in his arms. Beneath a pallor of
age and dust the wood was golden. The plank was at least two
feet wide. "My brother never threw anything away. He was even
going to save these. Build cabinets with the pieces. I was going to help him. That's what I promised him, anyway. I was
never home much. Always traveling. Lived in Washington.
Busy. Important man. That was me. Simon kept telling me he
needed more help around here. I never took him seriously."

"I expect Simon was very proud of you—"

"Always busy. That was me. World traveler. Make an ap-
pointment to get me home. Give me a list of family chores.
Be efficient. But Simon"— Gib patted the board—"he took
time. He knew the wood. He loved every board and every
stone of this chapel and the Hall and he remembered every
person who ever set foot here."

He pointed to the exposed beams of the roof and walls. "Chestnut. Tough as iron. Last forever." He nodded at the section of plank in his arms. "Pine. Softer wood. Easier to work with. But it doesn't last like chestnut."

"Well, when was the last time the floor was replaced?"

"Never."

"What?"

"This was the original. Floor was . . . the only thing not built to last. Termites got it last year."

I stared at him. The chapel was built *before 1750*. But apparently a floor that only lasted a quarter of a millennium wasn't good enough by Cameron standards. I smiled uneasily. "You're going to put in a new floor and by gum, this time it better last at least four hundred years, right?"

He didn't blink. "That's my plan." He paused. "That was Simon's plan."

"I see."

"Replace the pine with chestnut boards. Hard wood. Toughest wood around. Termites—no way. Guarantee—Simon's floor will be here a thousand years from now."

"Chestnut? I thought all the chestnut trees were gone."

"No more like 'em. Gone. Giants of the earth. Extinct. The blight got 'em in the thirties. Disease." He wavered, then steadied himself. "It's a waste of your time to listen to this. No reason you should give a damn. Right?"

"I don't waste my time. You're mistaken if you think I listen just to be polite. I'm rarely polite for *any* reason. Surely you've noticed. But let's talk about *wood*. Where are you getting the chestnut boards from?"

"Logs my granddad put aside, sixty years ago, when the blight hit. In a storage barn."

"Camerons *really* plan ahead, don't they?"

Gib abruptly walked to the center of the chapel. He dropped the board he was carrying. It clattered on the plywood floor. He raised his fists and looked around angrily. "Termites. It's always the little hidden bastards. The little mistakes you think you'll catch before everything falls apart. You turn your back on the smallest detail and it's the one that ruins you. You watch everything you believed in die right in front of your eyes." His voice rose. "No place is safe. And there's nothing you can do about it." He faced me, breathing hard, his fists clenched. "Tell me I'm wrong," he asked hoarsely.

I shook my head. "But I don't think termites qualify as the *wrath of God*."

"You're right. The wrath of God came later. Do you believe in accidents?"

"Yes."

"I don't. Accidents are the consequence of deliberate choices."

"Oh, I *see*. You choose to get out of bed every morning and one morning you slip on the rug and sprain your ankle. But it's no accident because it wouldn't have happened if you'd stayed in bed for the rest of your life? No—sometimes accidents just happen. We just have to deal with that fact. All right?"

"How do we deal with it? You tell me how you've gotten through what happened to your family. That's what I want to know from you."

"My sister needed me. I had a purpose."

"Good. All right. But there had to be more to it than that. No one wants to feel useless." He hesitated. "I speak from experience."

"Oh? I didn't come all the way here to visit a *useless* man. I have better judgment than that. Tell me about your brother. Tell me what happened to him—"

"I don't want to talk about it." He pointed to the organ. "Play something."

I sighed, but he had asked me to do the one thing I secretly wanted to do. I walked to the front of the chapel and sat down on a claw-footed organ stool. I fiddled experimentally with the pull stops on the antique organ's enameled backboard. I pumped the foot pedals and played a chord. Dust wheezed from the pipes, but the sound was pure.

I played a simple recital warmup I'd learned as a child. Gib pulled his hat off and tossed it atop a stack of pews. Then he sat down unsteadily beside the organ and propped his arms on his updrawn knees. He bent his head and shut his eyes. I glanced furtively at the rigid slant of his cheekbones, the gaunt slopes beneath his eyes—his hair was mink-brown with that fleck of gray at the top of his forehead.

When I finished I pulled my hands into my lap primly. "I don't usually play requests." He continued to sit with his eyes closed. For all I knew he'd fallen asleep. "But I'll make an exception if there's anything you want to hear. Or if I'm just babbling out loud to myself while you're taking a nap, I guess I'll play whatever I want. Are you asleep?"

He pushed himself up to his feet with effort. "Good God, you're talented. You can't go on throwing yourself away on the jobs you take." I bristled with humiliation—the truth always hurts. Before I could do more than stare at him open-mouthed, he turned and walked outside.

I hurried after him. "Where are you going?" He lifted a hand, let it fall, then eased down the steps at the front of the chapel mound, placing each booted foot carefully.

He's out of his mind. He's drunk.

I followed him but kept several yards behind. *He can't walk far in his condition.* "Are any of your family home yet? Back from Knoxville?"

He halted at the base of the steps and faced me. He towered over me, large hazel eyes scowling under dark brows frosted with wood dust. The dogs gathered around him, licking his pants legs and his hands, which hung loosely by his sides. "Are you planning to walk to the house?" I persisted.

His left hand lashed out. In an instant that showed how quick he was despite the bourbon, he folded his fingers under the cusp of my chin, and smoothed his thumb across my cheek. "You have green eyes like a cat," he said. Appreciation softened his face for a second. "Cocked up at the outside corners. The sharpest *cat eyes*. What do you see when you look at me?"

"A man who needs to sit down somewhere shady and let the bourbon wear off. A man who might be worth talking to if he'd *just sit the hell down*."

He turned and walked down the footpath toward the main dirt road. He walked with the tired, lazy grace that liquor endows on some hard-assed men. I followed him to the road and around a curve. A long flatbed truck was parked there. Tall, thick stanchions jutted from its scarred wooden bed. The truck was obviously meant for rugged hauling. Gib swung a door open and climbed into the cab.

"Where are you going?" I called. He didn't answer or even seem to notice. The man needed someone, something; he needed help. I felt frightened and exhilarated, conscious of the light again—moonlight lingering in the sunlight—a certain thinning of the fabric between choice and fate. I owed him for our childhood whimsies. I owed him for caring enough to find me, and for the undercover cop he'd sent in Chicago. I told myself I couldn't let him drive off a ledge or wrap this ancient truck around a tree. And certainly not until I'd gotten my money from him.

I went to the back of the truck, latched both hands around a post, and climbed onto the bed. I faced forward so I could watch him through the cab's dusty rear window. Most of the dogs jumped up beside me, eager to go for a ride.

The truck was old and the engine made noises like a dyspeptic elephant when Gib cranked it. Smoke belched from the exhaust pipe. We began to roll up the road. I held on tightly. I was ready to jump out if his driving got too wild. One of the blue-eyed dogs sat down beside me and whined.

I put my arm around him. We both turned around and watched Gib. "This is more than I bargained for," I muttered.

Eight

The first time a boy caused trouble for me I was only eight. While the nuns were drilling us for our confirmation, Barret Walker III kept whispering inanely, "The Lard cooks in mysterious ways," and because I had a small crush on him, with his cocky attitude and smart-guy stance when the sisters punished him, which was often, I was too attentive to his jokes.

So during confirmation, when the bishop asked me to name the seven gifts of the Holy Ghost, I named every gift perfectly until the very last one, when I glanced at Barret Walker III, who mouthed *lard*, and without thinking I told the bishop solemnly that the seventh gift of the Holy Ghost was "fear of the *Lard*."

Afterward, Sister Mary Catherine insisted the faux pas indicated a rebellious nature and was no accident, no matter how much I protested my innocence. Maybe she was right. As I rode into the forest with Gib that day I thought of Barret Walker III and wondered if there was any way I could really excuse my own choices.

Maybe Gib was right, too. There are no accidents. Only consequences. I had no idea where we were headed or what might happen next. Gib drove through the woods for several

minutes, turned off on another dirt road, and drove through
more woods, to a clearing by the river.

I climbed out and looked at the building that stretched
along the river's bank; it was long, wide, and low, with a rust-
streaked tin roof. Sections of its sturdy plank walls could be
unlatched to prop up—like awnings—in hot weather. They
were all closed and fastened with iron clasps. At first inspection I assumed the building was a chicken house, but it was
too tall for that, and massively constructed, and besides, no
one would put a single chicken house in the woods by itself.

Around it were lopsided piles of old sawdust sinking into
the field grass like soft gray islands in a sea of green, already
decomposing to form weak mulch that hosted briars and other
hardy weeds. Several open-sided sheds were full of stacked
lumber, and in others I saw small mountains of uncut logs
peeking from thick plastic tarps. The rusted hulks of two
dozen old vehicles had been lined up outside one wall of the
building.

This spot was also the Camerons' personal junkyard, or
someone's joke of an automotive museum. In addition to
vintage pickup trucks and the rusted frame of a Mercedes
touring car that would break any car collector's heart, I recognized a couple of 1950-ish Fords and an old English road-
ster. But there were also skeletal frames from buggies, and
the iron rims of wagon wheels, and in one shed, several pieces
of antique farm equipment—large, spidery, horse-drawn de-
vices for baling or cutting or whatever, I couldn't fathom.

The clearing was beautiful in its own morbid way, with
the small river gurgling on the other side of the building and
wide old beech trees on either side, nodding in the warm
breeze. I could imagine blacksmiths shoeing horses under the
trees, and farmhands guiding mule-drawn combines up the
same road we'd taken.

Gib finally staggered from the truck, left the door open,
and stood with his feet braced apart, his hands hanging by his
sides, as he faced the building. I climbed down from the

truck's bed, watching the harsh movement of his shoulders as he took deep, uneven breaths; his fists clenched, then unfurled, then tightened again. He stood like a half-beaten but stubborn fighter.

Before I could think of anything to say he strode to the building's wide industrial door, jerked a heavy iron bolt from its latch, then slid the door on its squealing metal tracks. Gib went to the center of the open door and stood, braced as he had been before, silhouetted by the inky shadows. Then he disappeared into the darkness.

The dogs milled uneasily outside. Even the stately blue-eyed dogs were reluctant to follow him. But someone had to go in there with him.

I moved slowly, aware of every degree of bright sunshine falling off my shoulders as I stepped inside, squinting. I smelled fragrant wood, dust, and clay earth. I smelled stale gasoline, like a service station on a broiling summer day.

As my eyes adjusted I looked around, then spotted Gib—a tall, dark shape—moving by the wall to my right. I heard a click. Lights came on, bright pinpoints of bare bulbs hanging under dusty metal hoods in a line down the center of the rafters.

In the middle of the floor stood a waist-high contraption, about fifty feet long, of steel rollers and sidearm levers designed to feed logs from a storage platform at one end of the building.

I looked from Gib to where the feeder met its goal: a steel table beside a maze of gears and wide beltdrives. Berthed in the center of the table, a savagely effective sawblade gleamed in the light. The blade was at least four feet in diameter, with teeth that looked as if they could rip a house in two.

Or a man.

A sawmill. Oh, my God.

Gib took slow, leaden steps, scuffing dust motes into the air. He stopped by the feeder trolley. His jaw clenched, he slowly held his damaged hand over the rollers as if the device might burn him when he touched it. When he finally rested his hand on the metal track, his shoulders slumped and he bent his head.

Next he shuffled to the end of the feeder path, then laid his good hand on the long slabs of wood, already milled into rough sections two feet wide and a foot thick, and arranged neatly on the storage platform. He stroked one of the massive pieces. It was as if he had to touch each element of this place, to bless it or curse it.

I felt dazed, even more as I noticed details like the pristine layer of sawdust on the floor, still bearing grid lines in places, where it had been neatly raked. There was a lingering chemical smell from walls coated in perfectly unsmudged white paint. I looked at the steel gleam of the giant sawblade and the cloudy smudges that looked like gray spray paint on the sawdust around the base of the gray-hued metal posts beneath the feeder track. The building had been cleaned, scrubbed, repainted, and then closed up.

Gib fumbled with an old engine that had been mounted off the ground on a concrete pedestal. He opened a wide wooden window on the opposite side of the building, squinted in the added sunlight, took something small from his trouser pocket, and bent over the engine unsteadily. It roared to life. Its thumping noise filled the building, and pungent exhaust smoke wafted out the window through a pipe.

But the sawblade sat motionless, as if waiting for him to pull a switch or press a button somewhere. He contemplated the blade with eerie fascination, walking around it slowly, riveted to a single line of sight that linked him to the gleaming, dangerous blade. He never seemed to notice me, standing a few feet away. I debated both of our next moves as if action were an improvised duet I didn't want to play.

I sidled past him then hurried to the engine, studying it. The key. The key in an ignition switch was easy to reach. A small, smooth chunk of wood dangled from it by a thin chain.

The words "Sawmill Engine" were painted in fading black on the wood.

Gib curled his ruined hand into a fist and slammed it against a control panel on a post beside the sawblade gears. The blade shivered, then accelerated, soon spinning at full speed with a sinister *whirring* sound I could hear even above the earsplitting beat of the tractor engine.

Gib sank his hands into his dark hair and staggered toward the log platform. He jerked a large, pronged hook off a wall and jabbed its sharp tip into the end of a log atop the platform. He wrestled the log onto the feeder track. It shimmied precariously on the track's edge, nearly rolling off before he lifted a booted foot and shoved it. The log settled into place. He sprawled on his back.

I yelled, but he couldn't hear me over the engine and the blade. He struggled to his elbows, sat up, then rolled onto his hands and knees and wavered to his feet. He had a shell-shocked look of determination. Shuffling, wiping sweat from his forehead, he went back to the log, which was inching down the track toward the blade.

I grabbed the engine's ignition key by its homemade wooden key chain and jerked it from the switch.

Silence. Everything stopped—the engine, the sawblade, the log creeping along the rollers. Gib frowned at the saw-blade and the halted log. Slowly, blinking, he raised his be-wildered scowl in the general direction of the engine. When he saw me he scrubbed his good hand over his sweating face, and looked again.

He started my way, swaying, holding on to posts, walls, beltdrives—whatever helped him move quickly without falling down. "Give me the key," he ordered in a tone that could have sliced logs as sharply as any blade.

He bore down on me with his good hand thrust out and his momentum warning that this was no time for rational arguments. I bolted to the window, which was just a crude opening with no screen. The bottom ledge was waist-high. The key still clutched in my grip, I latched on to the ledge with both hands and threw one leg over it.

But he caught me from behind, wrapping both sweaty, dirty arms around my waist, pinning one arm but not the other one. I yelled but held on to the window ledge with my right hand and right leg still hooked over it.

He pried me off with a hard tug that sent him to the floor with me splayed on my back on top of him. I rolled off and crouched on my knees, furious. "Get your hands off me! Are you too drunk to realize I'm trying to save your life?"

He sat up wearily, then thrust out his good hand. "I'm milling those logs today. It took all my willpower to walk in here. I'm not walking out without doing the job. *Give me that engine key.*"

"Look, I don't know what you're trying to prove to yourself, but I know this isn't the way to do it. Does this have something to do with your brother?"

The mention of Simon made him bow his head. I crept closer to him. "Talk. Talk to me. I talked to *you*—to that photograph—for years. Now you talk to *me.*"

Gib bent his head nearer mine. His breath hot and quick on my face, he gasped for air. Then, "We came here to cut boards for the chapel floor. We were arguing about something that wasn't even important. We were in a hurry. I was always in a hurry. Simon caught his arm in the beltdrive by the blade. I tried to hold on to him, but the belt pulled him into the blade. The blade snagged my hand. Then it caught my brother and cut him to pieces."

I swallowed the bile that rose in my throat. Suddenly I could imagine the smell of blood, the carnage. Gib exhaled harshly. He must have been picturing the same thing but in horrible detail. "Okay," I whispered quickly. "Okay. It's over." He raised his head, looked at me, pressed his cheek against the top of my head, then put his arms around me and held me snugly.

I froze. It had been years since I'd hugged anyone except Ella for comfort—either to give or receive it. Gib represented every kind of easy protection Pop had raised me to reject. Suddenly, just being there, choosing to be in the valley and to follow Gib—made me despise myself. Who was the enemy? Who did I blame for what had happened to Pop, and then to Ella and me? Gib and his whole pioneer-American, patriotic family personified the Us in an Us-versus-Them world.

And I would always be one of Them.

But then I heard the whisper of Sister Mary Catherine's lectures, God bless her stern, unyielding soul. *You're a musical wonder with a pagan name and a heathen father, but you're a passionate child. Look into your heart and never forget to give that passion to the people who need you. That's all that will save you.*

Slowly I put my arms around Gib. We held on to each other and gave comfort.

For the first time in ten years, something in my life was pure, innocent, and simple.

Nine

Later Gib sobered enough to drive me back to New Inverness. He escorted me to the deep, stone-columned veranda of Hoss and Sophia's house, his stride showing only the slightest waver. He stepped ahead of me with easy grace, opened their beautiful stained-glass front door, then stepped back, gesturing for me to enter. I could see the dignified but not quite deferential attitude of a man trained to serve and protect.

"I'll see what I can do about having your car repaired," he said with quiet formality.

"I appreciate that," I answered the same way.

"We'll expect you and Ella at the Hall in the morning. I'll send someone to pick you up after breakfast."

"Thank you."

"There's nothing I can do about today except apologize and swear nothing like that will happen again. I had no right to lay my hands on you in anger, not for any reason. I had no right to upset you. I had no right to expect your help and concern. The fact that you kept me from hurting myself speaks well for your integrity and badly for mine."

"Oh, please, I'm not used to being worshiped."

"I've been turning into a drunk. An invalid and a drunk,"

he went on wearily. "This isn't the only day I've gone to that sawmill stoned out of my mind. It's just the first time I had the guts to unlock the door."

I glanced at him sideways, for safety. I could still feel his arms around me, and when I looked at him the sensation wrapped me up again. "Good for you, then. You unlocked the door."

"And I would have done more if you hadn't stolen my damned engine key."

I bristled, preparing for an argument. But there was the slightest glimmer in his eyes, like the sunny rim of a cloud. I snorted. *"Ass."*

"I'm going back this afternoon and find that key, *Nellie.*"

With a grim smile of victory, he left me standing there. I don't know which made me madder—his stubborn refusal to forget the sawmill project until he was strong enough and had enough help to do the work safely, or the fact that he'd just turned my ear-pleasing Italian family name into a down-home Tennessee nickname.

Sophia found me wandering in a daze up a front hall, and came with her hands out. "What has happened to you? My husband went looking in the valley."

"Vee!" Ella called, as she hurried down a handsomely carved staircase. "I was so worried! You've been gone two hours! What happened?"

"I met Gib at the chapel. He went to the sawmill. I followed him. He was drunk."

"You went *there* with him?" Sophia said in a soft, horrified contralto. I nodded. She moaned. "But no one goes there. They can't bear it. Did he—oh, he was never supposed to go there and try to use that terrible blade again—"

"He didn't," I promised. Miserable and bone tired, I pulled the sawmill engine key from my skirt pocket. "What's that?" Ella asked, but Sophia gasped. I dragged myself up the stairs. As I passed Ella I noticed her exasperated and puzzled expression. I patted her shoulder. "I'm fine," I lied. I heard

Sophia sigh, behind me, "Oh! It is true, it is *true*! The angels have sent you to work miracles!"

I was no angel. I desperately wanted to pack our things and leave.

But I did like the idea of Gib going back to the sawmill and searching uselessly for the key.

Ella and I sat in Hoss and Sophia's tiny restaurant at a table by a window. A high, white thumbnail moon perched in the early-evening sky above the mountains, which made astonishing dark silhouettes against the horizon. I couldn't see the evening star, and strange fears skittered across my nerve endings like a spider. I had no guiding light and I was lost in a wilderness of more than one kind.

Across the room the only other customers ate peach pie on thick blue plates. They looked like tired hikers—a man and woman, middle-aged, their dusty safari shorts and golf shirts smeared with sweat stains. The Eddie Bauer catalog must have lured them into the Tennessee mountains with visions of outdoorsy glamour. The catalog was probably off in a corner somewhere, giggling.

Ella picked at a plate of stewed squash, crowder peas, turnip greens, and cornbread, as she watched me anxiously. I sipped from a stoneware mug full of black coffee and ignored a bowl of gelatinous chicken and dumplings. Sophia came into the room smiling and sat down with us. She put a bottle of port wine on the table and three small glasses. "A celebration of your arrival," she announced with the lilt of a warm Italian vineyard in her voice. Then she told us Hoss had come back from the Hall in a decidedly glum mood. Sophia, who turned information and gossip in her plump hands like a fine pastry, relayed his report that the family was at odds over Ella and me.

"Olivia wanted to come greet you tonight and bring you both to the Hall as soon as she heard you were here," Sophia said. "But Gib said no, that you needed to be left alone tonight.

That he had upset you. So of course Olivia is not happy about that."

I groaned. "I don't want to take my sister over there and put her in the middle of some Cameron turf war."

"Don't think that way! They are not *fighting*. Gib would never argue with his great-aunt. She is an *elder*. But she feels bad for provoking him today, so she lets this other thing—you and Ella staying here tonight—she lets it pass. They have other troubles tonight. Hoss says it's about Cousin Emory."

"Cousin Emory?" Ella said in a conspiratorial whisper. Her eyes lit up with righteous concern. "Who's Emory?"

Sophia grunted. "Emory is a greedy *bastard*." She trickled deep burgundy liquid into the glasses. "An old bastard, and a *wealthy* bastard. And so is his son. Joe. A bastard." She lifted her glass of port. We dutifully lifted ours. *"Salute,"* she said. "To victory over the bastards."

We sipped politely. Ella feigned a swallow, then set her glass down. I hunched forward and studied Sophia eagerly. "Is there trouble with this dastardly Cousin Emory?"

"Old trouble with new dollar signs. He has made a wonderful offer to buy the Hall."

"Wonderful?"

"He has found investors—a company that manages hotels and golf courses. Millions of dollars they'll pay. The family would keep half-interest. And a hotel company would preserve the Hall and the valley—no changes to the main part! In Emory's words, 'Just a few improvements.' Hah! Condominiums to sell on the mountainsides, and a conference center on the river, and maybe a tiny golf course in the far pastures."

"That would be unthinkable," I said slowly. "It would change the nature of the valley."

"Ah, but all beautifully done. And very hard to say no to. Hotel people would manage the Hall. Emory, the *bastard*, claims the family would be on the board of directors." She drained her small glass then set it down hard. Her eyes glittered.

"No more worries. Everyone gets rich. Enjoys life. No hard work. Just stroll among the guests and smile like an actor and entertain with family stories. A wonderful offer. Emory knows it is seductive. *Bastard.*"

"They'll never do it," I said fervently. "From what I can see Gib would never—"

"Oh, but this is no new plan of Emory's. This is an offer he made to Simon many times. And Simon was tempted to take it."

"What?"

"Simon worried that the family could not always manage the Hall—that maybe no one after him would want to be responsible. He thought Emory's idea would be the best thing. To make certain the Hall is always cherished and cared for as a historic place. A public place, but beloved."

She downed another glass of port. "Simon and Gib argued over this idea last year. That day. The day Simon died." Her voice trembled.

"Oh, *no*."

She nodded as she filled her glass again. "Gib was upset with him for talking seriously to Emory. But Simon, he tells Gib, he says, 'You do not want to take charge. Our sisters have their children, their own work, their own lives. You have *your* work. But I am *tired*. Min and I deserve to have vacations. And what about my children? They'll want to go off to college someday and live somewhere else. Who will take charge when I am gone?'"

Sophia gulped more port. " 'Look at the chapel,' Simon insists. 'The floor is rotten! I am so busy I cannot take care of it soon enough. How can I let our heritage rot before my eyes because I am too busy and too tired to fix it!' And so Gib says, 'Goddamn, I will help you cut new boards *today*! Come on! I have to catch a plane back to Washington tonight!' So they go to the sawmill, angry with each other, in a hurry, and poor Minnie goes along trying to calm them down."

"Were you and Hoss there that day—"

"Oh, yes. Oh, yes. We went down there. That is why my husband cannot talk about Simon. He still has nightmares. In his mind he sees it all again and again. What we found in that sawmill is in my mind, too. I drink too much when I think about it."

"I'd like for you to tell me about the accident if you can," I said. "I need to know—" I paused, glancing at Ella, who had stopped spooning mushed cornbread over her turnip greens and was merely pushing crowder peas with her fork. I recognized the signs. She had a weak stomach. "Maybe we can talk about it sometime. Not over dinner."

But Sophia, unaware, said, "You ought to know *now*. You deserve to hear the story. After all, what new misery would have happened today if you had not stopped Gib from running the saw in his condition? He is not a drinker at heart, you know." She downed another glass of port.

I swallowed all of mine in one rich, pungent gulp. "Tell me," I said.

"I believe I'll go out back and sit in the swing," Ella interjected in a small voice. "Excuse me." She stood. I asked quickly, "You need any company?"

She managed a smile. "Not if I leave before I hear any more details." She patted my shoulder then walked across the small restaurant. I watched until she disappeared down a hallway and I heard the back door shut behind her.

"Your sister has a . . . a—" Sophia said, patting her fleshy stomach covered in a gold-embossed T-shirt. "Not strong," Sophia finally managed.

"No, she just has a soft heart."

"Ah! Not like you, eh?"

"Not like me, eh."

"All right, then." She took a deep breath. "Minnie calls up here from a phone at the sawmill. She is screaming, *'Help us, help us.'* Hoss and I, we drive quick down into the valley, and the sheriff is coming, too, and the men from the fire department in Hightower—everyone we can call quick.

"We go to the sawmill, and we run inside." She paused, cupping her glass in front of her, shutting her eyes, then opening them and staring fixedly at the dark port, like blood. "Simon is cut in half just below his heart. And Gib is holding him."

Specks of light danced in front of my eyes. I took a deep breath and cleared my head. "Go on."

"Poor Gib. His arm looks like it has almost been torn off below the elbow. His hand—pieces are missing. I see them—pieces of pieces, in the sawdust. He is covered in blood all over. Soaked. Blood and well . . . Gib looks across the floor at the, *the bottom half* of Simon's body, and Gib asks, 'Who is that?' because he is out of his mind."

"Gib was still conscious?"

She met my stunned gaze then nodded. "He is lying against a wall with Simon's—holding Simon's top half—in his lap. He is cradling Simon with his good arm to keep him safe. And Min is sitting covered in blood beside her husband and Gib, and she has pulled off her shirt—so she is sitting there holding the bloody shirt against Simon's—under, you know, his ribcage. 'I have stopped the bleeding, see?' she keeps saying to us. As if she could not believe or accept that he is gone below the heart. Of course she is out of her mind, too.

"My dear husband, my poor husband, he goes to Gib and he tries to pull Gib away from Simon's body, and Gib, you can see, he is not long to keep from fainting. But Gib still holds on until the last, and he says just before he passes out, Gib says, 'My brother is alive as long as I do not let go. Do not make me let go.'"

"Oh, my God," I whispered.

Sophia shook her head. "God was not there, I think. The opposite one was there. Laughing at us all. You know who. I do not speak the name of evil."

We sat in dark silence, her face red from port and emo-

tion, my head buzzing with alcohol and her lurid description.
"Hey. Another drink," Sophia said finally.

"I thought you'd never ask." She poured and I drank. "He
has to cut those boards," I announced. "Gib. He has to do it.
He has no choice."

"Oh, no! He cannot. Not alone. And no one in the family
can bear to go back in that place. Olivia provoked him today.
But she did not mean to make him go to the sawmill."

"Provoked him? What did she do?"

"She and Bea and Min went to the city to hear Emory's
new offer. Olivia only did it to make Gib notice. To make him
act. She knew he would not go with them. He will not think of
selling to Emory. But if he does not prove he can take Simon's
place there is no other choice. His sister Ruth has her own career, she cannot run things there, and Min and Gib's baby sister Isabel, they are not leaders."

"He tried to prove something today," I said. "He just
picked the wrong place to start."

"The sawmill was the *only* place he could start," Sophia
said wearily.

I got a little drunk myself, late that evening, with Hoss upstairs asleep and Ella curled up napping on a couch in the living room. Sophia and I sat on her veranda in the postmidnight
darkness. A single battered streetlamp cast a small pool of
yellowish light on the buildings and gas pumps across the
street, but outside the light's glow I had never seen such
pitch-black shadows in my life.

And in the mountains around us, nothing. Not a single
house light. Blackness. The night sang with choruses of tree
frogs so loud I had to lean toward Sophia to catch everything
she said. She rocked companionably in her wicker chair. I
pretended to rock companionably myself while I pumped her
for more stories about the Camerons. She was a cornucopia

of information. My head swam with details I mentally squirreled away for future consideration.

Suddenly we heard the roar of a vehicle and screeching tires. A large late-model truck swept out of the darkness of the state road then swung into the parking lot. Under the streetlight the truck gleamed an almost iridescent shade of purple. Five big-haired women climbed out of the back bed, laughing. They held a jeweled leash while a large, shaggy gray goat jumped down after them.

A goat.

A young man got out of the cab on the driver's side, and two more women popped from the passenger side. "Waaaaahooo!" he yodeled at the top of his lungs, throwing his handsome head back. "I'm bayin' at the moon 'cause I got stars in my eyes and women on my mind!"

His women, appropriately enough, applauded. He was lean and long-legged but when he yodeled again his jeans stretched so tight I thought he might split a seam. Or bruise something. Long, coal-black hair dangled in a ponytail down the back of his gray western shirt. A silver earring dangled from his left ear. He wore cowboy boots. One look at his skin, hair, and face said he was probably at least part Indian.

He bounded over to the placid-looking goat, kissed it between the eyes, then lifted its front hooves to his chest and began swaying in place. He was dancing to unheard music with a goat in the parking lot.

The women applauded again. They ranged in age from barely above jailbait to barely below menopause. None was particularly gorgeous, a couple were fat and a couple bony, but all wore tight jeans or tight, short skirts, shirts with colorful western piping, western boots, and plenty of makeup.

"That is Carter's harem," Sophia explained. "They go with him to Knoxville and dance at the big nightclubs. You know, square dance. Line dance."

"He doesn't look like he's got much rhythm left tonight," I noted dryly. "Either he's drunk or the goat's leading."

"Carter, he is a *sweet* fool," Sophia said.

"Who is Carter?"

"Carter MacIntosh. He is a cousin of the Camerons'."

"He's from around here?"

"Yes, now. But he was born and raised in Oklahoma."

I watched Carter MacIntosh dance with the goat and felt he wasn't much of a credit to Native American dignity. "How did Carter end up here?" I asked. "He followed a migrating goat herd?"

"His mother was Cherokee but his father was white. Nobody even knows the father's name. And so Carter's mother gave him to his uncle to raise, and then she disappeared. This was hard on Carter, and he got into silly troubles as a boy. So Simon and Olivia, they get a call from his uncle asking if they will keep Carter one summer when he is a teenager. He comes, he visits, he is better. He loves Simon and Gib and the sisters, and they are good to him. So every year he would come back. A couple of years ago he moved down permanently." She touched my arm. "Welcome to a place where it has taken all kinds to make a family. Carter is charming. You will like him. Your sister will like him, too."

I drew up like a cobra on alert. I had an instinct about the type of man Ella fell prey to. And she'd be sympathetic to outcast, mixed-race Carter, because we were mixed-race. We had enough problems without Ella getting warm and fuzzy over a supposedly kindred spirit. Especially one with a harem.

"How old is he?" I asked Sophia. He was still swaying with the goat while his ladies watched appreciatively. "In human years, that is."

"Oh, who knows. Younger than Gib and the sisters. Hmmm." She counted on her coral-nailed fingertips. "Ruth is thirty-two, Isabel is two years younger, so Carter is maybe, hmmm, twenty-four."

Two years younger than Ella. Good. Too young for her tastes. "He looks too cute for his own good."

Sophia nodded wistfully. "But he has had a bad day. Isabel and Ruth are mad at him. He was supposed to keep track of Gib all day, but Gib chased him away. They say Carter gave up too easily, but how can *anyone* tell Gib what to do, the way his mind is right now? But still, Carter is in trouble with Isabel and Ruth. They heard about what happened at the sawmill." She paused. "I told them everything on the phone after you came back. About you, too." She pressed her hand to her heart. "Keeping secrets would be very bad for my health."

I watched Carter MacIntosh parade among his entourage, laughing and hugging. He'd apparently returned them to their cars and pickup trucks, which they'd left in the parking lot earlier. Carter released the goat and threw himself into the midst of the chortling females, then devoted himself to a series of back-bending, flat-on lengthy kisses with each of his big-haired concubines. Even the goat looked embarrassed.

"I've never seen a hornier-looking beast," I said. "And the goat, too."

Sophia smiled sadly. "You cannot tell by tonight, but Carter has worked hard at the Hall the past year. They needed him. Don't be fooled by tonight. He is sweet. Before he moved to Tennessee he planned to marry."

"Oh? Up in Oklahoma?"

"Yes."

"And?"

"They found out about each other."

"Who?"

"All three of the girls he proposed marriage to."

I watched Carter with even less approval. He threw his arms around a pair of women and wandered to his truck. He got into the cab with them. The other five prodded the goat to jump back into the pickup's bed, then went to their cars, laughing and waving good-night.

The whole caravan peeled rubber onto the two-lane and disappeared into the dark summer night. A minute later Ella wandered outdoors, looking delicate in a gauzy rose-hued silk shift and thong sandals with white plastic daisies on the toepieces. She scrubbed a hand over her sleep-ruffled hair. She still looked like a little girl at times. "What was all that noise?" she asked.

I decided to tell her about Carter from the get-go, and lay it on thick. Every irresponsible, untrustworthy moment I'd witnessed. "Carter MacIntosh," I said. "A Cameron cousin."

"No! I missed him? Did he introduce himself? Oh, you should have woken me up."

"Well, let me put it this way," I said with steely intent. "His Cherokee name is probably Dances With Livestock."

Ten

Ella and I ate eggs and biscuits with cream gravy at the diner at dawn, while the Eddie Bauer couple invaded our small table and told us stories about their hiking adventures. They had been chased by a black bear in the state park near New Inverness. "I expected a few cute squirrels and some mountain scenery for my photo album," the woman complained. "The park ranger was a gap-toothed redneck who didn't warn us that there were large animals in the woods."

"Where did you buy your tickets?" I asked.

"Excuse me?"

"The tickets for the theme park. None of this is real, you know. The wildlife are all high-class robotic imitations. You didn't notice when the bear did a wheelie and rolled back in the woods on his little computerized monorail?"

My sense of humor failed to enlighten or entertain them, but it did make them sidle back to their own table and leave us alone.

"Are you premenstrual?" Ella asked gently as we walked across the sunrise-pink parking lot in a well-greased stupor.

"No, I'm pre-Camerons." Carter MacIntosh's purple truck zoomed into view. I reached in my leather tote bag. "I'll fend off Mr. MacIntosh and his goat with my pepper spray," I warned, only half joking.

Ella gasped at the potential social calamity of me spritzing one of our hosts. "Don't you dare!"

The truck careened across the cracked concrete and halted not more than a dozen feet from us. A dark blue minivan arrived seconds later and pulled in beside it. A young woman drove.

Carter MacIntosh vaulted from the truck, looking as hollow-eyed as a playboy with a hangover and a seedy reputation *should* look. But his charisma was still in full force, the long, glossy hair, the tight jeans, the honey-brown forearms bulging in a snug gray T-shirt. He flashed a pearly-white grin as he tromped toward us in red lizard-skin cowboy boots. Suddenly he veered toward Ella, then halted. His eyes widened as if he'd suddenly brought her into focus.

"Hello, Mr. MacIntosh," Ella said quickly, warding off trouble with melodic tones, her voice as lilting as a flute. "I'm Ella Arinelli and this is my sister, Venus. We're very glad to meet you. My sister saw you last night. Where did you leave the goat? I'd love to meet it, too."

His cocky grin fading, he gazed raptly at her. She gazed at him, too, as if he'd materialized from golden air. He nodded his head at me, and then with slower emphasis at Ella, almost giving her a small, courtly bow. His silver earring danced in the morning sunshine. The pendant was a tiny abstract figurine of a big-chested woman.

"Hello, Ella Arinelli," Carter said. He spoke her name as if he'd never heard a prettier sound. She reacted by smiling, and his eyes moved to her mouth hypnotically. A pink blush began to emerge on her cheeks.

My worst fears were leapfrogging ahead. She could be so naive where men were concerned.

"Gib thought you'd pack up and hitch a ride back to Chicago this morning," the woman called as she slid quickly from the van's driver's seat. "That's why he sent us so early."

I dragged my stare away from my sister and Carter. The woman was about my age. She was dressed in an ankle-length skirt of soft, crinkled cotton, with large tie-dyed stripes and zigzags of purple, rose, and yellow splashed across the material, and a bright yellow T-shirt. Her hair was lustrously brunette and fluttered around her shoulders in straight shanks. She wore no jewelry. She had a stain on her shirt, probably baby food, judging by the burping towel still draped absent-mindedly across her left shoulder.

Her hands were smeared with brightly colored paint. Thanks to Sophia, I was now a wellspring of Cameron information, trivial and otherwise. This had to be Isabel Cameron. Gib's sister. Divorced. Her ex-husband was a gambler in Atlantic City. She had moved home to the Hall with her baby son right after Simon died.

"Isabel," I said politely. "The artist."

Isabel smiled. "Yes!" She scooted shy glances from me to Ella and back to me, then she reached out her rainbow-colored fingers. I let her take both my hands. Looking relieved, she alternately shook and squeezed my hands before she let go. "We're all *very* sorry you were drawn into our problems yesterday. We decided it was best for just me and Carter to come get y'all this morning. Not overwhelm you. Gib suggested it."

I squinted at her. "Is he feeling better today?"

"He's feeling *sober* for the first time in days," she admitted. She clasped her hands in front of her then steepled them to her chin, nunlike and supplicating. She was pretty in an apple-cheeked way, and gave the impression of urgent sincerity. "Venus, you stopped my brother from doing something dangerous yesterday. Of course our aunt Olivia insists that's a sign of the good luck she expected you'd bring. She's waiting to meet you."

"It's all in the timing," I said, feeling awkward. "It was just a coincidence that I happened along when Gib went to the sawmill."

Isabel smiled sadly. "You took care of my brother when he wasn't able to think for himself. That's not coincidence. It's a blessing."

"Oh, yes," Ella agreed. She and Isabel smiled at each other.

Carter stepped closer to Ella. "I wished I'd stopped by Cousin Hoss's last night to meet you," he said to her. "I thought a lady like you only existed in my *dreams*. Are you sure we've never met?" Carter delivered that third-rate pickup line then blinked innocently, as if she brought fresh light into his vision.

My sister held out her hand. "I know just what you mean. I feel I've looked into your eyes before, too. You have the gentlest eyes."

I chewed my tongue. After a portentous pause, Carter squeezed her slender hand in his brawny grip carefully, as if it were fragile as an eggshell. Then he held her hand and gazed at it, studying the contrast. "I think," he said somberly, "that I'm talking to a flesh-and-blood angel."

Ella's free hand rose, fluttering, to her throat. She glowed with teary and sentimental appreciation. "Oh," she sighed.

"Carter, I thought you preferred *goats*," I snapped.

Isabel gave me a knowing glance. She shook her head and rolled her eyes toward Carter. He released Ella's hand. "Aw, last night was just silliness," he said quickly. "Me and some friends."

Before I could say anything else, Isabel linked her arm through mine. I looked down at the unaccustomed intimacy and had to force myself not to pull back. Isabel smiled at me. "Why don't y'all go gather your things at Sophia's and we'll take you to the Hall?"

"Why don't you ride with *me*?" Carter said to Ella. "I'll give you a tour."

Her eyes glowed. "Why, I think that would be—"

"Trouble," I interjected. I snared her by one hand. It was awkward but effective—me hitched to Isabel's arm, Ella

hitched to me. "Thank you, Carter," I said coolly, "but we
don't want to put you to any extra effort on our behalf. Besides, unlike your nanny goat, we Arinellis always travel in
pairs."

As we rode up the valley's crape myrtle-lined road in the
comfort of Isabel's minivan, Ella sighed and moaned with ecstatic, tearful adoration. Her eyes became glistening green
beacons sweeping the scenery, the historical markers, the
shadowed blue-green mountains, the wildflowers, and even
the buffalo.

When Isabel parked on a stone courtyard surrounded by
azaleas, the mansion's tall, carved front doors swung open.
Gib stood there with his legs braced slightly and the massive
doorway framing him in dark, strong wood. An ominous, magnificent, antique broadsword—as wide as a fist and easily four
feet long—jutted from the handle he gripped with his powerful left hand.

The image was so phallic I almost blushed. If his point
was to tell me he was the mighty sword and I was the lowly
sheath who stole engine keys, it worked. He was dressed today in a handsome black pin-striped suit. A folded bit of red
plaid material peeked vibrantly from his breast pocket. I
couldn't take my eyes off him. He carefully hung the sword
on an iron brace beside the entrance. He kept his right hand
turned against his coat so the deformed side was hidden.

Carter opened the van doors. He had donned a fringed
western jacket over his T-shirt. He helped Ella out as if she
were descending from a royal carriage. "Welcome, pretty
lady," he said. "We're gonna have a little party in honor of
you and your sister this morning."

I looked questioningly at Isabel, who nodded. I sat in the
open door of the van's backseat, gathering my canvas luggage
bag and trying hard to seem busy and not unnerved. Suddenly
Gib extended his good hand into my downcast line of vision.

"I'll take your luggage," he said quietly. "Welcome to the Hall."

I raised my head slowly and met his gaze. He was absolutely, perfectly inscrutable. "Thank you," I said.

And so I walked beside him up a stone walkway more than two centuries old, and we didn't say another word to each other as we entered the cool, smooth, flower-scented shadows of the Cameron legacy. As we passed the sword Gib touched his fingertips to his lips then placed the kiss on the sword's deadly blade.

"Tradition," he said, pointing to a small plaque set above it. It read: FAMILY, HONOR, HUMBLE SERVICE. A GENTLE MAN WILL FIGHT TO THE DEATH FOR THE SAKE OF SUCH BEAUTY.

I kissed my own fingertips and touched the sword. I looked up into Gib's shrewd eyes. "In honor of my parents," I said.

"You have no honor," Gib said. "Where's my key?"

I leaned close to him. He stood well over six feet tall and had the tiniest fleck of blood on the shaved line of his jaw. I perched on tiptoe then whispered in his ear. "Where's my money?"

He glared at me, but we had no time to torment each other further.

Ella and I halted inside a long entrance hall that opened into a large arched doorway on our right. Ella's eyes filled with more dewy appreciation. Gib nodded to Isabel and Carter, and they set our luggage at the base of a curving staircase made of gleaming rose-hued woods. Isabel smiled at me, but I noticed bluish circles under her eyes. I had a feeling some kind of family conference had gone on well into the previous night. Gib said, "We tried not to make this a mad rush. We failed."

The doors flew open. A voice boomed out, "Look at her, Olivia, she's no' a wee wish of a star now, she's quite a looker, our Venus." A tall, walrus-shaped woman with a jowly face and a short cap of gray hair advanced on me with her arms spread. She was clothed in swathes of white scarves over a voluminous white blouse and matching pants. Confronted by this giant white human moth, I blurted, "Hello, ma'am," and thrust out an intervening hand.

But she swooped past my hand and wrapped her gauzy moth arms around me, lifted me on my toes, and gave me a half-hug/half-shake. "I'm no' a 'ma'am,' you bloody beautiful child," she proclaimed loudly. "I'm *Bea*, you hear? And do no' be callin' me *Aunt Bea* because I'm no' a bloody dull old lady."

"Bea," I echoed in a strangled voice. This was the cousin from Scotland, then, the one who had arrived for a visit years ago and never left.

She let me down with another affectionate shake then advanced on Ella, who melted with welcoming outflung hands. "You've no' coaxed your sister Venus here just to dance a jig, I betcha," Bea said loudly. "You're the sensible one o' the two of you, you're the one who knows it's a shame to resist what's good for you!"

"Oh, I have no doubt," Ella enthused.

Bea grunted then let her go and slapped Gib's shoulder placidly. "Good work, dear Gibbie." Then she pivoted and my eyes followed her back to the open door.

"Here's Min," Gib said quietly. A woman walked into the hallway, smiling at me under soft wavy brown hair and a gently worn-down face. Min Cameron. Kind, motherly, devoted Minnie, the love of Simon Cameron's life, Sophia had told me. She was too thin for the pale gray suit she wore, and the color gave her pinched face an ashen tint. Her eyes were large and brown and terrible in their steady sorrow.

"I'm so glad Gib found you," she said to us, cupping our hands in hers. Even her voice was tired, a low pitch with long vowels, as if she spoke with as little energy as possible. "My husband and I welcome you both. I'm sure he's watching us all at this moment. I'm sure he's happy to know we found you. It's not about the money. I hope you believe me when I say that. We want to share our home with you and Ella the way we shared our home with your parents."

The mention of Simon cast an awkward silence on us all. I forced myself to say, "We're so pleased you invited us," but Gib stepped forward quickly. He waved for someone to approach. A lanky teenage girl and boy walked into the hallway. "This is my Kelly," Min said softly. "And this is my Jasper."

Min and Simon's children shook our hands with firm social grace. Jasper and Kelly. Twins. Sixteen years old and good kids, according to Sophia. I could see the past year's grief stamped in their solemn faces, but Kelly's eyes glinted with mischief.

"Neither of you looks at all Asian," she announced. "I expected someone more exotic." She gazed at me. "But I *am* fascinated by your cornrows. Is that a fashion statement or a symbol of cultural rebellion? I thought cornrows were passé."

"I'm retro," I said dryly. "This is a weave and it cost me two hundred dollars." Having been a precocious brat myself, I wasn't astonished by Kelly's cocky attitude. "I did it because the braids look good onstage. Cultural statements are for politicians and bad artists. For the record, I consider fashion statements to be a sucker's game."

"Venus, or in Greek, Aphrodite," she recited. "The ancient goddess of love. The planet second from the sun—also known as the evening star. A little smaller than Earth. Covered in dense clouds of sulfuric acid. No moons. *Venus de Milo*. A famed statue of the Roman goddess. Armless. Venus flytrap. An insect-eating plant. 'Venus.' A hit song sung by Frankie Avalon in 1959. I've researched your name on the computer."

"I think I'm flattered. Or scared."

"Enough," Gib said. He scowled at Kelly. "Apologize for that barrage."

Kelly lifted her chin. "I'm sorry, Ms. Arinelli."

"No problem. Apology accepted."

Unless I had lost count, the only ones missing were Gib's sister Ruth and his great-aunt, Olivia Cameron. Somewhere beyond the doorway that other Camerons popped through like refugees from a time machine was the legendary Olivia. I gazed fixedly at what I could see of the room.

A fair-haired baby scooted into the hall in his four-wheeled selfpropelled walker. A pacifier plugged firmly in his mouth, his chubby hands latched on to the walker's tray, which circled him like a doughnut, he played bumper-pool with several sets of legs, including my own, before he darted through an opening and rolled up the hall, bouncing off furniture and the closed doors of various rooms. He reached a point where the entrance hall intersected a second hall.

Ebb Hodger sprang into view and snared him. "I let him think he's ex-caping," she said, her big, streaked-brown hair bouncing in a tide of curls over her forehead. "He's faster than a pinched rabbit." She and the child scooted out of sight. I heard him rolling up the other hall with Ebb's running footsteps behind him.

"That's my son," Isabel confirmed. "Dylan."

"Dylan," Ella echoed. "Like the poet or the pop singer?"

"Oh, *both,*" Isabel said seriously, nodding.

"And where is your sister today?" I asked Isabel nonchalantly. "Ruth." I wanted to assess all the Camerons at once.

Isabel looked embarrassed.

"Come," Bea said, planting herself between Ella and me then taking each of us by an arm. "Enough of us. Herself is waiting without a bloody shred of patience."

I glanced at Gib for an explanation. His eyes shuttered, he ignored me. Bea guided us into a magnificent room with high ceilings and library shelves, deep leather chairs, heavy reading tables, chunky brass and copper lamps, and the slight, musty scent of a thousand old, leather-bound books.

Swords, daggers, and sinister two-headed battle-axes decorated a wall between bookcases, posed on thick brass hooks and wooden racks set on delicate golden fleur-de-lis wallpaper. A library table was adorned with lace and linen, bouquets of white roses in crystal vases, and two dewy bottles of champagne set in silver buckets.

But all of that paled next to the tiny woman looking back at me. I forgot about the mysterious Ruth. With one fine-boned, mottled hand steadying herself on the back of a tall, ornate chair, the queenly, astonishing Olivia Cameron waited.

She raised her hand and beckoned us. Bea gave me a small push. I moved forward. I was transfixed by the quality of Olivia Cameron's eyes, misty-blue, still vivid, framed in a face as wizened as an ancient tree. Long gray hair flowed around her shoulders and down her torso. Her chest was a thin scoop above flat little breasts. She was dressed in a black jumper over an ivory blouse with a cameo at the throat. Her legs and feet were knobby and blue-veined below the dress's hem. She was barefoot.

I stopped in front of her, less than an arm's length away. She tilted her head back, worked her mouth soundlessly, grimaced, shut her eyes, and reaching up, laid one small hand on the side of my face.

"Hello," I said softly. "Thank you for remembering my sister and me."

She opened her eyes and smiled. She crooked a finger at Ella, and when my sister stepped up tentatively beside me, Olivia touched her cheek briefly, and smiled again.

"Aunt Olivia wants to write to you," Gib said, behind us. "She doesn't speak."

I didn't have time to absorb that strange news. *Doesn't,* not *can't?* No one had bothered to mention *this* before. He handed his great-aunt a small spiral-bound notepad and a thin gold ink-pen, and she opened the notepad and wrote while Gib held the pad in his hands. When she finished he held the pad out for me to read:

It's about time.

She might be filled with the sly humor of the saints, I thought, or just an old lady's arrogant peculiarity. "Thank you for inviting us," I told her stiffly. Olivia pursed her lips angrily then pulled something from her voluminous dress pocket. She handed me an old 45-rpm record of "Evening Star," with a faded paper jacket. "A golden song for my golden girls," was written on it in Mom's hand.

I stared at it. "How did you get that?"

"It was with the money," Gib said.

A golden song for my golden girls.

I faced him. Inside I was shaking. "Then the money *didn't* come from the accounts my father used to bankroll his politics. It was part of a trust fund my mother set up for Ella and me. I thought the government had confiscated the fund along with everything else. But it's the profits from song royalties on 'Evening Star.' "

"Oh, that's true, Gib, it's really true," Ella cried. "I remember when Pop showed us this copy of the record and told us about the trust fund Mom and he created." Tears streaking her face, she took the record from me and caressed it. "I can't believe we have this back." She looked at the gathered Camerons. "Our father sent Simon something much more precious than money."

"We understand," Min said gently.

I kept a neutral expression but almost sagged with relief. The money my father had tried so desperately to save for Ella and me had come straight from the last of his innocence— and our mother's loving heart.

Gib watched me a moment, obviously astonished. I recovered and held his gaze evenly. "The money's clean," I said. "It belongs to me and Ella, and we've got no reason to be ashamed of it." Pride surged in me.

"I believe you," he said.

We stood around the library table in the elegant old room, sipping champagne and making awkward attempts at small talk with Min, Bea, and Isabel, while Olivia sat in shrewd silence and Gib studied me as if I were an exotic animal he'd bagged.

Eventually I met Olivia's piercing gaze again. I felt light-hearted. "You want us to sing 'Evening Star,' I know. We'll be happy to perform the song for you."

Olivia wrote fervently on her notepad.

> *Don't patronize ME. I'm crazy, but I'm not senile. This isn't sentimental politeness. Now that we've dispensed with the discussion of your money, there's work to be done. What have you learned in your world? What can we teach you from ours? I want more than one kind of music from you.*

For a minute she and I traded a prickly, unspoken challenge. I had underestimated *her*, while she had probably overestimated *me*. But I wasn't there to play helpmate for her; I'd come to collect the only inheritance the U.S. government hadn't been able to steal from Ella and me.

Gib made a small, sharp movement with his head, and I turned toward him instinctively. "The engine key," he said, holding out his hand. Murmurs of distress went up around me. Gib shook his head. "If we can't go back in there, nothing will change for this family," he said. "It's what my brother would want."

Min gasped. "Gib, no. I thought we settled this discussion last night. You proved how impossible it is yesterday."

"I would have done the work if I hadn't been interrupted." Gib frowned at me as he spoke. "I intend to do it now."

"I can't—" Min began again. Kelly clasped her mother's shoulder and the boy, Jasper, looked on.

"Mama, we've got to," he said.

"We do," Kelly added, her voice cracking.

"Uncle Gib," Jasper said in a raspy voice. "You know Daddy wouldn't want you to go there without me and Kelly."

"It's my duty, and he wouldn't want either of you to grieve for him there," Gib replied gently.

"I should get to choose where I grieve," Kelly said loudly.

"Shouldn't I?" Her voice quivered. "I can't let Daddy's job go undone."

"None of us can," Carter interjected, shoving his hands in his pockets and scowling. "And I don't want to keep tracking you, Gib. You're hard to follow."

Ella gazed at Carter so rapturously that I reached back and grasped her hand in a viselike grip.

Isabel said, "We have to try," gazing from one person to another. "We should do it together, Gib." She went to him and wound one arm through his.

"You go back to that sawmill again by yourself with another bellyful of liquor," Bea said flatly, "and you'll end up a dead man. Except for Venus here, you'd no' be alive today."

Min turned to me and grasped my hand. "You and Ella represent all the goodwill my husband extended to the outside world. All the goodwill this family offers. Aunt Olivia swore it would be a sign if Gib could find you and your sister and if you agreed to come here. I'm sure that sounds foolish to you, but we started to believe. We *need* to believe our family's future here is as strong as its past. You've already inspired us. Please say something else. We need your objective opinion."

I stifled the urge to back away from her. These people were desperate, grasping at whims. They must be coming apart at the seams. Who in their right minds would trust strangers for such serious advice?

But they all waited expectantly. My head buzzed with champagne and glorious relief over our money's true origins. All right, I'd try to help them. With the desperate appeal of a spunky 1930s musical star—Judy Garland with braided blond hair and a navel ring—I spread my arms dramatically. *Hey kids, let's fix up the old barn and put on a show!* "All right, then. How about—" I paused for emphasis, then "—all of you cut the boards together! And then you fix the chapel floor! You can probably finish the work today if you all pitch in!"

Silence. Gib studied me with an intensity that made me look away. God—what was I getting myself into? I glanced at the others. Carter, Bea, and Olivia all looked at me and then at each other, as if they'd brought a carnival barker into their antiques-and-broadsword midst. I faced Gib again. "Did you think I drove all the way from Chicago just to sit?" I asked at last. "You invited me here. You wanted me to stir things up. You gave me good news today. Let me repay you with good advice."

"I thought you were about to break into song."

"Gib, you can count on me to help at the mill," Carter announced proudly. "I've got a strong back and hands. She's right. We can get those boards cut and trimmed today."

"More than that," Bea said loudly. "There'll be no backing away once we start, dearies. I say we go on to the chapel with the fresh lumber and fix the floor. Venus and Ella can come along for good luck."

I held my breath. Gib watched his sister-in-law, the forty-six-year-old woman who had become, over the years, a second mother to him and his sisters. I saw the emotions pass across his face—sorrow and amazement and hope. She went to him and took his damaged hand in hers. "I'll try to walk back into that mill," she said. "I can't promise you I'll make it."

He nodded. I pulled the key from the waistband of my skirt and placed it on Gib's palm. His fingers closed around it, feathering my own.

But he left it in my hand. "I trust you to keep it," he said, with the slightest bow.

Eleven

Our small group stood in front of the sawmill door in the warm September sunshine, an hour before noon. Dylan had been assigned to a shady spot under a tree nearby. Ebb Hodger peered unhappily at the scene while she held him in her lap. Everyone had changed into work clothes, and we were armed with heavy gloves. I still felt like a fool but strangely exhilarated, too.

Gib opened the door. The darkness poured out like a disease.

"You okay, big brother?" Isabel asked with a gentle stroke of his hair.

"Never wanted to walk into this hellhole again," he admitted. He stepped inside. I followed along with everyone but Min. The wood-scented and oily sawmill air smothered all thought of victory. The mood was painfully intense.

Gib pivoted like a general on large, dirty workboots. "The sawblade itself is off-limits," he ordered to Kelly and Jasper, but they dodged him and went up to it anyway, drawn to what they feared most. They touched it gently, cautiously. Then both of them stepped back. "Mama can't make herself come in," Jasper said.

Gib left to talk to her, then came back with his head bowed. "She can't do it. It's too much for her to take."

Olivia, who had not changed her dress or put on shoes, held Bea's forearm lightly for balance. They advanced on me, Olivia's bare feet scuffing a pair of unbroken ski trails in the sawdust. Olivia wrote on her pad.

Speak for me. Do something.

"Ma'am, I'm not a miracle worker. I'm not even sure your family really needs or wants me here. I'm a stranger."

She stamped a foot and looked at Bea for assistance. Bea scowled at me. "Of course we want you here, as long as you're not going to stay a bloody useless complainer."

I walked outside. Two cars were parked there along with the large flatbed lumber truck. Min sat sideways in the open door of a large burgundy sedan, the kind little old Republican ladies drive to bingo-and-drinks at the club. Her face buried in her hands, she rocked slowly. Jasper and Isabel knelt beside her, and Kelly hung on the doorframe, one hand trailing along her mother's bowed head.

"Minnie Cameron," I said loudly. "Look, I don't want to be here. This isn't my fight, really. But since I am *stuck* with this situation I want you to get up and go in there and make your husband proud. Or I'll never forgive you for wasting my damned time." She stared at me.

Kelly said, wide-eyed, "You are *nuts.*"

"Yes, but I recognize a debt of honor when I see one. Minnie, you owe your husband the honor of finishing the chapel floor. He wanted that work done. You have to do it for him. Your determination keeps his memory alive. Doesn't it?"

Min pressed her hands to her mouth. "You're *right.*" She rose and staggered inside the building. She stared at the saw-blade and then at Gib. The material of her work pants trembled around her thin legs as she shivered then hunched over. "Min, come on, Minnie," Isabel begged, huddling with her pale, soft arms around her sister-in-law's shoulders.

"Leave her to settle herself," Bea said from a corner

where she stood beside a wooden stool Carter had fetched for Olivia. Olivia waved Isabel aside. Min hugged her stomach and retched water on the sawdust floor. Isabel crooned to her while Carter leaped forward with a red bandanna he pulled from his jeans pocket. He took Min by the arm.

But Min straightened. She wiped her mouth then stood as if at attention. She nodded to Gib. He started the blade.

Carter ran over to the towering stack of chestnut slabs and guided one onto the metal feeder track. Gib laid his hands on its peeled and flat-hewn surface. Carter and Jasper positioned themselves to catch the plank on the other end, where a second track waited to guide cut boards to a pallet.

It wasn't easy to watch their faces. Gib eased a slab of wood toward the blade. I shivered as I heard the deep, off-key whine of steel slicing hard chestnut.

A fine yellow mist sprayed into the air. Sweat poured down Gib's face, and Min stood rigidly, forcing herself to watch the blade. It sliced a single wide board from the square-hewn slab taken from a tree that had been cut by a Cameron before the birth of any of us except Olivia and Bea.

The board fell neatly into Jasper's gloved hands. Gib started the log back through in the opposite direction, never taking his eyes off its progress. And when the second board lay under his fingertips Minnie walked over to it and smoothed her fingers over the wood.

Olivia wrote on her pad and pressed the pad into my hands.

Exceptional miracle-working for your first day here.

Darkness. The moon was up again. Things crept through the forest, small creatures and larger ones, whose eyes caught the light as they moved. No one seemed to notice except Ella and me. I was grateful for the dogs who lazed at the edge of the cemetery below the chapel, keeping all of us safe inside our primitive circle of light. Stacks of fresh-cut chestnut boards sat in the eerie glow of work lamps run by a large gasoline-powered generator outside the door.

I drank in everything, the family most of all. I'd known these people forever and a day. Isabel was as fairy-fey as my own sister, divorced, easily fooled and hurt by men, eager to keep everyone happy. She glided about, dispensing nails and cinnamon cookies, humming gently to the sleeping son she carried in a brightly colored sling across her chest. Min kept to herself, stacking discarded old boards and policing the grassy chapel mound for bits of debris. Kelly and Jasper vied for her attention by competing with each other for buckets of nails and wheelbarrows of trash.

Gib, his eyes like dull topaz stones in a face smeared with sweat and sawdust, directed the others with calm, quick instructions. He organized the stacked lumber and the tools, and he lifted his head from his own hammering duties each time the electric handsaw buzzed outdoors. He listened protectively, and he watched like a hawk as Carter cut lengths of the new boards atop a pair of sawhorses.

I saw Gib order the irascible Kelly onto the chapel porch. "The area around the electric saw is off-limits," he said firmly. "The perimeter intersects the door."

"Uncle Gib, I'm not the President and you're not in the Secret Service anymore," she protested. "I'm not even old enough to *vote*."

"Pretend, for my sake," Gib ordered, frowning. His dedication to detail and methodical precision was obvious. He would have made a fine pianist, in that regard.

"More's the better," Bea answered, as she passed around a silver flask of finely aged Scotch whisky. I took a large swallow then tottered inside the chapel. The night was pitch-dark outside the stained-glass windows.

I carried a tall plastic cup of iced tea to Gib, who was on his knees hammering nails into a board. I tiptoed along the aisle across massive, exposed floor beams. Below the beams lay hard-packed black earth, the top of the ancient mound. I felt I was walking the backbone of some sleeping, mystical giant. Carter, Jasper, Kelly, Minnie, and Isabel were all working diligently at various spots. So was Hoss. Sophia handed him nails from a leather pouch.

Gib drank deeply from the tea I offered him. I squatted beside him and watched a trickle of amber liquid escape down his neck.

"Why didn't your other sister come today?"

"She doesn't approve of you."

"I see."

He handed the cup back to me. "Thank you." I started to rise. "No, thank you," he repeated meaningfully, amid the drumming of multiple hammers striking handmade iron nails from a dusty collection in a Cameron storehouse.

I dropped back to my heels and studied him. "I earn my keep. I tried to say and do whatever might help your family. In some strange way it seems to have worked. So think of me kindly when I take my sister and our money and get the hell out of here in a few days."

"You can't wait, can you?" he asked darkly.

I stood quickly, negotiating people and stripped floor beams, then finally made my way to the antique organ, which was perched on a section of planking across the open maw of the floor. I sat down carefully on the stool, which felt precarious, and put my hands on the yellowed keyboards. Olivia and Bea stood in the doorway, watching. Jasper fetched a folding chair and helped Olivia sit. She pressed her bare feet together atop one of the new floorboards then inclined her head regally.

Everyone stopped hammering for a moment to stare at me. I arched a brow at Gib. "I would like to contribute something to the moment. How about a little Beethoven?"

"I don't know Beethoven from a spider's hind leg," he admitted. "But I'd appreciate whatever you play."

I pressed keys, pulled stops, and played with my head bowed and my concentration focused raggedly on my own two hands. Then I gave what Arinellis give best. Music.

•   •   •

The chapel's floor was fully restored sometime after midnight. All it required was varnishing, which could be done later. Everyone stood with exhausted satisfaction. Gib reached across Olivia's shoulders and brushed his good hand across the braids behind my ears, feathering my earlobe as he did. When I stared at him he said, "There was a firefly in your hair."

"Venus was twinkling," Isabel announced. That brought a few genuine smiles from the dirty, tired group, and a fake one from me. I was already on emotional overload without Gib's casual caress.

Min did not have to cry to grieve, and one look at her pale, thin face and the poignant expression in her eyes said this milestone had brought small comfort. "It's done," she said, her voice raspy, and it was as if she were speaking to Simon.

"Bring in some chairs," Bea ordered. "Herself wants a ceremony." Olivia waved a hand with quiet command. Jasper and Kelly ran to obey.

The chapel had been wired for electricity years before, but ornate oil lamps, hooded with stained-glass shades dripping tiny prisms, still lined the walls, set on wooden pedestals high on the thick chestnut ribs between the murals. After we were seated, Gib raised a long match to the wick of a lamp.

"I love candles and lamps," Ella said softly. "I've loved them since the earliest times I can remember, going to mass and listening to the organ and the choir, enthralled with the purity of it all. The altar candles always seemed to me like promises."

"A light in the darkness," Carter agreed. He turned from his chair beside hers and patted her hand.

She leaned toward him. "I knew you'd understand." They gazed raptly at each other.

I kept my eyes on Gib and the lamp. A scrap of thread on the lamp wick caught fire and floated upward, glowing red

and gold before Gib closed his bad hand around it in a suffo-
cating fist. If the tiny flame burned his palm he didn't show it,
but his face was already pale and set, hollows shadowed beneath his cheekbones, his eyes remote. I watched him shake
the lamp slightly then study the wick as if it had a mind of its
own, threatening his family's priceless heirloom chapel.

Carter leaped up and lit the lamps on the opposite wall
before Gib could get to them. The lamps' flickering, pungent
glow gave the gathering a sepia-toned effect. Except for our
modern clothes, we could have been time-traveling. A hundred years, two hundred, vanished in the primitive gentility of
small flames.

The pews, each of which weighed several hundred pounds,
were still stacked atop one another at the back of the chamber.
We sat in a hodgepodge of metal folding chairs, a dozen worn-
out and pensive people, in the middle of the night.

Bea stood. "Herself," she said, gesturing to Olivia, "is
wanting each of you to give a speech. 'Twould no' be a Cameron event without a bit of wind and pomp."

Gib looked at Min questioningly, and she got up. But she
only touched her hand to her chest over her heart, obviously
unable to say a word, by the contorted emotion on her face.
She sat down abruptly, and Isabel put an arm around her.
Someone else rose to speak, but I was barely listening.

I was lost in my own commemorations. *Mom and Pop
stood up there before that altar.* They played the song they'd
written that very day on the old organ, and Gib watched them,
and heard them, my parents, who would go back to the main
house after the ceremony and make love to each other that
night, creating me when they did.

I missed them, missed them so badly it hurt. Gib carried
my history inside his memory, starting with the day he
watched, as a five-year-old boy, while my parents said their
vows in this chapel, not twenty feet from where my sister and
I sat. But he couldn't forget that I was a traitor's daughter any
more than I could forget he was a patriot's son.

I lost track of time. My head spun from the close, pungent air. The stained-glass windows had been opened but I was caught in a deeper miasma, the drone of solemn and grieving voices, the parade of those testifying to Simon's irreplaceable aura. This family still had a long way to go. There was soft crying all around me.

But not from me. I stared at Gib's broad back rows ahead of me, and traced the outline of his dark-haired head to keep my concentration, and my eyes ached from the pressure behind them. He stood and spoke last. The lamplight flickered on his face and hair, figuring him in pieces of shadow, and I was suddenly drunk from looking at him.

"I didn't want all of you to see this chapel in bad condition," he said in a low, strained tone. "We locked the doors last year and left them locked until this week. All the time—" He lifted his maimed hand slightly "—all the time this was healing. I thought about going back to the sawmill. I thought about my brother's love for this chapel. Our family's love for it. It represents more than faith. It represents the power of people from different worlds to create something sacred together. That's what Gilbert Cameron and Soquena MacIntosh created when they got married, two hundred and fifty years ago, right here, in this chapel he built for her." He inhaled sharply. "I'll never let it be sold to Emory's investors."

There were discreet glances and frowns throughout the group. Min bowed her head. Isabel blushed and looked away. Olivia clapped her hands—just once, for attention—and when Gib looked her way she nodded her head adamantly.

He went on speaking, but I felt light-headed and couldn't listen. "Vee," Ella whispered. She clutched my arm. "Vee?" I inhaled sharply and blinked. My eyes met Gib's. "—it's a song that was written here, and I remember the day we heard Max and Shari Arinelli perform it in this chapel, after they said their wedding vows. Simon always thought of 'Evening Star' as belonging to our family in a special way. The Arinellis helped us celebrate the opening of Cameron Hall as an inn, but more than that, they helped us feel like singing again after our parents died. That's why Max and Shari's daughters are here tonight. Because Aunt Olivia believes they'll help us remember how to sing." He paused, his eyes locked on mine, challenging me.

Everyone turned to look at us expectantly. "You okay, lady?" Carter asked softly, clasping Ella's hand atop her quivering knees. "We're all in your corner. Go sing your heart out. Make your folks proud."

I stood. My legs felt like heavy pendulums. I met Ella's nervous, beseeching look and nodded. She rose to her feet slowly, and followed me up the aisle. I sat down at the organ. Ella stood pencil-straight beside it. I began to play, and we sang in harmony:

> In the soft sky the evening star shines bright,
> On this night of dreams we find,
> The heart of hope in starlight.

Ella's voice was pure, a sweet dovelike warble, but mine had a rasp like an old cheerleader's or Janis Joplin's at her whisky-and-heroin pinnacle. I watched Ella's clothes shiver with the tremor of her arms.

> Brilliant trust within your eyes
> The past is past, there is a world beyond the night,
> Shadows fall, but the evening star rises,
> Half a heart plus half a heart become one in its
> sight.

I filled in the harmonies with my voice cracking on the higher notes. *This is for Mom and Pop. Sing. Sing perfectly!* I felt fractured inside. Ella muffled words here and there, and trembled harder, but her distress gave the song more poignancy, and of course most of the Cameron family were sobbing by then.

Somehow we finished. Finished, thank God. Sweat trickled down my back, and between my breasts, and under my
arms, yet my skin felt clammy. The Camerons seduced outsiders. That was easy to see. They enthralled the unsuspecting
then absorbed the new energy. I felt as if Ella and I had been
sucked dry like fruit. That we'd been stripped naked and casually examined for birthmarks. We had to collect our inheritance and get away from these people at the end of two weeks.
Not a moment later.

When the song was over Gib gave me a brief nod of respect, coaxing open small pathways between us. In music the
variations on a melody eventually define the melody itself. I
heard his silent message in sudden, fresh tones. He was a man
who had lost all surplus faith but not his kindness; his gaunt
hazel eyes must have been charming and warm before the accident; he didn't mean to look bullish as he hunched his right
shoulder a fraction higher than his left. He made subcon-
scious efforts to compensate for the ruined symmetry of his
hands.

So now he stood in front of me, exposed and quiet, in
plain clothes covered in dirt and the golden powder of ancient
chestnuts. "Thank you," he said. Confused at the contrasting
emotions fighting inside me, I only nodded.

Arinellis had helped restore the Cameron chapel. We had
contributed something these people needed, had helped build
a foundation that might last. I looked at the respectful faces
around us and then at Gib again. I wanted to hope.

Yet I'd already done what I'd been brought there to do,
and my inner voice was telling me that the next two weeks
would just be marking time.

Twelve

It had been years since the Camerons had lived in the grand central section of the mansion. In the late 1960s, when Olivia opened the Hall as an inn, she and the children moved into a run-down wing that had been added around the turn of the century.

The original manor house and the more recent family wing were connected at only two points: a sunny enclosed walkway with double doors that bore a sign saying CAMERON FAMILY QUARTERS, PRIVATE, PLEASE, and the Hall's enormous, high-ceilinged kitchen, which was the center of a maze of doors—one to a storage room; one to the ornate and spacious central dining room; one to a small back porch with scarred working tables, an industrial steel sink, and shelves filled with canned vegetables and preserves. A fourth door led into a handsome little breakfast nook in the family wing.

We hadn't met FeeMolly Hodger yet, the famous cook of Cameron Hall, because Ebb said FeeMolly had been *on strike* for most of the past year.

FeeMolly was Ebb's mother. And Ebb's sister's mother. Ebb informed me the next morning that her sister was named Flo. Ebb and Flo. They were in their thirties and both had been married and divorced a number of times. Between them they had four children in elementary school and two at home. We hadn't met Flo yet, either, because she was home with two sick children. Both sisters' preschoolers had strep throat. I asked about FeeMolly's strike. I couldn't resist.

"Mama won't cook for halfhearted mouths," Ebb explained as I wandered around the Hall's kitchen the next morning, groggy but freshly scrubbed, wearing jeans and a black T-shirt with Tchaikovsky Rules emblazoned in white across the chest. Ella was still sound asleep upstairs in a feather bed with a beautiful heirloom quilt tucked around her chin. "Mama's got a reputation to keep up," Ebb prattled on, as she sliced the most delectable-looking homegrown cantaloupe I'd ever seen.

The melon scent rose like a perfume in the whitewashed kitchen, where the islands and counters and tall cabinets were all crowded with baskets of fresh vegetables and fruit. "And she says," Ebb went on, "it ain't bad enough that The Cameron is gone, but the peck-and-poke of life around here died with him, God bless Mr. Simon's sweet soul."

"The Cameron?"

"Mr. Simon. Mama always called him The Cameron. Head man of the family. It's an old Scottish way of speakin'. Goes way back. Even if the family's headed by a woman she's called The Cameron. Mama tried calling Ma'am Olivia The Cameron once upon a time, but Ma'am Olivia wouldn't have it."

"Oh? She abdicated to Simon?"

"Oh, no'm, I wouldn't say Ma'am Olivia felt *decayed*, I think she just wanted Simon to have the title."

I bit my lip over the misunderstanding and swallowed a smile. "Oh."

"Anyhow, Mama says she can't set her mind to cook for the family if they just gonna chew the moon every day."

"Chew the moon?"

"Reach out for manna from heaven instead of pulling

their own spirits out of God's good dirt. Mama can't abide wishy-washiness. She wants her title back. Chief chef, Cameron Hall Inn. I reckon she thinks you and your sister are a sign the time's a-comin'. She got out of her water bed this morning and commenced packing her spice sack and sharpening her knives."

I didn't know what to say to this strange image.

"She sounds interesting," I finally managed.

Isabel came into the kitchen about the time Ebb finished the breakfast biscuits, set a sleepy Dylan in his playpen where Ebb could watch him while she scrambled eggs, then gave me a quick tour of the family-wing rooms. The Hall was filled with two centuries' worth of eclectic antiques, linens, rugs, and artwork, all just a little on the well-worn side, enough to make a person feel comfortable.

The family wing alone was the size of a large house. "I have a bedroom downstairs with Dylan, and Olivia and Bea are downstairs," Isabel explained. "Min's room is upstairs, and so are Jasper's and Kelly's rooms. And the guest room where y'all are staying. We have all the upstairs guest rooms of the central house closed off. To save on heating and air conditioning. We thought you wouldn't want to be stuck alone in the public part of the Hall, anyway."

"Where is Carter's room?"

"In a houseboat he set up beside the river." A houseboat? That was good news. Carter wasn't in the same house with us.

"Ruth lives in Hightower, with her husband and their little girl, but that's close by. It's the county seat. Believe it or not, it's big enough to have a two-screen movie theater and six gas stations." She smiled. "Practically a metropolis."

"Hmmm." As I pondered the missing Ruth I idly turned an interesting ashtray in my hands. Then I realized it was fashioned from sections of animal skulls and fanged jawbones. I set it down quickly. "Don't tell anybody," I said in a low voice, "but your ashtray has teeth."

Isabel laughed.

"This kitchen was built in the nineteen fifties," she explained when we circled back to our starting point. "When the first electrical lines were run in the valley Grandmother remodeled and put in the kitchen. Before that all the cooking was still done on wood stoves and fireplaces in a separate building."

"Until the *nineteen fifties*?"

She nodded. "We change slower than a possum spits," she drawled elaborately. Isabel pointed out a tall window with a low sill. Down a worn stone path I saw a stone cottage with three stone chimneys. "That used to be the Hall's kitchen," she went on. "This window was a big doorway, originally."

I was overwhelmed. I already felt I was cloistered in some mythological castle, even though the general look of the place was lived-in and smoothed-off, like the worn oval river rocks that had been used to build porch steps and garden walkways around the Hall. "What's the old kitchen used for now?"

"It's the inn's office. For a long time we just used it as storage for yard tools and junk. But Gib and Ruth and I cleaned it out and remodeled it for Simon's birthday a few years ago. Gib even managed to sneak our father's rolltop desk out of the central Hall and into the kitchen building without Simon knowing. Simon loved that desk and that office." Suddenly downcast, she added, "I'm sure you can tell how we all felt about our big brother. He was really more like a daddy to us. Especially to Ruth and me. And now all of us just feel like we're spinning in thin air. I guess yesterday was the closest we've come to touching ground since last year. Thank you for inspiring us."

I ignored the new dose of flattery. "Do you plan to stay here now that you're divorced?" The blunt question seemed to hit her between the eyes. She blinked. "I don't want to think about a new husband. Or a new home. I need to stay here and just *be*, for now. I'm so tired. We all are. Gib was in and out of the hospital for six months last year, with surgeries and physical therapy. Poor Min's been nearly catatonic. Ruth moved from Knoxville and resigned as an assistant district attorney there, and she's planning to run for district attorney here this fall—"

"Wait a minute. Ruth is a lawyer?"

"Oh, yes. A prosecutor. She intends to become the first female district attorney in the Hightower district. And she's got plenty of money for a campaign, because her husband owns a Coca-Cola bottling plant. Ruth and he moved to Hightower after the accident. Everybody had to come home and help."

"Ruth's a prosecuting attorney," I repeated distractedly, still mulling that information. I was surrounded by patriots, a former but still-dedicated government man, red-white-and-blue frontier history, and now Gib's unseen but disapproving sister Ruth, who represented the closest, most intimate arm of faceless authority.

"I need a cup of coffee," I said dully.

Isabel and I sat at a big pine kitchen table that could easily seat a dozen people. Cats strolled around our ankles. We sipped coffee, talked baby talk to Dylan, and helped Ebb string a bushel of green beans. I decided the kitchen was the geographic and social intersection of two worlds—the museum-quality public history of the inn and the quiet, cluttered, loving comfort of the home.

Or else it was the hole at the center of a vortex that could swallow Ella and me without a burp.

Ella, Isabel, Min, and I gathered for a late breakfast of sausage casserole, scrambled eggs, biscuits, and fresh fruit on a small porch off the back of the family wing, shaded by a large dogwood tree and orange trumpet-creeper vines. Min sat dutifully with us, sipping coffee but barely eating. There was no sign of Gib or Carter. I was reluctant to ask, but noticed how Ella craned her head eagerly at every noise.

"Where's Carter this morning?" Ella finally blurted.

"Oh, your car!" Isabel exclaimed. "I meant to tell y'all before. Gib and Carter left early this morning to take your car to a mechanic in Hightower." Isabel darted an apologetic look at Ella and me from under her dark, shy lashes. "They had to tow it."

"We don't need it this week anyway," Ella said.

I sat there in mute frustration, chewing my tongue and wishing Gib had let me supervise my own car's repairs. In the meantime Isabel fed Dylan from jars of baby food. Kelly and Jasper had already left for high school in Min's big, solid car, which they shared with embarrassed bickering. Neither one of them wanted to be seen behind the wheel. Each morning they drew straws. That day Jasper got the short end.

Olivia did not eat breakfast or rise before midmorning, and Bea took breakfast in her room, where she watched the morning talk shows as she drank boiling-hot tea and ate muffins dripping honey and preserves made from the valley's apple orchards and fruit vines.

"We have a satellite dish now," Isabel explained between small scoops of stewed beef, which Dylan, giggling, mouthed and spit obscenely. I kept wiping beef goo off my cheek. Ella smiled at him and left the beef spray where it landed. "Until a few years ago," Isabel went on, "the Hall had a huge antenna, but we could still only receive three TV stations. There was a hot debate in the family over installing the satellite thingy. Television is *so* distracting. I said it would be too harsh. The world is filled with such meanness and violence and people leaping into bed at every cold-blooded opportunity, if you believe TV."

TV pretty much had the world pegged right, I thought, at least the world Ella and I had known for the past decade.

"But Simon wanted to watch CNN," Min commented. "He liked to tape it all day and then run the tape back while we went over the inn's daily accounts after dinner. He'd watch for glimpses of Gib at presidential events."

When she'd stopped speaking she gazed out across the

grassy yard beyond the porch. Ella, Isabel, and I regarded her in silence for a minute, and she never noticed. Hummingbirds began to dive-bomb a bright red glass feeder hung among the vines. Ella and Isabel seemed to imitate the birds' high-pitched chitter. Finally a tiny ruby-throated male hummer perched on a leafy green tendril less than a foot away from their heads, peering down at them with apparent bird-loves-bird intrigue.

"I'm working on a watercolor mural of hummingbirds," Isabel noted, looking on Ella as if she, too, recognized a kindred feathered spirit. "Would you like to walk over to my studio and see it? I work in that old log smokehouse behind the forsythia hedge over there."

Ella nearly bubbled with acceptance. Every detail of cozy heritage and generous charisma filled her with appreciation. No more dingy dressing rooms and crummy RV parks. No more microwave meals in the cramped confines of our rolling metal home. For the moment, at least, we were in the Great American Homestead, with all the comfort that implied.

"Simon restored the smokehouse a few years ago," Min said, still gazing into the lonely distances. "We'd used it as a storage shed but guests were always curious about it, so he cleaned it out and turned it into a one-room cottage. We offered it as a separate rental for the guests."

"When will you reopen the inn?" I asked carefully.

Min looked at me, then away again. "I don't know. I'm not sure we ever will. Simon knew every guest by name. Most of them had been coming here for years. They loved him. We all loved him. I can't begin to imagine how the Hall would operate without him."

Silence. Awkwardly, I laid a piece of buttered biscuit on Min's coffee saucer. My idea of domesticity was peeling the plastic wrap off a pack of vending-machine crackers. "You should eat," I said, like an Italian mother. She looked at me, touched my hand gently in a show of gratitude, then shook her head and looked away again.

.   .   .

Min went for a walk alone—something she did every day, Isabel said, so Ella and I visited Isabel's studio. The best I can say about her art is that big-eyed bunnies, angels, jewel-toned birds, and fluffy kittens appeal to many people, though not to me. I could see, however, why her work was popular in decorators' galleries around the South. The bunnies, kittens, et al. were somehow southern, frolicking among the pastel fantasies of cornhusk baskets and magnolia blossoms.

"These would be fantastic in a child's bedroom," Ella said in a wavering voice. I went on alert. I knew that note of desperation.

"I'd be honored to give you one," Isabel promised.

My sister looked away, blinking hard. "Oh, I couldn't. I have no place to even store it. But thank you Bless your heart. Thank you so much."

"When you have your first baby you can come back here and pick out any original of mine that you like. All righty?"

Ella fumbled with her hands and struggled not to burst into tears. The last thing I wanted was for her to spill the story of her lost love, lost child, and nervous breakdown in Detroit. The less this family knew about us, the better. "What's your basic thesis here?" I interjected loudly.

Isabel blinked. "You mean, why do I love to paint?"

"Yes."

"I like to look at my work and believe the world really looks that way. I want to pretend I'm only looking through a window." She paused. "I don't like grim reality."

"I'm sorry about your husband," Ella said softly. She seemed to have recovered her composure, but smiled at me wistfully.

Isabel sighed. "He was a spiritual chameleon. Love is blind. I saw what I wanted to see."

Ella's eyes gleamed. "That's so true about love."

We walked back across to the Hall with Ella and Isabel

still chatting like hummingbirds and me all too aware of my cynicism. Suddenly Carter bounded from the back door of the family wing and held out a large wicker picnic basket.

"Brought y'all some lunch," he said. He looked at Isabel and grew a bit solemn. "FeeMolly made it up for me while I was in town. She says she's coming over tomorrow. And not just to cook for the week. For good."

Isabel clutched her throat. "No!"

"And Flo's coming, too. They sure are determined to start back fulltime. They consider our havin' the Nellies here a sign that all's right again and Minnie's ready to rock 'n' roll."

"I'll talk to Gib," Isabel said, fluttery with trepidation. "We can't upset Minnie with this kind of pressure."

He nodded. Suddenly his smile reappeared. He flipped the picnicbasket lid open and winked at us. "Lunch made fresh this morning by FeeMolly Hodger, the absolute best cook in the entire state of Tennessee."

"Where are Gib and my car?" I asked darkly.

"Gib's still in town and your car's on the rack at Charley's Auto World shop. I am sure sorry, but it's looking pretty bad. Probably at least a busted gas line and a burned-out transmission. But don't you worry. Gib told Charley to fix it up and he'd pay the bill."

"No, he can't do that."

"You can't turn down his offer, it's not hospitable."

"It's a gift," Ella echoed. "Please, Vee." She glided to Carter then looked through his basket, offering exuberant sighs and compliments on potato salad, chocolate layer cake, and fried chicken. I recognized this as the polite forerunner of her mating call. One time she fell in love with a man at an opening party for a local theater revival of *Mame*. He offered her a miniature egg roll from the buffet. When Ella and I got back to our camper that night she spent an hour mulling the romantic first encounter. "A man who speaks through food symbolism is very sensitive," she said.

"Some enchanted evening," I sang at her that night, "you may share some soy sauce."

Now I headed Carter off at the pass. I walked over and put a hand on Ella's shoulder. "Thank you, but we're not hungry. We just finished breakfast a little while ago."

Ella frowned at me. "Why, *I'm* still hungry."

Carter laughed and slapped one leg. "Well, then, come on, Ella Mae Nellie, you go picnic with me by yourself! Come take a look-see at the transportation." He grabbed Ella's hand and led her around the looming stone pediment at one corner of the Hall. I stood in the yard fuming.

"You've been hornswoggled," Isabel said lightly. "But don't worry. Carter's a good guy."

"There's good and then there's good."

"I can't make any guarantees on that. But he's a gentleman. A gentleman and a flirt, but a gentleman, I swear."

Then I heard Ella laughing. For the first time in years my baby sister laughed in long, hooting, carefree gulps. I ran around the corner and halted in surprise. In the middle of a finely graveled driveway shaded by huge, gracious water oaks, Carter patted his transportation on its hump. It was a two-wheeled buggy pulled by a buffalo. A dozen tongue-lolling dogs and a few brave cats circled the vehicle.

Ella pivoted toward me, her face glowing. "I'll be back after lunch! Do you mind if I leave you on your own?"

I shrugged as nonchalantly as possible. "It's not as if I can go anywhere." Ella hugged me then darted to Carter's outstretched hand and climbed into the cart. He climbed up beside her, gave me a mischievous salute, then said, "Giddyap," to the buffalo.

And so I watched my only family—the sisterly yin to my yang, a delicate soul whose trusting nature had necessitated many years of hand-holding and belligerent interventions on my part, the only person in the world who loved me and trusted me with unfailing loyalty and unselfishness—ride off down a dirt road toward the wild forest and the rhododendron-tucked mountainsides behind a shuffling brown buffalo, sitting next to a copper-skinned man with the luscious appeal of a rich candy bar. I remembered how women drooled over Pop's ethnic mystique, and I was convinced Carter played up his own brand of exotic seduction. I was sure he hoped to carve Ella's initials in his bedpost along with about a thousand other female monograms he'd collected.

And I was afraid he'd break her heart into pieces too small for me to fix.

Thirteen

Bea, unshakable Bea, who grunted softly when she walked and sipped a homemade dark beer she called her midmorning toddy, took me on a tour of the Hall's main section, the part that had been opened to the public as an inn. She offered me one of her thick brown brews and I drank it, immediately developing a glow in my brain that distracted my worries about Ella enough to make me hoist my beer stein in a salute to the Cameron family Scottish clan tartan, displayed in a parlor off the library.

"You're a bold young woman, Venus Arinelli," Bea observed with tipsy appreciation. "Are you sure you have no wild Celtic blood in your veins?"

"Anything's possible," I said. "Because what I know about my family tree wouldn't make a good stump."

"I say you're a Scot at heart, and more's the pity for any who cross you!" From that moment onward Bea and I had an understanding, a camaraderie, if not outright friendship. She had the aura of old rebellions about her. This was my hunch. Maybe I was drawn to her because of it.

"Nearly two hundred years old, it is," she told me as we explored the mansion. "The first Cameron's son built it after he made his fortune in shipping over on the coast of the Carolinas. Human cargo and tobacco. Slaves. There's always a bit of shame in every great family. Makes the whole lot more fascinating, eh, dearie?"

I stared at her. Was she trying to tell me most of the Camerons wouldn't hypocritically condemn my own notorious family history? "Eh," I said uncertainly.

Bea pointed out spur scars and bullet holes, door moldings where some visiting backwoodsman had lodged his hunting knife more than a century before, and creaking floorboards showing faded scorch marks from spilled oil lamps and beeswax candles. Places where some long-dead hunting dog had chewed a furniture leg. An ax mark where an athletic Cameron female had thrown a hatchet at a Yankee officer.

"She missed," Bea said proudly. "More's the better, since she married him happily, after the war."

"This valley must be one of those magnetic centers in the earth," I told her with beer-induced profundity. "But I don't know if I believe in whimsies."

"Shame, shame. Oh, but don't you wish you *did*, dearie?"

I didn't know what to say.

"Oh, indeed, there are forces at work here," Bea went on. "It's why the Indians settled here in the old times. Why, there were wild Indians before them who built the chapel mound. The hot springs are proof of mysterious powers under the surface. An earth center, this surely is. A powerful place. And this house is as potent as an old woman. Wearin' her wrinkles and her wisdom as jewels of the spirit. You can no' resist her courage."

"Don't you ever want to go home? To Scotland? Your family?"

"And desert my dear ones here? This is my family."

"But don't you have Cameron relatives in—"

"I'm no' a Cameron by name, dear child." She drew herself up proudly. "I'm a MacCallum!"

"Oh." This meant nothing to me.

Her bushy gray brows surged together over a nose like a pit bull's snout. She waved a hand at a relatively modern portrait of a handsome woman in a soft beige dress suit with padded shoulders. "Herself there, Coira MacCallum Cameron, was my mother's sister. My auntie, she was, God rest her bold soul!"

"O-kay," I said, drawing the word out.

"She arrived like so many Cameron conquests to this wild place—she was no' willing at all, not at first!"

"Is slavery a family hobby?"

Bea brayed with laughter. "She was won in a card game in the nineteen twenties, in the back room of an Edinburgh pub!"

"Won?"

"The young doctor William Cameron won her, so to say! From her own brother! He was no gambler, Coira's brother Robert. He lost a bloody fortune to William, and had no way to pay the debt. So Coira, bein' Robert's older sister and a strict, responsible Lowland Presbyterian, Coira says, 'I'll be going to your homeland in the woods and working for you, Dr. Cameron, for a year to pay Rob's debt. And then I'll bloody well come back home!' Because Coira, you see, was ahead of her time. She had taken trainin' as a nurse during the First World War. And William needed a strong-hearted nurse to assist him on his rounds. The bears and the muddy trails and the mountain folk with their fearsome ways—most nurses could no' manage it! But Coira had a MacCallum backbone o' steel!"

"But she never intended to stay here?"

"Aye, but there was a bit of hanky-panky between her and William during the long ocean voyage over from Scotland, and a few months after she arrived here, there could be no hidin' it. She was puffing up, she was."

"Pregnant?"

"Aye, like a cat's meow."

"So she felt she *had* to marry Dr. Cameron?"

"Oh, no, dearie, she thought he meant to collect his full debt from her, that's all. The first bairn they bred was quite the scandal. She did no' marry William until he convinced her his heart was true. And that was only after their second bairn was born."

"No!"

"Aye!"

I gazed, intrigued, at the woman in the portrait. I thought I now saw a gleam of rebellion in *her* eyes.

Bea went on, "And so I grew up in Scotland hearing tales of wicked Aunt Coira in America, and then when I was just past grown Coira died, poor soul, and William sent their lovely, grievin' daughter to board with me and my parents in the Highlands for a summer. And that's how I met my sweet cousin Olivia."

"Did she . . . speak then?"

"Aye, of course! She had a voice like a dove!"

"But . . . what happened to her?"

"Life happened to her. Terrible life. She lost the will to talk for herself."

"You mean she really can talk if she wants to?"

"She wants to. She can no' force a sound. Has no' uttered so much as a peep in more than fifty years."

"But if her larynx and her vocal cords aren't damaged, then what—"

"It's her soul that's damaged. Now let's say no more about it. Enough sad stories for today! What are you, you talker you? A bloody morbid Scotswoman at heart, eh? What kind o' family do you suspect I'd leave behind? *This* is my home, where I've been happy once and for all, and I'd have it no other way." She looked at me closely. "I have no husband. Never had. No children. I came to help Herself manage after Winny and Simon senior died."

"Gib's mother and father?"

"Aye. And I've been here ever since. I'm a queer old beastie, but they love me here."

Since I didn't quite know how she meant that, and my mind buzzed with unanswered questions about Olivia, I said, "Queer beasties seem to be the order of the day around here."

"Aye," Bea chortled, and slapped my back so hard my teeth clicked together.

"This house," she went on comfortably, as we walked upstairs, "is timeless, it is. A survivor. The chapel is the soul of the family but this house is the heart. It feels sad now, but Herself and I believe it will somehow come back to rights, even with Simon gone. We all miss him so. Gib, God bless his manly hide, will have to fill his big brother's shoes."

"I expect Gib can accomplish anything he sets his mind to."

Bea sighed. "It's not what he sets his mind to, dearie. It's where he puts his heart. And his heart's been torn out of him. Take no heed in what he says to you. He's not found his new place, yet. None of us have, really. Ruth is wanting to sell the valley—"

"To Cousin Emory?"

"Aye. His investors. She's for it, thinks it's the best plan for the future. Min's leaning in that direction, too, and so is Isabel. Gib and Herself have no' persuaded them to give up the idea yet and fight."

"But Gib and his sisters are so close and loving. I haven't met Ruth yet, but I assume she and Gib—"

"Aye, they're specially so. Since they were wee bairns it's been all for one and one for all. But it was a hard time, those early years. A pack of orphaned children, Simon and Minnie mere teenagers trying to be father and mother to the brood, Herself not able to speak, and me, well, a stranger in a strange land, for a time. It made the children what they are, for good or bad, but very, very strong, each in a way. Dear Gib decided early that he'd be the family gladiator. That no one would ever

hurt anyone he loved again. It's his whole nature. Protecting."
She gestured dramatically. "Lock the gates and fortify the
castle walls!"

"That explains a lot about him."

We halted on a stair landing where more exquisite oil
portraits and sepia photographs of long-dead Camerons lined
the walls like a gallery of ghostly jurors.

Bea nodded sadly. "He couldn't save his brother, and it
may be that he can't save the Hall. And it's killin' him inside."

"I don't want to cause him more trouble. I really don't."

"He needs your kind of trouble, I'm betting. You're a
tough she-girl, inside and out. Not so easily lovable like the
dear lassies who've trailed Gib about over the years. He's out-
grown the pets, he has." She looked me up and down then
tapped my head with her blunt forefinger and nodded. "Come
along. I've something to show you."

She led me to a suite in a corner of the second floor. It
was a sun-washed room with a high-plumped kingly bedstead. Tall windows fronted a small sitting room brimming
with wicker chaises, and there was a huge, claw-footed tub in
the bathroom.

"The best guest room in the house," Bea said proudly. "It
was christened with love from the very first." She faced me as
I gazed wistfully at the peaceful and romantic place. "Your
parents," she said softly, "stayed in this room."

By the time I realized it, she'd left me alone there. I didn't
sit on the bed. That seemed a sacred spot. Trembling, I sat
down in a wicker lounge in a small alcove nearby. I put a hand
over my heart and felt the rhythm of my own blood.

My heart's memories began in that room.

Ella was still gone. It was after two o'clock and Olivia had requested me for tea at four. I told Min I'd like to take a nap
first, then went back to the main wing and sat quietly by a
window in the bedroom Mom and Pop had shared.

Finally I heard footsteps and a knock on the door. I jumped up, ruffled my braids, and called out, "Just a second. Let me get awake." When I opened the door I looked up into Gib's wickedly amused eyes. "I saw you from the lawn. You nap sitting up by the window?" he asked. "Are you a cat?"

I patted my braids and gazed about, feigning ignorance while my face tingled. But retaining my dignity was hopeless around him. "Kiss my big furry tail," I retorted glumly.

"The static electricity might stun me."

"I was watching for Ella. She was dragged off by Carter and a buffalo. I can't hunt for her because *some self-righteous mountain man* towed my car."

"You'll need two days for the car repairs, Nellie," he said. He flexed his right arm in a careful way that said the arm hurt a little.

"Hmmm?" I replied vaguely, fixated on the arm, his soft chambray shirt, and old jeans. He was big, wholesome, and handsomely denimed. "What?"

"When I took a look this morning I was afraid I'd have to put your hatchback out of its misery. My first thought was that you'd twisted the axle. But you didn't, and Charley, my mechanic over in Hightower, says he can have it up and running in a couple of days. So stop giving me that beady-eyed once-over."

It was appreciation, nothing to do with the hatchback, but I scowled for disguise. "My sister has disappeared with your cousin."

"She's fine with Carter. You've got my word on it." He stood aside and gestured toward the hallway. "Why don't you stop worrying about your *grown* sister and teeter off charmingly downstairs? I'll show you something purty, I swanie."

"Something *what*? You *what*?"

"Something pretty. I swear."

"Speak English, not Tennessee."

He grunted. I stepped into the hall, avoiding any casual contact with his outstretched arm. If any other man had said

"Come see something pretty" to me I'd expect the "something pretty" would involve showing off a part of the male anatomy that, at best, resembled a sunburned salami.

But with Gib, I was depressingly safe.

It was sleek, black, and beautiful, and had an ivory smile I couldn't resist. I put my ear close to the keyboard then gently stroked an A, then a C-sharp. "Not bad," I announced, as the pearls of sound faded into a low tremble inside the piano's chest. Pianos lived and breathed, to me. Pop put the idea in my head when I was very small—that pianos were magical animals hiding in wooden shapes to fool people, and that to coax songs from them you had to tickle them. This grand Steinway was the most beautiful creature I'd seen in years.

"In honor of your arrival I hired the best piano tuner I could find," Gib said.

"He did a good job. It purrs."

"It what?"

"Nothing."

"This piano belonged to my mother," he continued. "My father bought it for her as a wedding gift. She was traveling with a gospel music show when they met."

"Your mother was a musician?"

"No. She was a secretary. But she loved to play the piano."

I played a few chords. "Good acoustics," I said. "Good ambiance." The piano occupied one corner of a cozy room known among the family as the Franklin Cameron Smoking Parlor. The Camerons could call it the smoking parlor if they liked, but from that moment on, the big, old-fashioned room, full of leather armchairs and comfortable clutter, would always be the *music room* to me.

"The guests loved this room," Gib noted. "They'd come in here when the weather was too cold or wet to hike or explore. They'd play cards, games. Talk. Read. And they'd sit for hours, listening to my brother's stories about our history. Simon loved to entertain."

"When are you going to reopen to the public?" I knew it was a loaded question.

"I don't know if we ever will. It takes everybody working full-tilt from dawn to midnight to operate the inn. Min's not up to it, and there are certain jobs I can't *hire* anyone to do for us."

"I've spent my whole life in restaurants and nightclubs, so I know you can find the right help if you interview enough people."

"I can't hire a host. I can't replace my brother."

I skimmed the keyboard, just playing a few scales, letting the moment cool off. I was comfortable with the piano helping me speak. "They didn't teach you to grin and bow and say howdy do in the Secret Service?" I finally said

"It takes more than that. Simon had a sixth sense about people. He knew how to make them feel comfortable. He never met a stranger. I'm the opposite. I'm very good at making strangers feel very *un*comfortable."

I remembered his chilling stare in Chicago. "You have to practice diplomacy and showmanship," I said. "And pretty soon you'll be an old pro at hosting—once you get past the urge to dole out kung-fu chops instead of handshakes."

"Good God." He almost smiled. The smile simmered then disappeared, leaving a quiet scrutiny that said he never quite knew what to make of me.

"I get the impression," I went on, "that either you'll run this place so it'll pay its own keep or you and your sisters will have to sell out to dear Cousin Emory and his demon seed. There isn't a third choice?"

"No. Taxes and maintenance cost a small fortune. However it may look, we're not the rich branch of the family, Nellie." He came over and leaned on the piano. I got goosebumps on my skin. Gib polished a tiny speck of dust on the piano's closed lid. He had chosen a perfectly discreet distance by anyone's standards but mine. And unfortunately it wasn't that I wanted him to move away. I wanted him to come closer. "My former *high-paying* civil-service job wouldn't pay the costs around here, even if I could go back," he said.

"The Secret Service offered you an administrative job, I bet. Min told me you were extremely respected as an agent."

"My life is here now. I'm responsible for this place and this family."

"I understand. You're The Cameron, now. I heard Ebb call you that." A frisson of excitement slid through me. The old-world honor was very appealing and solemn. There was rebellious allure in casting Gib as the chieftain of the Cameron clan, modern sensibilities and patriarchal macho considerations be damned.

His eyes flashed. "That title has to be earned." He lifted his maimed hand. "You say all I need to do is learn to smile at people and offer them a handshake. How many people will be happy to shake this nauseating victory for medical science? There are days when I wish the doctors hadn't saved any part of my hand. That they'd just amputated it. Then I could stick a decent-looking fake on the end of my arm."

I became very busy pressing keys and listening to tones. I played a few chords, tilting my head, my eyes closed as if I continued to assess the room's acoustics. When I opened my eyes I found Gib watching me closely. "Sit your tight-ass John Wayne behind down on this bench," I ordered, "and give me that perfectly likable bum paw." I reached out and grabbed his hand.

I think he was too surprised to resist. He studied me sharply but sat down. I scooted over a little to make room. He tried to avoid touching his left thigh against my right one. I planted my left hand over his damaged right one, then pried his fingers apart. "Relax," I said. "Piano teachers do this with kids. *Relax.* You're as stiff as a frozen octopus."

I pressed his thumb on a key, then his first finger, then his second. "One, two, three, then curl your thumb under and repeat. Start here and go to there." I pointed. Awkwardly, slowly, he performed the simple exercise. "Congratulations, Mr. Cameron. You just played a basic little ol' scale. And you played with two fewer fingers than mere ordinary beginners. Now *stretch* those fingers. Do this." I showed him another maneuver. "And we add the left hand. Voilà! Smack that key. Now this. Now together."

"What am I doing?" he muttered, as he played.

"You're playing Mozart!"

"Get outta here. Sounds like 'Twinkle, Twinkle Little Star' to me."

"Yes, but it's also the melodic theme of twelve variations Wolfgang wrote on *Ah, vous dirai-je, Maman*." I launched into an elaborate segment of the piece, got caught up in the glory of it, and when I finished I realized Gib was simply gazing from me to my hands with his lips parted in awe—a handsome, vulnerable sight that made me stare at his mouth, and at him. I hadn't played classical pieces very often over the past ten years. There was deep sadness in them for me, a lot of memories, because Pop had coached me, and each bar of the music was polished and polished again, until it was an ingrained part of me, part of my skin and soul, fingertips and heart, and he was so proud of my talent.

Finally I realized Min, Bea, and Olivia had entered the room while I was playing.

"My word, dearie," Bea said softly. "My word."

Min cried gently. "You have a beautiful gift," she said.

Olivia's eyes glowed. She shuffled, barefoot, toward me, then bent over a notepad she took from a pocket of her white cotton blouse, and wrote: *He forgets to hate himself when he's around you.*

Gib craned his head to read it, but Olivia put her notepad away. She rapped her knuckles on the piano's lid and waved a hand for us to continue.

Gib nodded to her. "Today, 'Twinkle, Twinkle,'" he said dryly. "But after I reach my musical peak? 'Chopsticks.'"

Everyone laughed. Gib's expression became strained. I think the unaccustomed joy in the Hall, combined with his cozy proximity to me on the piano bench, suddenly made him feel guilty. "I have work to do," he said abruptly, and left the room.

Troubled emotions flashed across Olivia's wizened, girlish face; tentative, then sad; a smile, then quick, dewy shyness. She sat down on the bench beside me. I pretended Gib hadn't insulted me and arranged her fingers on several keys. "Press them," I said. "That's a happy chord."

She pressed. Smiling sadly, she nodded at me. Then she took my hands in her small ones and looked at me firmly. She fluttered her hands like birds, then settled them on the keys, glanced at me firmly, then performed the strange ritual again.

"I belong here?" I asked. She nodded. "I don't think so."

Olivia settled back in a deep chair and I played a little Chopin for her. She eventually fell asleep with a smile on her face. I sat and watched her awhile, wondering if she spoke in her dreams.

In my nightmares, I could not make a sound.

It was sunset before my sister came back with Carter. I'd been watching out a big window at the end of the upstairs hall. The beauty of the evening registered on my frazzled senses like a fine wine I didn't want to be tempted to drink. The valley filled with soft darkness. Fat, black beef cattle gathered for dinner around a hay feeder in the front pastures. A silver mist rose along the river, and the sky above the mountains deepened into purple, pink, and gold jeweled by my namesake evening star like a diamond earring. To love it all, to even think about falling in love, was too useless. All too soon Ella and I would be back in a city somewhere, hunting for work. Even with one hundred thousand dollars to cushion us, our life on the road would return to the same frugal grind, at least until I decided how to use the money.

Carter dramatically leaped down from the cart, patted the buffalo's narrow rump, then held up his arms to Ella. She laughed and scrambled off with less grace but infinite adorable awkwardness, while Carter caught her by the elbows. They stood on the front lawn with his hands on her shoulders, and her hands on his forearms, and they gazed at each other mistily.

I rapped on the window. Ella jumped and looked up sheepishly. I retreated down the hall and into our bedroom.

When she came in she avoided my stern gaze and headed for the claw-footed tub in our bathroom with a packet of her favorite bath salts in one hand and two vanilla-scented candles in the other. "I can't wait to soak in that deep tub filled with hot water," she called in a high, too-cheerful voice.

"I think you might better take a cold shower," I retorted, and slammed the bathroom door.

The next afternoon, when she disappeared with Carter again, I was so angry I thought I'd explode. I slipped out of the house and made my way to a gazebo along the river, brooding over Carter's instant effect on my sister. I leaned on a railing and stared down at the water.

A car pulled up the road then stopped. I didn't recognize the woman who got out and started my way. *She looks like a high F-sharp to me,* I thought as she marched across the lawn. She was tall and upholstered—easily two hundred pounds—all of the round flesh firmly fitted into a soft blue blouse and a snug beige skirt. Her dark hair was wound into a plump French braid with tendrils escaping as if pulled outward by the static electricity of her attitude. She looked prickly.

"It's about time I took a look at you," she brayed, then smiled ferociously and strode to me, thrust out her hand, and pumped mine in a firm grip. "Ruth Cameron Attenberry," she announced. "I've been in Washington on state business. A legal seminar."

Aha. Gib's other sister. The lawyer who lived in High-tower with her husband and baby daughter. The sister who "disapproved" of Ella and me. "Nice to meet you, Ruth," I lied. "State business? Should I salute?"

She leveled a brusque hazel stare at me as she made herself at home in a white wicker chair. "Are you always a smart-ass?"

I squinted at her. Interesting way she had of putting things. "Oops," I said breezily. "My reputation precedes me."

Her nostrils flared. "I hope mine precedes me. I'm an assistant district attorney."

"Technically, then, you get paid by the government to be obnoxious?"

"You *are* a piece of work. The rumors don't do you justice. I heard in town that you had a big mouth and a chip on your shoulder. That's an understatement, obviously."

"Look, I'm sorry you and I are getting off on the wrong foot. I'm a little testy at the moment. Let's start over."

"Right." She dismissed my apology with a wave of one plump, manicured hand. "For the record, my brother insisted I stop by and welcome you and your sister." She made the word *welcome* sound like a chore. Her expression was anything but gracious. "I'm not happy about this visit of yours. I didn't agree to it. I'm also not happy about the money your old daddy foisted on my brother Simon. Listen up, now, missy, I'm going to be as blunt as a hound's snout with you."

I burst out laughing. She stared at me while I wiped my eyes. "I haven't heard so much deliberate, down-home lawyer bullshit since I watched a whole afternoon of *Matlock* reruns."

Color rose in her cheeks. Her mouth formed a perfect, flat line. "I'd like to know why you arrived early the other day and went after Gib when he was alone and drunk."

I leveled an unwavering look at her. "You make it sound like a sinister plan. I wanted to check out the circumstances here before we met everyone. I'm not accustomed to strangers issuing innocent invitations and offering me large sums of money."

"Oh, I bet you've taken gifts from strange men a few times along the road."

"You're obnoxious and catty, too. I'm impressed. Even Matlock isn't that complex."

"I find it very interesting that you had no significant qualms about driving hundreds of miles to learn more about the Cameron family and property."

"I find you very interesting, too," I said in the even, controlled voice I used when club managers wanted to negotiate a nooky clause in the contracts. "Why don't you stop playing coy little variations on your theme and get straight to the big movement."

"Fine. I think you and your sister came here planning to hop on the Cameron gravy train. You think your old daddy's hundred thousand bucks might be small pickings compared to the money you could wrangle out of my family. I'm here to say that if you or your sister pull any stunts I'll be all over you like white on rice."

Cold fury. And amazement. Somehow, no matter how cynical I'd become, this woman's gall got to me, probably because I had been suckered by the welcome the others had given us.

Ruth went on talking. "If you have any intention of ingratiating yourself with my brother or our great-aunt in return for money or other favors, I highly recommend you drop the idea. And if you think you can cook up some bogus legal offenses worthy of some jackshit lawyer's attention—if you think you can find some excuse to badger my family for more money—let me tell you why that dog won't hunt." She leaned toward me, her eyes glittering with disgust. "I'll make sure the IRS lives and breathes to audit every tax return you send in for the rest of your life. I'll make sure you can't even spit on a street corner without a federal agent showing up to ask you why. You think you've been harassed for the past ten years? If you try to milk my family for charity I'll make certain you and your sister can't even apply for driver's licenses without getting your asses raked over the coals."

"I have never," I said slowly, "met anyone more paranoid than I am. Until now."

"You'd better take me seriously. I think we both agree the world's not a gentle place to live. You either stomp or you get stomped."

"Now let me tell you something. You represent every power-happy, anal-retentive, prejudiced sadist who ever took advantage of people I love. I don't want anything from you or your family. The charm of being one of the dispossessed people of the world, ol' girl, is that being threatened loses its power after a while. I've got nothing to lose as long as I still have *my* family. You stay away from my sister, because if you give her the lecture you just gave me—if you accuse her of motives she can't even fathom—*I'll tell the whole freakin' world how Simon Cameron hid money for my father—and how the rest of you became his accomplices*."

That was a terrible bluff. I couldn't begin to imagine myself actually repaying Simon Cameron's kindness—or Gib's honest discharge of duty—with that brand of revenge. But neither could I give Ruth free rein to threaten me and Ella.

Ruth stood. So did I. She was so mad she was trembling. "I'll be watching you and your sister until the second you leave this place," she said in a tone like a sharp hunting knife.

"That won't be long, I promise you."

She walked down the gazebo's steps, stalked to her car, and drove up to the Hall.

I let myself start shaking after I was alone. Staring after her, I said under my breath, "I know you. The first time I met you I was six years old and you were Nanny Robicheaux. I've been fighting you ever since."

·   ·   ·

I was ready to sizzle. I made my way down a path that followed the river into the woods. The September day was still hot enough for me to appreciate the cold water.

In a quiet spot where laurel shrubs shielded both sides of the river, I pulled off every stitch of clothes and sank down in a shallow pool. I must have sat there for an hour, watching minnows scoot around me. I examined my prune-skinned hands and wondered how long I'd have to soak before I shriveled to the size of a raisin. I splashed water on my breasts then stretched my arms overhead wearily. At that moment, in full, nipple-to-the-air extension, I heard the bushes rustle behind me.

I forced myself to move as if I hadn't noticed. I stood slowly, then slipped into my bra and panties as if I had all the time in the world to dress. I faked a yawn as I pulled on my white T-shirt, jeans, and sandals. Humming loudly, I slid my hands into my jeans' back pockets. I closed the fingers of my right hand around my pepper spray.

I pounced into the laurel shrubs, screeched some incoherent but ferocious attack cry, and squirted pepper into sixteen-year-old Jasper Cameron's startled face.

"Please, ma'am," Jasper said miserably as I marched him up a forest path beyond the cottage, "just kill me before anybody finds out. I'd be happier that way."

"You should have thought of that before you decided to become a Peeping Tom."

We trudged along. Sweat beaded under my bath-damp hair. I'd told him I was taking him to his mother, and I wanted to hear him confess to her. I just wanted to make him sweat.

It was working.

His head up, his eyes watering badly, his jaw set and shoulders back, Jasper walked ahead of me with miserable dignity. "I'm not askin' for mercy, ma'am," he mumbled.

"Good. Because you're fresh out of luck, mister. I've got no sympathy. I'm having a lousy day." I waved my pepper spray at him. Poor kid. I had only caught him a glancing squirt, but his eyes were streaming tears despite ten minutes of fervent rinsing. He stumbled along in a Braves jersey and huge, knee-length plaid shorts. He was too polite and clumsy to be anything worse than he appeared to be: a clean-cut teenage boy with a bad case of naked-female fever.

"The right to privacy is as basic as the air we breathe," I lectured grimly as we marched through the forest. "You could say I deserved to be looked at because I sat naked in the river, but I think I deserved to be respected. You make a habit of spying on guests who stay at the Hall?"

"No, ma'am! I was raised to be a gentleman, ma'am."

"I've known a lot of so-called gentlemen who don't have your conscience then."

"Ma'am, I figured you didn't mind, uh, to be looked at, ma'am! Because you're a musician and all. You get up on stages in front of people all the time."

I gave his arm a threatening prod with the nozzle of the pepper spray. "That's right. I choose to let people look at me sometimes. But not offstage. There have been too many times when I had no say in what or how or who looked at me—or how they looked at my home, my personal business, my family. My privacy belongs to *me*. What you did isn't a joke to me."

"Ma'am, I apologize again, ma'am," he barked. "I didn't mean to look, ma'am, I just happened to be nearby and the chance came up. Ma'am."

That's not the only thing that came up, I expect. "You don't have to call me ma'am, mister."

"Yes, I do, ma'am. Title of respect to ladies, ma'am."

As if I weren't armed with a table condiment. "How old are you?"

"Sixteen, ma'am," he reminded me crisply.

"Old enough to know better."

"Yes, ma'am!"

"I'm not a drill sergeant. Stop answering me that way."

"It's a habit, ma'am! I'm joining the Marines after I graduate from high school!"

"Why?"

"Duty, ma'am! Service to my country! Family tradition of government duty!"

"You can serve your country much better by going to college and peeping into the open windows of the girls' dorms."

"I'm not a pervert, ma'am! I intend to make my daddy proud!"

Here was the crux of Jasper Cameron, I thought. His life revolved around still-raw memories of a beloved father. "Your daddy wanted you to be a Marine?" I asked quietly. We strode up a hill out of the woods, between grassy meadows rimmed in white board fence. I was suddenly immersed in bright sunshine, the fresh blue scent of the sweetest air I'd ever smelled, and meadows of golden wildflowers stretching up the hills to puff-cake clouds above the horizon.

"I decided on the Marines this year," Jasper said hoarsely, still marching ahead of me, face-forward, his shoulders hunching with emotion. "My uncle Gib served in the Marine Corps before he joined the Secret Service, ma'am. My daddy was proud of Uncle Gib."

"I take it, then, that your daddy was never interested in being a Marine himself?"

"No, ma'am. My daddy was a businessman and a preacher, ma'am."

"What kind of preacher?"

"No particular church, ma'am. But he was elected county commissioner and stuff. He could marry people and stuff like that. And he could preach sermons. He didn't have time to go to college. He studied religion on his own. He said he sort of made up his own rules as he went along. People trusted him. Asked him for advice."

"Then tell me why your daddy would be proud if you put

on a soldier's uniform and vowed to kill your fellow human beings if the government asked you to."

"I . . . ma'am, I don't intend to shoot people unless I have to. You're not a Communist, are you? I heard you might be."

I bristled. "Mister, I'd bet money you don't know enough politics to tell me the difference between a Communist and a toad frog."

"Communists want the government to own everything."

"Well, I don't believe in politics. I'm not a political joiner. I just want the government to stay out of my bathroom window. Why don't you decide what *you* would be happy doing after high school, instead of what your daddy might want based on what you think he was proud of about your uncle Gib?"

This convoluted question evidently escaped him. We topped the hill, and he halted, his shoulders slumping again. I looked across at the magnificent old mansion set atop the next hill, with the small, lovely river gleaming peacefully below it.

"Please just kill me, ma'am," he repeated. "I don't want my mama to know what I did."

"Move it." We walked onward. "Why don't you get yourself a nice girlfriend, Marine?"

"I don't know how to talk to girls, ma'am. I always say the wrong thing. Or I don't say anything at all."

"You're talking to me."

"I'm scared of you in a different way, ma'am."

"Why, thank you."

"I was hoping you might help me out, ma'am."

"How so? By taking more baths?"

"You're in show business. You know about men. If I could just get some swank goin'—you know, kinda convince the girls at school that I'm a man—"

"Letting the big dog hunt doesn't make you a man. Any male animal can find a hen for his rooster. The tricky part is being smart enough to keep the other end in charge. That's what makes you a man."

"Oh, geez, ma'am, you sound like Uncle Gib."

"Good." I pointed to his head. "Use your brain. Be responsible. Think deep thoughts."

"I'm not sure I want to, ma'am. The things I've been thinking the past year nearly make me crazy."

"I see. About your father?"

"Yes, ma'am. I was going to go help him and Uncle Gib and Mama at the sawmill, but then I didn't because Daddy was sort of in a bad mood, and it wasn't like him, so I made up an excuse and didn't go." He paused and took a deep breath. "If I'd gone I would've saved him. And Uncle Gib's hand, too."

Sweet Mary. "Halt," I said. We stopped. "Sit." I pointed to a fallen tree. He sat down. I paced, my hands clenched behind my back. "When my father died I thought I could have done something different that would have saved his life. But you know what? We *always* think of what we might have done if circumstances had been different. That's life."

"No disrespect, ma'am, but I would have . . . I would have made a difference at the sawmill. I just know I would have. I would've jumped right in ahead of Mama and hit the button to turn off the sawblade. I'm fast. I run track. I move a lot faster than my mama can move. But I was ill-tempered and didn't go to the sawmill that day. I wasn't responsible enough. I wasn't a man."

"So you think having sex with me would make you a man?"

He leaped up. "Ma'am, I'm not even going to look at you again, much less dare have sex with you!"

"Well, calm down, because I wasn't offering. I'm saying you can't blame yourself for what happened to your father. And you don't become a man by marching around like a military clone, or by proving you can maneuver your sex organ toward the nearest female."

His face was bright red and getting redder every second. "I won't be caught off-guard again, ma'am. I run track, I lift weights, I practice the martial arts. I won't be weak again, ma'am."

"Look, my grandmother was descended from a samurai family. I've read a lot about the samurai, because of that. And you know what? The toughest sonuvadog samurai warrior was also the gentlest artist, the best poet, the most sensitive musician. Because it was said that a man had to appreciate beauty in order to know what he was fighting to protect."

"That's sort of what our sign says by the front doors of the Hall, ma'am!"

"Well, families of good philosophical taste like the same mottoes. Or something." I rubbed my forehead. "March on, Marine."

His expression fell. He plodded forward. When we reached the front lawn of the Hall we halted. Jasper looked as if he'd drop through a hole in the earth if he could.

"You're pardoned, Marine," I announced. "Apology accepted."

He stared at me with his thick brown brows arched like caterpillars. "Ma'am?"

"At ease. Behave yourself, and your trespassing today is our secret. Okay?"

"Venus, ma'am, thank you. My aunt Ruth says you look like the kind of woman who hangs out in alleys and rolls college students. But she's wrong."

"Scram, mister. You're losing points."

"Thank you, ma'am," he said again with elaborate dignity. Then he bounded into the house through a side door.

"Mozart never had these problems," I muttered under my breath.

A dinner party in our honor was planned for that night. I dreaded it. Being feted by Camerons felt suspiciously like being served up as the main dish at a barbecue.

By the time Ella walked into our bedroom that evening I

was pulling on a pair of white silk trousers. "I hope Carter isn't right behind you," I said. "Undressed women seem to be the primary entertainment around here." I had the trousers half up my thighs, and had not yet donned the matching blouse. My breasts bulged over the top of a white bra. When Ella said nothing I went on. "Of course, I expect he's seen more than a few women in their undies. And out of their undies. I wouldn't be surprised if he's taken a peek at your undies already."

She busied herself at a suitcase, and jerked a brush from her cosmetic bag. She stroked her hair so hard, wisps of it fanned upward in static-electrified blond filaments. "He taught me how to drive his buffalo today."

"I just bet he did. How'd your hair get so tangled?"

"Let's change the subject." She began pulling her jeans and blouse off and throwing them ferociously into a corner. I stopped pulling my trousers up, my fingers still wound in the waistband.

"What's *that* supposed to mean? Throwing clothes. What?"

She sighed. "Nothing, Sis. I don't want to talk about Carter right now. I need to change for the party. Did you talk to Min about tonight? Do you think she expects us to perform? She's really forgetful—you can see it in her eyes, she's in some other world half the time. Carter and I watched her endlessly rearrange some flowers in a vase—he says she's spent most of the past year in bed or just sitting around her bedroom—"

"Listen to me. I've had a helluva bad day. But even so, I've never let strangers take advantage of us. Don't you trust me anymore?"

"What in the world?" She gaped at me. "What provoked you to say something silly like *that*?"

"Nothing. Never mind."

"You think you always know what's best for me," she said testily.

"We're getting out of here at the end of two weeks and we're not coming back again. I've been on the phone. I've got serious leads on studio work in Nashville." Before we left Chicago I'd sent out a dozen copies of our standard studio-audition tape, but I didn't mention that. "I've been concentrating on our business. You haven't. I only agreed to come here to collect our money and try out the Nashville job market."

"You hate studio work. You always say it's boring."

"We could stand a little boredom and security! We're not going to live off our inheritance. I'm going to invest it for the future."

"Because you don't trust me to handle our money, you mean. Because I'm not dependable. You've never relaxed since my, my *illness* in Detroit—"

"Please don't start that. Don't change the subject. I'm telling you not to fall in love with this place or this family or Carter, because it's all just temporary. It's a fantasy. We'll collect our money and we'll leave."

"What's wrong with you? Why are you raising your voice at me? I haven't done anything."

"Well, good, keep it that way. *Don't* do anything."

"Fine." Her mouth set, she threw a pale gray shift with a faux-pearl collar over one arm. "I thought I'd wear this dress tonight."

"It's too sexy for a dinner party. Tone it down."

She looked me straight in the eye. "It is *not* too sexy. It is *perfectly* appropriate and you know it. You just don't want me to attract attention. I think you'd like for me to become a nun. But I like being treated well, I like being sexy, I like Carter, and *I like being here.*" She strode into the bathroom and slammed the door.

I paced, thinking furiously. Forget the Nashville job market. In the morning I would make some phone calls to booking agents I knew out west.

I had to get Ella far away from these people.

Fourteen

"Them's the Nellies," Ebb whispered to her lookalike younger sister that night.

Flo whispered back loudly, "I see 'em. I got eyes."

"Hello," Ella said, smiling. "Carter told me this place wouldn't be the same without you two and your mother."

Flo gaped at her. "I heard right," Flo said. "You're a real lady." She and Ebb set silver hors d'oeuvre trays on a massive buffet beside the bar of the music room then headed out the doors as hurriedly as they had come, darting glances at us. "Don't that hair hurt your head?" Flo called to me. "All them braids wound up in a knot like that?"

"I have a tough scalp," I replied.

Flo guffawed. "I heard you got a hard head."

Twenty-five guests had been invited to the party in our honor that night. Olivia arrived as if at the head of her own royal procession, trailed by Kelly and Jasper, and balanced on Bea's arm. She proceeded, barefoot, toward the piano. She was dressed in an apple-red skirt and pink blouse with a huge antique cameo brooch at the throat. Her hair dangled around her in gray curlicues. Bea, who was dressed to the nines in a yellow satin dress with an overjacket outlined in yellow beaded flowers, helped her sit in the armchair beside the piano. Bea sat in a straight chair next to hers.

Hoss and Sophia Cameron arrived, greeted us exuberantly, and stood near us with their drinks—a martini for him, a rum and Coke for her. The room filled with people over the next half hour. Ella and I were formally introduced to a dizzying array, not close to a full house by Cameron Hall standards, but pound for pound an expensively coiffed and well-heeled crew of family and old friends.

Carter wasn't anywhere to be seen, thank God. I sat at the piano, improvising jazz riffs from segments of old tunes. I felt safely barricaded. Ella shifted uneasily on a delicate wooden chair beside the piano bench. I noticed her glancing at the doors every time someone new arrived, then the spark in her eyes fading when it wasn't Carter. She knew better than to ask about his whereabouts while I was listening.

A man who'd been talking to Gib suddenly headed our way. He had the clean-cut, no-frills decorum of a solid suburban businessman in gray pinstripes, his gut a little thick but his attitude muscular, his chin just beginning to go soft. A carefully clipped mane of pepper-gray hair framed dark blue eyes and weathered skin.

I'd already noticed him because he watched Min somberly and with a certain wistfulness when she didn't realize he was looking. "Ms. Arinelli," the man said to me in an educated magnolia-and-bourbon accent, "what I know about music wouldn't fill a termite's pocketbook, but when I listened to the record of you playing some classical piece—I can't even remember its name—but when I heard you on the record you made—well, I could understand a little twelve-year-old girl learning that kind of technical skill but not that kind of emotional passion. You played your heart out."

Who in the world was this man who knew I'd been a soloist on an obscure album of young musicians? The album had been produced by a small company that specialized in classical music, and only five or ten thousand copies were made. Pop proudly bought a thousand of them to give away to friends and customers at the nightclub.

"What's your point?" I asked sharply.

"Vee, this gentleman is offering you a compliment," Ella said anxiously, twisting her earrings as if dialing for satellite signals to pinpoint danger. "How . . . how do you know such an obscure detail about us, sir?"

His eyes widened. "Min, introduce me before these young ladies decide I'm sinister," he said quickly as Min came to the piano.

"Oh, he's as harmless as can be," she said to us, and I watched him deflate a little. Her one comment turned a daring senior wolf into a toothless, aging poodle. "Venus, Ella, this is an old family friend from Knoxville. Bo Burton."

"Reginald Aster Burton," he corrected, recovering enough charm to grin and bow gallantly. "But going by *Reginald* got my behind kicked in reform school, and when I was serving in Korea my sergeant said *Aster* reminded him of a daisy. He didn't put it quite that way but I got his point. So I'm Bo. Old Bo to the whippersnappers"—he said that with a jaunty tone and amused eyes—"at the field offices. B-e-a-u Bo to the ladies who are intent on romancing me." He flashed the quickest hopeful glance at Min, who never noticed. I realized she'd made a point of standing a full yard away from him. "But enough about me. It's a joy to meet you both. I've got a pair of daughters not many years younger than you two. They call me Bo Daddy."

"He's a talker," Min said dryly.

"I'm in charge of the state forestry commission. Of course I'm a talker. I have to talk about trees all the time. That takes a gift for gab." He laughed. "Minnie, you think I'm more fun than a pine beetle and twice as nice as a wood borer. I know you do, deep down."

"You make my leaves itch," she teased gently. Then she stiffened as if humor were a betrayal, and she filtered into the people around us. He tracked her departure with a slight frown until someone called him away. He nodded to us, smiled, and left.

"Widower," Sophia whispered in our ears. "He and his wife visited here for many years. Their daughters, too. Now he's all alone and so is Minnie. He is a handsome man, a good man, and only fifty! So many years of strong *hmmm hmmm hmmm* left in him yet! But does she see him that way? No! Some other woman will take him before she notices! A shame!"

"How does he know so much about me?" I asked.

Bea jumped into the conversation. "Dear Gib is a thorough boy, and he found a copy of the recording you made as a wee girl, and we've been listening to it for months. Aye, and here." She handed me a note. I glanced at Olivia, whose shrewd eyes flashed as she inclined her head in acknowledgment. I read: *Don't worry so much. Play.*

I looked at her, and at Ella, but I was still gauging the danger involved, and she was, too. I began a song but halted as we heard the loud tapping of silver on crystal. Isabel was drumming a spoon against a wineglass. When silence reigned she gestured to Gib. He moved to the center of the room. "Aunt Olivia asked me to welcome all of you to the Hall." Gib, resplendent in a light shirt and leather suspenders, moved aside with a slight gesture of his hand toward Olivia, who nodded regally. Then Gib motioned to Min. Her back straight, her head up, she looked at the guests with tears slipping down her cheeks.

In her hands she held a small brass bell. "It's so good to see all of you again," she said. "I . . . don't remember a lot of our conversations from last year, but I know most of you were here to share our grief over my husband and to offer all the help you could to us, and to Gib, while he was in the hospital. I'm proud you came back to share tonight with us."

Kelly and Jasper stood behind her, their heads bowed. Isabel moved to stand near Gib. She put an arm around

Kelly's shoulders. Gib stared fixedly into space, turned oh-so-discreetly to hide his damaged hand by his side.

Min raised the small bell. "All of you—and every guest who visited this house—can tell stories about the small touches of humor and hospitality my husband incorporated. This wasn't a business to him. He believed he had a calling to welcome people to this house, that he and his brother and his sisters and Aunt Olivia and our sweet Beatrice should open this lovely old home of the Cameron clan to friends, relatives, and strangers alike. He believed that the world would be a safe and joyful place if we all treated one another like family. And each night, when he walked through these downstairs rooms and rang this bell to call our guests to dinner, he was offering fellowship to everyone who could hear the sound. Thirty years ago, tonight, he rang this bell the first time." Her voice faltered.

Mom and Pop were here that night. They heard the bell. Ella cried softly beside me. Min went on, "When I ring this bell tonight, my husband will be listening"—now half the people in the room were wiping tears from their eyes—"and all of our guests, past, present, and future, will be with us in spirit."

She lifted the bell.

Gib took a champagne glass from a table behind him, raised it with his ruined hand clasped around the stem, and added in a strong voice, "To my brother's love for the Hall and this family. To my brother. And welcome to Venus and Ella Arinelli. Thirty years ago your parents stood in this room." He paused for a moment, his eyes directly on mine. With neutral diplomacy he said, "We hope their good wishes watch over us all. And we're glad we found you."

"Good show, dear Gib," Bea said under her breath. Olivia reached across me to the piano keyboard and began pounding a high D with her forefinger.

Everyone, startled, turned to look at us. I held up both

hands to show it wasn't my doing. Olivia blew Gib a kiss, then sat back in her chair, her expression firm and proud.

Min and Isabel gazed at Gib with adoration.

And so, God help me, did I.

It had been years since we'd been invited to anyone's fine table, years since I'd maneuvered a piece of real silverware in my hand. The soft, lace-edged tablecloth and napkins embroidered with a Cameron crest caressed my hands; the chandeliers seemed too bright; I was reliving the luxuries of childhood, when Pop spared no expense, and every night Ella and I ate dinner with him at a private room at his nightclub, with white tablecloths and white-aproned, bowing waiters, and Pop helping us slice little-girl portions of prime rib into bite-sized pieces, or pull delicate roasted quail meat from the tiny quail bones, while he led us in solemn critiques of the jazz or classical selections he played on a stereo in the room.

Every night, a music lesson, and a very private, formal family dinner. I loved that memory so much. A butler door swung open. Ebb and Flo paraded into the room carrying a magnificent china soup tureen between them.

Min motioned for them to begin serving. She sat at a far end of the large table, with Gib at the opposite end, and Ella far away from me, placed beside a stately woman who owned *Southern Scene*, a sumptuous, upscale magazine that had been considered the bible of regional travel and entertaining for decades. They were already chatting like old friends.

Carter had finally arrived. He'd turned himself out in gray linen with a gray western-style jacket fitted with black piping around the shoulders, and a collarless shirt with a pearl stickpin at the throat, to match the pearl stud in his earlobe.

"You're a looker, all right," Hoover Bird MacIntosh boomed cheerfully as he gazed at Ella.

"Pretty as a goddamned daffodil," his wife, Goldfish, echoed. They were Carter's adoptive parents from Oklahoma. His uncle, Hoover Bird, had shoulder-length hair pulled back with a silver clasp. Goldfish, red-headed and big-busted, wore a dress suit in an eye-aching shade of neon blue.

Ella blushed then offered gamely, "Carter mentioned to me that he had to pick you folks up at the airport in Knoxville. Was your flight late?"

Uncle Hoover Bird grinned. "We got a late start out of Oklahoma City. Had to switch planes. Had some computer trouble."

"Oh? I'm so glad you could get a later flight."

"They didn't take a later flight," Gib interjected. "They switched planes."

Ella looked bewildered. I'm sure I did, too. Carter cleared his throat. He took Ella's hand. "Darlin'," he said soothingly, as if bad news were coming, "they've got a couple of Cessnas and a little jet."

I stared at him, then at Gib. Gib arched a brow. Uncle Hoover Bird announced, "Oil money. We struck oil on our ranch during the early sixties." Rich. Carter wasn't a ne'er-do-well relative. He was a rich ne'er-do-well relative.

This didn't make me feel any better. Carter and Ella leaned close together and gazed at each other like cats watching butterflies flicker against a windowpane.

Darling, he had said.

We went upstairs to our bedroom. Ella slept in the main bed, a lovely canopied number done in soft yellow. I opted for a plush wicker sleeping couch in a sitting room. Ella opened a curtain. "Oh, Vee, look." Moonlight glittered like silver on flower gardens and the swimming pool. A small apple orchard stretched in moon-shadowed charm alongside a large vegetable garden surrounded by a split-rail fence. It was a scene of astonishing, heart-melting beauty.

Gib stuck his head in the open door of our bedroom. "If you hear the dogs barking it'll only be that they're chasing off deer and rabbits," he said. "Or maybe a bear after the seeds in the bird feeders. I chased off a mama and her cubs a few weeks ago."

"We won't be going out to watch the bears," I promised. He said good-night to Ella, who was already sinking luxuriously into a chintz armchair. "Ebb will bring up some hot tea in a minute," he added.

"Oh, bliss," she sighed. "Thank you. This is all so wonderful. I feel like a princess."

"Good for you," Gib said gently. "We pride ourselves on our hospitality." He glanced at me. "Are you feeling like a princess, too?" he asked dryly.

"No, I'm the evil queen." His eyes slitted, he smiled and nodded an ungallant agreement. He crooked his finger at me. When he walked off I trailed him down the hallway. We stopped at the top of long, simple stairs with a newel post of golden wood. "Chestnut?" I asked.

"Yes." He frowned. "There's something I don't understand. Why haven't you asked to see your money?"

I stalled. "Why haven't you offered to show it to me?"

"I don't even like to talk about it."

"Fine. Neither do I. On the day Ella and I leave, just bring it to our car. We don't have to discuss it. Or look at it."

A sardonic smile crooked one corner of his mouth. "Don't you want to count it and see if it's all there?"

"Oh, I will. I'll sit in some hotel room somewhere, juiced on Dom Perignon, naked, with hundred-dollar bills scattered around me, and I'll laugh wickedly as I count the whole stash. Just think of me that way."

"Subtract the money from that mental image, and you've got a deal."

The evening had certainly mellowed him. Suddenly awkward, I changed the subject. "Everything you've done for Ella and me since we got here has been gracious. Thank you."

"No problem. You and Ella are Company. This is how we treat all Company."

"My sister enjoys being part of a family group. She loves children and she loves the friendship of women who don't make her discuss duet arrangements and badger her to practice her violin. I appreciate the kindness everybody around here has offered her. She deserves to enjoy being here."

"Nothing for yourself? All for Ella? Never admit you seriously need anything or anyone to look after *you*, hmmm?"

"You summed me up. Congratulations. You can relax— I'm not looking for a man to lean on."

"I wish you could see me and my motives clearly."

"I do. Pure and simple. Duty to your family, honoring your brother's wishes, putting up with me to humor Olivia—I understand your motives."

"Thank you for cooperating with me. Being kind to Olivia, and Isabel and Min. Even if you're only doing what you have to do to pick up your money."

Wounded, I tossed back, "Speaking of the missing link in your family, I know Ruth didn't come tonight because she still doesn't like your inviting Ella and me here."

"Sorry, but that's true. I think I can safely say, however, that even Ruth will keep her opinions to herself and treat you both well in person."

I decided not to tell him how wrong he was about his sister's politeness. I didn't want him to know how I'd threatened her, either. I shrugged. "She was a little cool when we met."

Gib, unaware, nodded. "My sister's blunt but fair. We agree on matters of principle about family togetherness."

"Except for the little problem of her wanting to sell the Hall to your cousin Emory."

He scowled. "She'll come around. I'm working on her attitude."

"How about Min and Isabel? Can you change everyone's attitude? Can you and Olivia bring about some major shift in the Cameron universe?"

"We're trying. You're part of it. You and the memories of how we started. That's what you and Ella represent."

"Oh? That's not very logical."

"You go on trying to be logical. I used to appreciate logic. Lately I've just been operating by instinct." He spoke quietly, leaning closer to me. "And instinct is a powerful motivation, Nellie." I found myself leaning toward him, too. Then his gaze went to my mouth, and suddenly we were on the verge of kissing. We swayed together as if pulled by some invisible force. I quickly took a step away from him and gripped the balustrade at the top of the stairs.

He recovered fast. Nodding good-night to me, he started down the stairs, leaving his obvious rejection in the air like skunk musk. "Where do you go at night?" I called after him. "To your *cave*?"

"The Waterfall Lodge," he called back. "It's where I live, for now. I like the peace and quiet."

"Oh, yes, Sophia told me about it. Your great-great-grandfather built the lodge when he and your great-great-grandmother weren't getting along. After a year she had the servants hide decomposing trout in the lodge to flush him out and force him to move back to the Hall. I admire a woman who knows when to call on dead trout for help."

Gib managed a short, explosive chortle of laughter. I listened to the rich baritone sound fade until he closed a door behind himself downstairs.

Fifteen

"Good morning," I said brightly to the half-dozen visitors who had stayed overnight. I sat down reluctantly in a chair Gib held for me at the dining table and looked over cantaloupe and strawberries piled in an etched crystal compote. I surveyed Ella's and Carter's empty chairs. I hoped Carter wouldn't show up for breakfast. "Ella will be down in a minute," I announced to the assembled—Gib, Min, Isabel, Goldfish, Hoover Bird, and Bo Burton. "She was just about finished dressing when I left our room."

I began spearing strawberries with a heavy sterling fork. Then I realized that Goldfish was peering at me and nervously biting her pruny, pink-rimmed lower lip. In tight white jeans and a button-popping white blouse, with her eyes made up elaborately in rainbow hues, she looked like an aging L.A. hooker. "Hell, honey, your sis just headed for the hills with Carter," she said. "I saw 'em going out the back kitchen door. He brought up a couple of riding horses." Goldfish went *pluuuff* in dismissal, pawed the air with red-tipped nails, and hooted. "Don't worry, honey. Your sis'll have a fine time."

"I see," I said, as a knot of anxiety and fury formed in my stomach. I started to get up.

Gib put a hand on my shoulder and bent close to my side. "Don't make a scene and ruin Min's mood this morning. Do that for me and I promise I'll help you find Ella after breakfast."

I looked desperately at Min, whose eyes were a little brighter with the crowd around at the table. She was even smiling at a joke Bo Burton had just told.

I had no choice. I'd never find my sister in the mountains around there without Gib's help. But I knew the truth, deep down. For the first time in my life I was willing to make a compromise.

Because Gib Cameron asked me to.

Gib stopped his jeep at the top of a mountain hiking trail so narrow I'd spent the entire steep ten-minute drive battling small tree branches.

"Hunting the elusive Ella," he said in a mock-documentary whisper. "This variety of the little-known yellow-crested violinist appears friendly but is, in fact, only seen when lured out of hiding by her sister, who warbles the ritual song of female kinship." He cupped his left hand around his mouth. "Give-men-no-nooky," he yodeled softly. *"Givemennonooky."*

I plucked leaves, twigs, and several caterpillars from my braids. "I don't dislike men. I just dislike men who are smart-asses."

He jumped out of the jeep and walked to a rocky overlook. Above us to the right a tiny stream trickled from a crevice in the mountain's craggy, lichen-covered side. The sound was as soothing as a fountain, and the air was scented with water and green, ripe life. I stood beside Gib and looked down a hundred yards through a jungle of laurel and trees, into a glen where the tiny stream bottomed into a small, lovely pool surrounded by tall ferns.

I caught my breath. In front of us and below us was a world

for dreaming. A world like some fabulous fantasy medieval landscape drawn in one of those dragon-and-elf computer games or calendars. Sheer towers of mountains, breathtaking views, cliffs, flowers, clouds, shadow and light—a dreamscape from a modern Eden. The earth had birthed rocks; it was seeded with fist-sized and football-sized rocks in harmony with every stone hoe, shovel blade, rake tine, or pick point wielded in the attempt to clear this unconquerable forest.

When Gib dropped to his heels I squatted beside him. The rocky grotto of the creek glen below us made a very seductive setting. "They haven't been there," Gib said.

"How can you tell?"

"If they'd ridden in on the trail down there we'd see where the horses trampled some of the ferns. So we can cross this off the list. They haven't been here at Arrowhead Pond."

"Arrowhead Pond?"

"Hmmm. Up in an attic at the Hall we've got a collection of arrowheads from those bottoms that date back a thousand years. That's what the scientists say. When I was a boy I used to come here alone all the time and hunt for more."

I looked at the wild territory below, above, and all around us. We were a long way from the Hall. "No one worried about you? You roamed all the way out here and no one worried?"

He smiled below solemn, worldly eyes. "In our family this is the *backyard*."

"Didn't you have friends?"

"A few. I was a loner."

"And later on?"

"What do you mean?"

"When you were grown?"

"I get by, Nellie. I'm just careful about the company I keep. Quality, not quantity."

You never know who might be dangerous. Who might hurt you or the people you love. "Really? Sophia said—" I halted. "Never mind. Let's keep looking."

I started to rise. He put his bad hand on my forearm. The

contact—and his new willingness to use the hand—sent warm tremors through my skin. I stayed still.

"Play fair," he said. "Finish that sentence."

"She said at least a dozen of your former lady friends converged on you after the accident. A *dozen*. That's not the batting average of a true loner."

"A dozen over a lot of years. Not exactly a league record, either."

"I'm surprised at least a couple didn't stick around. Have you got a few hidden somewhere?"

"Most of them are married now."

"But not to you, I take it. At least not recently."

"I've never tied the knot. I didn't want the commitment. I traveled too much. Put my career first. I saw how hard it was for other agents to keep their marriages together. And to be honest about it, I thought I had the best of everything and I didn't have any big urge to fall in love. Now don't start analyzing—"

"I understand perfectly. I'm the same way."

"Hmmm. I don't think so."

"Who are you to tell me what I—"

"I *want* to love somebody. I'm not sure you do at all."

I was silent. How wrong he was about me. How hard I must look, more isolated and cold-blooded than I realized. "You're the wrong one to lecture me," I said finally, keeping my tone as light as I could. "Out of all those women who cared about you, you couldn't pick even one who was special."

"Ditto," he countered. "Ella tells me you haven't been out on a real date in years."

He got me right in the solar plexus. I stood and took a deep breath. "That's meaningless information. Don't use my sister to spy on me. She's an easy mark and too sentimental. That's not fair."

Gib squinted up at me, unshaken. "All's fair in love and war with Camerons," he said.

.   .   .

Carter's houseboat, vintage 1930s, was set on short, massive, saltwater-pickled sections cut from a pier salvaged off some inland waterway in Florida. The river gurgled outside his front steps. A punching bag dangled from a low limb of a shade tree beside the strange home. Flying on a dual pair of flagpoles on the bow were the Stars and Stripes but also a Cherokee tribal flag.

"He brought the houseboat with him from Oklahoma," Gib explained. "It's a MacIntosh family heirloom."

I stared at a saltwater houseboat from a state located at least a thousand miles in every direction from the nearest ocean. "That makes sense," I said.

"They've been here." Gib pointed to hoofprints in the yard near Carter's purple truck. He knelt and touched the in dentations. "It's been a while, though. The dirt crumbles around the edges of the impressions. Takes several hours of drying in the sun to crumble like that."

"Can you tell if he coaxed my sister indoors and put any moves on her?"

"Not unless he left a note. 'I snared the unsuspecting babe. Hahahaha. You'll never get her back.'"

"Thanks for the comedy, Daniel Boone."

Gib stood. "Don't joke. My ancestors knew Daniel Boone, Daniel Boone was a friend of theirs, and—"

"Right, right, but you're no Daniel Boone. Very cute."

"Actually, I'm a *damned* good tracker. When we were teenagers Ruth and I used to hunt wild pigs with the Hodgers. Ruth had an incredible eye for the trail marks, but I was even better."

I had no doubt that Ruth could run a wild boar down and scare the tusks off him, but I kept that opinion to myself. "Fine. But we're not looking for a wild pig, we're looking for my sister. Even though she doesn't oink she ought to be easy to locate."

Gib shrugged. As we walked back to the jeep he said, "I should have mentioned one little mitigating fact."

"Yes?"

He smiled wickedly. "Carter's the best. Nobody can find him when he doesn't want to be found."

"Try," I said in a steely voice.

He patiently took me along every road, every drivable hiking trail, every moonshine hollow, ridge, overlook, creek bottom, and hidden glen of the great valley and the mountains around it, until I was drunk with history and scenery, swept along in the rich, ancient veins of a place so wonderful I was dizzy at times. He was trying to distract me. It worked.

We sat on a mountaintop—a bald, he called it—among a meadow of wildflowers dotted with large rhododendrons. The sky seemed to go on forever, and the warm wind blew small clouds of exploding dandelion seeds into the air.

The Cameron Valley was two miles long and a mile wide in the center of the Cameron Mountains of northeast Tennessee. Gib said it took a good hour to walk the valley by following the river through the heart of it from east to west. There were another two thousand acres of Cameron land around the valley, all steep mountain terrain. "We don't count it except when taxes are due," Gib said. "Then we're *sure* it's ours."

"Gib, face it. To most people this is the hind end of nowhere."

"That's not what you're thinking when you look at the valley. I don't see that kind of quick dismissal in your attitude. Can't you just admit you understand the appeal?"

"Why don't you tell me what it means to *you*?" I waited in contented victory. He couldn't resist, and I'd enjoy hearing him talk some more. His voice was deep and rich, the mountain accents long and smooth. He had taken these wild southern mountains with him in his heart all over the world, and that showed in his voice.

"I don't have words to describe how I feel about this place," he said.

"For God's sake, you obviously haven't had a long conversation with anyone other than your own bullheaded self in the past year. You've forgotten how."

He looked at me quietly. "You go right to the point, don't you? Excuse me." He made a plucking motion at his neck. "There. I got the arrow out."

"Somebody has to get to the point around here. Beating around the bush seems to be the family hobby."

He smiled slightly. "All right. You want my poetic description. People love the sense of grandeur here. The past. Something big. Something special. But human. Warm. We're not special people—just ordinary people thankful for a special place. And what we own is what we are. The hundred-year-old bearskin rug from a bear Lucy Cameron stabbed with a pitchfork when it killed her pet pig. Esau Cameron's fifty-year-old Harvard diploma with the corners burned off, from a fire in the main chimney during the winter when the snow was so deep it covered the doorways.

"We have a Confederate saber with teeth marks on the ivory handle. Because the next generation of Cameron babies after the Civil War were all given their father's sword to cut their teeth on."

"That's a joke."

"No, it's not. It really happened. Don't look at me that way. We're not eccentric, we're patriotic. My father was a geologist. A scientist. He worked for the government. And my mother—I guess you'd call her an artist of some kind, though she made her living as a secretary. That's what little I remember of them, and what I've been told.

"All in all, we're caretakers in mountains so old they make the Rockies look like teenagers. Breathe the air in our valley and you feel right. Like you've inhaled a balm."

He halted. I was leaning forward and caught up in his words. I loved them. And I loved the way he spoke so freely and comfortably about the land and its people.

And me, dammit, I listened so closely I forgot again that I was hunting for Ella. I blinked. "Don't stop." That came out in a husky and fervent tone. He and I traded a long look.

"I promise you one thing," he said finally. "Your father was about the only guest we ever had who chose not to visit again. That says something about his determination to forget everybody who ever treated him decently. And obviously he wanted to forget the kindness your mother believed in."

I sat back. "You should have stopped before you reached that last part."

"I know," he said.

Everything of real importance in the valley seemed to be situated near water. Pioneering wisdom at work, I guessed. When we reached a thick log-and-stone lodge by a large waterfall deep in the woods I thought nothing was left to amaze me, but the beauty of the place and the comfortable strength of the small lodge left me speechless. The waterfall hung in silvery patterns among dark, brooding rocks, forming a small grotto not a dozen yards from the lodge's front porch.

One of the blue-eyed dogs leaped off the porch and ran over to Gib's side of the jeep. A pair of cats strolled from behind a large wooden barrel on the porch. The barrel overflowed with ivy and tiny white wildflowers. A machete hung from a leather scabbard nailed to a post. An ax leaned beside a chopping block and a pile of small logs in the yard. The windows were covered on the inside with thick quilts. I could make out the patterns. "This is my place," Gib said. "I'm going in and phone the Hall. Just to see if they've shown up there yet. I'll be back in a minute."

After he disappeared beyond a heavy door under the stone-columned porch I got out of the jeep and went to the waterfall. I stood at the edge of its shallow pool, watching minnows and letting the wet, cool mist billow over me. I shouldn't have been disappointed that Gib hadn't asked me to step inside his personal living space.

"Nope, no Ella back at civilization," he admitted when he strode outdoors. He stopped when he saw me. I moved, suddenly embarrassed, from beside the pond. My clothes were damp and my face was covered in dew from the waterfall. I'd become enthralled in my own small rite of communion. "You look happy. Or maybe it's just the damp T-shirt," he said. Something in his eyes made my legs weak and my back arch.

"You live like a hermit," I said. "You need decent curtains on your windows, at least."

"When I want more light I pull back the quilts. When winter gets here they'll help block the drafts around the windowsills. I'll build a fire in the fireplace and get in bed about ten feet away, and I'll pull a stack of blankets over me and I'll read Tolstoy and Tom Clancy with an oil lamp while the wind howls outside. And I'll drink a shot of good sour-mash whisky before I go to sleep."

I could picture him naked under a mound of quilts in that dark, isolated lodge, while firelight and lamplight flickered across his face. I could picture him being the naked center of a warm flannel cocoon, and I could picture me inside the cocoon with him, and I could imagine he would be like whisky, fine and smooth and liquid, inside me.

"You should get an electric blanket," I said.

He smiled at my breasts. At least I was convinced that was his only focus. "I should get electricity, first," he answered.

"Last stop," he said. It was late afternoon. Neither of us had had anything to eat since breakfast, and only spring water to drink. I felt giddy and light on my feet.

Brainwashed.

We went back to the sawmill. Gib's choice. We sat beside the building on a sandy section of the riverbank under a thick-waisted beech tree, and I busied myself pretending to watch minnows in the river and prying white slivers off the beech's curly bark. Searching for a neutral subject, I finally blurted, "According to the historical anecdotes I've heard so far, I'd say your family takes a lot of pride in regularly capturing unwilling prospective in-laws."

Gib smiled a little as he idly flicked smooth river pebbles into the swirling water beyond our feet. "It's best to hear Cameron stories in the context of the bigger picture. A University of Tennessee professor wrote a paper on our history some years ago. Not the first time professors and history types have dissected us, but he sure as hell went further than most. He said we never grew out of the 'feudal Highland-Scots mentality that pervades sections of the eastern Tennessee mountains.' You get the drift."

"Ouch."

"He did say we prospered by capturing, buying, or bribing new blood into our family. I guess he meant to make a name for himself by coming up with a catchy thumbnail analysis of us. Made a lot of the family mad. Anytime outsiders put the facts on paper they sound peculiar."

"So enlighten me."

His gaze grew distant. "Simon believed our ancestors survived in the mountains not because they kept outsiders out, but because they brought outsiders in. They took a chance. I never used to agree with him on that. I wanted to build a fort around us and bar the gates. But since last year I've decided we're not safe—no matter what we do. I want you to understand why we Camerons don't forget people like your parents."

"I'd like to understand. I'm listening."

"We pride ourselves on never turning away a stranger. In the old days that kind of hospitality wasn't just politeness. People up here in the mountains knew it could be the difference between life and death. Strangers who traveled the Cherokee trace down through this valley knew they could count on the Camerons for a meal and a bed. Hurt, sick, hungry, lost, freezing to death, chased by somebody or something that meant to kill them—they got help once they reached here."

"Are you saying my father broke some kind of generational legacy? That he insulted your family's entire history because he rejected the Camerons' friendship after my mother died? Sweet Mary Mother of Jesus! I thought I'd heard my father accused of some heinous things, but dissing the Cameron hospitality code is the most far-fetched yet."

"Maybe to you. Not to me." Gib lifted his ruined hand then looked at it with disgust. "Look, I know I'm not all I used to be—I'll never be able to do some of the simplest chores without help, I can't manouvor my hand, and the docs say I should have one or two more minor surgeries to loosen up the tendons and get rid of the scar tissue. But I am the head of this family now. Call it patriarchal bullshit or whatever you want to, but that's what I am and what's expected of me. I take my family's reputation seriously."

"You're *not* helpless or pitiful or impaired in any meaningful way," I said impatiently. "Someone used to tell me a fable about rolling stones gathering no moss. Well, a stone that rolls *too* fast can't take time to accumulate any wisdom. But when you chip a piece out of that stone it rolls slower, and even if it's not as smooth and pretty as it used to be, it takes on a different quality."

I hadn't done the fable much service with my dry summary, and I didn't mention that it had been one of Pop's slyly political bedtime fairy tales. I could picture him sitting in a chair between Ella's and my twin beds, solemnly spinning proverbs for us. I had been enthralled by his rough beauty and the throaty song of his voice.

Gib looked doubtful. "So this here rock," he drawled, "does it stop to smell the roses?"

"Sorry. I mistook you for the type who appreciates a little Zen with his proverbs," I retorted. I looked at him morosely and that made him worse.

"Thank you, grasshopper," he added.

"Oh, to hell with you." I started to rise.

"Apology offered," he said quietly.

I sank back down on the riverbank. After all, I was stranded in the middle of the woods with him—again. "Apology accepted," I admitted. "I know the fable sounds trite, but I'm only saying that you're youngish and *not* hard on the eyes, and you've got money and position and a respectable family. *And* this incredible place. And a blue-blooded pioneer American heritage that makes me feel like I ought to be sitting in the hold of a ship off Ellis Island waiting for permission to salute Old Glory."

His face tightened. "I'm not asking for anyone's pity—I'm just trying to explain. I have to reach out in ways I wouldn't have done before. I had too much pride before. Hell, you ought to understand that."

I looked away. "Maybe."

He ran his good hand through his hair and exhaled sharply. "You want to hear another story about wild-eyed Camerons? The first sawmill on this spot was run by waterpower. It was built by Robert Cameron, Gilbert and Susan's youngest son. He inherited the valley. He went to the Carolina coast as a young man, made his fortune in shipping, married into a big Charleston shipping family, then came back and built the Hall. Cameron Hall. Showplace of the Tennessee mountains. There was nothing else like it when they opened the house in 1805. Robert had a society wife. Charleston society. She didn't want to move to the frontier. So he kidnapped her."

"He kidnapped his own wife?"

"Her and their firstborn baby, plus her lady's maid, her pet goats, and a handful of house servants. Kidnapped the whole kit and caboodle and carted them up here. Locked his own wife in the new mansion for at least a year. She smug-

gled letters to her family, and a couple of her brothers organized a militia and rode up there to rescue her."

"This is your own brand of fable, isn't it? This didn't
really happen."

"No brag, Nellie, just fact. The brothers got sidetracked
by adventure and went on over the next mountain. They pio-
neered Attenberry County and that's why there are Attenberrys next door to Hightower County and Cameron Hall today.
All because Dorothea Attenberry Cameron's brothers came
to rescue her but ended up being our neighbors."

"She must have hated Robert! *And* her idiotic, attention-
deficit-disordered brothers!"

"Oh, now *that*'s a female take on the situation. Once
Robert finally gave her a chance to run away she didn't do it. I
can't speak well for his technique, but then, how else would
he get an ocean-loving city wife to try out life in a mountain
pioneer mansion? They lived to be old people and she died in
the Hall. By her own choice."

"Brainwashed."

"Won over."

I began to laugh. Maybe it wasn't appropriate, considering that we sat only a few yards from the sawmill and its horrifying memories, but my nerves were shot and I feared I
might cry from simple emotional overload.

Gib sat motionless, looking at me with real appreciation.
Finally I quieted down and scrubbed my fingers over my
eyes. I was blushing, and I looked away, then back. He still
watched me.

"Don't take this as a cheap line or a come-on," he
warned, "but you're wasting yourself behind all that fake hair.
You're different. It's the shape of your face and the quality of
your skin. Your face is graceful, Nellie, and you're a little
gold-colored. I've never seen anyone like you. When I was
hunting for you I got hold of one of the first newspaper photographs of you performing on the piano as a girl, when your
hair was still black. You couldn't have been more than five or

six. That's the look you ought to go back to, Nellie. Be who you are. Don't hide. I'll do what I can to make sure you and Ella aren't harassed anymore."

"You think it's so simple," I accused, because now I really had to struggle not to cry. "You don't know."

"Hell, yes, I understand. I know about holding on to things. It's the same reason I won't let everything my brother built up just fall apart. If you and your sister remind my family of better times and make my great-aunt happy, then—" He halted, frowning at me.

I finished darkly, "We have value. You've done your duty. Sure. Ella and I are only here because we serve your purpose. You despise our father and you only tolerate us."

"I understand your loyalty to your own father." He spoke in a low, controlled voice. "But do you have to be *proud* of a man who threw away his family's future for the sake of a bunch of gutless murderers?"

The question was a slap. I felt sick at my stomach. "As long as I've got breath to defend him, I will." I added bitterly, "Do you have to be *proud* of a system that steals from and destroys its own innocent citizens?"

"I'll be proud of *the good, God-fearing American government* until the day I die," he answered.

The river filled up the silence between us, its water singing as it tumbled and swirled around rocks worn too smooth to resist being left behind.

Sixteen

Ella and Carter didn't return until sunset. They rode up the Hall's picturesque main drive as if they'd been on a brief outing, Carter expertly guiding a tall, muscular gray horse and Ella wobbling on a fat little red one, who seemed so gentle she could barely lift a hoof. I watched wearily as they made their way between stretches of broad, emerald lawn and waist-high azalea shrubs so old their trunks were knotty wands. Nothing was new there, except Ella and me. I stood on the Hall's cobblestoned front courtyard with my hands on my hips.

Gib walked out of the Hall and waited beside me. He smelled of cinnamon, delicious and edible. FeeMolly Hodger had arrived and was baking righteously. She planned a leisurely late-evening feast on the deck by the pool. I tried to ignore Gib.

"What do you plan to do?" he asked curtly. Our afternoon conversations were a wall between us. "Give your sister a spanking and restrict her phone privileges?"

"Ella and I look after each other. That may seem quaint to you, but it's the only way we got through the past ten years. She doesn't know how to deal with men like Carter. You of all people ought to understand, since you know how sick she was after her last romantic escapade."

"That doesn't mean she's in trouble with Carter. Consider the possibility that the two of them are just having an innocent good time."

I stared at him. "Do you honestly believe your woman-chasing cousin isn't trying his best to nail my sister?"

"To some people, Nellie, a little casual nailing could *be* an innocent good time."

"Oh? Then why haven't you partaken of Carter's harem in town? I'm sure he'd share."

He scowled. "My *hammer* does its best nailing on long-term building projects."

Ella waved at us as she and Carter stopped their horses in the courtyard. Carter jumped down and held up his arms to her. She made an effort at appearing nonchalant as he swung her off her horse, but even in the shadowy light I could see that her hands trembled and her face was pale, except for large blotches of pink in her cheeks. Carter had a somber, almost urgent look. I ran to Ella and cupped a hand along her face. "You're hot! Are you sick? What's wrong? What did he do to upset you?"

"Nothing, Sis." But she looked at me with a feverish glow in her green eyes, and smiled wanly.

I glared past her at Carter. His gaze was trained hypnotically on Ella, and he made no effort to notice me. Ella swayed toward him and he grasped her outstretched hands. They looked at each other as if they kept discovering small miracles. My sister's head tilted back, her lips parted. Both she and Carter seemed caught up in reverent, soulful communication.

I'd expected to see hints of flirtation, silliness, or outright lechery. Not this bewildering seriousness. "What did you do to her?" I threatened loudly.

"Vee, shhh," Ella whispered, never taking her eyes away from Carter.

"Whoa, Nellie," Gib said, shouldering into our tight triangle. He stood a head taller than his cousin and looked down at him and my sister with a troubled frown. "Carter?" he asked. "What's going on here?"

"Tell them the news," Carter urged softly, winding Ella's hands to his chest. "I want to hear you say the words." Ella sighed dreamily and nodded. They faced us.

"Vee," she moaned. She held out her arms. Her face glowed with excitement and a sudden tide of tears. She laughed. "Carter and I are in love!" She flung her arms around my neck and hugged me wildly, while I stood there dumbstruck, staring over her head. I watched Gib give flinty scrutiny to his dewy-eyed younger cousin.

"Is this a joke?" he asked.

"No way, no how," Carter answered. "I've been waiting for Ella all my life. I don't care how fast it sounds. I love her."

"And I love him, Sis," Ella echoed.

"You're not in *love*. You've known him all of three days."

Ella drew back, crying, and tenderly took my face between her hands, as if to soothe me. "Three days have been a new lifetime to me already. I'm inspired. Mom and Pop must have felt the same way. There's magic here. Carter and I—we want to honor the same spirit they honored."

I took her by the shoulders. "Wonderful. We'll toast your inspirational ideas at dinner. That'll be plenty of honor for Mom and Pop's sake."

"Tell them the rest, darlin'," Carter said softly.

Ella flew back to his side, and he put his arm around her. "You say it," she whispered.

Carter's eyes gleamed. He grinned at Gib and me. "Everybody said the Nellies would be good luck! A fresh idea or two! Well, me and Ella are gonna prove it! We're getting married *tonight*!"

·   ·   ·

It is safe to say Olivia was the barometer for every emotion from curiosity to shock. She sat in the library room with the rest of us standing around her like a royal court.

Ebb and Flo craned their heads to peek from around the hall doorway. Ebb's mounded bangs stuck beyond the door-case even when Ebb and Flo were discreetly invisible. Fee-Molly didn't emerge from the huge central kitchen, but rumor had it she was already creating a wedding cake.

My body felt like a drum being beaten from the inside. This was no party to me, no celebration.

"Ella and me ask you for your blessings, Auntie," Carter said to Olivia respectfully.

"Ma'am," Ella added gently, "it would be such an honor to me if you approved of our marriage. I promise you I consider marriage vows a sacred trust."

Olivia nodded.

"We want to call Cousin Hoss to perform the ceremony in about an hour," Carter went on. "We want to be married at the chapel *tonight*, Auntie. It's important."

"Why Hoss?" I echoed. I was only trying to stall while I cleared my head. There wasn't going to be any wedding.

"He's the local judge," Gib said, his arms folded across his chest. He stood beside me. We were united in resistance.

"What about the license? The blood test?"

"Hoss can issue the license. And the state of Tennessee doesn't require a blood test."

"I should have known. I suppose checking Carter for webbed toes is out of the question."

Olivia motioned for me to come closer. She drew her notepad from her dress pocket and wrote: *You disapprove of this impulse so bitterly. Why?*

Stunned by her mild response, I said, "How could anyone approve of this?"

She wrote: *I understand your fears. But you have to let her make her own decisions.*

"Vee," Ella moaned, "I really have to have your blessing." I hesitated, studying her urgent, pleading expression, and felt torn apart.

"We need to talk in private," I said.

She came to me and hugged me tightly, then stepped back. "We will. I know we have to. But that doesn't change the fact that Carter and I dearly intend to be married tonight. Have faith. I know this seems foolish and frightening to you, and it changes everything about our future, but I believe in my heart and soul that it's *time* for us to change. It's time for new paths, Sis."

"Paths? You don't even have a *map*. Or a compass." I swept a hand toward Carter. My voice rose. "Or any significant idea who this man *is*."

"Faith. Intuition. Just trust my instincts for once. We want your blessing. Please. *Please.*"

"I can't give my blessing to a wedding with a stranger."

"I'm afraid I have to agree," Gib said. "Carter, there's no reason why you and Ella have to rush. You can get to know each other first. Hell, Carter, at least take Ella on a few dates and go see a movie or two."

"I know her heart and soul already," Carter answered with quiet confidence. "Before I met her I was a boy playing at being a man. Now I'm ready to *be* a man. This isn't silliness. This is Ella. Ella Arinelli. Who believed in me from the minute we met, just like I believe in her."

Olivia wrote for a while then handed the pad to Bea, who drew herself up proudly and read in a ringing voice, " 'Take joy where you find it and accept passion where it must be celebrated. I give my blessing on Ella and Carter. We need a wedding here. Tonight. Yes.' "

I gazed at Olivia bitterly. She returned the look with quiet challenge, as if saying I had no choice, and she hoped I accepted her edict. "My sister isn't a Cameron possession," I said in a low, even voice. "You can't agree to this just because you think a wedding would be good for family morale. I'll fight you on it."

Olivia stared at me calmly. One gray brow arched slightly. She nodded toward Carter and my sister, who were mesmerized by each other even as we discussed them. *You've already lost,* Olivia's expression seemed to say.

" 'Do we all know what this date is?' " Bea continued to read Olivia's written statement. " 'What special event today's date marks?' "

"Yes," Ella said softly, looking at me. "Vee and I just couldn't bear to talk about it. But it's why Carter and I decided we have to be married *right now*."

Silence. My throat closed. I wanted to scream, drag Ella out of there, cry for corrupted joys and symbolic pride, and kill Carter MacIntosh with my bare hands. "What's everybody talking about, Mama?" I heard Jasper whisper.

Kelly added, "What's today?"

"It's an anniversary," she answered gently. "We've been waiting for our guests to mention it first."

I saw pinpoints of light and my knees went weak. I felt Gib's strong left hand in the small of my back, steadying me. That made me arch away from him, and the renewed defense made him nod approvingly.

Because thirty years ago on this date, Mom and Pop had gotten married at the chapel.

"Is the sonuvabitch in that room?" I asked quietly. Gib stood in the hall near a closed bedroom door. The perfect body-guard. He looked troubled, but firm.

"The sonuvabitch is getting dressed for his wedding," he murmured. "And no, I won't let you go in there and kill him."

"He can't marry my sister. He doesn't have what it takes to care for her—he has no clue what she needs, how fragile she is. You know what I mean."

Gib took me by one arm and led me a discreet distance away from the door. Then he said, "You think I approve of what's happening? This kind of half-cocked idea is the last thing we need right now. Are you saying she hasn't told him about Detroit?"

"I don't know, but I doubt she has. She wants to pretend Carter's special. She wants to believe nothing bad will ever happen to her now that she's here."

"For the record, my cousin is probably the most stand-up, decent-hearted man she's ever met. And he sure as hell ought to be warned about *her*."

"Warned?"

"Pull in your claws and don't look at me that way. You want to be honest about this, well, so do I. Ella's a sweet soul, but she's got a history of mental problems."

"Mental problems? She's sensitive and highstrung. She had a nervous breakdown following a traumatic romance and a miscarriage. That's not a *mental* problem."

"Whatever you want to call it, she's not likely to turn into a rock of stability overnight. I think a man ought to know exactly what he's getting in a wife. I'd say the same thing if we were talking about alcoholism or a heart defect or any kind of disability."

"How *could* you?" I grabbed his maimed hand in both of mine. "You of all people should have compassion for someone who's not perfect—whether it's physical or mental."

His scarred fingers closed over mine like thick clasps. "I can't *hide* my hand no matter how much I try. I don't make excuses for it. And I wouldn't deceive a woman into loving me or marrying me with the idea that somehow she's going to work a miracle and make my hand normal again. *Truth* is the issue."

"Then you tell Carter that my sister spent a month in the psychiatric ward of a Detroit hospital. And you tell Carter she's been pregnant, and she lost the baby. *You tell him*. And make sure he knows she also had a nervous breakdown ten years ago, after our father died. Go ahead." I stepped back, trembling, furious, heartsick, and jerked my head toward the closed door. "Tell your cousin the brutal facts. He'll appreciate you for protecting his interests that way. Go ahead."

Gib's stony, frustrated expression said I'd made my point. "Goddamn," he said, shutting his eyes briefly. He looked at the closed door. "You win. Ella has to be the one to tell him."

Min and Isabel came around a corner in the shadowy hall and looked from us to the closed door anxiously. I quickly released Gib's hand and stepped back. "I brought this for Ella," Min said. She held out a slender jewelry box and opened the lid. A magnificent strand of pearls was coiled neatly inside.

"*Something borrowed,* for good luck. I thought she'd like to wear these. They're mine. My husband gave them to me on our twentieth anniversary." She touched the pearls gently.

"And *something blue,*" Isabel added, holding out a lovely pale blue handkerchief with initials embroidered in one corner. "This belonged to Great-grandmother Vameer. She was a Yankee schoolteacher from Maine. Great-grandfather hired her to teach the local children. He sponsored the community school. When he met her at the train station in Knoxville he was drunk. She hit him with her valise. If you look at her handkerchief—see, right there?—that's a tiny stain from his blood. The valise's metal clasp cut his lip."

In the middle of chaos I was being confronted with more Cameron heirlooms and another peculiar Cameron love story. My mind was on fire. "You've been kind to my sister and kind to me," I said to Min and Isabel, "but I'm sorry, there's nothing joyful about this marriage. It won't last."

Min smiled sympathetically. "That's what my family said when Simon and I eloped. We were so young."

"It's not the same situation."

"Oh, yes, it is. Olivia took me in immediately, no questions asked, the same as she's taking in you and Ella. For better or worse. When you marry a Cameron you marry the whole family. I'm serious."

"Venus," Isabel interjected gently, laying a hand on my

arm, "I knew my husband for two years before I married him, but that didn't help. We can't promise you that your sister will be happy with Carter, but we can promise you she'll be accepted here. And so will you. This kind of impulsive marriage isn't all that bizarre. Not by our standards."

"I don't want to insult any of you, but I have no reason to think your cousin has what it takes to make a *normal* marriage work, much less this . . . this *excuse* for a wedding ceremony."

The bedroom door flew open. Carter stood there, solemn yet preening in dark trousers with a buckskin fringed jacket. He adjusted a turquoise bolero at his collar then realized I was staring murderously at him. "I was about to come see you," he said. "To beg you to give your blessing on us. For Ella's sake. You're the be-all and end-all to her, sister-wise."

"I'll make you a deal. Call off this wedding and I'll give you our money. You can have all of it."

Gasps. Min and Isabel looked stricken. Gib blew out a long breath and shook his head. Carter's gaze dulled and his chin rose proudly. "You think I'm a half-breed Indian welfare case? I've got money in the bank. I don't deserve what you just said."

"I don't know *what* you deserve. I don't know *you*. All I know is that you're going to wreck my sister's life."

"I'd say her life's *been* a wreck for a long time. I'm not going to be disrespectful to you, Miss Vee. You're Ella's sister. But your daddy just about *did* wreck you and that sweet girl, and I thank you for loving her and looking after her as best you could, but now I'll take over for you, and I swear to God you'll never have to worry about her again. I swear to you."

"You won't keep that vow longer than it takes to use her and throw her away," I said in a low, strained voice.

"You're wrong. For the first time in my life I feel like I'm whole instead of *half*. I'm not on the outside of the candy store with my nose pressed to the glass. I've got the other side of my heart now. You don't know how it is to grow up feeling that you're not a whole person. Not Cherokee. Not white.

Well, your sister *sees* me. *Me.* Clearer than anybody ever has before."

"I don't give a damn one way or the other about your bloodlines. My father could teach you a lesson or two about the courage it takes to grow up half-white and unwanted." I turned to walk away, then looked back in defeat. "You're marrying *his* bloodline, and you'll *never* live up to it."

Ella was dressing for the wedding. A clock on the fireplace in our guest room chimed ten times. "I'll wear this white blouse and the gold linen skirt that goes with my suit, and my gold pumps, and—" She halted. I was simply staring at her from the center of the room. Her shoulders sagged. She stood there in an ivory knee-length slip, wiping her eyes, then wiping her wet fingertips on the silk. She'd been crying since I shut the bedroom door. "Go ahead and talk to me," she begged.

"You can't do this. It's insane."

"All spiritual devotion is reckless. But I feel to the core of my being that this is what I *have* to do. We sat for an hour on a mountaintop just watching the eagles glide in the sky. *Eagles,* Vee. We didn't say a word, and it felt perfect. And then other times we talked so quickly we finished each other's sentences."

"What happened when you weren't talking or watching birds of prey?"

"We talked about sex, but then he said, 'I want to be different with you. I want to be sacred.' I agreed. And he asked me to marry him. And I said yes. It was so easy, Vee. So right."

"Did you tell him about Detroit?"

"No. He doesn't need to know that."

"Yes, he does. He's acting like a sweet kid in love because he doesn't know the responsibility you're handing him. Don't make him go into this blind. If you can't be honest with him about what happened to you and how sick you were—"

"I'm well now! I can have more babies—I'm sure of it. *And I'm not crazy.*"

"I didn't say you are or ever were *crazy*. I'm saying you have a history of special health concerns, and the man you're going to marry ought to know about them."

"I've finished grieving. I can move forward. I'm full of hope—more hope than I've ever had before. This is different. With him—it's special. You can't change my mind."

I felt weighed down, trapped. I needed to push my hands against the air and spread invisible walls. "You can't marry this man," I repeated between gritted teeth. "People won't understand. They'll gossip. They'll say you want his money, his name."

"I'm used to gossip. So are you."

"We're a team. An act. You can't break that up."

Ella smiled. "We're a great team, but we're not much of an act, and you know it. I want to retire from show business. I love this valley, Sis. I love this family. There's an old Victorian farm cottage beyond the east pastures."

"Gib showed it to me. What's the point?"

"It was built by one of Carter's relatives. It needs a lot of work, but Carter's been making plans to restore it. He took me there and carried me over the threshold, and he said he could picture me in that house with him and our children! Oh, Sis! I'll have a home! And children! And a husband I truly love. And you'll always have a home, too. We'll both be part of this family."

I said softly, "You're marrying a stranger because you're desperate to replace your lost baby and you want to guarantee a home for us."

"No! Oh, dear Lord, no. Don't think that!"

"I won't let you do it."

"Vee, I'm not marrying just to have babies and a place to live! I'm marrying for absolute and total, passionate, honest *love.* To build a home and a family with my life's partner."

"I'll make a deal with you. We'll find a permanent job in

Nashville. We'll sell the RV and get an apartment. You can visit here. Carter can visit you. Take it nice and slow, see how you feel about him as you get to know him better. How's that for a compromise?"

"It's very safe and reasonable," she said, "but I don't need to create artificial safety with Carter. I *am* safe with him. I've never felt that way before with a man."

"He's two years younger than you. He doesn't have a real job or any apparent ambition. He has a two-bit harem in town. You don't even know his family, other than his aunt and uncle."

"Age makes no difference. And of course he has a job— he's taken care of everything around the Hall, and the outbuildings, and the livestock this past year—and the Camerons are his family. The MacIntoshes and the Camerons take care of each other."

"You're *my* family. I thought you trusted me to build a future for us."

"I'm trying to stand up for what's best for you, too. We can't go on the way we were. I love you, Sis, but I've fallen *in love* with the right man, finally. The only man for me. Please try to learn to love him as your brother-in-law." The thought was so preposterous I could only gape at her. The clock chimed ten-fifteen and I flinched.

She took my icy hands. "Give him a chance. Give this family a chance. Feel the difference these people can make in our lives. And the goodness we can add to their lives. They need us, Vee."

I bit my tongue. "Sandsprings Resort," I offered, watching her with urgent, strained enthusiasm. "I'm sure we can have six months if we want it. Starting the first of October. The main lounge."

Ella loved Sandsprings. It was in northern Florida, a few miles from Daytona Beach. We'd wintered there twice before. The weather hovered around sixty degrees most days, and the clientele were mainly snowbird retirees and old folks nesting on fat pension funds. Sandsprings guaranteed good tips, few hassles, and long, peaceful walks along the sand dunes of the Atlantic coast. "I'll call the manager right now," I said.

"Vee," she replied sadly, shaking her head. "Please stop. *I am going to marry Carter MacIntosh tonight.*"

I felt as if my brain exploded with fear and frustration. I flung up my right hand.

And I slapped my sister.

Pop never struck either of us. Never. And I'd never dreamed I could be provoked into hitting Ella.

She didn't shed a tear. That's how horrible it was. She turned to stone and so did I. Her eyes were the only life in her for a few seconds—wounded, the pain showing in deep green shadows, but then forgiving. She made a mewling sound. I threw my arms around her and held her tightly. She wound her arms around me.

"I'm not deserting you, I swear," she whispered.

"I'll be here for you when it all falls apart," I answered.

Seventeen

Ella Akiko Arinelli and Carter Walking Eagle MacIntosh were married by Colonel Harold "Hoss" Cameron, Retired, in a plain civil service at the two-hundred-and-fifty-year-old Cameron Catholic/Scottish/Cherokee chapel, just before midnight on our parents' thirtieth wedding anniversary.

I don't remember many details because I could only concentrate on standing beside Ella in silent duty, dressed in a black silk tank top, black toreador pants, and five-inch stacked-heel black Mary Janes. In that getup I hoped I represented unsentimental pragmatism and the last gasping hope for our all but extinct family tree. My head whirled with the lamplight and the faint smell of burning oil.

"The bride and groom can kiss," Hoss said at the end, and they did. I went dutifully to the creaky old organ and played something dignified, I can't even remember what. When I finished I sat there until Gib finally took me by one arm and whispered, "Just hold on," and I let him guide me from the chapel.

Back at the Hall he stayed beside me. We watched Ella and Carter accept champagne toasts from Hoss and Sophia, then Hoover Bird and Goldfish, and finally Olivia.

My sister was an ornament now. A Cameron possession. The latest in a long line of women and a few men who'd been bribed, coaxed, bullied, forced, or seduced into settling in the wild Cameron Valley.

She and Carter ate slices from FeeMolly's two-tiered wedding cake with an impromptu decoration of fresh purple and white pansy blooms on top. Bo Burton snapped pictures. I played the theme from the late-sixties movie version of *Romeo and Juliet* on the baby grand in the music room. Gib leaned against the piano with a flute of champagne cupped in one brawny hand and his face starkly composed. He had changed into a charcoal-gray suit for his role as Carter's best man. His expression grew darker as he listened. "Now there's a happy wedding song," he said drolly. "Lovers who kill themselves. I bet your next selection will be that happy little 'They'll never see each other again' tune from *Dr. Zhivago*."

"Did you know," I said dully, "that the Japanese see the ending of *Romeo and Juliet* as the *only* correct way to tell the story? To them it's a play about two people who disobeyed and dishonored their families. Romeo and Juliet *had* to kill themselves. It was the only way they could restore the balance."

"By God, *there's* a cheerful thought. You want that ending for Carter and your sister? Would that make you happy?"

"Don't you dare—" I began, but he put a finger to his lips. Ella was headed our way. She was flushed and fluttering. Her eyes gleamed but were swollen from crying. I stood.

"We're leaving now," she told me. I felt the hush in the room, everyone trying to look away, to pretend not to listen. "We'll be at Carter's place tonight and come back over during the day, tomorrow. If you need me you can call."

"You mean he has a phone?"

"Of course he has. Please, Sis, give us your blessing."

All I could make myself say was, "I want you to be happy. I hope you will be. I'll be here when you need me."

Not if, *when*. Carter came to us and took her by one hand.

His eyes flashed. His mouth was tight. "Thank you for what generosity you've given us," he said formally.

I stared at him and said nothing.

Ella hugged me hard. Against my ear she whispered, "I'm fine. I'll see you tomorrow."

"Use condoms," I whispered back.

She kissed my forehead, began to cry again, then smiled at everyone and turned back to Carter. They left the room. I felt the blood draining from my face. It took all my willpower not to run after them and beg her to tell me this was a joke, that she'd changed her mind.

I walked numbly out one of the back doors and across the lawn, into the apple orchards, until I bumped into a wrought-iron bench and sat down. I folded my hands on my lap and gazed into the darkness.

What was I up against? Only one of the founding families of Tennessee. All-American aristocracy with a Native American bloodline to clinch the title. Revolutionary War heroes, Civil War heroes, you name it. Sitting squarely in an 1800s manor house that looked as if it belonged among the heather and lochs of Scotland.

The Camerons were everything Ella had always wished our family could be.

A minute later Gib spoke. "I'm here, just over here, nearby. No need to talk to me. Just so you know you're not alone." I couldn't believe what was happening to us. After just a few days in their company I was being asked to accept the most intimate family ties with strangers. After years of trusting no one, I was suddenly expected to trust *everyone*.

Gib was wrong. I knew exactly how alone I was now.

She was radiant. When Ella and Carter finally strolled back to the Hall late the next afternoon, she was pink-cheeked and bright-eyed and unable to break the habit of admiring Carter with long, distracted looks. He returned the favor and held her hand as if she were made of the most delicate crystal. Her glow faded only when her eyes met mine. I knew my scrutiny was merciless. When she hugged me, I could only think how separate she was from me now. That a stranger had come between us in every sense of the word. "Do we have your blessings today?" she asked.

"You know I want what's best for you," I said.

"That's not a blessing."

"It's honesty. That's better. You know you can always count on me."

Ella regarded me with an aura of confidence that was blossoming more every minute. She tilted her head gently. Her hair slid across her left eye like liquid honey. She pushed it behind her ear. It was the most sensual and natural movement, as if she were finally, fully aware of herself as a woman. "I can't discuss what happened between my husband and me because it's sacred between a husband and wife. You know that. But I will say that he's wonderful and it was beautiful." She paused, smiling widely. "Every time."

"What brought Carter to this spirit of sanctified privacy? A concussion? This is a man who was group-kissing women and dancing with a goat last week."

Ella smiled as if I were teasing. "It's important to me that you get past your doubts and accept my choice. I love you, Sis. What is it about *me* that you love?"

"That's not important."

"Why do you love me? I'm not very useful."

"I love you because you collect feathers and believe in angels."

"Is that all?"

"Because you love people. You believe in the goodness of people. You're kind. Because you remind me of our mother."

"If you love me, how can you find nothing to love about Carter?"

"Excuse me?"

"I love him, and you love me. I see qualities in him that I cherish. If you value my spirit then you should realize my spirit at work through the people I love."

"You married a man like Pop. An outsider. That's the attraction, isn't it?"

She took my hands. "Oh, Sis. You're so wrong. I didn't marry a man like Pop. I deliberately married the opposite—a man who knows how to love people openly and wholeheartedly. A man who puts family ahead of everything else. Pop tried to make us think that we were everything to him, but he let us down, Sis. If you can't bring yourself to give me and Carter your blessing, then you're saying you've turned out just like Pop." Tears crested in her eyes. "He was always embarrassed by me. I wasn't smart enough, strong enough, talented enough. If you judge me the same way I can't bear it."

In for a penny, in for a pound. I'd thrown all I could at her. Now it was time to dig a trench and settle in. I had almost pushed her too far.

"I'll put some faith in your choice," I said carefully. "I'll show you how much I agree with you on one point. I say we sell the RV. I expect we can clear ten thousand dollars on it. We'll put the money in a joint account. You won't have to ask Carter for money."

She clapped her hands to her throat, looked at me in joyful disbelief, then threw her arms around me. "Sell the RV, oh, thank you, Sis," she cried. "I knew you wanted to stay here. I knew it. Actually, Carter and I have already talked about the RV," she admitted. "He has a plan. We'll take care of it while we're on our honeymoon."

I stared at her dully. "I bet."

That afternoon, Ella packed her bags. She kissed me on the cheek and said she knew I'd be fine for a few weeks with our new family. She and Carter planned to visit the rest of Carter's kin in Oklahoma. Carter promised me she'd come home with the biggest diamond wedding ring he could find in Oklahoma City.

After Oklahoma they'd fly to Chicago, clean out the RV, sell it, rent a truck, and haul everything Ella and I owned back to Tennessee. We'd be a snail without a shell. Absolutely exposed—we wouldn't have a home we actually owned ourselves. And Ella would be gone for upwards of a month.

A whole month. I thought I'd die from worry and loneliness before she even left. She and Carter went to the airport with Hoover Bird and Goldfish. I watched my sister drive away with strangers.

Shock, anger, and frustration boiled up inside me. I hated every Cameron in the valley. And yet I couldn't leave, I couldn't ignore them, and I couldn't pour out my fury.

I was totally on my own in the mountains of Tennessee with a troubled family who collected in-laws like a hobby, and a man who knew how to torment me more than I tormented myself. Gib avoided me. I didn't see him at all that day or the next. I stayed in my room.

I began to have nightmares about being stripped naked and deserted in the woods, so I wandered the hallways at night. I walked in the shadows of sepia-globed night-lights on rubbed chestnut baseboards, and portraits of long-dead Camerons watched me. One of the blue-eyed dogs kept me company, bumping my hand with his nose. Even the cats began to follow me.

I heard Dylan's coo of sleep behind the closed door of the room he and Isabel shared downstairs. He slept in a mahogany crib that had been hand-carved as a wedding gift to a Cameron a hundred years earlier. Bea and Olivia shared a two-room suite. I heard the murmur of an aria from a radio inside the darkened anteroom, which was fronted by a pair of glass-paned double doors hinged by a brace of gold gooseneck handles.

Jasper didn't sleep in the Hall. Since spring he'd camped in an old woodshed outside Carter's houseboat. Bea explained to me that Carter kept an eye on him, and in stormy weather Jasper darted inside Carter's place and slept on the couch. But usually he slept in his father's sleeping bag, using his father's gear.

In the big master bedroom down the hall from mine, Min never shut the door. It had been her and Simon's bedroom, and she said she couldn't stand the loneliness behind a door at night. I let myself peek in on her one night, only once, feeling guilty and invasive, but the door was open. I craved evidence that other people were simple in their unguarded times.

Min slept sitting up in an old recliner, the moonlight showing her angular body and the delicate shape of her small breasts under a simple cotton nightgown. She had an opened Bible on her lap. Beside her a window let the soft night breeze come in, lifting sheer white curtains like slow wings. Kelly had abandoned her own bedroom to sleep with her mother in the past year. She made a question-mark shape under the coverlet of a broad bedstead. Snuggled alongside her were another of the blue-eyed offspring of the dog in the wedding photo and several of the friendlier cats, including a calico whose tail had been unnaturally bobbed by an angry fox, I'd heard.

We were creatures missing pieces, all of us.

The courthouse in Hightower was a large, modern brick building beyond the town's tree-lined streets and turn-of-the-century town square. A small billboard had been erected on the lawn. Painted on it was a tall thermometer with cash amounts labeled up one side. The thermometer's bright red level was stuck on $507,200.

What Crime Pays Back in Debt to Hightower County Citizens, proclaimed a slogan in thick, satisfied letters. Smaller script underneath explained: *Dollar Values of Property Seized in Narcotics and Other Crimes.*

I got out of the hatchback and stood at the lawn's edge, morbidly fixated on the billboard. No wonder Gib and Ruth wanted Pop's money out of their family. The shocked citizens of Hightower might have to raise the temperature on the thermometer of public righteousness. I walked up a brick path lined with hedges pruned into imposing square blocks of greenery. As I climbed a short set of steps to the lobby doors I passed a row of small newspaper boxes filled with stacks of local church pamphlets. So much for the separation of church and state.

Inside, in the two-story atrium lobby, one wall displayed high school students' posters celebrating the start of the Hightower Highlanders' new football season. Stomp the Attenborough Indians, one poster shouted in red paint designed to look like dripping blood. The lobby's other wall contained a giant brass plaque listing the Ten Commandments.

I supposed at least one or two troublesome ACLU lawyers were buried in cement somewhere in the building's foundation. I looked for Ruth's name on a directory, then trudged up a wide staircase. A cleaning woman said, "Hello, there, ma'am," as I passed her on the second-floor landing.

"What?" I snapped.

She paled. "You look a mite lost, that's all. You need some directions, ma'am?"

Suddenly, I realized she was merely being polite. Sociable. "I'm looking for Ruth Attenberry's office, please," I said, shamefaced.

"Right down yonder. Second door on the left." She pointed. "The judge brought in some fresh cider from his orchard this morning. Help yourself to a cup at that table in the hall."

"Thank you."

My jaw set, I strode quickly past the facade of folksy hospitality. I'd entered the bowels of the legal system, trapped like a peach pit Ruth couldn't stomach, and no amount of small-town southern comfort changed that fact. I walked through an open office door and halted. There was Ruth, reared back in an upholstered chair at an ornate wooden desk. She was angled away from me; I couldn't see her face but I saw her large, stockinged feet and plump legs propped beside a green-globed desk lamp. The skirt of her beige suit was hiked up above her knees. Pungent-smelling white smoke wafted into the air above the high chairback. Papers rattled.

"I imagine you suspected I'd come to see you, sooner or later," I said. "Now that you think my sister's proved your theories about us being trollops and gold diggers."

"Yep," she answered without turning around. "I can smell the stink of corrupt moral values a mile away." She took her feet down and pivoted in the chair. A slender, almost delicate little cigar was perched between her fingers. Her lap was full of legal documents of some sort. A gold fountain pen gleamed in the brunette hair above one ear. She bared her teeth in a smile.

"What did you expect? That I'd send your sister a wedding present? How about a shovel to help her dig into Carter's money?"

I shut the door and sat down in a hard wooden chair across from her desk. "Listen, you smug, self-righteous harpy, your own *family* is apologizing for your rudeness. 'Ruth's so busy.' 'Ruth's not a chit-chatter.' Of course they don't know the half of it. Don't Min and Isabel's opinions mean anything to you?"

"I leave the nice-nice duties to them. They're darling souls and that's their job in the family. Kicking ass and taking names is *my* job. Mine and Gib's. I expect *he* hasn't apologized for my lack of enthusiasm toward the lovely Arinelli sisters. Because he agrees with me. You're trouble. Both of you. But even I'm surprised how fast your sister moved. She got all over Carter like a greased snake."

"I can tell this conversation is a waste of time. You pick the weapons, I'll pick the hour. You want a blood duel, I'll give you one. Get up, girlfriend, and let's commence with the ritual bitch-slapping contest. Because that's what it's going to take to settle this, isn't it?"

"Lord have mercy, how you *do* talk. I don't have any intention of mud-wrestling with you. The situation's more complicated, now. You and Ella are family." She snorted derisively when she said that, but I was amazed that she admitted any alliance at all.

I stared at her. "I doubt my sister will be *family* for any longer than it takes your cousin to dump her."

"That's the problem. I have to fake a certain level of decorum until he wises up."

A chill went through me. Surely Gib hadn't told her Ella's medical history. "You mean when he realizes he's married a woman who expects a mature, faithful husband?"

"Considering the kind of male role model y'all grew up with, I'd think Ella would be happy enough just knowing her husband doesn't run with a crowd of left-wing sociopaths who fry federal judges."

I leaned toward her and said in a low, calm voice, "You were only a little girl when your world fell apart, but it affected your whole attitude, didn't it? I should have known. It explains so much about you and Gib and Isabel—and Simon, too, no doubt."

"What the hell are you talking about?"

"Your parents. How they died in England. Killed by IRA terrorists. You've always wanted to find those bombers and punish them, but you can't, so you channel your energy into this superjudgmental, law-and-order mentality."

"When I want to hear cheap psychological analysis I'll turn on a TV talk show. I believe in fairness and justice. It's that simple."

"Fairness and justice require an open mind. You've already decided my sister and I are treacherous scum. The only reason I give a damn is that I don't want Ella hurt. That's all I came here to say. Take out your private war on *me,* not her."

"It seems to me we're in the same boat. I have to tread lightly because my cousin thinks he loves her—and you have to behave because your sister says she loves *him*."

"Agreed." I stood. "Thanks for your time."

She smiled coldly. "What do *you* believe in, Venus de Milo? Don't let your reach exceed your grasp. That's how the statue probably lost her poor little arms. Being greedy."

I went to the door, opened it, and gazed back at her innocently. "Now that I'm certain you're a toothless threat, I *believe* I'll enjoy a tasty cup of apple cider on the way out."

She threw a law book at me.

Isabel slipped inside my bedroom one afternoon while I was attempting to jot down notes about a piano composition. I wasn't making any progress; my moods were all bad, I worried constantly about Ella, and that didn't contribute much creative energy. She and Carter had been gone for days.

"You're so mad at us all you can barely see straight, can you?" Isabel asked meekly.

I sighed. Being mad at Isabel was like being mad at Ella, which was the emotional equivalent of kicking a kitten. I just couldn't do it. "There are a lot of Camerons in this part of the world," I said finally. "But only two Arinellis. To y'all this was just another colorful Cameron marriage, but it changed my sister's life, and mine, completely. And I wasn't offered any choice. The situation was forced on me."

She nodded sympathetically then held out a pot of hot tea and tiny cream-cheese sandwiches on a silver plate. "Ella and Carter will be fine," she said gently. "You really should try to feel at home here, even though you've only been here a few weeks." I shook my head. She set the tray down then laid a hand on my shoulder. "We don't want to upset you more than you are already, believe it or not, but there's something we haven't told you. You need to know. It might make you feel better toward us."

Oh, no, I thought with queasy dread. "I'm beyond surprise," I said calmly.

"You've noticed that this bedroom has a yellow theme?"

That was an understatement. Everything, from the curtains, the bed, the chairs, the throw pillows in the window seat, the rose-printed wall-paper, to even the lampshades, exuded a soft shade of yellow. It was like sleeping inside a large, sunlit egg.

"Somebody likes yellow," I said blankly.

Isabel nodded. "This bedroom is decorated in yellow because of your mother. She sent a gift when you were born. That yellow chenille bedspread. We did the room to match it."

I looked at the bed with a smothering sense of stark overload, surrounded by meaning, portents, memories, star-crossed spirits, and trouble. I realized I'd been sleeping under my mother's bedspread.

"I need some time to myself, thank you," I said. Isabel's brows shot up in embarrassment. She apologized for upsetting me then hurried out of the room.

I decided to put as much distance between me and everyone else as possible from then on. I spent my days walking the roads and paths of the valley.

One afternoon I hiked into a hidden glen not far from the chapel. Amazed, I stared at the cottage there. It was simple but lovely, painted red with white trim and a white board porch with white rocking chairs on it. Flowers bloomed in old washpots set around the stone steps, and the window boxes overflowed with ivy and impatiens. White lace curtains moved gently in the open front windows.

I felt like Goldilocks discovering the three bears' place. I could almost smell their tempting porridge.

A brass plaque hanging on a porch post said,

SCHOOLHOUSE COTTAGE. THIS FORMER ONE-ROOM
SCHOOLHOUSE WAS ESTABLISHED FOR THE COMMUNITY'S
CHILDREN BY QUENTEL MARONIA CAMERON IN 1902.

Another Cameron historic site, I noted with resignation. These people probably even posted signs over the biggest rocks. *Davy Crockett stubbed his toe here, 1822.*

But it was a place where I could retreat and brood in private. The infamous Venus Arinelli was taking command of it now.

Eighteen

Maybe they were glad to get rid of me, or maybe they felt sorry for me. I couldn't tell. But no one seriously opposed my plan to move to the cottage.

Everyone walked out of the Hall and gathered around me as I left. "Are you sure you feel more comfortable going off to stay there?" Min asked.

"Yes. I'm just not used to living with people."

"Those years she spent with the lamas in Tibet affected her social skills," Gib noted. He set my luggage in the rear of the car and slammed the hatchback.

"Brother, hush," Isabel rebuked gently.

He nodded curtly to me and walked back into the Hall. I watched him go with a sinking heart. He was as unhappy as I was. He was stuck with me and my hidden money indefinitely. Plus he'd let his cousin marry without learning my sister's unstable background. My family secrets were a growing albatross around his neck.

Min smiled gamely. "Of course you know you're welcome to move back into the Hall whenever you want to. Don't you want at least one of us to go over to the cottage with you? Then you can look around and maybe change your mind."

"Thank you, but I can find my way. I'm looking forward to just being quiet and absorbing everything that's happened." Olivia wrote on her pad and held it out to me: *Gib lives in the lodge. Carter and Ella live in the houseboat. You now live in the schoolhouse cottage. Nothing odd about that. You are all satellites of my personal moon. Part of my galaxy. That's all that's really important.*

"Olivia," I said evenly, "I don't want to be disrespectful to you. But you don't own me. I'm only staying in this valley because my sister needs me here when she gets back."

Olivia wrote: *Oh? Which would be worse? To be needed, or to learn you are, in fact, no longer needed at all? You are part of this family now, like it or not.*

Bea read the notes over our shoulders. "Herself, oh, Herself," she said, chortling and waving a tall mug of warm beer. "We're no' so grand as stars in your orbit. We're mere bugs in your web, you dear old spider, and aren't we knowing that for a fact?"

Olivia eyed her narrowly then wrote: *Drink your morning toddy and be quiet. Some days you annoy me.*

Minutes later, as I drove the car down a shady, forest-draped little road deep in the valley below the Hall, Kelly leaped out from the woods like a lanky teenage cat.

She waved a cigarette in one hand. I stopped the car and she sauntered over to my open window. I tried not to gape at her transformation. Until then she'd been a clean-cut Junior Barbie. Now she could pose for one of those Calvin Klein ads where the models look as if they're in need of drug rehab. She wore a sloppy white tank top, low-slung baggy jeans, black nail polish, and tiny barrettes in her short, dark brown hair, which looked as if it had been styled with axle grease. As she leaned down in a cloud of unfiltered smoke, I was nose-to-cleavage with her small breasts and her put-on expression of apathy.

"What's happening?" she asked rhetorically. "I thought maybe I could hang out with you a little. Like I could be myself around you, 'cause you understand. I can't wear this stuff at the house. Nobody's cool with it. But I figured you wouldn't care. So maybe I can go to the cottage and show you where to put your crap and all?"

Being an expert on my own self-protective attitude, I recognized cocky bullshit when I saw it. I indulged her. "Sure. Get in. So what's the latest news from hell on earth?"

She brightened. "Life sucks." She swaggered around to the passenger side. Her lower lip twitched nervously. After she took her place in the passenger seat I borrowed her cigarette and took a puff.

"Man," she said in an awed tone, as she studied me. "How come you're only wearing a couple of little hoop earrings? I want to see you with all your holes filled up. *Man,* did it hurt when you got that one up in the top of your ear pierced?"

"Yep, the needle went into the cartilage and it hurt like a bitch. I don't recommend it."

"You're not wimpin' out, are you? I mean, you ought to put on all your earrings and be proud."

"My ears need a rest. The jewelry was for my act. It looked good onstage, but it's no fun to hook it with a fingernail. I tore one of my holes, once. Had to have stitches. It's no fun to have your holes stitched, either."

She giggled wildly. "Uncle Gib says you have a pierced belly button. When he came home from Chicago he told Aunt Ruth and Aunt Isabel all about it, and like, he was saying *exactly* how you had a little gold ring with a little gold chain that went around your waist, and how it looked like you'd sprinkled some gold glitter around your belly button, and how your belly jewelry reflected the stage lights and stuff when he went in that lesbo nightclub to see you the first time, and so he's telling this story and all of a sudden Aunt Ruth said, 'Good godawmighty, did you get out a magnifying glass?

You've spent more time describing her navel than you've spent talking about the last five women you *dated*.' Uncle Gib gave her this kind of one-eyed squint he does when he's pissed off, and he got *real* quiet."

I should have laughed. I should have enjoyed knowing Gib was a secret slave to my allure. But a wave of intense longing went through me, and I was suddenly aware of my navel as if he'd kissed it.

"Can I see it?" Kelly babbled on. "Your navel?"

I pulled up my T-shirt and she peered at my stomach. "Hey, that looks like a little silver barbell. Can you feel it all the time?"

"When my clothes rub against it."

"Is it sexy?"

"To who? Me? Sure. And it makes me feel centered. That may sound strange, but—"

"No, I get it. Chakras and shit. Center of your energy. I know. I read a Shirley MacLaine book once."

I took another long pull on the cigarette and blew smoke rings as I drove, then crushed the butt in my ashtray, among cold wads of chewing gum.

"Not your brand?" Kelly asked.

"I quit smoking a few years ago. Got rid of most of my bad habits. They catch up with you if you don't. You have to weed them out. You ought to quit while it's easy."

"What kind of drugs do you do?"

"Aspirin."

"You know what I mean."

"Unh-uh. None. They cost too much, they're bad for your health, and the world's crazy enough without confronting it with your head all messed up. You don't want anybody taking advantage of you because you're wasted."

"But what about the, you know, the thrill of experimenting with your inner dimensions? All that sixties stuff. I thought you were some kind of hippie."

"You want to experiment with your inner dimensions?

Write poetry. Write a song. Hug your mother. And for the record, I'm not old enough to have ever been a hippie. In fact it's safe to say all the hippies disappeared by the time I was old enough to notice. Disco music and their own aging baby-boomer greed did them in."

"Shit."

"So tell me—do you like to scurry around the woods with this secret, gothic look or do you just like the excitement of leaping out of the bushes at visitors?"

She blinked. "I wasn't trying to scare you, I promise, I—" She halted, then quickly restored her apathy. She shrugged. "Yeah. Sure. I'm the queen of the Goth fan club. Wanna see the bruises from my needle tracks?"

As I drove I glanced over at her. She looked as sinister as Cinderella playing dress-up for Halloween. "I could tell you some stories about musicians who shoot up," I said casually. "They drool in their food and fall asleep in the middle of a conversation."

She puckered her black-lipsticked mouth. "I'm really not interested in that kind of nasty stuff, anyhow. But it's cool to talk about—you know? People should walk the edge so they can really know what the abyss looks like."

"Trust me, you don't have to walk up to the edge to know how evil it is. You can stand back and watch other people dive right in."

She gave an elaborate sigh. "You mean people you love?"

I hesitated. Then, "That's exactly what I mean. And I'm not just talking about drugs."

"You mean any kind of evil you can't stop from happening?"

"Exactly."

"Like what happened to my dad and Uncle Gib."

"Right."

"Uncle Gib's the big man around here now. Mama has abdicated all power. See, we got this *real* male hierarchy thing going on in our family."

"I don't think it's a matter of sexual politics. I think your mother needs more time to mourn and recover. And from what I've heard she's never been the kind of person who felt comfortable as a leader."

"I wish she'd just be comfortable as a mother, you know. It's like we can't talk anymore. Like she's shut up inside herself."

"She loves you and Jasper like a mother tiger. I've been watching. Just cut her some slack for a while longer."

She shrugged. "She told us to respect Uncle Gib like we did Daddy. But my dad was cool. I bet he wouldn't have cared if I'd smoked some weed."

"I see. Hmmm. You've tried a more evil weed than tobacco, eh?"

"Yeah, a guy at school grew a bushel of pot behind his grandpa's pigpens. He gave me a bagful a couple of months ago, but Uncle Gib got wind of it. Like he smelled it on my clothes. You know, 'cause he got trained to know about drugs in the Secret Service, I guess. He didn't tell Mama, but he threw my stash in the river and took me over to the sheriff's house and made me watch a film on *brain damage*."

"Well, maybe he overreacted, but he's probably worried about you. You know, when you're feeling confused it's too easy to make some really dangerous choices."

"But I wouldn't! I told him it was no big deal! But he said"—she puffed out her chest—" 'Bad habits grow from small roots.' Sometimes he's got like this old-man righteous asshole attitude."

Teenage angst looks at every issue through the backward end of a telescope, reducing all outside concerns to a single effect on Self. I remembered how I was at her age and how crazy I was after Pop died, but I decided tough love was the best approach. "Look, if you imagine I'm going to let you come hang out with me so you can toke and smoke and get high, you've got another think coming. I mean, we can be cool, but we're not going to be that cool. Okay?"

She muttered obscenely for a minute. Then, "I just thought you could give me some advice. Nobody else around here has a clue. Nothing exciting happens around *here*. Nothing good. It's haunted." She shrugged, but her lip stopped twitching. "Would you teach me to sing?"

I blinked at the sudden change of subject. "I'm not much of a singer."

"Yeah, but I bet you know enough to teach me how to breathe right and project my voice and all."

"All right. I'll teach you what I can. Why?"

"I sent in an application for a beauty pageant. Miss Teenage Eastern Tennessee. It's in December. There's a talent competition."

"Why do you want to be in a pageant?" She shrugged. I noticed the choker necklace she wore. Attached to the short, thick chain were a crucifix, a tiny, faded-gold bell, and a half-dozen car keys. "Quite a collection of stuff you've got on that chain there," I offered.

"This is junk from the bottom of my dad's jewelry case," she said, fingering the necklace and giving a shrug. "I just think it's neat to wear it. You know—so when people look at me they'll be looking at him, too, kind of."

Here was another heartsick Cameron soul. I understood too well. She wanted to represent her father to the world in every way she could dream up, even if avenues such as beauty pageants didn't make much sense. "I know the name of that tune," I said.

When we arrived at the cottage I said darkly, "Your uncle Gib didn't show me this place when we were touring the valley."

"Probably 'cause he figured you'd want to move there right away if he told you about it. I guess he was right."

"It's a special place."

"Yeah. Dad used to rent it to people. Some people think it's the *supremo* place to stay."

I exhaled wearily as I got out of the car. The woods felt like a humid green fortress. Kelly leaned on the car's hood and extracted another cigarette from a crumpled pack in her jeans pocket. "Want one more?"

I was feeling vulnerable and defeated. "Yeah." We smoked in companionable silence. "Where's that path go?" I gestured toward a pretty little sunlit trail that wound off through the forest.

Kelly flicked ashes. "Down the hill. It's a back way to the chapel. We got walking trails all over the valley. They were Daddy's idea. His and Mama's. Jasper and I used to go with Daddy and help him cut the blackberry briars back from the sides every summer. There's miles of trails around here. We used to take a knapsack full of Cokes and candy bars, and when we got done with the briars we'd sit up on the eagle cliffs and Daddy'd sing."

"What kind of songs did he like to sing?" I asked gently.

"Real bad country-western. Like 'You Can Keep My Wife but Give My Truck Back.'" She smiled a little. "And he liked Simon and Garfunkel. Maybe 'cause his first name was Simon."

I gestured toward the cottage. "Your dad put up that historical plaque?"

She nodded, fingering her necklace with the tips of her black-painted nails. "It was his idea to fix up Great-great-grandma's schoolhouse and let people stay in it. It's got a big tub with water jets in it."

I got dizzy and crushed the cigarette under the heel of my sandal. Camerons had trails and roads all over the place, too many buildings, houses, and historical markers, and I couldn't imagine where Ella would fit in, much less me.

Kelly followed me around like a lost puppy while I toured my new quarters. I ran my hands over the cottage's handsome Adirondack-style wood chairs and tables. Touching soothed me. Ella teased that I always tried to coax music out of any object I laid my hands on.

In the main room was a massive stone fireplace and a chintz couch that looked like it might pull out into a bed. I tested it and it did. I sat on the mattress and studied the wall across from me. It had been left in the original whitewashed planks, with an antique chalkboard set among landscape paintings of the valley and the grand, plain-spirited Hall.

Make yourself at home, Venus, was written on the chalkboard in a feminine style I recognized already as Isabel's handwriting.

In one of the nearby paintings a Cherokee village of low huts stretched along the river, with a large, round council house at their center. I absorbed that past through my fingertips. I touched the chalkboard message, smudging it. Didn't trust the sentiment. I scrubbed my hand over the words and erased them. The only bedroom was sumptuous with comforters and richly colored pillows and thick copper lamps, the bed, kingsized with tall log posts. Off the bedroom was a decadently luxurious bathroom with a giant whirlpool tub. The bathroom had a huge, low-set garden window that opened to face a small deck and the woods beyond.

With Kelly right behind me I wandered into a small but modern kitchen, bright and cozy with gingham curtains and a red-checked table in front of a bay window. The kitchen was stocked with mouth-watering tasties and smelled of sweet, ripe peaches stacked in an earthenware bowl by the kitchen window. There were tins filled with what appeared to be fresh homemade cookies, and a basket of fat, soft muffins wrapped in gold foil.

Home, sweet home, for however long it lasted.

"I'll come back tomorrow, if it's okay," Kelly said. "I've got to go get ready for church. I have to change in the woods. I left a knapsack."

"Sure. Come back and we'll talk about that pageant business. Even if you change your mind about doing it, I'll still teach you the basic techniques of singing."

"Great!"

I walked out on the porch with her. "So tell me something, Kelly, because I've tried to avoid asking this. It's not very polite."

Her face lit up. "Hey, I'm cool."

"Can your great-aunt Olivia hear okay? That is, she can't talk but she's not partially deaf, is she?"

"Oh, she can hear fine. She can hear me say 'goddamn' a mile away under a bushel basket."

"What happened to her voice?"

With a bored expression, as if telling a fact she'd repeated thousands of times at her tender age, Kelly explained, "She quit talkin' after she killed her husband with rat poison. She put it in his dinner. He foamed at the mouth and died having fits."

The hairs rose on the back of my neck. Kelly noted my stunned expression and grinned. "Neat, huh? But it was fifty years ago. She hasn't killed anybody since then. Besides, don't worry, she really likes you. I can tell. I gotta go."

After Kelly loped into the woods with a wave good-bye I stood on the cottage porch, thinking about Olivia being a notorious husband-poisoning widow from decades past. My sister was somewhere in Oklahoma with a stranger she'd married. I was secretly falling in love with Gib, a disapproving, damaged man who scared and excited me with his hard loyalties. And now I was related by marriage to a psychologically mute old murderess.

> IN THIS VICINITY, FIFTY YEARS AGO, OLIVIA CAMERON PROVED THERE'S NO MARRIAGE THAT CAN'T BE A LITTLE MORE EXCITING. SHE DEMONSTRATED THE FINE ART OF COOKING TO PLEASE A MAN. OR POISON HIM.

I wondered where they put the historical marker for *that*.

Nineteen

I stayed busy composing new duets on my keyboard and plotting career strategics for the future, when Ella and I would undoubtedly need them.

It made no difference to me that each night, when Ella called me to chat, she sounded blissful. Not only was she having a wonderful time on her extended honeymoon, she was being treated like a queen. Carter had given her a diamond ring so extravagant that she couldn't mention it without crying. Hoover Bird had presented her with an heirloom hand-woven MacIntosh family blanket, and he had also bestowed on her a Cherokee name that meant *dove*. She and Carter were heading to Chicago. He'd already lined up a buyer for our RV. They would be home soon.

Home, she said easily. It rang in my ears.

When I got off the phone one night I sat on the cottage porch in the dark and realized Ella Arinelli was now officially Ella Dove MacIntosh. I was the only one left who bore the Arinelli name that Grandpop had brought to America so proudly.

"I'm the last of the Mohicans," I said out loud.

My words echoed back at me.

·   ·   ·

One morning I sat in the cottage's sunny kitchen nook, drinking breakfast tea and eating toast covered in apple butter. Giant acorns popped the roof like gunshots, and I looked out once to see deer in the yard and a fat woodchuck sniffing among wild muscadine vines. I rinsed my teacup three times out of sheer boredom and feared I might start talking to squirrels unless I found a routine to cling to, soon.

Olivia and Bea arrived in a golf cart. They drove around the valley at odd times of the day and night in their cart, though I'd glimpsed them only a few times before. I went outside gratefully. A large tabby cat stood between them on a purple shag-rug bath mat on the dash of the golf cart. The cat leaped down and sniffed the hatchback's left rear wheel, then turned and peed on the tire.

"Good morning to you, child," Bea shouted. She was dressed in pristine white overalls, a flowered shirt, and a large straw hat. "Have the wild beasties and the ghosties not scared you back to the bosom of the family, yet?"

"No, but that cat's insulting me, and the huge kamikaze acorns around here are making me nervous." An acorn pounded the cottage roof, bounced, hit the roof of the golf cart, bounced again, and nearly beaned the cat as it finished spritzing my car. Olivia smiled. I walked over to the cart and she laid one of her hands, like bones covered in thin yellowed paper, on my wrist. She handed me a note.

Emory is coming today. He plans to make his final presentation about the Hall's future. We vote today. You must come and help me.

I held her gaze firmly. "Why should I help you?"

She scowled then gestured to Bea, who was suddenly serious. Bea clicked her thick fingers. "If respect isn't in your heart by now, your help will mean nothing. But Herself believes you have the knack for seein' us as we need to be seen, for good or ill. We're puttin' our faith in you, dearie. It's up to you whether you want it or no'."

"What if Emory's right? Maybe y'all should go into partnership with his investors."

"Then perhaps we're no' regarding the situation with anything but our tired, wishful hearts. If you think our time here should come to an end, say so. For believe me or not, dear Gib sets store by your thoughts. He says you're too honest for his own good, but he means that as a compliment."

"I'll go just to see how the dastardly Emory operates. But I don't intend to get involved. I'm only doing this because I want to study how this family reacts to stress without luring unsuspecting visitors into disastrous marriages."

Bea hooted. "We'll turn you loose on Emory with that sharp sense of humor of yours and you'll gut him like a trout!"

"I hate to disappoint you but I and my sense of humor have to change clothes first. Excuse me." I gestured to the black silk pajama top I wore with ragged shorts made from sweatpants. Olivia's fingers tightened on my wrist. Her eyes gleaming, she glanced at the placid-looking Beatrice with silent communication. "Oh!" Bea exclaimed. "It's slippin' my mind." Bea looked at me slyly. "She wants to see your belly jewel."

I opened a button on my pajama top. Olivia studied the silver stud in the rim of my navel. She smiled. As I buttoned up Bea chortled. "Half the county is talking about you. You're said to be a godless and forthright woman with your belly jewels and your wild hair and your lonely ways!"

"Good."

Olivia pulled out her pad from the golf cart's driving console, scribbled calmly for a minute, then handed it to me.

People are nervous about women who take charge and do what must be done. I approve of you. Keep everyone on-guard.

I looked at her narrowly. Now I understood why she wanted me to meet Emory. She thought I might become her private attack dog—a young version of Herself, the new voice for deadly experience.

I'd met men like Emory Cameron before, men who had the flavor of silver spoons so firmly ingrained in their taste buds that their tongues had turned to silver plate. I walked into the library, took one look at the tall gray-haired patrician in his golf shirt, crisp khaki slacks, and diamond pinkie ring and thought, *Capitalist pig*. Which was a ten-cent cliché I'd never heard even Pop's most fanatical political cronies utter seriously. I almost laughed aloud for thinking it.

Gib entered the room a second later and nodded to me. He angled slightly in front of me with his shoulder as he escorted me to Emory. Gib made the introduction and Emory shook my hand, smiling as he said, "I never know what kind of folks I'll find taken underwing here. So you and your sister have joined our home for wayward strangers? Aunt Olivia's support of ne'er-do-well women does get more peculiar with every passing year."

Capitalist pig, I almost said. But Gib took me by one arm, escorted me to the door, and said in a low, deadly tone, "Everybody's in the dining room. Go tell them I'll be there in a second."

"Would you prefer I go back to the cottage and keep my nose out of this? Obviously I'm making you uncomfortable. And Emory is a—"

"I know what he is. He and I are about to have a conversation about what he just said. Out." He touched the tip of my nose with his forefinger, I took a startled step backward, and he closed the double doors to the library. I stood there blankly facing the matched curlicue carvings of the doors.

"What are you doing here?" Ruth asked behind me, "if I may be so nosy about the newest and least likely member of our enormous family tree?" I pivoted. She lurked there in oversized pin-striped glory, looking every inch the swank, go-get-'em prosecutor.

"What do you *think* I'm doing here, Perry Mason? I was invited by Olivia. But at the moment I'm trying to decide if Gib's in there defending my besmirched honor or agreeing with dear old asshole Cousin Emory."

"Well at least you've pegged Emory right. I give you points for good judgment about him." She grunted. "Gib *never* agrees with Emory, so you can safely assume he's in there defending whatever honor you've got."

"I'm surprised Emory isn't putting his best foot forward, if he wants y'all to cooperate with his ideas."

"He's a smug prick. He thinks we're desperate now."

"So you're saying that's not the case. Good."

"No, I'm saying we *are* desperate and we'll probably end up taking his offer, because it makes sense, but we don't have to like it. Or him."

"Oh."

We walked down the central hall. Ruth grunted, "By the way, keep your mouth shut during this discussion. You shouldn't even be here." She strode before me into the dining room, where Olivia and Bea were already seated, along with Isabel, who held Dylan on her lap. A burly young man with a thick face and thinning red hair commandeered one end of the long table, where he fiddled with a videotape. A portable TV and VCR sat on the end of the table, facing us. "Joey, this is the older sister of the woman who ran off with Carter," Ruth said brusquely.

"Ruth," Isabel rebuked.

"Her name's Venus Arinelli," Ruth added with grudging etiquette. "Venus, *dear,* this is our cousin Joey."

He stood. He was tall and also of the golf-shirt, country-club variety, like his father. He crunched my hand in his handshake, then corrected Ruth in an annoyed tone. "Joseph." He gave her a slit-eyed scowl and sat down.

"Joey used to visit here when we were kids," Ruth went on blithely. "We've always given him credit for inspiring us. See, he's older than the rest of us and we consider him an elder. When we were kids he'd sneak around and beat up on Gib, until Gib got big enough to take boxing lessons from old man Gummer over in Attenborough. Mr. Gummer was an Army heavyweight boxing champ back during World War Two. After Gib learned how to box we didn't have much more trouble from *Joey*." She grinned at her cousin, who chewed a gold fountain pen and flipped through a thick folder of documents, while his face turned red around the hairline.

"I remember when Ruth bit Joey," Isabel ventured delicately, as if she were complimenting all involved. Bea and Olivia watched us with shrewd silence.

Ruth grinned. "Yep. Caught him stealing brandy out of the liquor cabinet. Bit a chunk out of his arm. I think I was about eight years old at the time. That was when I first knew I wanted to be a lawyer. Good godawmighty, it was so satisfying to catch a criminal and make him yelp." She turned to me. "See what I mean about Joey being an inspiration?"

"Why, yes," I said primly.

He raised his head and stared at me. "I hear that you and your sister work as entertainers. In bars."

He made it sound as if we were strippers. "We're musicians. We perform piano and violin duets. Pop music and standards. Most of our venues have been large hotels and restaurants."

"Oh? I heard my cousin found you in a lesbian nightclub. Do you and your sister have a large lesbian following?"

Bea slammed a fist on the table. "You're about to find yourself tossed out the door on your *arse*, Joey."

I held his stare and neither one of us gave an inch.

"Large, small, medium," I said evenly. "Lesbians of all sizes."

"Is homosexuality a personal lifestyle choice of yours, or just a business?"

"*Music* is my business. My only requirement is that I play for people who have ears and brains. For example, I can see that even *you* have ears."

"Since your sister married into our family," Joseph went on, "with such *rare passion*"—he emphasized the words—"I assume she, at least, is bisexual? Or maybe the lure of money converted her."

"Stop this," Isabel said.

Olivia laid a gold-headed cane on the table. Bea clamped a hand on it. "Easy, now, dear. The child's got him well in sight."

Gib and Emory walked in at that moment with Min, who moved with thin, straight-backed dignity. Emory's face was frozen in politeness, and so I bit my tongue. Min touched my shoulder as she passed by on her way to the chair Gib held for her. "You've been introduced to Emory and Joseph?" she asked.

"Yes, indeed. Thank you. I already feel as if I've known them all my life. It's really astonishing how familiar some people are. From the first minute you talk to them, you know exactly what they're all about."

Min frowned in bewilderment at that exuberant response, Isabel covered her mouth, and Ruth said under her breath, "Too bad you never got the chance to bite back."

Oh, I would, I would.

Gib stood in the back of the room with his arms folded over his chest. He wouldn't have attended this session if he didn't fear surrender might be the only wise route. Yet it was obvious this was tearing him apart.

"Let's review the situation," Emory said. He stood behind

the television as if it were a podium. He nodded to me with more deference than before, but it was only a cold facade. "I'll go over some facts since we have a new member of the, hmmm, family, here, who may not be familiar with the details."

Joseph handed him a sheaf of papers. He leafed through them idly, as if refreshing his memory. "Financially, Cameron Hall Inn, Incorporated, is still in the black, even after being closed for more than a year. Simon and Min managed the inn's profits very well for a long time. They made solid investments and smart improvements. They operated on a sensible budget, and thus, thank God, the inn has been able to weather this storm—for now.

"But if this property remains idle for another full year, the taxes and maintenance costs will eat you folks alive. You'll be headed toward serious trouble financially. And this valley, this grand old house, in fact our entire family legacy, will be jeopardized.

"I need an answer today, folks. I can't put my investors off much longer. I realize that none of you have any deep affection for me. I'm a plain-spoken man. You may not agree with my ideas, but you know I sincerely care about preserving this legacy for generations to come."

Emory paused, cleared his throat, sipped from a glass of iced tea Joseph handed him, then looked pointedly at Min. "Min, you're tired. You don't have the heart for the hard work required to manage the inn. You know Simon felt my plans had a lot of merit. You know he discussed them seriously with me, and with you, and with the family."

"The only thing I *don't* know," Min said hoarsely, "is whether he would have ever gone through with it."

"I believe he would have, Minnie. He wanted what was best for you and Jasper and Kelly. He wanted what was best for his brother and sisters, and for Bea and Olivia, and for this valley, and the house. He wanted you to relax and travel and never have to worry about a houseful of paying guests again. He wanted you to know how it felt to stay in five-star hotels where *you* are the guest. And he wanted your children to love this place but never be slaves to its upkeep, the way the two of you had become."

"I don't think he was quite *that* way about it," Min said. "What he really wanted was what I wanted—a little more help so that we could have some free time. It should have been simple, really, and—"

"Minnie, are you prepared to consign your children to an uncertain financial future—risk their college educations— for the sake of argument?"

Her shoulders sagged. "No, I'm not."

"Good. Isabel?" He pivoted to the other side of the table. "Isabel, honey, you are the sweetest young woman I know. Your little paintings can make a decent living for you and Dylan, but will it be enough? You have to be both mother and father to Dylan now, and you don't want him to look into your eyes one day and ask you why you didn't do what was right— why you turned your back on the kind of money that would not only guarantee a wonderful future for him but also give you the freedom to paint your kittens and rabbits to your heart's content."

Isabel fretted and blushed. "I appreciate that concern, really I do, but I keep thinking that I have enough freedom already, and that money isn't everything."

"Tell your son that money isn't important, when he's a young man and he wants to know why his friends have so much more than he does."

"That would take a bloody miracle," Bea said darkly, "since it's a boon day when a teenager is no' discontent with life."

Emory's face took on an expression of stoic patience. He ignored Bea's outburst and turned toward Ruth. "You're young, and you have the talent, brains, and ambition to win the election for district attorney up here next fall. Hands down. I don't doubt that you'll move right on up the political ladder. Governor Ruth Cameron Attenberry someday. I can picture that. United States Senator Ruth Cameron Attenberry. I can picture that."

"*President* Attenberry," Ruth said. "Picture *that*."

"I can. I honestly can. But that kind of ambition takes full-time dedication, and you know it. And it takes money. Think what kind of start you'd get, Ruth, with the political nest egg you'd have if you and the others here form a partnership with my investors."

"Well, Emory, it's always intriguing when you say these things, but I picture myself as a populist, you know, a woman of the people, with grassroots support—"

"Be a populist, Ruth. But be a realist, too."

She frowned. "Look, I'm the only one here who's fully committed to your plan, but I think it's safe to say Isabel and Min agree with me but haven't been ready to vote before. This deal *is* going to happen for you, all right? You don't have to go through this litany of our individual worries each time."

"I'm only presenting the logical argument, Ruthie." Emory looked at Olivia. "There's certainly nothing I could say to you that I haven't said a thousand times over the years, is there?"

Olivia wrote on a notepad, then pushed the pad to Bea. Bea read, "'You speak to our fears and our vanities, not our true hearts.'"

Emory sighed. "Despite our unpleasant disagreements you have to believe that my dearest wish is that you and Bea spend your last years here in serenity. Free from worry," he went on with strained patience, "knowing that the family's interests are cared for and protected, and that your loved ones will always have a home here, at the same time proud in the knowledge that you've entrusted this property to the most skilled professional management-and-development people in the hotel industry."

Olivia looked at me for some show of drama and response. I glanced away, stone-faced. There was a lot of common sense in Emory's perspective, oily though he was. I couldn't honestly argue he was wrong. Olivia rapped her cane on the table. I jerked my gaze back to hers then, and she tried to communicate through ferocious scrutiny.

Why should I care? I wanted to say. She'd shown me no mercy when she'd encouraged Ella and Carter's wedding. She was an arrogant old woman who wanted everything her own way. I was her pawn. She'd invited me and Ella to her private kingdom not out of concern for us but to liven up her own depressed brood.

"Let's stop at this point and watch the tape Joseph and his team put together," Emory said. "It's something new. I think it's going to finally convince y'all to make a decision."

Joseph pressed the VCR's play button. A misty, gorgeous aerial view of the mountains appeared on the screen. "I hired a photographer and sent him up in a small plane to get these shots," Joseph said. As the aerial camera moved with slow grandeur among the mountaintops, ethereal dulcimer and flute music rose. It had a vaguely Celtic lilt.

A melodious-voiced narrator intoned, "Welcome to the Cameron Mountains of eastern Tennessee. A place of breathtaking splendor and beauty. A place where hospitality and history merge into a unique experience waiting for you, our privileged guest. A world that will replenish your soul with its charm and majesty. Welcome to a land so rare that to glimpse it is to never forget the magic. Welcome to"—the music swelled dramatically—"Cameron Hall Grande Resort!"

The name *Cameron Hall Grande Resort* appeared in elaborate scrolled letters. The announcer began describing the resort while the video segued artistically from handsome shots of the Hall and the valley to glorious full-color architectural drawings of planned additions, which would all be discreetly situated to preserve the ambiance of the wild valley. A tennis center. A conference center capable of hosting groups of two to three hundred. A spa. A rustic but luxurious hotel overlooking the opposite end of the valley. A state-of-the-art riding stable with a show ring.

"And at the heart of it all, the Inn at Cameron Hall," the announcer went on. The Hall appeared on the screen again, obviously filmed for some earlier production, since the trees around it were vividly colored in autumn reds and golds. "The Inn at Cameron Hall," the announcer repeated, "where you will be hosted in luxurious historic surroundings by the Cameron family themselves. Where five-star gourmet meals are offered with down-home southern hospitality. An inn where your every modern wish is granted but the spirit of serene good-living remains in every smile.

"And yet," the announcer continued solemnly, "your visit to Cameron Hall Grande Resort offers so much more." An intricate color drawing of a handsome stone-and-wood building appeared on-screen. "A place where the history and culture of the Tennessee frontier is cherished and preserved. A place where the curious visitor and the serious researcher can study the Cameron collection of pioneer and Cherokee Indian artifacts. A place filled with rare books, documents, and photographs. A facility with computer links to major historical and genealogical libraries throughout the Appalachian Mountains. A place where the love for two hundred and fifty years of Cameron heritage can be summed up in the heart and soul of one man who epitomized home, family, and hospitality. The Simon Cameron History Center."

Min gasped. The tape ended with more shots of the mountains, the ethereal background music fading into poignant silence. I felt as if I'd been greased with a foul perfume. Emory Cameron had mastered the art of manipulation. He'd pinpointed Min as the most vulnerable link in the family, and set up a major dilemma for her and the others. "Oh, God," Min whispered. "That would be *wonderful.*"

"I knew you'd like the history center," Emory said. He rubbed his hands together. "I suggest that you all take a vote on the proposal right now."

My gaze shot to Gib, who unfolded his arms and said, "You didn't include me in your argument."

"I believe you already understand what's at stake, Gib. I have faith in your unimpeachable sense of duty. You don't like me at all, but you wouldn't be here today if you weren't ready to listen."

"You don't want to talk about my part in this situation because there's no way to sugarcoat it." Gib held up his maimed hand. "There's no persuasive speech you can aim in my direction."

"All right, Gib. You want me to lay it on the line? I will. I know you've had job offers. You could walk out of here tomorrow and work for some of the most respected private-security firms in the country. You've been asked to come on as a full-equity partner with some retired agents who have their own high-level security firms. With your background, you could even start your own firm.

"Or you could work for any one of a dozen major national corporations who'd hire an ex–Secret Service agent to coordinate security for their facilities and personnel. And I believe in my heart that if you're honest about it you'll admit right now that you'd dearly love to take one of those job offers. Stop kidding yourself. Stop hanging on. You're not doing the future of your family any service by deceiving them and yourself about your true wishes."

Silence. We all looked at Gib. I clenched my hands under the table. "The only important truth is this," Gib said. "The day we went to the sawmill Simon and I had a helluva argument over the future of the valley. Everybody knows that. But what I remember most is that he didn't want to accept your plan. He was just worried that you were right and there might not be any alternative. I tried to convince him there were other choices."

"You're avoiding the point," Emory said in a soothing tone, as if pressing for honesty were painful to his sympathetic nature. "My plan *is* the only sensible way to go. Simon knew that deep down. I don't see how, considering your disability, and your lack of expertise managing this kind of business, I just don't see how you can find enough help—and the right kind of expert help, the kind of people who could really allow you and Min and your sisters to take Simon's place and position the Hall for future success."

Silence. Isabel began dabbing her eyes. "Let's get it over with. Let's vote."

"I have to agree," Min said dully. "Aunt Olivia, please forgive me."

Ruth cradled one of Olivia's hands in hers. "Aunt Olly, I don't want to vote against you and Gib. Please don't make me do that." Ruth gazed up at Gib. To my shock, there were tears in her eyes. "Big brother, I wish I agreed with you about leaving things the way they are, but I just don't see how we can do that."

"I have a plan," Gib said. Silence. Everyone stared at him. He dropped his hands to his sides, the maimed one, as always, slightly hidden behind his right hip. His left hand curled and uncurled slowly. "We contact everyone on the inn's mailing list. Put the word out. We reopen the first weekend in January. That gives us the rest of the year—three months—to get organized, to learn new routines working together, and get the Hall in top-notch condition."

Emory sighed patiently. "Very few people visit here in the winter months unless they've just come to the mountains to ski. The weather's too unpredictable. You see, Gib, you're not even aware how a simple problem such as that guides the seasonal business of managing an inn."

"He's right about the winter months," Min said gently.

Gib took a deep breath. "Of course, I know that. Winter bookings are slow. That's the point. We'd only have a few guests until spring. We could handle that—we'd practice on them. We won't take reservations for every weekend, either. Just the first and third weekends of each month, to start. We'll have plenty of down time to analyze and correct our mistakes and then prepare for the next round of guests. I say we try it."

"I say you stop procrastinating and vote," Emory countered.

"Gib, can't you admit that Emory's plan is reasonable?" Ruth asked quietly. "It takes wholehearted commitment to supervise this place. None of us wants the responsibility, and we're not going to judge you if you don't want it, either. It's not as if we'd be selling out. We'll be partners with these investors of Emory's. We'll still have a home here. We'll have a say in how the valley's developed, and we'll still control the Hall."

"We'll be tenants on our own land."

"You'll be honored partners," Emory countered. "Consultants. Board members. And you'll all be rich."

"But you'll be the richest of all, you bloody bastard," Bea said.

Emory sighed. "I'll be investing a lot of my own money, Bea. Of *course* I expect a healthy return on it."

Joseph stood. "Just take a little bitty vote," he prodded in a smooth voice. He grinned at his father. "Like Daddy here always says, There's no time like the present."

"Sit down, Joey," Ruth ordered, "or I'll bite a plug out of your present."

Tension crackled in the air. "Agreed?" Emory said, smiling. "All right? Accept my proposal, or reject my proposal. Accept or reject. We'll go around the table. Minnie, you first. *Accept?*"

Her face went white. Tears slid down her cheeks. Isabel began to cry, too. Ruth frowned into space. Gib's stony resistance began to lose ground. It was something barely defined, but I saw defeat sinking him down as if with invisible weights.

I couldn't let him go down alone. Crowded behind my conscience were all the years I wished I had known what to do for Pop at his most vulnerable moments, all those years I'd spent agonizing over how I might have made a difference if

I'd only recognized how alone he felt. If I did nothing for Gib now, if he was forced to turn his family's legacy over to Emory, he'd never recover. Some part of him would be angry and sick with defeat for the rest of his life.

I owed him a measure of loyalty; I owed his brother, Simon, a huge debt of gratitude; I owed this entire family for caring enough to want us here, even if it was for their own purposes. I could make a difference, for once. "What about *my* vote?" I blurted.

Everyone stared at me. Ruth snorted. "You don't have a vote. You shouldn't even be hanging around the voting *booth*."

"I certainly *do* have a vote. All of you have been trying to convince me that my sister and I are full-fledged Cameron kin now. Well, *fine*. But that means you have to put your, your *democracy where your mouth is*. Therefore, I deserve a vote. In fact, Ella gets a vote, too. And why doesn't Carter already have a vote? And Bea? How did she get left out?"

I met Gib's eyes and saw a certain gleam, challenging and intense. I couldn't tell if it was admiration for my bravado or just plain curiosity over the meltdown I had started.

Emory rapped the table with his knuckles. "Family votes that involve property issues are voted on solely by Aunt Olivia and her immediate heirs."

"Why? The rest of us have to live here, too. The vote affects us."

"Legally, it makes no sense for anyone other than direct heirs to have a say—"

"Legally, these property votes are informal and only Aunt Olivia's vote really counts," Ruth corrected. "Her name's the only one on the deed."

"She can make the decision herself, alone, if she wants to," Gib noted.

"Herself has ne'er been a true tyrant and ne'er will be," Bea said. "She does no' want to force her choices on her loved ones."

No, she prefers to coax, bully, and charm us, I thought with a sudden admiration that surprised me. "So what you're saying is"—I looked innocently from Gib to the sisters and Min, then to Bea and finally Olivia—"that Olivia can choose who votes today and who doesn't."

"Exactly," Gib said.

"Nonsense," Emory countered.

Olivia tapped the table with the head of her cane. She pointed at me. "Me?" I said. "Do I get a vote?" She nodded regally. "And Ella?" She nodded again.

Ruth groaned. "When pigs fly."

"And Carter?"

Another nod.

"And Bea, too, then," Isabel added eagerly.

Olivia nodded.

I grinned. "So we can't take a vote, because Ella and Carter aren't even here."

Olivia nodded.

"Gib?" Isabel said, as a small, hopeful look spread across her face. "You're really interested in reopening the Hall?"

"Is this serious?" Ruth interjected. "Have you and Venus de Milo here been cooking up something together?"

"What we've been discussing is hard to describe," Gib said, staring at me. "Why don't you try, Nellie?"

"Well, if I have to spell it out for everybody, I will. You can't tell me on the one hand I'm going to have the exalted position of musical director of Cameron Hall, while on the other hand you decide to make this deal with Emory. You promised me a place in this family, dammit. Not a job working for a bunch of investors. Or for Emory. For you, Gib Cameron. I consider your word to me as good as a signed contract."

"Musical director, my ass," Ruth said. I'd made that up. She knew it, too.

"Just grease up my little pig wings, Ruthie. Y'all have to remember that Ella and I were raised by a father who owned a successful nightclub in the French Quarter of New Orleans. We don't just know the *music* business. We know audiences, customers, the general public—their care and feeding, their habits and habitats. They're a strange beast, but fairly easy to tame. So I have no doubt that we can help Gib and Min and everybody manage the inn pretty well. For one thing, I'll play the piano in the evenings. I'm sure Ella will assist me. Not only by playing duets for the guests but . . . well, my sister is a perfect hostess. Between her and Min and Isabel, the gracious southern hospitality factor should be pretty well covered. There. That's all I have to say. If I'm out of a job before I've even started, then I want to know *today*."

"This is ludicrous," Emory said. He looked as if his eyes might pop. Olivia looked at me with quiet pleasure.

"No, it's *not* ludicrous," Min said suddenly. "If Gib feels that he's ready to try—just two weekends a month starting in January—then we have to try. And if Venus—who is new to our family—if a newcomer like Venus has so much faith in our ability to start over, then I'm sorry, Emory, but we just have to make the effort."

"I was ready to tell my investors we had a deal!"

"Tell them you were wrong," Gib said.

"I've been placating these people for a long time. All right, all right, here's the bottom line." He jabbed a finger at Gib. "I predict that the opening weekend is all it will take to prove I'm right. One weekend." He swept his hand at Min and the rest of us. "That's all y'all are going to need to see that you can't manage here without Simon. So I'll come back for a vote in January. Right after the opening weekend. And it has to be a final vote. No second chances after January, Minnie. No history center named after Simon. And no college money for Dylan, Isabel. No campaign nest egg, Ruthie. If you turn me down in January you'll regret it for the rest of your lives."

"Your money men will wait until January," Ruth said

brusquely. "They think we're sitting on a gold mine here. They'll wait."

Min said wistfully, "Could you run the tape back and let me see the part about the history center again?"

"Run it back," Emory ordered, snapping his fingers at Joseph, who hurried to comply. Min leaned forward with one hand knuckled to her lips, intensely studying the drawing of the center again, while the narrator described the wonderful facility that would bear Simon's name. My eyes stung and I stared at the table. I had no idea if I'd done the right thing by interfering or not.

"You wouldn't drop this history center from the plans, would you?" Min asked Emory. "I mean, if we told you this winter that we agreed to your development idea, this history center would still be part of it?"

Emory came to her and clasped her hands. "Minnie, I *want* to honor Simon. I promise you that we'll build the history center in his name. But Minnie, you don't need to wait. Don't be confused by Gib and his . . . consort's wishful thinking." He stared at me. "Young . . . lady, you and your sister have ingratiated yourselves into this family in a very remarkable and sudden way. I have misgivings about your motivations." He glanced around magnanimously, finally settling his gaze on Gib. "Let's not mistake unflattering ambitions for serious loyalty."

Min drew her hands away and gave him an icy look. "That's not fair, Emory. Venus hasn't done anything to deserve that, and I'm ashamed you said it."

"Absolutely," Isabel agreed with head-shaking indignation.

Ruth looked grim. "I couldn't care less about Venus's part in this. She's irrelevant. The family's objections to voting right now are sustained, Emory. If I were your judge I'd suggest that you plea-bargain."

"This meeting's over," Gib announced. He had a look that could wilt flowers. He'd learned it in the Secret Service, no doubt, where agents deliberately made eye contact with people in crowds, analyzing, warning, threatening them without a word. I'd read somewhere that the best "eye men" could make a heckler shut up or ward off much worse.

The look worked because it was backed up by a Zen-like concentration that bespoke total dedication and lack of self-concern. Even though I understood the mechanism—music is built on attitudes, and presenting music to an audience is an exercise in reckless wing-walking and crowd control—I was afraid when Gib looked at Emory that way. Gib said to him softly, "Don't ever walk into this house again and insult anyone I invited under this roof. You think I'm not up to filling Simon's shoes. Well, hell, I agree with you. But my brother wouldn't allow you to insult a guest or a family member, and I won't either."

Emory held up both hands. He pivoted toward me. "I'm sorry. I meant nothing but the most sincere concern."

"Oh, shut up, you bloody fool," Bea said.

"I'll be back in January."

My tour de force of total showmanship had changed the course of Cameron history—at least for the next few months. And it was quite possible I'd doomed these people and the place they loved so deeply. These people included Ella now. And by extension, me.

I skittered a glance at Olivia. Her silent mouth quirked at one corner. Her eyes glowed.

Whether I'd meant to or not, I had served her purpose grandly.

"Why did you do it?" Gib asked. We stood in Simon's office. The shades had been drawn for over a year; the big, comfortable space smelled musty.

"Because to me Emory and Joseph represent all the smug, judgmental, self-entitled *haves* in a *have-not* world. I don't like them. I've dealt with men like them for years."

"That's not good enough. Why did you do it?" he asked again.

"Because Emory's plan would change everything that's *brave* about this valley and your family."

"Why?" he insisted.

"Because I need a job to do here." My voice rose. "I have to stay busy or I'll lose my mind worrying about Ella!"

"Why?" he said between gritted teeth.

I sank into an old wooden desk chair with rumpsprung damask pillows. I shut my eyes. "Because I'd like to stay here and help you if I can."

He touched my cheek with the backs of his fingers. I looked up at him breathlessly. He sat down on the edge of the desk. "By God, Nellie," he said in a soft voice, "if we can't do this together then it can't be done."

"Was Emory right? Have you had job offers?"

"Yes."

"Would you really rather move on? Tell me. I'm not really part of your family, so you can't hurt me with the truth." What a lie, but it sounded good.

"There have been days—" He paused. Then, "Weeks, months, when all I could think about was walking away from everything here. But not now."

"Why?"

He looked heavenward. "Oh, why does she ask *why*?" Then he looked at me, arching a brow. "Turnabout is fair play?"

"Why?" I persisted.

"I'm getting stronger."

"Why?"

"I'm accepting what happened to my brother as an accident. I don't blame myself as much. Going back to the sawmill was a turning point."

"Why?" I said.

"For God's sake. Because I'm starting to think I might actually belong here, running this inn, under the right circumstances." He slapped his legs. "Now, the first thing we have to do is get to work on that mailing. I'll go through the inn's computer files. I'll get Min to help me. But there's a helluva lot to do, Nellie. We'll be busy for the next three months. Painting, polishing, fixing. There'll be menus to discuss with FeeMolly, food supplies to order, liquor and the wine cellar to be inventoried and restocked, plus the Hall will have to be cleaned from top to bottom—all the guest bedrooms, the communal rooms—and you have to do whatever it is you do to plan your musical performances or whatever you call them."

"I'll go to the cottage," I said dryly, "change into some grungier clothes, and be right back to start disciplining that darned lazy piano of yours." I hurried to the door.

"Nellie," he called. I halted. His voice, deep and warm, went through me.

"Hmmm?" I glanced back at him.

"*Why* have I stopped thinking about leaving?" He paused, then nodded to me. "Because it's interesting to see what you're going to do every day. So far, you've put on a helluva show."

"Oh? The prospect of aggravating me gives you a reason to get up every morning?"

He laughed, flicked a switch on a desk lamp, and turned away.

Twenty

"You're the *what*?" Ella asked. She stood in the library still holding her cosmetic bag and wearing a filmy peach-colored dress that Carter had bought for her during a shopping trip in Chicago. A pea-sized diamond perched on the third finger of her left hand. Like a hen on a nest of eggs, it sat on a cluster of smaller diamonds.

Our RV was history, my sister was gloriously happy for the moment, and Carter was being dutifully polite to me, as I was to him. I think Ella was shocked that I calmly welcomed her back with the news of my new status.

"I'm the Hall's musical director," I repeated. "And you're my assistant." I looked at her over the baby grand, where I'd spread out lists of several hundred pop tunes and classics. I'd offered to discuss the selections with Gib—not because I wanted his input, but to honor his detail-oriented angst. "The inn's re-opening in January," I added.

She laughed, bounded over, and hugged me. "I knew you'd fit right in here as soon as I gave you a little push!"

"You didn't give me a push. You jumped off a cliff and I jumped after you."

Her smile faded. "I've never been happier, Vee. I'll just

be patient and let you see for yourself until you're convinced." Her gaze went to the lid of the piano. She caught her
breath.

I'd placed Mom and Pop's wedding photo there.

"We'll work seven days a week until the end of the year, if we
have to," Gib said, surveying clouds of dust motes that rose
every time he pushed a fist into the cushions of a couch in an
upstairs bedroom. He glanced out the window. "The lawns
need to be fertilized and mowed one last time before winter.
There're tons of leaves to get up. The gardens have to be
plowed. And every pipe in this house has to be checked for
leaks and loose insulation. All the chimneys have to be
cleaned, and—"

Ruth grunted. "This is a crazy idea. We need more than
three months to get ready. And we need an army to get this
house back in spotless condition. We should have voted for
Emory's proposal."

"Either leave or get to work, but don't complain," Gib
ordered.

She grimaced. "I'm just playing devil's advocate."

I coughed. "I can easily picture you with a pitchfork and
a forked tail."

She looked at me. "I picture you the same way."

I smiled.

Isabel and Min stayed in the office with Gib all one October afternoon, compiling the mailing list, writing a promo-
tional letter, and running off thousands of address labels.
Ruth called her businessman husband, Paul, who was one of
the Attenborough Attenberrys and therefore a distant relation
to his own wife's family. She had him send a delivery man
from Knoxville with more envelopes and stamps.

Ella and I were so tired from wrestling linens in twenty
bedrooms in the main house that we didn't bother to read the
one-page form letter printed on the Hall's handsome crested

stationery. My job was placing folded letters into the envelopes. By midnight the last envelope was done and we all got up and just stood there looking at one another, over head-high stacks bound with rubber bands.

"Maybe I'll sleep soundly tonight," Min said. "For the first time in months, I'm tired in a way that feels comfortable."

She wandered away for a glass of water, Isabel followed her, Ruth went to a phone to tell Paul she was on her way home, and Jasper and Kelly staggered into the den of the family room and collapsed on a couch. Ella stretched languidly and blushed as Carter clumped into the kitchen. He'd been at the barns all day. "I've just about got that roan mare trained not to bite anybody," he said. "I tell you, Gib, I'll use her on trail rides and the guests won't have to worry about a single nibble."

"Sounds like a plan," Gib said. "Next you can work on Ruth's bad habits."

Carter guffawed as he swept Ella into his arms. "You ready to go to our little land-boat and snuggle for the night?"

"Mind if I bite your ear?" she cooed.

"I can't wait."

"Good-night," Ella called as she disappeared with Carter out the kitchen's porch door.

"Good-night," I said flatly. Gib and I were left at the table. I noticed an extra letter had fallen on the floor. "I'll toss this in the trash." I walked out onto the back porch, where moths fluttered around a small light fixture overhead. I glanced over the letter as I started to drop it in a tall galvanized trashcan.

My eyes stopped at the sight of my own name.

This fall we welcome several new additions to our family. Our Oklahoma cousin, Carter MacIntosh, has joined us as manager of the stables and livestock. Carter will be offering guided horseback trail rides and buffalo cart tours of the valley. Carter's wife, Ella, will be one of our new hostesses at the inn. Last but not least, Ella's sister, Venus Arinelli, a world-class concert pianist, will perform nightly on the baby grand in the Hall's music room.

I read that last part several times.

"Is something wrong?" Gib asked quietly. I turned. He was leaning inside the porch's screen door. He held a short, fresh cigar between the thumb and forefinger of his bad hand, and awkwardly moved the cigar to his lips as he watched me. He flicked a kitchen match nimbly inside the palm of his good hand, and the flame cast provocative shadows on his face as he lit the cigar.

It was an impressively macho trick, striking a match on his own skin. But the contrast between that and the stiff, distorted fingers of his right hand was distinct. He fumbled with the cigar and finally wedged it between his fingertips. When he took it from his mouth and exhaled, his expression had become strained.

"My hand must be hypnotic," he said, "because you never answered me."

"Maybe I needed a minute to get myself together." I held up the letter.

He relaxed a little. "You don't like being included? Min wrote it, but Ruth and Olivia and I agreed on the wording. Is it a problem for some reason?"

"No. It's . . . just been a long time since anyone referred to me as a concert pianist. Much less a *world-class* concert pianist."

"You think that's false advertising?"

"I don't know anymore."

"Well, look at it this way. You've got a reputation to live up to." He flicked a thin cap of ash from the cigar tip, studied his clumsy, scarred fingers for a moment, nodded good-night to me, and walked out onto the porch, past me and down the steps.

"Thank you for remembering what I used to be," I said.

He turned in the darkness. "I'm looking at what you are now. And it's true."

He walked on, disappearing in the night.

I folded the letter and put it in my pocket.

Gib, Min, and I crowded into Gib's jeep and went to the tiny post office in the back room of Hoss's store in New Inverness. "Glory be," Hoss enthused as we carried in a half-dozen large boxes filled with stamped and sealed envelopes.

"So many people to contact! I never would have thought!" Sophia sang out, reaching over the scarred wooden ledge of the office window to take each box.

"About five thousand," Gib said. He took the last box from Min and levered it over the ledge. Hoss and Sophia stacked it atop the others.

Min looked at the head-high pile of boxes wistfully. "Simon and I never sent out big mailings like this. We kept a list of guests from the very beginning, but after the first few years we never had to solicit new business. We had to turn people away unless they booked rooms months in advance."

I nabbed a package of peanuts from a shelf above a fat, humming, dew-speckled soft-drink cooler. "Well, with five thousand on this mailing we should at least get a one-percent return. So maybe fifty people will book rooms during the winter weekends. That'll be a nice, modest start."

"Except that Simon and Min used to get fifty people a day," Gib said, scowling.

"Well, we'll practice on our fifty during January. See whether you can master the fine art of hosting." I grinned at him fiendishly.

He grunted. "I was the agent in charge when the king of a Scandinavian country and two of his mistresses wanted to go out of the White House and eat real American soul food in Washington after midnight. If I could get that clueless bunch through dinner at a rib shack where the locals tried to shake down the king's personal valet for pocket change, I believe I can make a good impression on the plain, ordinary guests we might entice back to the Hall."

"Well, well, well, you're getting uppity now that you've got a mission in life," I joked. I wiped my hands on the legs of the baggy blue overalls Min had presented to me as a joke. "You're a hillbilly now," she had said wryly. But I had stitched rows of gold sequins on the shoulder straps and I wore the overalls with my Tchaikovsky Rules T-shirt underneath. I heard that after Ruth saw my customized outfit she told Isabel I looked like a circus clown. Thinking of that, I nibbled peanuts delicately, and frowned.

"You don't know how to eat goobers," Gib said. He dismissed my little bag of store-bought nuts with a shake of his head.

"What? I'm as southern as you are."

"You grew up in New Orleans, city girl. It's not the same. Come on. I'll show you." We walked outside. Min stayed behind with Sophia to look over cruise-ship brochures. Her expression said she was tired and impatient. Sophia was trying to coax her to come along on the Hightower Garden Club's seven-day winter cruise in the Caribbean.

Out in the bright October sunshine, with just a hint of cool autumn in the air, I followed Gib to the jeep and got in. He drove up the state route toward Hightower, then swung off on the roadside where a ramshackle fruit stand sat under the trees. Smoke wafted from a fifty-gallon steel drum set on a makeshift grate over a wood fire. The yard was outlined with empty fruit crates, and the top of each crate was crowded with jars of fresh honey, homemade jellies, pickles, and relishes. The scent of apples and cinnamon curled deliciously from the tailgate of an old pickup truck, where mounds of fried apple pies lay cooling in a shallow cardboard box beside a bubbling pot of oil on a gas grill.

A small old man spotted Gib and came out of the fruit stand, waving like crazy. "I re-COG-no-sized you right off!"

he said. "I threw up my hand and started a-woving 'fore you set foot on the ground! Hit's been a long spell since I seen ya out and about!"

Gib introduced me to Golwat; that was his name—first or last, I couldn't tell. I learned later that Golwat lived in an old one-room lumberjack's shanty high up in a hollow, and he got a pension from his years as a railroad lineman, plus what income he made at his fruit stand. He was FeeMolly's *man friend*. Ebb and Flo's biological father had died when they were children. Golwat had been FeeMolly's casual paramour for years.

"I could use you if you need a little work this fall," Gib told him. "FeeMolly needs extra hands to shuck and peel and slice. She got a late start on her canning this year. You come by the Hall anytime your arthritis isn't acting up."

"I sure will be there," Golwat promised. "I got my ear full of news about the Hall already. God bless." He pointed at me. "Ma'am, you done got The Cameron out in the 'shine. Good to see him."

I smiled diplomatically but noticed Gib's frown at the title Golwat gave him. "We need some boiled pinders and whatever else the lady wants," Gib said.

Golwat hustled to the steaming steel drum and lifted a ladle made from a large clean coffee can wired to the end of a broom handle. Rich brown liquid drained from holes in the can's bottom. He dumped boiled peanuts into a double paper sack.

I gathered several hot fried apple pies on a paper plate then turned around with money in my hand, only to find Gib paying the elderly man already. As we drove away I said, "Deduct that from my salary."

"You said you didn't want a salary."

"Maybe I should change my mind so I'll have a salary to deduct your gifts from."

"Consider boiled peanuts and apple pies a perk of your grand title as musical director. Here. Eat the peanuts this way." He pressed the tip of a steaming brown peanut shell to his lips. Then he sucked for a second. "Get the juice first," he explained. Next he parted the soggy shell with his tongue and sucked the peanuts out. Then he neatly spit the empty shell out his open window. "Biodegradable litter," he said.

Watching him work a peanut with his lips and tongue had pretty much put me in an altered state of mind. Peanuts, boiled or otherwise, were the last thing I could think about. "Demonstrate your technique again," I said.

He did. Slowly. I'm sure he knew peanuts had ceased to be the motivation for either of us.

Min ran into the kitchen at dawn two days later. Gib, Isabel, Flo, and I were groggily testing the first experimental cups of coffee from a ten-gallon commercial percolator Flo had unpacked from a storage room. FeeMolly had ordered bags of a new gourmet bean she'd seen on a cable cooking show. "I don't like this blend," Isabel announced.

"Too tangy," Gib said.

I coughed. "I think the spice scent singed the hair in my nose."

"Dear God," Min moaned. We all turned quickly. Gib grabbed her arm. She was as white as a sheet. "Dear God," she repeated. "There are one hundred and twenty-two messages on the answering machine in Simon's office. I counted them. The letter's only been out for two days *and there are one hundred and twenty-two messages*."

We hurried en masse to the old kitchen building and gathered around the desk. The red signal light on the answering machine was flashing so fast it almost flickered. Gib pushed the playback button. Isabel grabbed a notepad. "I'll make a list."

We listened in silent amazement as one excited caller after another requested a room. A terrifying number asked specifically for the opening weekend. When the last message ended Min studied Isabel's notes. "Oh, my Lord. All of these people want to book the first weekend in January? Gib, this isn't a *slow* seasonal start. *This is a full house!* And these are professionals!"

Gib frowned. "What do you mean?"

She pointed. "He owns a travel agency. She's with the state tourism commission. He's a reviewer for *Tennessee Travels* magazine. She's a travel agent. All of these people are *experts.*" She sat down weakly. "We're going to be *reviewed.*"

Gib bent over her and rubbed her limp hands. "I promise you we'll make Simon proud," he said.

But when he met my eyes he was worried.

Ella and I were suddenly caught up in daily meetings conducted by Min, who lectured on everything from proper check-in procedures to which bed linens to use in the guest rooms—soft brushed-flannel sheets and pillowcases in the winter, she said. Gib, Carter, and Jasper worked constantly outdoors, pressure-washing the Hall's stone walls, painting the wooden fences along the front pastures, mulching, raking, mowing, pruning.

Like everyone else on the place, I helped with any chore that needed doing. I cleaned guest rooms, washed windows, set out the winter cabbage plants in the garden and the autumn seedlings for the flower beds. I shooed raccoons from the garbage, chased a possum from the dogs' dishes, and captured the litter of half-grown kittens who regularly darted around the halls.

"Those weeds are my lavender plants," Min said very gently one day. "They'll come back in the spring if you don't pull them up." I was in the herb garden out back, vigorously plucking withered plants from the ground.

"Oh, shit. I'm sorry." I began frantically shoving lavender roots back into the loamy soil. Min knelt down and helped me.

"They'll be fine," she soothed. "They're pretty tough. Slow down. There. That's it. Baby them a little." She looked at me curiously. "You and Gib have been like whirlwinds around here. Did y'all make a pact to outwork each other?"

"I can't speak for him, but I'm just a naturally obsessive person."

"I used to be. Believe it or not, I was a dynamo. Simon and I were up at dawn each day, always talking, planning, working."

"Everyone says you've been a lot perkier in the past few weeks. You're doing great."

"Look at this." She held out a lean, pale forearm and pushed up the sleeve of her sweater. "Dry skin. That's not the least bit 'perky.' "

"Use some of that honey-and-wildflower lotion Isabel makes. She taught Ella how to mix it up and Ella gave me a bottleful, and it's great. Of course we all attract bees now, but—"

"I'm drying up." Her expression all at once serious to the point of despair, she clutched her hands on the knees of her denim skirt. "I'm forty-six years old and I'm so lonely for my husband in bed, *and I am drying up.*"

I didn't think of her as a mother figure, I thought of her as an older sister, and that was very appealing to me. "You're not old," I advised calmly. "And you need to let yourself think about, well, Min, about *dating.*"

She bowed her head. "I've never said this to anyone but you. There are times when . . . all I can think about is Simon. But there are times when I am so desperate—in bed by myself at night—that I think any old handsome stranger could walk into the room and I'd jump on him."

"That's healthy. You should want to make love. It's not healthy to do without." I bent my head close to Min's. "Bo Burton," I whispered slyly.

"Ack!" She got up, her face turning bright pink. "Oh, he's a big, sweet, silly dog! I was friends with his wife! *Good* friends. And Bo was good friends with Simon! Why! Oh, you! Vee!" She hurried back into the house, obviously flustered beyond coherence.

Bo Burton. He was the one for Min. Any man who could fluster a woman that way had the inside track on her desires. Yes. The Camerons had meddled in my life, so I would meddle in theirs.

On one of the rare mornings when no major chores or meetings were planned, I walked out on the cottage porch and halted, stunned. The forest's tentative autumn colors had fully bloomed, overnight, into brilliant reds and golds. A late frost had turned autumn spiderwebs into silver lace hanging among the tree limbs. I went out in the yard, tilted my head back, and turned in a circle, slowly.

I ran for my keyboard, set it up on the porch, and worked all morning on my music. I wanted to write songs to those mountains, to celebrate them, to find where they were inside me and turn the emotion into sound.

And then I put on new hiking shoes I'd bought in a shop in Hightower. I took the peeled-birch hiking stick Jasper had made for me, and I walked blindly into the forest. I wanted more inspiration.

Gib tracked me to a high mountain bald late that afternoon. I was relieved to see him and upset at the predicament. I'd been enchanted by the mountains. Gib tried to look nonchalant despite the fact that on his back he was packing a first-aid kit, water, food, thermal blankets, a portable ham radio, a rifle, and his machete. "I was just wandering through the neighborhood," he said.

"Carrying gear for an expedition?"

"You know the Boy Scout motto."

"Always be gentlemanly and pretend the chick's not lost?"

"Something like that. When we couldn't find you I was afraid you'd been carried off or eaten."

"All right, I admit it. I got carried *away*."

He radioed to the Hall, where Ella insisted on speaking to me in tearful disbelief. "I wasn't lost," I lied. "I was exploring."

Gib and I walked back down the mountain into a deeply sided lane that wandered through the low coves and hollows. "I was just following this old trail," I explained. "I thought it must come out on a public road somewhere." Gesturing toward the steep sides, I added, "Someone must have bulldozed this trail years ago. I mean, it's cut so deep in places."

"This trail was here a *thousand* years ago," Gib said quietly. "And probably for thousands before that. It wasn't cut by machines. It was worn into the earth by buffalo herds and war parties and traders between the southern tribes and the northern ones. If you knew where to look for what's left of it, you could follow this trail all the way to Canada."

I halted. The ground felt rich beneath my feet. "I read somewhere, there's a theory, that prehistoric Asian tribes came over the Bering Strait and settled in the Americas, and that the Native Americans are their descendants."

He nodded. "So you're feeling a little déjà vu? Reclaiming the old prehistoric stomping grounds?" But his teasing was gentle.

"Did you know Elvis might have been a Turk?"

"What?"

"His ancestors came from a part of the mountains where there were descendants of Turks and Moors and Portuguese and all sorts of Mediterranean people who had been brought to the New World by Spain in the fifteen hundreds. These beautiful black-haired people and their languages. Elvis is a town in Portugal. It's not spelled the same as our Elvis, but still—"

"I could believe Elvis was a Turk," Gib admitted. "I could believe he was from Mars after he entered his sequined jumpsuit phase."

"Oh, don't humor me. I'm giddy."

"There are no outsiders here. Nobody who belongs more than any other kind. Your Asian ancestors may have walked this path when it was just a twinkle in the mountain's eyes. And since they begat the Indians, and since I've got a little Indian blood in *me*, we're probably related, Nellie. So you *are* family. Blood kin. Make you feel better?"

"Your line of reasoning is more outrageous than mine. And that's saying a lot."

"You set out into the mountains because they called to you. Your instincts heard and responded. You're home." He cocked his head and listened. "I can hear them right now." He crooned in a droll, singsong voice, "Welcome back, modern descendant of really old Asians. Don't forget to pack a compass."

"You fool," I said, but couldn't help laughing.

He pointed. "Look. Up there. That ridge. My grandfather's cousin Jonathan Cameron shot and ate turkeys to keep from starving when he was trapped up on that ridge with a broken leg. It was right after his wife left him. She was afraid to live in the mountains. And she was mad as hell because she'd found out that Jonathan was running whisky. In fact he'd become the local liquor baron. We're talking nineteen thirties. Depression era. The family was nearly bankrupt. Jonathan saved the day by bootlegging liquor. Cuban rum he bought off the South Carolina coast. Local sour-mash whisky. Until he crashed his car up on Hodger's Ridge one night with the revenuers after him. He managed to get this far before he collapsed. He nearly died up there before anybody found him."

"What happened to his wife?"

"She came back to take care of him while he recuperated. She stayed and he went legit. They kept a couple of turkey feet and Jonathan had them gilded as an anniversary gift. In the family we've always called that story *The Thrill of Victory and the Agony of De-feet*."

I stared at him. "Is that story true?"

"Of course. I can call their granddaughter in Atlanta if you insist. She inherited the gold turkey feet."

I shook my head. "I guess by Cameron standards that's a perfectly credible tale."

"Not a *tail. Feet.*"

We walked for a while in companionable silence. There was human history, drama, joy, and romance embedded in the land of that valley: the old hedgerows, the faint outlines of houses, cabins, barns still visible in the grass, the tumbled stones of chimneys, the remnants of old fences and old roads. As for the deep path in the woods—I was amazed. Centuries of human and animal traffic had cut the broad path into the hillside. Trees draped it in a golden tunnel.

We were walking back in time. This was the same path the first Cameron walked on his trip there from the coast, another world, half a world away from his homeland, the possession of a woman who must have seemed completely mysterious and dangerous to him.

"It's worth it," I said to Gib. "This valley. It deserves to be left just the way it is. It's worth fighting for."

"Nellie," he said, looking at me intensely, "I think you're coming around. Watch out that you don't fall in love here."

Flustered, I made a big show of scowling at him. He'd never catch me sighing over commemorative turkey feet.

Bea and Olivia held court every afternoon in the private sitting room between their bedrooms. A person had to be invited. Some days the guests were family members, some days a visiting friend. Tea was served with serious formality, in one of Bea's finest china tea sets imported from Scotland and carried in by FeeMolly herself on a heavy sterling tray.

The tea was served scalding hot in teacups as thin as eggshells, so they turned blazing hot as soon as they were filled; there was no way to hold one in any but the most proper manner, clutching the delicate handle, pinky finger stuck out, desperately trying to avoid a burn.

The sitting room Bea shared with Olivia was fascinating and a little creepy—part natural history museum, part Victorian tea parlor, part downtown sports bar. Clusters of bright silk flowers sprouted from odd vases, iron stew pots, and old jars. Frilly flowered drapes decked a row of windows with large velvet bows at the sashes. When the windows were open the room's fringed lampshades shimmied like dancers.

A large poster of the Atlanta Braves was framed on one wall, surrounded by a collection of bats, balls, shirts, and ticket stubs. Most of the items were autographed. Nearby was a shelf full of German beer tankards.

The walls collided at corner knickknack shelves filled with turtle shells, snake skins, jawbones bristling with bear, bobcat, and wild boar teeth, arrowheads, pottery shards, and musket balls. At the center of the room visitors chose high-backed wing chairs and sat around a lace-covered table, facing Bea and Olivia. Olivia sat in a fat, firm mission-style chair with colorful cushions and wide oak armrests, her bare feet propped on a plaid footstool that rocked. Bea sat in a mammoth burgundy leather recliner with controls on the side to make the backrest vibrate.

On that quiet early November afternoon, Ella and I were invited to tea along with Min and Isabel. Afterward, Olivia fell asleep in her chair. Bea placed a Braves stadium rug over Olivia's feet and legs, then touched her fingertips to Olivia's cheek. "She'll sleep sound for the hour. I'll be in the kitchen watching *Oprah* with old FeeMolly." Bea shuffled out of the sitting room.

I cleared my throat. Glancing at Olivia, I whispered, "I can't resist asking this any longer. Is there some reason why she never wears shoes? Why she never cuts her hair?"

Isabel blinked. "She stopped cutting her hair and wearing

shoes at the same time she stopped speaking fifty-plus years ago. It's one of her mysteries."

"What hurt her soul so badly?" Ella asked.

"No one's told you all about her past?" Min asked. "We'll tell you. She doesn't mind."

I shook my head. "I learned enough to decide she needed her privacy. I wouldn't want someone prying into my history, so—"

"She wants you to understand her as much as possible," Isabel said.

Ella, Min, Isabel, and I huddled like the witches in *Macbeth*, stirring the strange, intoxicating brew that was Cameron history. Isabel began to tell us the story.

Olivia Maureen Cameron stopped speaking when she was thirty years old. She hadn't said a word since 1945. Not for any reason. She never made a sound of any kind. She didn't even talk in her sleep.

It wasn't that she didn't want to speak. And nothing was physically wrong. Over the years doctors diagnosed the condition as everything from guilt-induced trauma to psychosomatic illness. She'd been called crazy, stubborn, and just plain odd. In the family, they finally accepted her condition as permanent and harmless.

She had been a pretty young woman. Small framed pictures of her showed an elfin, dark-haired debutante with mischievous light eyes.

She had a sharp mind. She graduated from a women's college in Nashville, won awards for just about every sport and club young women could excel at back then, and was the belle of the ball in Tennessee society.

She wanted to go to Boston and work for a women's magazine there. She was a writer—always had been. But her parents wouldn't have it. Journalism was no career for a woman, and they didn't want her up there being corrupted, in their view, by wild-living northern women and unscrupulous northern men.

Then her mother died and Olivia went to spend a summer with Bea and her family in Scotland. She loved Scotland and became close friends with Bea. She begged to stay with Bea's family indefinitely. But her father made her come home.

A year later she was engaged to marry an older man named J. Ogden Owens, of the Knoxville Owenses, a rich railroad clan. J. Ogden was a widower. His first wife had committed suicide after their baby died in an accident. J. Ogden was also a state senator, and he planned to run for governor. Some suspected he wanted a smart, pretty young wife with the right connections to stop some ugly rumors about his first wife and child.

Because there was gossip that J. Ogden had a violent temper. Yet he could be a charmer, and he was brilliant, handsome, and rich. By the rules of that time a high-strung, hot-blooded gentleman was entitled to a temper.

He and Olivia had a wedding the newspaper society columnists called the biggest of the decade. They honeymooned in Europe, then settled into one of the Owens mansions in Knoxville. Over the next few years Olivia lost two babies in miscarriages, and then she had one, a boy, who barely lived to be a year old.

He fell down a set of stairs and broke his neck. At least that's what was said at the time.

When her boy died Olivia was already pregnant again. She gave birth to a girl named Katherine Maureen. In Olivia's albums there were pictures of her, and baby bonnets, and tiny, embroidered gloves, all pressed for safekeeping. Olivia called her Katie. Katie was a few years old when J. Ogden ran for governor—right after World War II. He won.

He would have become governor of Tennessee. Olivia would have been the state's first lady.

But a week before the inauguration, Katie fell off a balcony at the house in Knoxville. At least the servants gave that account of the accident.

Two days later, Olivia poisoned J. Ogden Owens, her husband, the governor-elect, at breakfast. He died in grotesque, writhing agony by suppertime.

I studied Olivia as she slept. Her hands were small, bony, and long-fingered, with plain oval nails that had the yellow patina of old age. Hardly dangerous-looking now. But her face was composed even as she slept. She was never off-guard.

"So she really did kill her husband," I said. "Just like Kelly told me."

Isabel said, "Hmmm, she certainly did a revenge thing on him," which was an absurdly frivolous description but somehow appropriate. "She poisoned him with strychnine in a bowl of bread pudding."

"Traditional," I ventured. "Ladylike, yet effective. I like that."

Min smiled, and Isabel's eyes flashed with appreciation. "Not a pretty way for him to die."

"But he deserved worse," Min said. "Aunt Olivia told the family lawyer, 'He shook my babies to death. I knew he was dangerous but I was ashamed to speak up. I let him kill my babies.' "

I looked at Ella hurriedly. Babies. She clasped her throat. "You mean Olivia suspected him in the first death but didn't—or couldn't—leave him?"

Min carefully arched her pale brown brows and lifted her hands, palms up. "We'll never know. Those are the last words anybody heard her speak. She didn't speak in her own defense at the trial, she didn't plead for mercy, she didn't explain anything. The Owens family claimed she was crazy, that she must have killed her own children and then murdered her husband on top of it. Her father used all of the Cameron family's influence to keep her out of prison or the state asylum."

"Oh, my God," I said.

"Her poor babies," Ella sighed tearfully. "And poor Olivia."

"Her father brought her home to the Hall," Min noted. "She's been here ever since."

Isabel rose and gently adjusted the blanket around Olivia's legs. "After our parents died she became the head of the family. She'd outlasted the scandal. Simon was only a teenager, and Gib was five, and Ruth and I were just babies. Minnie, here"—Isabel smiled at Min gently—"Min married Simon the next year, and Bea came from Scotland, but it was up to Aunt Olivia to keep us all together. Emory wanted to send me and Ruth to be raised by Cameron kin in Georgia, and stick Simon and Gib and Aunt Olivia in one of his rental houses in Knoxville."

Min stood also, and tucked the bottom of the lap throw around Olivia's thin, bare feet. "She feels she should have done something to help you and Ella years ago."

"She couldn't have done anything to help us," I said stonily. "No one could have."

"When Gib told her he'd located you in Chicago, he said you and Ella had been harassed and mistreated, and that was something none of us had ever suspected. Aunt Olivia went to her room and stayed for two full days. She barely moved. Just sat looking out the window."

Isabel nodded fervently. "She does this kind of thing sometimes. She does it like a vision quest. A meditation. When she finally came out she gave Gib a note she'd written. She said if we didn't help you two then we couldn't help ourselves. She wrote about all the tragedy that's been part of your family and ours. She believes there was a reason your parents came here—some kind of fate. That it meant your family and our family needed each other to survive. She told Gib to go and find you and do whatever it took to bring you here."

"Oh, my," Ella said, wiping her eyes.

I reached over and gently brushed a strand of Olivia's long hair from her cheek. She looked like a withered little girl. "Don't let her silence fool you," Isabel whispered. "She's still a fighter."

"I know," I whispered back. The government had tried to punish her for evils and tragedies she couldn't control, and she'd spent the rest of her life punishing herself.

I understood her too well, and that scared me.

Twenty-one

I'd already noticed a half-dozen magazine clippings about FeeMolly Hodger's cooking awards, which included a citation from *Gourmet* magazine. Each article had been matted, framed, and hung on a wall in the Hall's huge kitchen.

One morning when I walked into the kitchen I peered with amazement at a new clipping from *Southern Cuisine*.

FeeMolly Hodger was born in 1932 in a log cabin deep in Hodger Hollow, which is next to Take Home Ridge and just over the Cameron River Valley from Oscar's Shed, all of which are tiny, isolated hamlets in the Cameron Mountains of eastern Tennessee. Mrs. Coira Cameron—society matron, Scottish-born nurse, and self-taught midwife—attended FeeMolly's birth along with her husband, Dr. William Cameron. The unsuspecting Mrs. Cameron innocently wrote "Female" on the yet-to-be-named baby girl's birth certificate, and the Hodger clan concluded that the matriarch of Cameron Hall had named their daughter for them.

You see, kinships, clan alliances, and community loyalties still run as deep as pioneer legacies in this

magnificent wild country high in the ancient Appalachians. The Hodgers have worked for the Camerons for
generations, with bonds of fealty that hark back to revered
old-world traditions.

And so "Female Hodger" was ordained in an old
ritual by Coira Cameron and the baby's proud Hodger
parents, who puzzled over their new daughter's name and
finally bestowed it on her with phonetic sincerity. Today
"FeeMolly" wears her quaint moniker with the pride of a
mountain oath and the confidence of a master chef, commanding her kitchen on the Cameron estate with fierce
devotion.

I stepped back, astonished at the long tendrils of human
fellowship that reached to and from the heart of the Cameron
heritage, where I had been conceived as surely as a ripe seed
dropped in rich soil. I was beginning to have absurd flashes of
belonging, as if I, too, could claim a place there, since it was
Gib who had named *me*.

"I have to say something to you, flat out," Ebb interjected.

A little dazed, I pivoted toward her and shoved my hands
into the pockets of my jeans. "Yes?"

She stopped kneading biscuit dough in a broad stoneware bowl to stare at my long, ropy, fake-blond braids. Her
own hair was an enormous brown-teased poof above a shim-
mery gold-lamé headband, a true marvel of hair architecture.
Yet Ebb gazed humbly at my cornrows and the pile of
Medusa-like strands I'd bound up with a red silk scarf. "I
ain't worthy to hold your rat comb," she said. Seriously.

After a stunned moment, I nodded to her just as seriously. "I consider it an *honor* to be admired by someone who
has mastered the art of hair elevation beyond all known human limits."

"But *you're* the hair queen to look up to," Ebb said in big
round tones of reverent gratitude.

"We'll share the title," I insisted.

Her eyes glowed with pride. We shook hands.

"I couldn't live over there in the woods like you're doing," Flo confessed one day as she was helping me bleach my roots. "It's haunted. The whole danged valley is full of haints, but 'specially over yonder near the chapel."

I laughed. Our childhood home in New Orleans was supposedly haunted, like everything else in the old sections of the city, where ghosts could easily whisper from every shady courtyard and every festoon of Spanish moss. It never worried me. Catholics talk to so many saints, invoke so many spirits anyway. Pop let me believe that Mom, Grandmother Akiko, and Grandpop Paulo were still with us, keeping us safe. He even ventured that every time I heard music they were watching over me, and every time I *made* music they were right beside me.

Like Ella, I grew up looking for portentous signs in fallen feathers; I tried to interpret them after Mom died. Our Grandmother Akiko was the one who started the whole feather angelic-communication idea in our family. She wrote dozens of poems on the subject. I had her books of haiku.

After we were grown and Ella became obsessed with the feather mythology, I backed away from it, disavowed the nonsense as nonsense. I felt I had to balance her whimsy with brutal pragmatism, or we'd never survive.

So I was well equipped to deal with dead Camerons, Cherokee and white. But when I was alone I crossed myself. It wasn't the ghosts of the dead I had to worry about so much as the spirits of the living.

Particularly, as it turned out, FeeMolly.

"The rush of air in my ears is my favorite intoxicant, next to a good stiff drink!" Bea yelled as she wheeled the golf cart at top speed between the hedgerows of the courtyard that fronted the Hall. Ella and I clung to the cart's side roof supports. Cold wind buffeted us.

Bea had picked us up at the horse barn, where Ella was gamely admiring Carter while he assisted a pregnant mare in labor. It had taken me an hour to lure her away from the spectacle of Carter crooning gently while he inserted his arm up to the elbow inside the vagina of a large, grunting horse.

I needed Ella in the music room at the Hall, to rehearse a new duet arrangement I'd written. Guests at Cameron Hall paid an average of $250 per night for their lodging, food, and now, formal entertainment. I was determined that when the first guests arrived in January they'd marvel at the Hall's live, first-class music every night. I tuned Ella's violin for her. I used every opportunity to redirect her overheated newlywed attentions toward the music business.

"Pigs!" Ella shouted to Bea suddenly. "Pigs!"

I thought she was losing her mind until a dozen small, pink pigs—all squealing hysterically—emerged from newly planted beds of purple winter pansies. The miniature herd darted in front of us.

"Out of the byway, you wee devils!" Bea yelled, steering wildly. Isabel burst from a small door in the long column of white-trimmed windows in the Hall's left wing. Waving her arms and looking like a large plaid butterfly in a wool jumper and sweater, she loped past us, chasing pigs.

"The piggies arrived an hour ago!" Bea shouted over her shoulder at us, still maneuvering the golf cart to dodge piglets. "They came by special courier! An English pig farmer shipped them to Minnie"—Bea swung the cart to the right up a stone walkway—"because dear Simon married the Englishman and his lady friend at the chapel here a few years back"—Bea jerked the golf cart to a halt—"and they promised him some midget English piglets when their first bairn was born." As she wound the golf cart among another pair of pigs she blew out an exasperated breath that upended the brim of the straw hat she wore with a brown jogging suit. "Leave it to a bloody Englishman," she growled, "to no' ask a by-your-leave to thrust his pork upon you without a bit of warning!"

A small pig leaped up on the wide stone entranceway directly in front of us, skittered across wet, newly washed stone, and tumbled off the opposite side, oinking as he went. Ella bit her lower lip. I burst out laughing. Then I glanced back and saw that Isabel was crying as she chased the other little porkers. She looked like the picture of overworked frustration.

"Oh, poor Izzy," Bea said gruffly. "Venus, if you'll be so kind, you and Ellie go help Izzy darlin' with her arrogant bacon."

"Carter says I'm good with animals," Ella noted. "He says it's because they sense I won't hurt them. While we were visiting Hoover Bird, Carter taught me to handle a pet raccoon."

At least he didn't teach her to dance with a goat, I thought. "Why don't you go on inside and change into your white dress," I told Ella. I crawled out of the golf cart and flexed my shoulders under my quilted jacket. I stuck my gloves in the back pockets of my jeans, then rubbed my bare hands. "Both of us shouldn't be subjected to miniature frozen pig wrestling."

I heard a disgruntled shriek. FeeMolly came waddling around the far corner of the mansion's right wing, her red leather walking shoes crunching on the pebbled path between flowering shrubs and daisies, a meat cleaver hoisted in her right hand. I'd never really talked to her, because she ignored me and everyone else when it suited her. She came and went at odd hours, before sunlight and after dusk, and when she commanded the Hall's kitchen no one but Ebb and Flo were allowed access without permission.

But now she was on a rampage. Her beady-eyed face was flushed and angry. She was built in fat, widening tiers of breast, belly, and butt. She sported thick gray hair dyed at the temples with red skunk streaks the same color as her stretch pants and shirt—which were covered by a red chef's apron.

"Hit don' matter t'me ifn' I has ta skin a *swamp rat* fer stew!" she yelled at Isabel, who jumped at her approach. Isabel had managed to herd most of the piglets onto the lawn, where a U-shaped row of low, clipped boxwoods hemmed them in.

"Shag and I are going to herd them to the cattle barn," Isabel called. She pointed to the blue-eyed dog who was already hunkered in front of the agitated piglets. "Shag's got them under control now. Just give me a chance."

"Sun's set on the *gimme*! Ain't nobody out chere can pertect 'em!" FeeMolly bellowed. "They got in my winter cabbage patch, and by Jesus now the only cabbage they gonna git are the ones floatin' in the stew wit 'em!"

I'd never heard a dialect like hers, not the most traditional coastal Gullah or backwater Cajun, not anything remotely like the drawling mountain gibberish she chattered ferociously.

"You'll not be cleaving the piglets!" Bea bellowed with grand Scottish dignity. Ella ran over and stood defensively beside Isabel, in front of the pigs. Isabel cried, "No, no, FeeMolly!" and snatched up a small pink pig in her arms. "They're pets!"

"They is *stew*! Out of my way, younguns!" FeeMolly brayed. The sight of a maniacal three-hundred-pound mountain chef advancing on my sister with a meat cleaver sent me running frantically into the action. "Stop it!"

"I'll bring herself out here!" Bea called, and barreled up the walkway to the front doors.

There was no time to wait for Olivia to help. I planted myself in FeeMolly's path. She halted, pointed the cleaver at me, and intoned, "Hain't got no nevermind fer you, you funny-headed heathen! Be along wit ya!"

"You just leave the piglets alone," I insisted patiently. I unfurled one hand in a finger-pronged power gesture, posed before her face as if I were about to cast a spell. I remembered it from Mrs. Duvelle's voodoo lessons, as a child. "You're not going to threaten my sister, Isabel, or the pigs," I said with hypnotic intent. "No."

FeeMolly grabbed the end of one of my braids and sliced it off half-way up. I launched myself at her cleaver-wielding arm, latched both hands around her wrist, and hung on. She began slapping me in the head with her free hand. Tiny stars shot across my vision. I would end up with a concussion. But if I let go of her arm I might end up as human pâté.

Isabel screamed. Ella ran over and grabbed FeeMolly's other arm. "Please, FeeMolly, please calm down!" Ella shouted.

"You git yo' sis off me! She gonna git her head knocked clare inta next morn!"

"Please, don't, please," Ella panted.

It was like trying to hold down a blimp in a tornado. FeeMolly swayed while Ella and I staggered back and forth. Ella bounced against me and fell down. I levered one arm over FeeMolly's cleaver arm. She whacked me in the back of the head with her free hand.

I sank my teeth into her forearm. She uttered a screech and drew back her fist. I was certain the next time she hit me I'd be out cold.

Gib was suddenly among us. "Stand down!" he ordered in a voice like a drill sergeant's. FeeMolly had a death grip on my hair. He pried her hand away, barking out orders in a calm but steely tone, and wrenched the cleaver from her. Ella scrambled to her feet.

"Stay back," Gib said. "She'll hit you when she's this upset. Nellie, pull in your fangs. *Nellie.*"

I ducked under FeeMolly's arm. My mouth was filled with a taste like sweaty clams. My jaw throbbed. My head ached. Gib angled between FeeMolly and me. I straightened slowly, wobbling but still on-guard.

Ebb and Flo ran up to us. "Mama's hormones are a little iffy right now," Flo said. "The doctor just adjusted 'em."

I shook my head. "*Freddy Krueger* has more excuses. She meant to cut me!"

"Aw, she was just foolin' around," Ebb said.

"From now on you come to me if you have a problem," Gib told FeeMolly, "I'll take care of it. No more chasing people with knives. It's not polite. All right?"

She stared at him glumly. "Don't gimme no more req'-tion papers."

"What? Is that what's put you in a mood? Look, you don't have to fill out any requisition forms. Just tell Ebb and Flo what kind of supplies you need and they'll fill out the form I gave them."

"Misser Si never keered over fixin' no paper! You learn 'em up! Place's goin' straight to Beelzebubber if'n yer gumption wants on ya! Misser Si God bless Misser Si God bless I miss'm."

Gib's expression turned as unyielding as a rock wall. "A little formal organization isn't too much to ask. I have schedules. I have checklists. This is the way I run things. I miss Simon, too. But I'm in charge now. You need to remember that."

"I put diapers on ya," FeeMolly barked. "Don'cha order me, *boy*." She drew herself up, worked her mouth, then spat on the ground at his feet. I stared at the frothy white blob of spittle near the toe of Gib's worn leather loafer. Embarrassed for him, I stole a glance at his face. He was still as stone.

Olivia arrived then, on Bea's arm. Min ran outside with them. "I thought the pigs were still locked in the old chicken coop."

Isabel sighed. "The door came open while I was feeding them."

"Now I am 'bout ta be *eatin'* 'em!" FeeMolly announced. She snatched at the cleaver Gib held.

Olivia raised one fine-boned finger, commanding, chastising, regal. FeeMolly deflated, and began to look forlorn. "Misser Gib hain't s'much's gotta sharp stob to dig us outta mizry," FeeMolly explained to her. "He puttin' his law, his *law* down on folks 'stead of goin' along kind-like, after Misser Si."

Olivia pointed firmly toward the Hall. FeeMolly clamped her mouth tight, then glared at my chopped-off braid on the ground, and at me. "Next time I be chip-chippin' on you like you is tough hambone, mop head." She glared at me and then at Gib, again, then waddled away.

Olivia, her face compressed in deep thought, picked her way up the mansion's steps. Bea lumbered after her. "I'm sorry, Gib," Isabel said tearfully. "FeeMolly's just on edge like all the rest of us. Today feels so strange."

Gib bent slowly, wearily, and retrieved the foot-long section of my hair. The remnant of neat, pencil-thin synthetic braid unraveled between his fingers. "You missing any pieces other than this?" he asked.

"No." I gestured toward the shorn-off section still connected to my scalp. "But I think I'll go inside now. I feel a little frazzled."

"Would you like your end? Can you glue it back on?"

"No, just throw it away."

He tucked it in his back pocket. "Contrary to local opinion, if you change your mind I won't ask you to fill out an official req'tion paper."

I arched a brow. "You plan to document even your smallest req'tions?"

Finally a little humor leavened the grimness FeeMolly had put in his face. "*None* of mine are small."

I snared a pig and held it up. "They came from England. They came by air freight. Therefore they're real, honest-to-goodness *flying pigs*. And flying pigs are good luck, in my opinion."

His mouth worked. He squinted at me as if I'd sprouted pig wings myself. "I believe whatever you say," he promised drolly.

I wished it were that easy.

Twenty-two

I needed protection from FeeMolly, everyone joked. I found a bodyguard, or rather, she found me.

She had maniacal green eyes, black fur with a lightning-bolt smear of white between her ears, and the personality of a feline chain saw.

"That black kitten inherited a hell-raising spirit," Gib said, "or else she's part panther." And then he added, "I say you and she are a perfect match."

She was the only offspring of an unspayed tabby cat who had taken up residence at the Hall during the last winter and a pampered Siamese tom who escaped from the mayor's wife in Hightower and went walkabout in the mountains. My cat was only half-grown but already fought with every other four-legged animal in sight, including the small, troublesome English pigs. Min banished her from the Hall because she climbed drapes and chewed silk flowers. She was in serious danger of living the life of a loner in one of the barns.

But she showed up at my cottage one day and eyed me from the edge of my own porch as if I smelled like food. Haughtiness was an art form to her. I found her curled up asleep on the porch welcome mat after a cool night, and I let her in the kitchen and gave her a tepid scrambled egg.

She ate the egg, licked her paws and my fingers, then jumped into my lap while I played the keyboard. As my hands moved, her head swiveled as if she were watching Ping-Pong. Finally she curled up and went to sleep, purring.

"That wildebeest slept in your lap and purred?" Isabel said incredulously, echoing a sentiment I heard from Ebb, Flo, and Min: "She bit the pee out of me for just *lookin'* at her wrong," Ebb noted. "I mean to tell you, that cat come over and *bit my ankle out of spite.*"

"She and I obviously have an instinctive bond," I said proudly. I'd often wanted to bite people.

I'd never had a pet before. Pop had been allergic to animal fur, and Ella had had asthma as a child, so pets were out of the question. Suddenly I cherished this small, lonely, odd creature who deserted all its kindred kitties at the Hall to keep me company through the dark, cold nights in the mountains. Min gave me a litter box and a bag of cat necessities, including a paper bag filled with dried catnip from the herb garden.

"We never got around to naming her," Min said wistfully, as if even the smallest domestic niceties had fallen apart during the past year. "She's your cat now. You name her."

This duty became more profound to me than I'd ever admit out loud, and I thought about it for several days. I watched my housemate scale the walls, doors, kitchen cabinets, and *me* with a velocity approaching the speed of sound. She was quick, she was fast, she was merciless. I had cat-paw skid marks on one shoulder and both legs.

"Allegra?" I said to her one night, testing.

She raced across the cottage's main room, skidded on the wood floor, then slammed into my ankles before leaping onto the kitchen counter, where she swatted at nothing then convulsed into a fuzzed, madly devilish-eyed stalking routine. "Allegra," I confirmed happily. "I think your brain's set on high tempo. *Allegra.*"

When I walked to the Hall each morning I took her with me. She quickly decided to ride piggyback in a knapsack Kelly loaned me, and sat regally with her small black head poking out the knapsack's unzipped top.

I arrived one chilly morning just as Gib stepped out a back door. He carefully held something in his cupped hands. He halted and I did, too. He studied me and Allegra with a frown. "Do you dress for effect?" he asked finally.

"Have cat, will travel."

Besides the cat-bearing knapsack I was wearing a baggy white sweater, cutoff jeans, and black army boots with neon laces. I had all my braids wound up on top of my head with a long red scarf threaded through them. "The cat's just the icing on the fruitcake," he countered.

Something moved in his hands. He opened them slightly and I saw a rectangular, clear-plastic mousetrap with a frantic live mouse bumping around inside it. A dab of yellow showed where cheese bait had been placed in one end of the tiny box. "Dead mouse walking," Gib said. "Aunt Olivia believes it's bad luck to kill any animal inside the house, so I give the mice a head start for the woods. What happens to them after that is their own problem."

"So this is your idea of fun. Wrestling Mickey Mouse into a box—" I began.

Allegra sank her front claws in my back, launched herself to my right shoulder, and then in a flash of black fur made two leaps—one to the ground, and another squarely at Gib's mouse-bearing hands.

He took a step back, but Allegra hung from his shirtfront, yowling, with the trap caught between Gib's chest and her underside. Through some fluke of plastic-mousetrap engineering the trap's door popped open.

And the mouse popped out.

At which point Gib tried calmly to pull Allegra off his flannel shirt while she scrambled to nab the mouse. The terrified mouse wriggled between Gib's shirt buttons. It disappeared inside his shirt.

"Don't hurt my cat," I called, running over and tugging at Allegra.

"The damned mouse is plowing a furrow through my chest hair," Gib said through gritted teeth. "And your cat is digging post holes."

Allegra climbed him in pursuit of the large, moving, flannel-covered mouse-bump. Gib cursed, fumbling with buttons that his right hand couldn't manage. His face carved with frustration, he gave up and jerked his shirt open, ripping buttons. The mouse shot up to his shoulder then disappeared down his back. He shrugged the shirt down his arms and dropped it—and the mouse inside it—to the ground. The shirt moved wildly as the mouse hunted for an escape. Allegra pounced on the undulating shirt, got her head under the edge of it, and scooted beneath the fabric.

The mouse shot out one sleeve, headed straight across the open lawn, and disappeared into the zinnia beds. The zinnia blooms had long since fallen off, leaving only tall, drying stalks. Allegra raced after her prey. She was still covered in Gib's shirt.

We watched his shirt go humping across the lawn and into the rattling zinnia stalks like an armadillo wearing a plaid dress.

I faced him reluctantly, my face compressed in an apologetic wince. He glared at the flower bed and then at me. "I never thought I'd see the day," he said darkly, "when one of my shirts would run away from home."

"I'm sorry. I am, really. I—" My gaze went to his bare chest, which was broad, well formed, and elegantly haired, leading down to a handsome belly.

A small, gold ring gleamed in the rim of his navel.

I jerked my gaze up to his face. His brows flattened and he looked grim. "The woman at the piercing parlor in

Knoxville didn't warn me it would itch for six weeks. That's what I get for trusting a woman who had more metal stuck in her face than a bucktoothed tenth grader."

"I—you, I can't believe it—"

"Why? You can't believe I'm capable of getting a hole punched in my skin? There's nothing to *that*, Nellie. If you mean you can't believe I want to associate with the social and political ideas of the pierced-parts crowd, well, you're right. This is only a piece of jewelry, Nellie. Not a personal statement."

"Why did you do it?"

"Because I've always wanted to be a pirate. I told her to put a ring *in my ear* but she missed."

"I'm serious. Why did you do it?"

"Because it helps me to concentrate on some other section of my hide besides my hand."

"Why?" I insisted, my voice rising.

"Because I want something to rattle me every time I close my mind to new ideas. Something to remind me that I'm capable of taking new directions. I touch my belly ring and hear you haranguing me. You telling me what to do. This"—he jabbed a finger at the ring—"is *your* opinion, Nellie. This is your voice. This is *you*."

I reached out. I didn't think. There was nothing calculated about it. I just reached out naturally and touched my fingertips to the tiny gold ring protruding from his skin. The flesh around it was warm and slightly pink. When he breathed his stomach shifted in tight shivers.

"Be careful what you touch," he warned in a low, uneven tone.

"When I had mine pierced I had to leave the tops of my pants undone for weeks. I couldn't bear to have them scrape against the ring."

"There's a mental image," he said.

"Does it hurt?"

"Not at the moment."

"Put antiseptic on it every day. Keep it clean." I drew my hand back. My hand trembled. "I shouldn't have touched it so much until it's completely healed. Germs."

"I'll take my chances."

Both of us were caught up in something helplessly provocative. We stood there in the yard, in the clear cool morning sunshine of late autumn, and I said, "Let's see if there're other surprises," and with no guile at all I walked around him, looking at his back and shoulders, while he stood still. I touched his skin here and there. "Allegra scratched you," I said. "You're bleeding a little." I showed him my fingertips with traces of his blood on them. "Do you want me to get something to put on it?"

"My shirt," he said distractedly.

We walked over to the zinnia bed. His shirt hung on a few broken stalks. He examined it a moment, then put it on. "Your buttons," I murmured, dazed. Several were missing. The buttonholes were torn.

"I have trouble with buttons, anyway," he told me.

He struggled with his shirt buttons, the two knotty, stiff fingers of his injured hand refusing to perform that simple task. Color rose in his face. Protective sympathy swelled inside my chest; I understood lost dignity.

"That's a damn fine belly-button ring you got there, sir, and thank you for letting me help with your buttons." With that warning, I pushed his hands aside. Standing close to him, I fastened the buttons that were left. He watched me. His chest moved swiftly. My hands shook.

"I can't have a simple conversation with you," he said. "You make me want to pull my hair out or howl at the moon."

"You're a brave man, Gib Cameron," I whispered. "Or maybe we're a good influence on each other."

"Stranger things have happened," he said gruffly.

We stepped away from each other when we heard the back kitchen-porch door swing open. I looked around sheepishly. Gib became very busy rechecking his torn buttonholes.

"Good morning," Min called. She gazed out at us like a tall, benignly curious praying mantis in a shapeless jumper the rust color of old leaves. "I thought I heard a commotion out here."

"No problem, Minnie," Gib said. "We were just headed indoors." She nodded, eyed us both with her head tilted, then discreetly withdrew inside the house. Gib and I walked across the lawn. "No one but you knows about this," he said, gesturing toward his stomach. "I'd like to keep it that way."

"No problem."

That night I fed Allegra an entire can of tuna and stroked her fur with a soft wool sock she loved. She deserved special favors for her part in uncovering Gib's secret.

My contentment didn't last long.

"I have some extra bleach for you," I said to Ella. "Your hair's starting to take on a kind of reverse skunk stripe when you part it in the middle."

A full two inches of silky black roots showed at her scalp. She smiled. "In a couple of months it'll be long enough to cut the blond section off. I'll have a full head of short, black hair. Carter's thrilled that I'm changing it."

"I bet. He'll get to pretend he's with another woman."

"Don't start."

"Well, I for one don't intend to throw away years of carefully cultivated bleached roots and synthetic braids. This is me, and it's going to stay me."

"Stop trying to sound smug. You're a softie at heart. I know you're helping Jasper practice his social skills around girls. And I also heard that Kelly brings you poetry and you set it to music for her. And you're going to teach her to play the guitar."

"No, I said I'd teach her the basics and then you could take over, because you've developed *such* an interest in the guitar," I said sarcastically.

Carter had bought my sister a red-and-silver Gibson, the Cadillac of guitars. Ella had taken to it like an old friend. She was now playing country-western music. "We're goin' to have us a bunch of musical babies," Carter told everyone who'd listen. "They're going to grow up to be country-music stars. They'll all be TV spokesmen for big pickup-truck companies. And at the awards shows, Ellie and me will insist we gotta be seated between Garth Brooks and Reba McEntire."

"You're not playing guitar because you want to head a dynasty of country yodelers," I insisted to Ella. "You're doing it to please Carter."

"I wish you and I didn't argue every time we try to have a serious conversation," Ella said sadly. "We could *both* have nice lives! We could trust people! Love people! But the only way we can do that is if you stop rejecting every single living human being who might, just might, have a painfully unpleasant opinion about us!"

"What has that got to do with—"

"You always do it! You always assume the worst! But people shouldn't have to pass some kind of loyalty test!"

"I will never," I said through gritted teeth, "betray our family. And neither will you."

"*Betray?* Oh, *Vee.* You're hopeless. I give up on you," she said in a tired voice. She had never said anything like that, in that tone of voice, to me before. She clasped her chest. Tears streamed down her face. She brushed past me and left the house, slamming the screen door.

After that argument, she and I didn't speak one word to each other for a week.

Their names were Bobby Jim and Wally Roy. They were two of Ebb's boys, both of them under the age of ten. They wore camouflage pants and T-shirts for casual dress. For toys they had four-wheeler dirt buggies decorated with squirrel tails. They hadn't been hit with many smart sticks.

Bobby Jim and Wally Roy were yelling and racing around on their dirt buggies, but everyone except me and Kelly was out at the back orchards harvesting the remnants of the fall apples. One of the inn's trademarks had always been FeeMolly's apple butter. Ella had suggested that all the guests for the opening weekend find gift baskets of apple butter and fresh muffins waiting for them in their rooms. She came up with these small, Martha Stewartish ideas with an ease that impressed everyone; her most recent projects included designing new table arrangements for the dining rooms.

Through the music room's open windows I could hear the faint sounds of Ella playing guitar. Laughter drifted to me on the breezes. I swore I could smell the sweet aroma of a wood fire. Min and Gib had set up an iron stew pot filled with mulled cider.

I wanted to be outdoors drinking cider and pretending to be aloof while everyone else laughed. Instead I was in the music room with Kelly, who presented me with the sheet music for the piece she'd chosen to perform. She still insisted she was going to perform in a teenage beauty pageant. I looked at the music incredulously. "If you don't mind my asking, why in the world do you want to sing 'Don't Cry for Me, Argentina'?"

"I feel Evita Perón made an important statement about political corruption."

"For or against?"

"Okay, so maybe she was all show and no substance, but she was interesting. She looked glamorous in the movie."

"Would you consider, hmmm, something more conventional for a beauty pageant? Say, a nice tune from a musical that doesn't require a companion primer on Latin American politics? Something from a Disney musical would be bland and harmless."

"Oh, *puh-leeeze*. Do I *look* like a white-bread kind of girl?"

"Well, frankly, yes."

"I want to be seen as daring and brave."

"It's not a matter of how you see yourself, it's how the judges will see you. Do you really think you can sell them on the image of you as the wife of a South American dictator? You have to be able to act the song's emotions, not just sing the words. You have to *be* Evita Perón."

"Look, I can be cute or I can be different. Trying to be cute isn't going to win me any points. I have to be something else."

"You're already something else," I said gently. "I like you."

"You're being polite."

"I'm never polite if I can help it."

She studied me with the trademark Cameron squint, but her lips quirked and finally, she grinned. "Different can be good," she said.

"You win." I set her music on the piano's backboard. "So it's the song from *Evita*, eh? All right, we'll determine the best key for you to sing in, and I'll write the accompaniment for it, and we'll work on your delivery."

"Excellent!" She thrust out a hand. We shook.

Bobby Jim and Wally Roy crept up through the shrubbery to the music-room window, pressed their noses and tongues to the glass obscenely, then snorted with laughter and ran away.

Kelly and I traded looks of disgust. "Buffoons," I said.

I should have known they were up to something.

Late that afternoon, I gratefully hurried outside. Everyone had moved to the back rows of the apple orchard to harvest the last round of ripe fruit. The orchard was dotted with stepladders. Isabel, Min, Jasper, Ebb, Flo, Ruth, Paul, Ella and Carter, Gib—each was perched in a tree or waiting below to catch the small, tart, dusky-red winesaps and place them in large latticework produce baskets.

Olivia and Bea supervised from queenly armchairs with a table between them, where a jug of the mulled cider sat alongside stoneware mugs and a bottle of dark rum. "Here's for you, Rapunzel," Bea called, and handed me a mug.

I took a deep sip, expecting warm spiced cider with a hint of rum. "Holy moly," I said between strangled coughs. "No one should climb up on a stepladder and handle fruit after drinking one of these."

"Oh, yours is a wee bit stronger than the others," Bea admitted. "You have to catch up on the sippin' we've been at all afternoon."

Gib watched me as I stopped beneath his tree. I was at eye level with his thighs and hips. I looked up at him with a warm, giddy sensation already creeping through my brain. "Nice big apples," I said.

"You should see the stem," he replied.

Chortling under my breath, woozy with sexual insinuation and rum cider, I hurried away, as if helping Isabel carry a full bushel basket were suddenly my mission in life. Ella waved at me from across the orchard. I waved back. Carter was up in a tree. Ella stood beneath, looking pink-cheeked and pastoral in a print dress with a handsome sweater in some geometric Cherokee pattern woven in it. She caught apples in a large gingham apron she wore, then gently set them in a basket by her feet.

I didn't go over to see her, not with Carter there. There was so much tension under the facade of our daily routines. I didn't know what to do, what to say, and I couldn't bring myself to pretend otherwise. Our argument still hung in the air. I knew my kind of pride could be disciplining or self-destructive, and I was always tormented by the debate over which it had become.

I got drunk. Not sloshy, overtly drunk, just drunk enough to hum Debussy off-key while I lugged baskets of apples to the kitchen's back porch, where FeeMolly and Golwat sat peeling apples and smoking long pipes. An old radio hung from an iron hook on an inside post. Some twangy Loretta Lynn song was playing.

"Loretta Lynn," I said cheerfully. "I saw the movie. You know. Her biography. With Sissy Spacek."

FeeMolly only grunted. I was looped enough to feel magnanimous. "I'm sorry you and I started out on the wrong foot a few weeks ago," I told her sincerely. "I really respect your work here and wish we could be friends."

"What you care 'bout us'n folks, mop head? You ain't nothin' but a flutter-by. I seen ya come, I be seein' ya go. Misser Gib need better'n you. Gully-witch. Haint. Booger. Fly away 'fore ya cream turns to sour clabber in the churn."

"Well, thank you for listening," I said, then wandered back to the orchards, embarrassed and depressed, my skull beginning to tighten with a rum-induced headache.

After I toted the last basket of apples I slipped away to the broad, peaceful deck around the pool, which Gib and Carter had already covered for the winter. I found a lawn chair situated where it couldn't be seen from the tiers of windows across the back of the Hall. I stretched out on my back and watched wisps of white clouds ride a sky turning gold with sunset. I thought about Ella and FeeMolly. I was not popular.

My head hurt. I fanned my braids over the backrest of the lawn chair and let them dangle. The clouds hypnotized me. I dozed off and dreamed, in odd and worrying patterns, that FeeMolly had turned into a giant red-haired snake that hissed at me. *It's true, what she said is true,* I dreamed. I became a bird and flew past her. A flutter-by. I circled the Hall, trying to land, but couldn't remember how. I looked desperately for Gib. FeeMolly hissed again.

I woke up with Gib's hand on my shoulder. It was almost dark, and the air had grown cold enough that I shivered. "Good God, quit wandering off without a word," he scolded mildly. "It's dinnertime."

"I have a rum-and-apple-cider headache. I was a little stewed."

"That was Bea's goal. She likes to get people crocked and see how they act. It's her hobby. She uses it as a gauge of character."

"Well, my gauge is stewed, too."

"You did fine. You held your liquor well, you kept working, and you didn't turn *ill*."

"Wrong. I do feel ill."

"No, *turn ill*. Mean. Angry. You're not a mean drunk. Under that crabby exterior you're a mellow soul."

"I'm a spicy, rum-soaked soul. I'm a fruitcake." I sat up, rubbing my forehead. The scalp at the crown of my head felt as tight as a piano wire, and itched. My hair seemed to have coagulated into one heavy planklike weight. "I need aspirin," I moaned. "My head feels peculiar. Maybe this is what a migraine feels like."

"Hold on. Let me turn on some lights before you get up. I don't want you to stagger onto the pool cover." Gib walked over to a small metal box hidden at a corner of the deck. He flipped the lid up and pressed a switch. Around the deck and pool the landscape lights came on.

"Thanks," I said. I stood, then clasped my hands to the top of my head, massaging.

"Good God," Gib said. He stared at my hair. I took one look at his face and quickly ran my hands farther back.

"What? What?" My fingers touched an alarming texture. Sticky, matted. My hair was stiff. I jerked my hands down and looked at them. Dabs of orange paint colored my fingers. "What? What?" I grabbed the ends of my braids. The entire mass moved. I smelled the chemical scent of orange spray paint.

I swayed. *"Somebody painted my hair."*

Gib strode to me and grabbed me by the shoulders. "Sit down. Sit." When I was safely planted on the lawn chair he guided my head between my knees. "Breathe," he ordered.

I gulped air. After a few minutes I straightened shakily. "My hair," I moaned.

His face grim, he stood and examined the ruined, spray-painted braids, trying to pry them apart. It was useless. "I promise you I'll find out who did this, but I'm sorry, Nellie. That's heavy-duty paint and there's probably not a damned thing that'll save your hair."

Someone had turned my do into bad graffiti.

My symbol of pride, rebellion, ambition, and disguise. Ruined.

Within an hour Gib pinned the crime on Bobby Jim and Wally Roy. "How can you be sure?" I asked him. Everyone gathered in the den of the family wing. My head was wrapped in a towel he'd brought me. I had refused to walk into the house with the horror exposed.

"Years of law-enforcement training and high-tech investigative practice combined with instinctive deduction skills," he deadpanned. He turned to Ebb, who was red-faced. "Your boys have orange spray paint on their fingers. And they stashed the empty cans in their four-wheelers."

"I'll kill 'em," she said.

"Let's see your hair, Sis," Ella said gently. "Come on—it's only hair."

"Not even real hair, for the most part," Ruth noted.

"Maybe it can be fixed," Isabel mused.

"Ebb can fix any kind of hair damage," Flo soothed. "She's got everything in the world out in her truck." Ebb operated an informal mobile beauty-and-barber salon, upon request.

"Can she fix *this*?" I challenged dully. I pulled the towel off. Flo shrieked. Ella and Isabel gasped. Min put a supportive hand on my shoulder.

The central section of my hair was bright orange from the top of my head to the ends of my braids. The paint had penetrated all the way to my scalp on top. Farther down, the spray paint had combined with my synthetic weave to glue my braids into a fist-thick mess.

"Nothing's going to get this stuff out of my hair," I said with stony control—my only hope of holding back tears of rage and embarrassment. "Ebb, get your electric clippers. You're going to shave my head."

She clutched her chest. "Oh, Lord, I'd sooner cut my heart out."

"Cutting out hearts comes later, when I get my hands on Bobby Jim and Wally Roy. But my hair is"— I took a deep breath —"beyond saving." I wrapped the towel around my head with the melodrama of a coroner shielding the squeamish from a horrifying corpse. "Shave it."

Ebb was the only one I allowed to witness the process— one big-haired pro to another. We sat in Min's bedroom. I stared at myself in a mirror over the dresser when the deed was done. "I look like a fuzzy peach," I said.

Ebb wailed, "I feel like I just tore up a masterpiece and throwed it out the window."

I made a tight turban from a dark silk scarf of Min's, then anchored it with a softball hat of Kelly's. Sporting the Hightower Highlanders logo but feeling naked, I walked numbly into the big, friendly den of the family wing.

Everyone tried not to stare, but they couldn't help it. Ella covered her mouth and left the room, Carter following her anxiously.

"You look, well, you look fine," Gib lied.

I stared at Bobby Jim and Wally Roy, who had been herded into the room to wait for me. They were teary and terrified. Ebb whacked both of them on the fanny. As if the words had been knocked loose, Bobby Jim spouted, "I'm sorry, ma'am, for paintin' your hair." Wally Roy echoed the sentiment precisely.

"They'll pay for you to get some new hair wove onto yours as soon as yours grows out enough," Ebb assured me.

"That won't be necessary." I held the boys' gazes with intensity. "Why did you do it? That's what I want to know. Did you think it was funny?"

"We—" one began. Then halted. The other chimed, "I dunno," and stopped. They fixed their eyes on the carpeted floor.

"You don't have to buy me some new hair. But you do have to answer my question. Why did you do it?"

"Granny told us to!" Bobby Jim blurted.

"Big mouth!" Wally Roy shouted, and punched him in the head.

FeeMolly.

FeeMolly gave no ground, refused to apologize, and looked as if she'd spray-paint me herself if I crossed her path. "I showed your true colors," she snarled, and then she turned to lumber out of the den. But Olivia stopped her with a raised hand. The silence was heavy. FeeMolly stared at her with obvious concern. Olivia wrote on a notepad then handed it to Bea. Bea motioned for Gib, who walked over and read the note.

"I agree," he said to Olivia. "Min?"

Min read the note. Her eyes sad and her face drawn, she nodded. "If you'd just apologize to Venus," she said to FeeMolly.

FeeMolly drew herself up, all three hundred pounds in stacked defiance. "I'd a-ruther die."

Bea scanned Olivia's message then nodded. "You've insulted Herself with your meanness against one who's done you no harm," she told Fee-Molly. "You'll be leaving Herself's employ."

In the stunned moment that followed, even FeeMolly blinked in amazement and turned dark red.

"No," I said quickly. Everyone looked at me. FeeMolly and I traded brittle stares. "I don't give a damn about getting an apology from you," I said. "You wouldn't mean it and it wouldn't mean anything to me. Keep your job. You can't scare me off. I won't let you."

"You crazy," FeeMolly growled. But she spat in her palm then thrust it out. After contemplating her silent surrender for a moment I spat in mine. We shook. It was slimy. She tried to break my fingers, I think. I dug my thumbnail into her knuckle. I caught Gib, Olivia, and the others looking at me with troubled expressions.

But I'd saved FeeMolly's maniacal hide, and I'd pointed out once again that I didn't need charity from Camerons. I think FeeMolly knew it, too. She waddled out of the room, cursing under her breath, but with deep sighs of relief.

"Granny's been bested," Wally Roy said in an awed voice.

But my hair was the loser.

Twenty-three

Late that night I sat naked in front of the cottage's bathroom mirror, crying.

I heard someone drive into my yard, peered out a window, and saw Gib getting out of the jeep. He carried a bottle in one hand. When I opened the door I was safely ensconced in a head scarf, with sunglasses over my eyes, my robe belted securely around me, and Allegra perched in my arms defensively. Gib stared at me. "Excuse me," he said, "I'm looking for Nellie, but I've obviously come to the house of the Invisible Cat Woman."

"The less anyone can see of me at the moment, the better. I wish I *were* invisible."

"I'm glad I decided to check on you while a few inches of skin still show." He held up the bottle. It was a dusty flask of brandy from the Hall's cellar. "This is the best hooch in the county since Camerons stopped making their own. I thought you might at least like to sip the good stuff while you scream and tear out your—well, never mind."

Tear out my hair. "Too late," I deadpanned.

Gib walked past me to the kitchen, opened the brandy, poured a large amount into a glass he took from a cabinet, and handed it to me. Allegra leaped aside and disappeared into the bedroom, popping her tail. I took a deep, reckless swallow from the glass. Fine brandy went into my blood like a hot bath. "I'm going to get drunk twice in the same day," I said dizzily. "What next? I've lost my sister, my career, my RV, and now my hair. I don't have much left to donate to the Cameron cause."

"How about yourself?"

"You're not getting *that* tonight."

"I meant your loyalty. Your enthusiasm. Your trust."

"I'm already working like a dog for this family."

"Only because you're stuck here with Ella. Whatever you do, you do for Ella's sake."

"That's right. But you get the same result, either way. So don't look a gift Arinelli in the mouth." I took another swallow of brandy. My face burned with humiliation. "So why did you come here? Were you afraid I'd hang myself with my chopped-off braids? Not to worry. Take a long, hard look at me. I'm a survivor."

He scowled. "Right now I suspect that underneath that scarf you look like an onion with a fungus."

He was right. Miserable, I set my empty glass on the counter, wandered over to a couch, then sat down, hugging myself. Gib watched me a second, then sat down beside me. "Will you let your hair grow out the natural color?" he asked.

"I suppose."

"I hope you do. I didn't like the yellow cornrows."

"Look, I wasn't all that fond of them myself." I gestured toward my head. "But for years Ella and I tried so hard to disguise who we were."

"As Golwat says, it's time you let people re-COG-no-size you."

"I don't want to be re-COG-no-sized. I felt safer with that fake hair on my head."

He reached out slowly. I froze. He removed my sunglasses. My eyes were swollen and red. He slid a fingertip under my turbanlike scarf and tugged gently. It slid off. So there I was—my head shaved, my face puffy and distorted. I sagged with defeat for letting him expose me without any fight at all. "I re-COG-no-size you," Gib said gently. "Hello, Venus."

I leaned toward him gratefully. I couldn't help it. "You shouldn't have come here tonight. I'm not capable of dealing with you."

"You're safe. Can you accept that just for once, or do you want me to leave?" He smoothed his bad hand over my head, which was splotched with orange on top, the skin itself stained a bright pumpkin hue. "It amazes me that you've never pulled away from the sight or the feel of my hand. Even now."

I sighed. "I'm surprised you want to touch *me*. I've never felt uglier in my life."

"It's a good thing I have a strong stomach." I managed to laugh, but the drink had already gotten to me, and sleepy fatigue was starting to intrude. Gib slipped one arm around me. I buried my face in the crook of his neck. "You don't care about me so you don't care what I look like," I murmured.

"That's right, I don't give a damn," he confirmed in a gruff whisper.

"Good." I fell asleep in his arms, amazed at my sudden contentment.

He was gone when I woke up on the couch the next morning. I felt like Sally Field at the Academy Awards. He liked me. He really liked me.

I bathed, dressed in a long wool skirt and thick sweater, wound a paisley scarf around my head, and set out walking. I took the road from my cottage to the Waterfall Lodge. Long bands of cold morning light filtered through the leafless woods. My breath clouded the air in silver puffs.

When I reached the lodge the jeep was out front but there was no sound, no sign of Gib being inside. The waterfall gurgled and splashed melodically; the air in the shady glen was damp and clear gray, open to interpretation—the color of rain. I couldn't see a light through Gib's curtains, or rather, the quilts he'd tacked over the windows on the inside. I gingerly stepped up on the porch and thumbtacked a bulky white envelope to the heavy frame door.

He opened the door as I finished forcing the pin into the hard wooden surface.

We studied each other awkwardly. He was in a half-buttoned flannel shirt and old jeans. He held an open copy of a Beethoven biography in his left hand. "This is not for effect," he said, nodding toward the book. "I was really reading it. Trying to understand what you see in his music."

"I . . . brought you a tape." My attention distracted by the fine, dark chest hair that showed between his open shirtfront, I gestured vaguely toward the envelope tacked to his door. He pulled the envelope down and read the note printed on it.

These are some of my original compositions. I record them on my keyboard and use my synthesizer to expand the orchestral effect. I just thought you might like them.

His quiet, intent gaze turned to me. "Ella told me you write music," he said. "She said you have hundreds of songs. Compositions. Whatever you call them. Songs and arrangements. She told me. But she also said you never let anyone listen to them. Not even her. Why me?"

"The tape is a thank-you gift, for last night. Your kindness. Your brandy. For loaning me your shoulder to rest my bristly orange head on." Silence. He watched me, and I watched him. His door still stood open. I glimpsed dark log walls. "Interesting place," I said. "You've seen mine. How about letting me see yours?"

"I can't invite you inside this lodge, Nellie. Or to be frank about it, I *won't* invite you inside. We need to stop this flirtation business before it goes any further. And I say that being fully aware that I started it, last night."

Startled—humiliated, because he'd seen obvious intentions I didn't want to admit myself—I retreated to the yard. He caught up with me easily and we both halted. "What did you expect?" he asked. "Did you come here to offer yourself to me?"

I could have died. Disappeared into a puff of overblown, self-certain, feminine vapors. I hurt beyond measure. "The least you could do is *pretend* you care. Live up to your gallant reputation. It was hard for me to come here."

"If you think it's easy for me to turn you away you don't have any idea what's going on inside me right now."

I stared at him. "Then, why—"

"I don't want to wake up every morning wondering whether it's the last time you'll sleep in my arms. Worrying that you'll leave. I need permanent people in my life. I need to count on a woman for the long run."

"How can I promise you I'll stay? I believe with every breath in my body that my sister's marriage is headed for trouble sooner or later, and there won't be any place for us here, then. We won't be family anymore. Because there's no doubt in my mind that blood is always thicker than water with Camerons."

"You still don't have a clue, do you? You don't really trust me or anyone else here. And you're convinced I'll betray you. Me and everything I represent."

"You've never shown any sign of respecting my family—"

"I respect *you*. I respect Ella. You've both earned it."

"You know what I mean."

"You mean forgive what your father did? Make excuses for him? Hell, no, I'll never do that. The difference between you and your sister is that she doesn't demand that the whole world apologize for turning him into a criminal. He made his own choices. Stop defending him and live your own life. You have a home in this valley. All right? I mean that. I want you to stay."

"Ella and I don't belong here," I said urgently. "We were

raised in the city. We've spent our whole lives in cities. We have a career in music."

"Your sister act was getting you nowhere, and you know it."

"At least we were self-sufficient and hardworking, and we were *good* at our work. Don't try to make me believe you've changed your mind about us. You still want us out of your sight and our money off your conscience. You and Ruth, too—neither of you want any goddamned daughters of Max Arinelli in your family permanently. Admit it. Stop lying to me. *Admit it.*"

He regarded me intensely for a long, uncomfortable moment. Then he pointed to his jeep. "Get in."

"What?"

"Get in or I'll put you in it myself." He meant it. I climbed inside his rust-streaked, knobby-wheeled, kick-ass old vehicle, sat rigidly on the sun-faded upholstery, and stared at him as he slid into the driver's seat beside me. He deftly mated two raw wires that dangled under the steering wheel. A spark leaped between them, and the jeep started.

"Where are you taking me?"

"We're going to have a long talk," Gib warned. "And there's only one place to do it."

The hot spring gave off a fine mist of steam like a clear soup broth. A meadow was all that separated us from the deep forest. The historical markers stood guard beside the stone gateposts of the valley's entrance. I glimpsed the paved public road curlicuing through enormous oaks and beeches, but not another human being in sight. Across miles of mountains tangled in forest, God alone knew what kind of wild, hungry eyes watched us.

Gib got out of the jeep and pointed to the spring. "Let's go."

I eyed him warily as I walked over. He reached out firmly but slowly, gauging my reaction. His hand settled under my elbow. I hissed, "You're going to throw me in the water?"

"I'll show you where to sit down. So you won't slip on the rocks." I looked down at gray ledges descending into a clear bottom. Gib then stepped down the natural stairs while I gaped at him. When the water reached his waist he said, "Come on in," looking up at me and still holding me by the elbow. "The water's good for what ails you."

This was a dare. I stepped onto a ledge, then down onto another, and slowly sat down. Water as warm as a bath covered me from the breasts down. It had a briny mineral smell but felt like a massage on my back muscles. Even my hands felt soothed. Gib had the gentlemanly good grace to concentrate on my face, at least when I was noticing. "You soak up well," he said.

"I could drown in all this wet wool." I turned away and focused steadily on a bit of soft green moss at the pond's edge. It was just barely hanging on, like me. "This is a hot tub. I want a tall tequila sunrise with a paper umbrella. If I go back to the Hall dripping wet and say you convinced me to sit in the spring with all my clothes on I'd better smell like I've been drinking. That's the only excuse that'll make sense."

"Go ahead and take your clothes off if that makes you feel better." Gib settled deeper beside me. "The fewer clothes, the fewer details. Because the Devil's in the details."

"The Devil's in the details," I repeated, nodding, "and if you and I have one thing in common it's that we spend all our time keeping tabs on the Devil." I sank down in the water up to my neck, then gingerly leaned my turbaned head back on the rounded rock behind me. "Look, let's stop pretending we misunderstand each other. Whatever you've got to say to me, just say it."

He looked me straight in the eyes. "Last year? All those girlfriends who came to see me at the hospital? There wasn't even *one* who hadn't been dumped by me. I'd always been in charge. I was the one who called the shots and moved on when I got bored."

"Well, you certainly must have left some decent memories behind if they ran to your side when you needed them."

"No, they made polite visits to the hospital, but then ran like rabbits when I asked them to marry me."

"You did *what*?"

"I was drugged to my eyeballs, I was full of tubes and metal pins, and I had nightmares about the sawmill and Simon every goddamned time I closed my eyes. I wanted someone to love me so much she'd stay beside me and keep all that pain away somehow. I must have asked four different women to marry me."

"You weren't being rational. They knew that."

"Listen, these were women who wanted nothing better than to marry me when I was somebody important. These were women I'd walked out on because they couldn't stop talking about marriage."

"I see. But being proposed to by a man who obviously isn't being picky anymore is not a compliment—"

"There was more to it than that. They couldn't take this." He raised his ruined hand. "And they couldn't take the fact that I wasn't going to be the man guarding the President anymore. It was a hard lesson for me to learn, Nellie. To make a needy fool of myself. To realize most of what I'd been was an image. To be rejected for not measuring up anymore. Maybe it was a lesson in humility I needed, but it hurt. So don't think I have no idea what you're feeling."

I could sense the humiliation and misery he'd been through. He realized I felt sorry for him. He became awfully quiet. We pretended to listen to the birds. Finally I said, "I never understood why my father loved his politics more than he loved us." Those were the hardest words I'd ever spoken. "Why Ella and I weren't more important than his . . . ideals. His bitterness. I swore to myself I'd never make that mistake. That Ella would always come first. By God, if Pop couldn't take care of us, then I'd do it for him."

Gib levered himself up to a higher ledge, so that only his

lower legs dangled beside me in the water. He took something from his jeans pocket. Holding it awkwardly between his thumb and scarred forefinger, he rested his maimed hand on the knee closest to me.

I looked at the small white pebble in his grasp. I struggled for a second with the knot in my throat. It was white quartz, like mine. My nerves were shot, my life was unraveling. But I wasn't so bad off I'd cry over our sentimental rocks. Not yet, anyway. "Part of your valuable wishing-rock collection?" I said.

Smiling thinly, he nodded. "I was sitting right here when I gave the other one to your mother."

Now he had me. My breath seemed to catch. "Do you remember anything else about her?"

He nodded, again. "I was only five years old, but that weekend was a turning point in my life. Because your mother almost drowned here."

I stared up at him in shock. And listened.

Twenty-four

"The story of that time has been told and retold so often by Bea, and Min, and Simon over the years that it's taken on a life of its own. Aunt Olivia wrote in her journals about every word that was said and reported and done that year. So I'm not making up much detail, Nellie, or embroidering any more than can be helped, and some of it's even word-for-word. And all of it's the truth, as far as we're concerned.

"I was scared and confused and only five years old. It sounds odd to say, but that's why so many details have stuck in my mind. What I don't remember exactly I remember as it seems to me now. Plus I've made it my business to study that year since then. As if I could figure out something in the atmosphere.

"Nineteen sixty-eight was the year my parents were eaten by the world. That's how it felt—like the world was a big hungry Thing that had opened its mouth and swallowed them.

"That January they loaded a half-dozen suitcases into Dad's Cadillac. He was so proud of that car. It was an old fifty-six model with tail fins the size of a cartoon space rocket. He worked for the government, specializing in geothermal research.

"I don't remember much about him, but it's all good. I've heard that his science interest centered around the valley's hot spring when he was a boy—trying to understand the thermal makeup of the warm water and the geology of the minerals in the water.

"He wasn't much of an outdoorsman—at least not in the sense of hunting and fishing and raisin' hell in these mountains, and that alone set him apart from his father and most of the Cameron men who grew up here. He had bad asthma, I know that much, and when he was stuck in the house he read all the time. Mother did, too.

"There wasn't a lot of money in our branch of the family then. The Hall was shabby, but I remember feeling that we had the most wonderful life here.

"That day they left for London, Mother sat in the Cadillac's passenger seat and cried and waved. Isabel was only three months old, and Mother hated the idea of leaving her to be bottle-fed so soon.

"But Dad really wanted Mother to see London with him. She'd never traveled outside the country before. The trip was a conference on nuclear energy. Only supposed to last a week. She looked so pretty in a blue coat with her hands covered in a pair of bright red gloves she always wore. She was dark-haired and on the short side, soft and curvy, more fashionable then than she would be now. I'd guess back then people called her bohemian.

"She wrote poetry and recited Shakespeare. She played the piano and roamed the mountains looking for wild plants to collect. She kept a garden and she made papier-mâché Christmas ornaments that looked like lopsided angels.

"That day she blew kisses to us, and the air was so cold they steamed.

"I stood there trying not to cry, and Simon took my hand. He was tall and skinny and on the quiet side—I never in my life then or later heard him raise his voice—and until that day it's fair to say his dreams were simple. He'd joined some tiny little church over in Hightower, and he wanted to go to college and then seminary to become a minister. He was only sixteen then.

"Standing out there that day, it was only me, him, and Aunt Olivia. Ruth was barely old enough to totter around without falling. 'Aunt Olivia's in charge but you're the man of the house,' was the last thing Dad told Simon. But he told me, 'You're the *assistant* man of the house.'

"I was so proud of that.

"They never came home from that trip. The bomb the IRA hid in the lobby of their hotel in London killed a dozen people. Including my folks. Gone. Caught up in some gutless bastards' private war on innocent people.

"Scotland Yard forwarded their luggage and Dad's twisted-up gold wedding ring, because the detectives found it in the debris. They'd been able to make out Dad's and Mother's initials engraved inside it. That was all we got to touch. That ring.

"Their bodies came home in sealed coffins. That made it harder. Never seeing them again—not even their bodies. I remember sitting up in a hideaway spot near the attic of the Hall. Hiding there every day. Afraid to come down and find out they were still gone. I had nightmares for years that they'd gotten lost in England and were trying to find their way home. Even as a grown man I can't help looking for them in crowds, wherever I go."

"Right after that, we moved into the Hall's right wing, which had been closed off for decades. When I was a little boy, the pipes clanked and the faucets sputtered, the toilets stopped up because tree roots had taken over the drains to the septic tank, and half the light fixtures wouldn't work because squirrels and mice had chewed through the wires. The furniture coughed dust and the windows—they'd been covered by shutters outside and drapes inside—were caked with years of crud and mold.

"Hoss was in Europe with the Air Force but he sent money to pay for repairs, and so did a few other kin, and we used that to fix up the old wing so we could live there.

"Aunt Olivia wrote on her notepad: 'The Hall makes up in charm what it lacks in new amenities. I plan to open it as a hotel.' She sent that to a friend who ran the state tourism office. He wrote back and said we needed more amenities.

"Amenities. Amen Ities. Ities. Itty Bitties. Little. Amen. Prayers. 'We need more itty-bitty prayers?' I asked Simon, and when Simon finally figured out how I'd come to that conclusion he grabbed me and hugged me until I thought my eyes would pop. 'We need all the prayers we can get. I'm putting you in charge of Itty-Bitty Amens.'

"I started whispering 'Amen,' every hour every day. I'd wish on my rocks and say amen.

"When Bea came over from Scotland she said we had plenty to offer the public—not just history and FeeMolly's great food, but fresh air and wildlife and mountains that make people forget their troubles. She pointed out to the tourism honcho that there weren't many inns where people could sleep under heirloom quilts and breathe in history.

"But Emory told everyone who'd listen that she and Aunt Olivia had lost their minds, that no one would be fool enough to drive over an hour from the nearest city and pay good money to vacation in a drafty old stone-block mansion.

"Nobody could scare Aunt Olivia, though. She and Bea sat down and wrote an advertising brochure. Simon used the wording for years after that, even after he and Min hired an advertising rep to handle the inn's marketing. I remember a part about visiting our waterfalls, and sleeping on feather beds, and playing checkers in a parlor surrounded by Cameron Scottish memorabilia. 'Find your own serenity at the heart of the sacred Cameron River Valley,' the brochure said.

"Simon read that sentence to me, and to Min, over and over, like a protection. Aunt Olivia and Bea packaged up stacks of the brochures—the first ones were nothing fancy, and I helped stuff envelopes and carry the boxes to the car.

"We mailed them off to the state tourism offices and anywhere else Olivia could think of. And then we waited. And we waited. At least a month. I remember it feeling like half my life. Because just like Emory predicted, not one soul called to make a reservation.

"I used to sneak outside and eavesdrop on Simon and Min so I'd know how scared to be. They'd hide in the rose arbor down by the river, snuggling, and kissing, crying sometimes, making out, and talking. I knew things were bad. They'd only been married a few months. They were just kids.

"Old friends called to ask why in the world Aunt Olivia was demeaning the Cameron name, opening the Hall to paying guests. Strangers. But no strangers called to make reservations. Sometimes at meals we'd all sit there just quiet. Just full of this mood—the unspoken dread. We were going to have to leave. Go to Knoxville. Live in the city, turn the Hall over to Emory and his part of the family.

"I started carrying a stick and walking the perimeter of the front cattle pastures. I don't know if I was patrolling for enemies or looking for help. Both, I guess.

"Then one day early in September the phone rang, and everything changed. I remember Bea and Min running out of the office they'd set up in a storage room off the kitchen. Min was whooping, 'We've got customers!'

"Bea told us our first guests would be a married couple named Arinelli. We spent about ten minutes looking at the name written in the brand-new ledger Aunt Olivia had bought. Arinelli. I remember spelling it and trying to pronounce it.

"Max and Shari Kirk Arinelli. We didn't know then that they weren't really married. I doubt Aunt Olivia would have turned 'em away if she'd known, but she probably would have insisted they reserve two rooms.

"Your mother told Bea she saw one of our brochures at an information booth at the Nashville fairgrounds. She said she and your dad were touring with the Decca Records stage show, and they had a weekend off before they went on to the next city. They wanted to see the mountains and relax.

"The Grand Ole Opry's weekly show was all most folks thought of when anyone said 'show' and 'Nashville.' Bluegrass or country and western. But Min was a big music lover—she'd brought her stereo and all that when she married Simon—and she recognized your mother's stage name. Shari Kirk. She ran and got her stack of forty-fives and found a song your mother had recorded. I guess it hadn't hit the bestseller charts or anything, but Min liked it.

"Celebrities. That's what we had coming. Min started shrieking and we played the record right then—it was 'Summer Sometime'—and it had a little Motown flavor to it, which made it pretty exotic around here. Simon and Min slow-danced, and so did Aunt Olivia and I, and then Aunt Olivia and Bea.

"Fifty dollars a night. That was the going rate when we opened the Hall to the public. A luxury price for those days. It was one reason people said the inn idea would never fly. But we were out here miles from nowhere, with no restaurants, so the price had to include meals, otherwise we'd have had a lot of starving guests. Bea insisted on keeping the bar in the library stocked, too. Put it on the honor system. Fix yourself a drink, write a note on the bar register. Pay your tab when you leave.

"That was uptown lodging by most people's standards at the time. The county was dry. We were practically bootleggers for having a bar. There was no such thing as a liquor license. If the county sheriff hadn't been married to Hoss's niece we'd have been in trouble.

"But we were ready to entertain Max and Shari Kirk Arinelli.

"Show-business people.

"I wondered if they'd look real."

"Your parents showed up on a hot, bright Friday afternoon in a little red Mustang with the roof down and the radio turned up so loud we could hear it over the engine as the car came up the front road.

"We were all peering out the windows from behind curtains. I'm embarrassed to admit it, but Min snapped pictures. The snapshots are in Aunt Olivia's albums, along with Olivia's journal entries.

"Your mother looked like no woman we'd ever seen outside of the drive-in movies over in Hightower. She had blond hair cut in a sort of flip, and over it she'd tied a see-through white scarf with yellow polka dots. She wore big black sunglasses. She was so pretty. She smiled all the way up the driveway—the biggest, whitest smile I'd ever seen in my life, and she looked excited.

"When your dad stopped the car in the courtyard she stood up in the convertible and faced the Hall and put her hands together like a prayer against her mouth. 'What's she doing?' I whispered to Simon. 'She thinks this is a church?'

"Before he could answer Bea told me, 'She's happy to be here. The place has taken her soul in.'

"You know who she looked like the most? She looked like a blond Mary Tyler Moore. She was wearing white pedal pushers and a gold-colored top, with a fat white beaded necklace dangling down the front. Gold and yellow were her colors.

"Your dad jumped over his car door—we thought that was pretty cool, like James Bond—and he came around to her side and held up his hands. And she leaned down and gave him a little kiss on the mouth.

"And he smiled.

"In general, though, he looked less easy with himself than she did. I don't think he ever laughed that weekend. We got the sense that he was dead serious about music and life and your mother and anything else that crossed his path. He kept to himself a lot, kept quiet, and watched us. He didn't know what to make of us, I guess. Whether we were real. We felt the same way about him.

"He had jet-black hair, and his eyes were hooded and deep set. It wasn't that I'd never seen anyone who wasn't lily-white. But your father was odd to me. He wasn't quite like us and he wasn't Cherokee.

"For years Bea has told people he had a face like a boxer and eyes like a panther. Plus his hair was long—long enough to touch the top of his shirt collar in back.

"This was a helluva shock. Among our MacIntosh kin up in Oklahoma there were men who wore their hair down their backs, but that was Indian tradition, so it was all right. And they were family.

"Not to mention the fact that your dad was dressed like something out of a San Francisco coffeehouse. He showed up at the Hall in baggy white pants, a floppy blue shirt that wasn't tucked in, and white loafers *with no socks*. Not even Indian Camerons went without socks and their shirts tucked in.

"Min said, 'That man looks like he's got some Indian blood.'

"Bea said, 'No, he looks something like a Chinaman.' Bea's word, not mine. Aunt Olivia thought he was Hawaiian. 'Maybe Korean,' Simon put in. 'Like Dr. Su, Dad's friend at Oak Ridge.'

"It was almost funny. There we were hiding behind the curtains with Min taking photographs and Bea and Olivia debating a stranger's bloodline like he was a prize bull. And I remember thinking when you dig a deep hole, people say you'll dig all the way to China. That maybe the man had popped through a hole.

"Aunt Olivia started gesturing toward the front doors. Bea jumped. 'Herself is right! What are we doing? We're standing here gawking like forest brownies watching dew fall!'

"When your folks stepped inside the front hall your dad looked around like somebody might be waiting to jump him. But your mother clapped her hands, and smiled and said, 'Oh, Max. It's a different world,' and then she noticed me. I had hidden and was sneaking peeks from just inside the library doors. Of course Isabel and Ruth gave me away—Isabel was making baby-babble noises and drooling down the front of my shoulder, because I had her in a knapsack on my back. I had one hand wound in the shoulder strap of Ruth's overalls so she wouldn't run back to the fresh flowers in a vase by the hall coat stand. She'd already eaten the blooms off some tea roses.

"About the time your mother noticed me, Ruth stamped one of her hard little bare heels onto my toes. I think I went *ooooph* or something, but I kept a straight face.

"Your mother hurried over and dropped down in front of me. She took off her sunglasses and looked into my face, and smiled. 'You're covered in baby girls,' she said. 'And I'd say you're doing a good job taking care of them.'

"I was only five years old, but I already appreciated a pretty woman when I saw one. I told her, 'I look after the ladies around here, ma'am.'

"She was too sweet to laugh at me. Your father came over to me and held out his hand and said, 'Glad to meet you, you must be the ladies' man around here.'

"I was too little to get the joke, but I said, 'Yessir, can't keep 'em off of me,' and he smiled—and your mother burst out laughing then. He and I shook hands. That was the first time a grown man ever offered me his hand. It meant a lot to me.

"You see, I do have distinct memories of him, Nellie— good memories. I studied newspaper pictures of him when I started looking for you and Ella. I noticed the small scars on his chin and his eyebrows and the one across the top edge of his lip. I noticed his broken nose.

"He'd had a helluva hard life as a kid. I know that explains a lot about him. How he turned out. His politics. I try to remember that when I make judgments about him.

"But when I was little I didn't know he'd been beaten half to death in gang fights when he was growing up after World War Two. I just thought he looked different.

"He asked me if I had time to escort your mother around over the weekend, because he had work to do. And I told him I had plenty of time for an extra girl.

"He shook my hand again. And your mother didn't laugh at me. She said she'd be honored.

"That was the best day I'd had in months."

"We couldn't treat your folks like customers—we weren't clear on that aspect of running an inn yet. They were a test—they were the first paying visitors. They were the only guests in the house.

"At supper Bea set them at the big dining room by themselves but it seemed—well, too fussy and too lonely for two people. All that china and crystal and a table big enough for twenty. Bea asked them if they'd like to join the family and they looked kind of relieved and said yes. So there they were the first night, in our little Formica dining room of the family wing.

"FeeMolly overwhelmed your folks with all the food she rolled out. We still have the menu in a scrapbook Aunt Olivia keeps. Quail casserole and all sorts of homegrown vegetables, homemade yeast rolls and pies and cakes—not to mention the best wine in the house. Your dad said we couldn't go on treating strangers this well or we'd go broke. Your mother said the brochure told the truth. That we made them feel like family. She said neither one of them had any family, and I remembered being sort of embarrassed for them. Aunt Olivia wrote on the table with a pen: *You're our good-luck charm. So we'll dub you honorary family.*

"I think that pleased them no end. I think that was when your dad began to relax a little.

"After dinner he played the piano and your mother sang for us in the library of the main rooms. All sorts of songs, our own private show—your dad on the piano and your mother singing. This went on for hours. We all loved it. I sat on the floor with one arm around Shep—he was one of Bea's imported sheepdogs—and the other clutching Isabel, and I didn't want that night to ever end.

"They were magic, your folks.

"The next morning your mother got up early and she asked me if I'd show her around—go walking with her. She wanted to come down here to the hot springs. Your dad was working on musical arrangements. I was so proud that your mother thought I was man enough to escort her around the valley. This was important to me. But I told her I had to take my baby sisters, too. Simon had put me in charge of them.

"She said she'd be glad to help me baby-sit. It was clear she loved children. So off we went. I hoped the mailman or the sheriff would drive up and see us. I wanted to show her off. She was dressed in a yellow bathing suit, with an open white shirt over it, and white shorts, and white sandals. Her toenails and fingernails were painted bright pink. She put a broad yellow sunhat on her hair and tied it beneath her chin. We have a picture of her.

"Anyhow—we set off down the road, your mother pushing Isabel in her stroller and me pulling Ruth in a toy wagon. It was a nasty-hot day for September, and the trees didn't shade the spring quite as much as they do now. But when we got down there your mother shucked her shorts and sat down in the water. I didn't understand why she wanted to sit in warm water on a hot day. I'd never heard of a hot tub. Maybe she hadn't either, in nineteen sixty-eight.

"I had on shorts and a T-shirt so I sat like this with my

feet in the water, with Isabel asleep in her stroller and Ruthie splashing around in the shallow edge.

"I asked your mother why she and her husband didn't have any kids, since she liked kids so much. I remember she said something about wanting babies worse than anything else in the world. I didn't understand why she didn't have any if she wanted them so much. I thought she might be like Min's Aunt Beebee. Now Beebee—at least this was the way I heard it when I was little—Beebee couldn't have babies because she kept looking under the wrong cabbages in her cabbage patch. Also known as barking up the wrong tree, in terms of the husbands Beebee picked out.

"I said that to your mother—the cabbages theory—and she laughed. I remember that. Then she got quiet and said she'd look under all the cabbages in her garden if she got the chance. That she would love to have babies.

"That's when I gave her a rock.

"I always carried some of my wishing rocks in my pocket, rubbing them like worry stones or fetishes. I told her my mother said they were pieces of the evening star, and that it was good luck to wish on the evening star, but that she'd have to come down here at dark and wait until she saw the star in the water, and then wish. Your mother asked me, How does the star make a reflection if there are trees overhead?

"I'd wondered about this technical point myself, but my mother had always explained it away—you had to trust that the reflection was there. That the evening star would make your wish come true when the time was right. That was the trick. Timing.

"I told your mother that was why some of my wishes never came true. I just couldn't get the timing right. She asked me what I wished for the most. A toy, a trip to Disneyland, what?

"I told her I wished my parents weren't dead.

"Your mother started crying. At the time I had no idea how a child saying something like that would upset someone with a soft heart. So she was crying, and I was embarrassed and confused.

"Then all of a sudden she said she felt too hot, and she started to get out of the water, but she didn't make it. She fainted.

"Just went limp. Slid down in the deep center here. I grabbed her under the arms. I wasn't strong enough to pull her out of the spring, and I couldn't let go or she'd drown. So I only managed to keep her head above water. Ruth looked like she might fall in the deep part at any second, and I'm thinking, *What do I do if Ruth falls in, too?*

"I started yelling for help. Shep always watched Ruthie like she was a lamb, so he decided that Ruthie was the reason I was yelling, and he took hold of her by the back of her sundress and pulled her out of the water's edge.

"Ruthie never liked being herded like mutton on the hoof, so she pitched a fit. I'm yelling at the top of my lungs, Ruthie's screeching, Shep starts barking—and all that time I'm desperately trying to hold your mother's head above water with my arms going numb.

"It must have been only a few minutes but it felt like hours. Suddenly your father ran down the road. He'd started after us the way he said he would, and then heard the commotion. So he comes running full tilt and jumps in the spring. He gets one arm around your mother and one around me, and he pulls us both out.

"Then he starts rocking your mother in his arms and shaking her a little, telling her to breathe, to wake up, and he looked like he was scared out of his mind. She came to and started crying again.

"He held her and kept rocking her—and he's checking the pulse in her wrist, and he puts his hand over her heart, and he asks her 'What's wrong?' about a dozen times.

"Finally she manages to say, 'I'd die to have your babies.'

"And he looked stunned. He said, after a minute, 'You know I love you and I wouldn't have a life if you died.'

"I didn't forget that. Words like that, with death still such a part of my thoughts every day—I remember that's exactly what your parents said to each other. They kissed, and your dad looked over at me and put his arm around me. Your mother apologized for scaring me, and your dad told me I saved her life.

"I saved her life. I'd finally made a difference in the matter of life and death. I couldn't do anything about my folks being killed, but I could protect other people. I never forgot how that felt, that day, realizing the power to overcome grief by serving others. The power to make sense of the world by stopping some of the senseless pain."

"Your dad wouldn't let your mother walk back to the Hall. He sent me to get Simon to bring a car down. When we all got back to the Hall your dad carried her upstairs.

"When your dad told the family what I'd done at the spring Simon went to the liquor cabinet and fixed me about a thimbleful of brandy, and he and Bea and Olivia drank a toast to me. I thought I'd burst with pride.

"Your folks came downstairs a little while later. They confessed to Bea and Aunt Olivia that they'd lied about being married. They asked if we'd let them hold a ceremony in the chapel that afternoon. I think your dad knew he'd almost lost your mother at the spring, and it made him take stock of how he felt about her.

"Aunt Olivia had Bea put the word out—and within a few hours we had a minister, and a photographer, and flowers, and even a wedding cake.

"Your dad played the wedding march on the chapel's antique organ—but the sound was majestic. And afterward he played a song he and your mother had written, and your mother sang with it. Words she'd written that afternoon.

"And that song was 'Evening Star.' About my star. My wishing star. I will never in my life forget that song. We all went out front of the chapel with your folks, for pictures. I sat on the steps with my arm around Shep. I remember thinking that we would be all right, now. That the evening star must be watching and listening again.

"The next afternoon, when your folks were getting ready to leave, they told Aunt Olivia they'd promote the Hall to everybody they knew. As it turned out, they mentioned their wedding to a reporter in the next city, and he wrote a feature article about the inn, and we got a lot of business from that. We got our start, because of your parents' wedding here.

"Before she left your mother put her arms around me and told me she'd made a wish on the star, that she'd wished for a baby girl, and that if her wish came true she'd name her Venus after the evening star, and maybe one day her daughter would come here to look at herself in the spring. That way I'd get to see her. And she'd bring me good luck.

"She told me she'd come back to visit and she'd count on me to take care of her daughters the way I took care of my sisters, and the way I took care of her, when she fainted.

"I promised her—I swore to her on the wishing rock—that I would do that.

"Take care of her daughters.

"Take care of you."

Twenty-five

Take care of my daughters, Mom had asked. She tried to make certain Ella and I would have a second family, at Cameron Hall. Gib had saved her life—and by extension, mine, too. I wouldn't exist if it weren't for him.

"What are you thinking?" Gib asked. "I didn't tell you the story of that weekend to make you more unhappy. But you don't look happy at all right now."

Maintaining control was critical. Here was a man who was man enough to share a stunning, intimate story with undemanding sentiment in his eyes and his voice set in the earthy cadence of a parish priest reciting a workingman's mass. I loved simplicity as much as I loved the complex elegance of music. Music was nothing without its silences.

I took a deep breath. "Thank you for telling me about it. I just need a second to recover. I'm sitting here where my mother almost drowned, and you've told me a story I never heard before. Pop never talked about it."

"Does it help you understand that I *want* to remember your father kindly?" he asked. "That I'd like nothing better than to put aside what he did later on?"

"Can you do that?"

"You'll never know—and neither will I, nor anyone else—whether he meant to associate with killers or not, whether he knew what his friends intended or not. I can only tell you that you'll be judged on your own merits here, and nothing but. You and Ella."

I didn't say so, but I knew I'd have to defend Pop one way or another for the rest of my life. Maybe Mom worried that he would need more help than other men to keep his path straight. "He adored my mother. He worried about her. She had a weak heart," I said. "A heart valve that didn't close right. And the wall of her heart was thin in one spot."

Gib, who had leaned forward with his elbows on his knees, turned his head to look at me. "You're saying she had a congenital problem? It caused her to faint here?"

"Maybe. Her heart is what killed her. Heart failure while she was under anesthesia during a hysterectomy. Pop always said she thought she'd die young."

"That may be so, but there could be another explanation for why she fainted that day."

"What?"

"She was already pregnant with you."

After a long moment, I nodded. "She always told me I was born nine months after she and Pop got married here, but it was actually eight months. Maybe she just didn't want me to worry that Pop only married her because she admitted she was pregnant."

"I don't buy the idea that he felt forced to marry her. I think he admitted how much he loved her that day."

"I know he loved her."

"Try to keep in mind that your mother had a lot of faith in the future. Maybe not her own future, or your father's, but yours and Ella's and mine. Try to stop worrying so much and have some faith yourself."

"You think I'm cynical for no good reason?"

"No, a lot of people have let you down. Including me."

"You? No. I had no expectations."

"Then why did you keep the rock? And the wedding picture?"

I was silent. "Why?" he persisted.

"Because I liked to believe in you."

"Then I did let you down. I should have come after you years ago. You and Ella. I knew more about your father's arrest than most people. I could have found you, if I'd wanted to."

I faced forward, staring blindly into the forest. "Thanks for the honesty." I straightened automatically, trying to keep a show of pride.

"I'm sorry," he said wearily. "I had a career to think about. There were friends you could have turned to. I thought you would. You disappeared too fast for me to have a chance."

"I didn't know who to trust."

"So you're human. You don't have to explain anymore."

"Fine. Neither do you."

"Yes, I do." He paused. "I was only about twenty-six. First-year rookie. And I lived and breathed for my work. I'd been meant for it since that day here at the spring, when I learned how it felt to keep someone else from dying or getting hurt. I didn't want to risk losing my career. Plus I didn't want to hurt my family's reputation. Simon and Min had finally turned the Hall into a success. A moneymaker."

Who was I to be disappointed by his failings, when I had my own to consider? "I doubt I'd have trusted you enough to accept your help," I managed. "By then I'd learned not to trust *anybody*. Particularly if you were with the government. I still feel that way about government agents."

"I'm the government. You're the government. Every citizen of this country is the government. Your father only had legitimate reason to blame the people who made the Asian American policies when he was a boy, and the people on the street who treated him like dirt because he was mixed-race. That's not 'the government.' "

"Then I'll tell you what the government is. It's men who come into a house with two teenage girls who don't have an attorney yet, and they call in some beefy women in uniforms who take the underage girl to a juvenile jail because there's no adult supervision in the house, and then they push the older girl around—literally *push* her into corners and yell at her and threaten to arrest her. It's men who smile while they're pawing through your lingerie or your high-school yearbooks or your jewelry box. Or personal diaries. It's men old enough to be a father to you, men who are dressed well and supposed to be upstanding defenders of justice and the American way, men who know they can play a little grab-and-tickle with a girl who's scared and has no one to turn to for help."

He stared at me, and I watched the effect of my outburst settle in him. "I didn't learn any of that in my research on you," he said, in a low voice, and I knew he was shocked. But I didn't want pity from him, not from him. I wished I hadn't said a word.

"They don't write it up in the official reports," I said wearily.

"If you can remember any names, tell me. I'll locate the bastards for you. I'll make it possible for you to confront them face-to-face. I can do that for you."

"I don't remember names. What difference does it make now, anyway?"

"This kind of thing goes on because people won't talk about it."

"No, it goes on because the system is corrupt, and when the government comes down on people who have no money or power, nobody gives a damn about constitutional rights."

"That's not true. A lot of good people care. I care."

"*Then listen to that tape I gave you.* Because obviously music is all I can give you—and all you'll take from me— without both of us being scared of the future and fighting over the past."

We sat in silence for a minute, struggling with the reality of mistakes and regrets. His shoulders hunched, his mouth set in resolute lines, he dropped the white pebble from his hand into mine. Then, in a quiet voice, he said, "You think you can learn to love an ex-government man?"

I took a deep breath. I wanted so badly for him and his family to recognize the basic decency of me and my family. I wanted so badly to trust him with everything I held dear, the way my mother had.

The water of the spring was too warm, suddenly. I felt dizzy. But my heart was strong—I wouldn't let myself end up heartbroken like Mom and Pop. I eased out of the water and sat on the spring's grassy edge. When Gib reached out to help I drew back instinctively. "I can't." He stopped his hand in midair. "It's nothing personal," I promised quickly.

"The hell it's not," he said.

The next morning, around dawn, I walked to the river along an old path cushioned with fallen leaves. I went to the wooden-and-stone gazebo on a bank of ferns overlooking the water, and sank down in a willow chair. I listened to birds sing and the river burble seductively, and I prayed.

How do I deal with all of this?

Nothing came to me—not a whisper, not a thought, not a stray feather.

But suddenly there was Gib, cresting a pastured ridge against the gold-and-red morning, silhouetted like a tall earth-bound wizard in his old fedora and the cane gripped in his ruined hand. Walking the wild hills was a lonely, powerful habit Camerons seemed to take to heart like their Highlander ancestors. I watched him, fixated, as he crossed that space of open ridge. He halted and looked down at me.

I was sure he knew it was me there in the gazebo. We held each other's distant scrutiny for a few seconds before he turned abruptly and walked into the forest, headed in the direction of his lodge by the waterfall. I had a bad feeling he'd been walking all night. Into the wilderness for my sake. And me for his sake.

The cusp of the sun lit up the ridge and colored him in gold. I found myself crying. I didn't want to need him or his family because, like Gib, I didn't want to need people I knew I'd have to give up. I didn't want to lose anyone else in my life.

But I loved him secretly, without any doubt at all.

I stayed frantically busy to keep from thinking about Gib or at least to exhaust the temptation. He seemed to be doing the same. No task was too big or too demanding. He moved truckloads of hay into the barns for the winter; he mulched the gardens; he was constantly roaming about the Hall and the outbuildings doing some handyman chore with a toolbelt hanging from his waist.

I went to the Hall one day for rehearsals with Ella, piano lessons that I'd begun to teach Jasper, and singing lessons for Kelly. That day I had my head wrapped in a purple scarf. I felt like a grape. I needed to find some private time and tell Ella the story Gib had told me about Mom and Pop. I knew it would mean as much to her as it had to me.

Ella sat with her back to me in the music room of the Hall, playing guitar. Unfortunately, Carter lounged nearby. They were rarely separated, which made it nearly impossible for her and me to hold deep conversations. I knew she liked it that way.

She was wearing a large straw hat. I gazed at her in bewilderment as I placed a handful of sheet music on the piano. "Hello?"

"Hello," she said, without turning around.

"You look real fashionable," Carter said to me.

"No, I look like I belong to a gang that attacks wine stewards."

"Well, that, too." He grinned. "Anyhow, Ellie figured you and her could use a different kind of rehearsal today. You should do some songs with piano and guitar. I'm sure the guests will like it."

"That would mean writing new arrangements. No, we'll stick to piano and violin."

Ella turned around. She removed the hat. She had cut her hair off down to the dark emerging roots. Now it was a soft black cap, maybe an inch long all over. I stared at her. "Isn't she cute as a bug?" Carter asked.

Ella managed a teary smile. "I didn't want you to be the only one with no hair. Now we'll both grow out together."

For the first time in weeks we shared something other than anger, disappointment, and sorrow. We were both nearly bald, like novitiates in some spartan nunnery.

I went to the piano and sat down. "Let's improvise some duets with the guitar. Maybe that's not a bad idea."

Ella couldn't stand it. She had to come over and sit beside me and hug me. "You don't have to say anything," she whispered.

"Birds of a feather go bald together," I managed. "I love you."

Carter cleared his throat. "I won't ask you for a blessing on your sister and me—not yet—because I know you think I haven't earned it, but I have to say that you are a classy lady who holds her opinions as gentle as a wren on the nest. When they've gotten too big for the circumstance you let 'em go."

His analogy made about as much sense as a nineteenth-century German tone poem, but I nodded. "I'm trying to give you the benefit of the doubt."

"Something's happened to you," Ella said. "You're different."

"I'm hairless. It affects my brain." I put my hands on the keyboard and cleared my throat. "Let's get started. You pick and I'll grin." She laughed then reached for her new guitar.

What had happened between Gib and me was a sharp small stick jabbing me in the stomach. I didn't know who I was anymore.

Twenty-six

We were only weeks away from the Hall's opening. The skies poured rain, and the wind coming down off the mountains was intoxicating, bringing a brisk scent like cold, wet granite and chimney smoke. Thanksgiving weekend had come and gone. The highlight was a flock of wild turkeys parading across the front lawn without a clue that a couple of their tame brethren were roasting inside the Hall's kitchen ovens. After the turkeys wandered away Ella ran outside and picked up a dozen large feathers, proudly adding them to her collection.

The first day of December, all of us began putting up Christmas decorations. This went on, nonstop, for an entire week. Since the inn's opening weekend followed closely on New Year's Day, Gib and Min had decided the holiday decorations should be left up until then. Frankly, we wanted to dazzle the reviewers. Blind them to the reality of Simon's absence, if necessary.

Ella went into Christmas overload. After years of glumly decorating only a tiny fake tree we anchored to the RV's dresser, she was as excited as a child.

A spectacular Christmas tree now stood in the front foyer

of the Hall. It was easily thirty feet tall, and covered in hundreds of ornaments contributed by guests over the decades. Smaller trees were decorated in the music room, the dining room, and the sitting area at the end of the upstairs hall. Even the guest rooms had small Christmas trees, and elaborate wreaths were hung on each door.

But in the family wing, the Christmas atmosphere was fragile and poignant. A single delicate tree stood in the den, adorned with cherished heirloom ornaments and whimsical ones made by the family. Some were yellowed, papier-mâché angels with crumbling wings, made by Winny Cameron, Gib's mother. They smiled quaintly from the green boughs.

When I was growing up, the nuns talked about finding the Holy Spirit in a home. I felt it, looking at that sentimental tree in the den. So much about the Camerons was gracious, kind, respectful, serene. There was an ingrained security among them, maybe a temporary security for Ella and me, but I craved it more every day.

I looked in my bathroom mirror in the mornings and watched a bristly, dark-haired stranger emerge. I continued to artfully braid and wrap scarves around my head and sock a floppy cloth hat over that, before I left the cottage. I wasn't sure yet who this stranger might become, so I refused to reveal her to anyone else.

I wouldn't say I coached Kelly to a level where she could win the Miss Teenage Eastern Tennessee beauty pageant, or even the pageant's talent competition, but on a cold, clear night a week before Christmas, at a cheesily decorated high-school auditorium among the big-city lights of Knoxville, Tennessee, I can honestly say that Gib's niece, my determined student, Kelly Cameron, was the best, the proudest, and certainly the *only* sixteen-year-old Evita Perón the audience had ever seen.

It was a major Cameron family event, requiring a caravan

of five cars for the long trip to the city. I went early with Kelly, Min, and Ruth as a backstage assistant. I led Kelly in relaxation techniques and voice warm-ups. Ruth counseled her to watch the other contestants for pageant violations like stuffing their dress bodices, which could get a girl disqualified.

When Gib ushered the rest of the family into their seats at the auditorium Bo Burton arrived, too. He showed Min the bouquet of pink roses he'd bought for Kelly. Just as I'd suggested in a private consultation, Bo plucked one rose from their midst then presented it to Min. "And a rose for the most beautiful mother a pageant contestant could have."

Min flushed. "I'm too old to be silly about a flower." She thrust the rose at a startled Isabel then excused herself and went backstage.

"What did I say wrong this time?" Bo asked me wearily. I pretended not to hear him. My matchmaking was supposed to be our little secret. I felt Gib watching me.

"You're accusing Minnie of having womanly vanity," Bea said loudly. "She's no' used to being flirted with, man!" Bea slapped him on the back. "You must take matters into bold consideration, or she'll never get your wee meanin'!"

"My meaning is getting more *wee* by the day," Bo said.

Gib guided me to a quiet corner in the lobby. We stood, casually hidden, around the corner from a case of football trophies. "I should have known," he said. "Bo's as subtle as a tank. So are you."

"I'm only trying to help."

"How's Kelly?"

"Pretending not to be nervous. She's so scared her fake eyelashes quiver."

"Poor kid."

"But if you want to know the truth, Ruth is more nervous than Kelly is. Min is very calm about everything."

"Ruth takes competition seriously. If you think she's intense, you should see Jasper. He's outside pacing the sidewalk. I don't think males should be allowed to come to these things. This is a female event."

"Listen, Pop used to throw up before my piano competitions. He tried to hide his problem but I found out as I got older. Now *that's* pressure."

"Too much pressure on you to meet his expectations," Gib corrected with a troubled tone.

"No. I loved it. I had nerves of steel."

"No, you'd just never admit it when you were afraid."

I changed the subject. "Kelly's a trouper. I've armed her with every tactic I know—concentration, delivery, mental attitude, you name it."

"Now wave a magic wand over her and turn her into a Barbie like the other girls in the pageant." Gib sighed. "I don't want to see her get flattened."

"Go walk the pavement with Jasper. You're as antsy as any daddy."

"Kelly's been asking me to teach her the basics of tae kwon do. I think she should switch to that. Martial arts. Forget the eyelashes."

"Nonsense. I've got to go backstage again. Ruth's idea of preshow encouragement is to tell Kelly they can sue the pageant organizers if anything goes wrong."

"Hey, you two!" Ella glided up to us. She looked lovely and plush in a pleated blue jacket and skirt. Her hair had grown out enough to lie flat, courtesy of Ebb and Flo's hightest styling mousse. It gleamed like onyx. Mine was still a bristle. I'd wrapped a black silk scarf around my head that night, to match the suit I wore.

Ella smiled and touched Gib's coat sleeve. "You've been gone so long Carter thought you went to buy a bottle of bourbon."

"I should."

"Would you mind getting Aunt Olivia a Coke at the concessions stand? I told her I'd get it, but I have to make a quick run to the rest room."

"I'll get the Coke. Go ahead."

I strode over to her. "Are you feeling all right?" I touched her face. "You're a little pale. What's Carter done? Did you two have a fight?"

"Oh, Vee. Stop obsessing." She smiled, then disappeared into a nearby women's room.

"Yeah, quit obsessing," Gib echoed somberly. "Go worry about Kelly."

"Okay. Do me a favor. Buy the Coke but then wait outside the bathroom and walk Ella back to her seat."

"Sure," he agreed darkly. "I like to hang around women's rest rooms."

"If anyone stares at you just say you need a date."

"Scram," he growled. "And stop worrying about Ella."

"See you from the wings. Tell the whole clan to applaud like crazy every time Kelly sets foot onstage." I darted away, frowning.

Kelly was in the middle of "Don't Cry for Me, Argentina," belting out the melodramatic lyrics to a somewhat flabbergasted audience of several hundred people. They had just finished clapping enthusiastically for a pie-eyed redhead who tap-danced and twirled a baton to the love song from *Aladdin*. The redhead was more their type.

But Kelly was selling Eva Perón, really selling the piece, accompanied by a tape of my customized arrangement of the song, which played with fairly decent quality over the auditorium's sound system.

"The truth is, I neeeever left you," Kelly sang, spreading her arms wide. "All through my wild—"

The electricity went off. Not an uncommon occurrence on windy mountain nights. The music stopped, the microphone went dead, the lights faded, and small emergency lights snapped on, offering just enough illumination to prove

Kelly stood in the center of a glitter-draped stage with her mouth frozen open in horror.

"I'll have somebody's ass in a trap over this," Ruth snarled, standing beside me in the wings. I ran to an old upright piano that had been rolled just offstage during rehearsals. I gave it a shove and it careered out of the wings. I pushed the bench out to it, sat down, and played the opening to Kelly's song. She looked at me desperately. *Sing,* I mouthed to her.

And she did. I thought her lungs might burst. She arched her back and bellowed the song with great melodramatic flourishes, striding back and forth on the dim stage in her tailored faux-glam padded-shoulder pin-striped suit, and then she teetered on her stacked-heeled pumps down a short set of stairs at the center of the stage and worked the audience, extending her arms as she walked a few yards up the center aisle, turning to either side, making eye contact, then backing slowly toward the stage and climbing the stairs as she sang the last few bars.

As she finished she nodded regally, just as I'd taught her to do. I didn't care if she won or not, if there was applause or not—I was so proud of her, and remembered so many times when Pop's firmly ingrained bravado helped me through tough moments in public. I suddenly realized that I'd taught her the discipline and confidence I'd carried straight from him, and from Mom, and before them from Grandpop Paolo and Grandmother Akiko, and even my grandmother Big Jane Kirkelson, who must have been a confident woman if she played guitar in truck stops.

The audience went wild with applause. They gave Kelly a standing ovation. She nodded again, outwardly composed, though she transmitted a visible body tremor that made the back of her skirt shimmy. I ducked down behind the piano's high back and quickly wiped tears from my eyes.

Thank you, I whispered to the knowing ghosts around me.

Kelly waited until the applause began to fade and then pivoted and walked slowly off. I followed. The instant she was out of public view Ruth grabbed her in a bear hug. "I did it," Kelly said, hiccuping with relief. Min stepped out of the shadows. "I'm so proud of you," she said.

Kelly raced to her. They hugged tearfully. "Do you think Daddy would be proud, too?"

"Oh, *yes*."

Ruth clapped her on the shoulder. "Sweetie hon, you may not win the pageant but everybody in Knoxville is going to hear about your performance."

"I did everything the way Aunt Vee said."

Aunt Vee. Tears burned my eyes. I covered desperately by straightening my ludicrous turban.

Ruth glared at me. "Well, doesn't that just take the cake?" she drawled. "Madame Swami has won a convert."

Propelled by the pageant, we were all cheerful for the holidays. Bo Burton barnstormed us on Christmas Eve. The man terrorized the livestock, the dogs, the cats, and any nearby wildlife when he arrived without warning in a forestry-service helicopter, dropping languidly into the front pasture like Santa Claus with rotary-blade reindeer.

"I brought Maine lobsters!" he bellowed as he and the chopper pilot lugged a huge ice chest up through the front shrubs. All of us gathered on the front courtyard to watch him.

"Did they sprout wings?" Min asked dryly.

"Minnie, these lobsters are too heavy to fly on their own! These lobsters are so big they'll even scare FeeMolly!"

"Not unless they know how to use spray paint or a meat cleaver," I muttered. Beside me, Gib gestured to Carter and Jasper. To me he said, "Watch this. He loves it." Then he called to Bo, "You have anything else to carry? Need some help?"

Bo stopped melodramatically, his brindled hair stirring like the mane of some mad professor, his long cloth coat

winging back from broad candy-striped suspenders and a
Frosty the Snowman tie. He spread one hand over his heart.
"More? More? Of course there's more. There's an ice chest
full of champagne and caviar."

"He's brought food like this every Christmas for years,"
Gib told me. "When his wife was alive she'd get out of the he-
licopter with her arms full of tins of homemade cookies and
cheesecake. And every year Simon made the same joke about
the Burton Christmas gifts. He'd walk out to meet them all
hunched over, swearing they'd broken his back the year before. They loved that routine of his." Gib hesitated, frowning.
"I don't know how to clown around with Bo. Suggest something funny I can do, Nellie. Quick. Somebody needs to keep
up the tradition."

"It's already taken care of."

Jasper darted from around a corner of the house, pushing
a large wheelbarrow. He zigzagged across the lawn, grinning
determinedly. "Daddy told me to never help you carry pack-
ages," he called to Bo, "unless I brought a wheelbarrow or a
truck!"

Bo laughed heartily. Gib blew out a breath and seemed to
feel relieved. I touched his arm briefly, and when he looked at
me I hid my sympathy behind a jaunty expression. "See? You
don't have to keep up all of Simon's traditions by yourself.
But if it makes you feel any better, in my eyes you'll always
be a *natural* clown."

His mouth turned up at the corner. "Thank you so much."

Kelly loped to Bo and threw her arms around his neck.
She pecked him on the cheek. He kissed her forehead. She
turned and grinned at Min. "Come on, Mama, your turn." Apparently, this was another tradition.

But Min fled toward the Hall's front doors. "I think I hear
the phone," she said.

Bo's jovial smile faded as he watched her run.

.   .   .

Christmas morning. I was expected at the Hall by eight A.M. for an elaborate family breakfast, to be followed by champagne mimosas and the gathering Bea called "the wee sharing of the gifts" around the Christmas tree in the music room.

It was a crisp, blue-sky day, with a heavy frost glinting like silver. I dressed in red leggings, a long white sweater, a shimmering gold scarf, and a gaudy Santa cap. I gave Allegra a Christmas stocking, which I'd stuffed with a six-pack of albacore tuna, two cat toys, and a fresh bag of catnip. Then I tucked her in my knapsack, which was bulging with tapes of new music I'd written. I took my walking stick and stepped outdoors.

A small brass historical marker had been planted neatly beside the path to my front door. A red bow was tied around the post.

> SCHOOLHOUSE COTTAGE. HOME OF THE LEGENDARY VENUS "NELLIE" ARINELLI, MUSICIAN, EXPLORER, PROTECTOR OF PIGS. ORIGINALLY FROM NEW ORLEANS, LOUISIANA. SHE PUTS HOT-PEPPER SAUCE ON HER GRITS. KNOWN FOR HAVING BLOND, BLACK, OR ORANGE HAIR. LIVES WITH A SMALL PANTHER NAMED ALLEGRA.

I must have read it a dozen times. I wondered if it had been Gib's idea and decided it had to be. I touched the raised brass letters. I laughed at it, and myself. I struggled not to cry like a sentimental fool, because I already looked silly enough. Finally, I took the bow off the post and tied it around my wrist like a Christmas corsage.

Allegra and I hiked to the Hall.

The family's mood was bittersweet that Christmas morning. Amid so much splendor, they remembered the past year's holiday, when the Hall was dark and all anyone could think of was the accident, and Simon. They were aware of their contrasts just as Ella and I were aware of ours; Christmases past had been depressing, small, and lonely but Christmas present glittered like warm wine and diamonds.

"I like my historical marker," I said to everyone, most pointedly to Gib. He nodded. "Whose idea was it?"

"Santa's," he said dryly.

"Okay, but who snuck over in the middle of last night and set it in the ground?"

"Santa's elves."

"They left large shoe prints with ribbed treads." *Just like your farm boots.*

"Mountain elves on steroids. Getting bigger every year." He paused. "Why, you're learning to track elves. Pretty soon you'll be able to find your way back home when you go hiking."

"If I could speak to the elves personally I'd say, 'Don't be smart-assed when someone is trying to say thank you.'"

"I'm sure the elves would point out that you're giving elfhood a bad name with that pointy-tailed hat you're wearing."

"Well, I have a surprise."

I glanced around the room. Bea, Olivia, Jasper, Kelly, Min, Isabel, Ella and Carter, and Bo Burton watched me expectantly. Even Ruth and her taciturn husband looked curious. Finally I met Gib's shrewd eyes. I pulled the hat and scarf off and ruffled my black hair, which was now a sleek but decorous inch long. "Here she is," I announced. "The boring woman with no braids."

There were broad smiles. "You look like Audrey Hepburn," Min said. "Really."

I darted a look at Gib. The unguarded gleam of appreciation on his face flooded me with warmth. "Pshaw," I said.

Ella smiled at me. "You do look like Audrey Hepburn a little."

"I've always thought of you as a *Katharine* Hepburn type," Gib offered, regaining his neutral expression.

"What? Smart and vivacious?"

"Cranky and domineering," Ruth interjected.

"Protocol!" Bea announced. "Each to his or her own chair, dearies. Make a round of it. Starting with Min."

The gifts were small and inventive, token presents, in keeping with family tradition. Min gave inspirational books. I handed out carefully wrapped cassette tapes. "This is a collection of pieces I've written during the fall," I said. "I call them *The Cameron Suite.*"

"You wrote a symphony about us?" Isabel asked.

"No, no. To be technical, it's a series of instrumental pieces—synthesized with backgrounds and complex tracks on my keyboard—that are thematically linked."

"Like a John Tesh concert?" Jasper asked hopefully.

"Hmmm. Yes." *Trust a teenager to crush you totally,* I thought, but kept my elitist opinion to myself.

"This is a treasure," Bea said, tucking her tape in her pocket. Olivia's eyes gleamed. She held her tape in both hands, on her lap.

Gib said nothing. I had no idea if he'd ever listened to the other tape I'd given him. His approval meant so much to me I'd rather not know.

When her turn came, Isabel stood. "Ella and I have grown so close in the months since she and Vee came here. She's become a new sister. We've had so many long talks about life and men, and art and men, and children and men." Everyone laughed. I forced a smile, thinking that Ella had more in common with Isabel than with me. "And we've talked a lot about spirituality. About living it, and about dealing with tragedy through faith, and about expressing faith. And so"—she gathered a stack of small, flat parcels wrapped in gold paper and bows—"here are some new paintings of mine. Thank you, Ella, for inspiring them."

Angels. When I pulled the gilded paper off my gift I looked down at a fierce blue-and-white-robed angel with braided hair, carrying a fanged black cat and a keyboard. She was beautiful, in the stilted folk-art style that had become popular.

"Wow," Carter said. "My angel is one dancing dude." He tapped a finger on the painting. "Is that my goat, Izzy?"

"Yes," she said cheerfully.

"Mine is sweet, and I love all the doves around her," Ella enthused.

"Mine's wearin' MacCallum plaid, and an archangel she must be," Bea proclaimed. "And look." She held up Olivia's painting. "Herself with a scroll and feathered pen like a razor-sharp spear." Bea pointed next at Ruth's angel portrait. "Why, it looks as though Ruth is pounding the clouds with a judge's gavel."

I laughed. Ruth snorted at me. I craned my head and peered at Gib's gift. His angel was a crew-cut Marine in flowing Marine-blue robes, carrying a sword.

Isabel had finally found the perfect symbolism for the Cameron sanctuary, the fierce devotion to home and family. She was painting wrathful, protective, warrior angels. "Say something," I whispered to Gib.

Gib lifted his head and nodded to his baby sister, who waited eagerly. "Good work, Sis. Semper *Fly*."

She smiled with relief.

Finally, Ella handed out her gifts. She and Carter traded quick kisses and soft, meaningful looks. Ella slid her arm around my neck and hugged me briefly while Carter maneuvered a large box in front of me. Her eyes were teary and glowing. "You have to open yours first," she said.

I sat there, unmoving. Everyone was looking at me with their unopened gifts propped on their laps. Gib leaned close. "Don't look so nervous."

I unpeeled pale silver-and-white wrappings tied with an elaborate bow in which a small white paper dove was anchored. I opened the box and found a tiny box atop mounds of tissue paper. I unwrapped that box with trembling fingers.

Inside was a small crystal grand piano. "Thank you," I said, giving Ella a puzzled but relieved look. "It's beautiful."

She was crying urgently, watching my reaction. "Look through the rest of the box."

I shoved tissue paper aside. Underneath was a small over-night bag. "Just what I needed," I said carefully, frowning.

"It's packed; I packed it for you," Ella said.

"I'm going somewhere?"

"You and Gib are."

"What?"

Gib stood. "Take your bag, Nellie, and put on your coat. We're going to Virginia to get the rest of your Christmas present."

Twenty-seven

Gib made mysterious phone calls when we stopped at a gas station somewhere in the rolling hills south of Richmond. We'd been on the road for five hours. He'd consumed, along the way, two hamburgers, four cups of coffee, and one long, thick cigar. I'd refused all of his offers for convenience-store food, beverages, and smokes. I wanted explanations, which were the one thing he wouldn't give.

"We'll be there in an hour," he said as he slid back into the jeep. I was wearing my quilted parka, but the jeep was drafty and I was nervous. I shivered. "Don't you think it's time you let me know what this is about?"

"You'll know soon enough."

"Ella knows. Just tell me, too."

"She wants it to be a surprise. She and I agreed."

"She knows I don't like surprises. So why didn't she come with us?"

"You'll have to ask her when we get back. I don't pretend to understand women."

"You've made that obvious."

From the pocket of his heavy canvas coat he pulled candy

bars and a packet of venison jerky. "Dried Bambi strips," he noted drolly, offering them. "A specialty of the store."

"I'm not hungry. I really *don't* like surprises, Gib. And if this trip is a joke, it's a bad one."

"It's not a joke. But whether you'll like it, I can't predict." He briefly consulted a coffee-stained map he pulled from a thick folder of maps stuffed behind his seat, then he hotwired the ignition and clamped a stiff, dark brown section of jerky between his teeth.

And on we went.

It was late afternoon. The sky had clouded. The Richmond-area radio stations were predicting snow. We'd traveled along two-lane blacktop through nothing but brown, wintry farmland and forest for the past thirty miles.

I looked around anxiously as Gib turned the jeep onto a broad, unpaved road that wandered off through two pastures. A small sign by the entrance warned in large reflective letters: Restricted. No Access. No Trespassing.

"What kind of place is out here in the middle of nowhere?"

"A big one."

He drove along the well-kept road in a cloud of gravel dust, with fenced pastures on both sides; cattle grazed at open-sided hay sheds. I still couldn't fathom what type of warehouse existed in the gentrified Virginia farmland. We passed through a short stretch of forest until the road abruptly changed from gravel to sleek pavement. We rounded a bend and faced a towering chain-link gate with an official-looking gatehouse. Gone were gentle farm fences and pastures. Twelve-foot-tall chain link stretched threateningly as far as I could see in either direction, dotted at intervals with large No Trespassing signs that warned of armed security. In the distance were at least a dozen enormous, utilitarian gray-steel buildings.

"Where are we?" I asked in a low voice. "And how often do the inmates try to escape?"

"This is to keep people out, not in," Gib answered calmly. A guard in an unmarked khaki uniform stepped briskly from the gatehouse. He wore a large pistol at his waist and scrutinized us seriously. Gib introduced himself and held out his driver's license but also some kind of laminated special pass. The guard nodded pleasantly. "Mr. Cameron. All right, sir, go to Building C."

He pushed a button, the gate whirred open, and we drove in. As Gib guided the jeep down the lanes between the buildings, their shadows slid over us. I found myself pressing my spine into the seat's backrest. Overwhelmed, I was stiffening into resistance. "I feel small, and I don't like it."

"We have met the enemy," Gib quoted with grim humor, "and I'm sorry to admit that this time the enemy is *we the people*."

I gave him a puzzled frown. At that point a small door popped open at the end of one building and another khaki-outfitted man stepped from inside. I saw lettering on the steel facing. Building C. He waved at us, Gib nodded to him, then parked next to the door. I sat in frozen silence. Gib came around to my side and opened the passenger door. I warned quietly, "I'm not getting out until you explain why you brought me here. And what *here* is."

We traded a look, mine searching, his troubled. He held out his hand. "It's a U.S. government warehouse." He closed his hand over my arm carefully. "And I brought you here to reclaim what was taken from your family."

I felt dazed as we walked into the shadowy interior of Building C, but a small part of my brain began to buzz with the enormity of it. Around us stretched mammoth rows of heavy steel-girdered shelves; the building's peaked steel roof seemed a mile above my head, and stacked neatly onto the high concourses were hundreds or maybe thousands of wooden crates, each labeled with stenciled codes in black lettering. As we walked down an aisle, guided by the man who had waved us toward the warehouse, I looked at the computer bar codes pasted on each crate, as well.

Gib kept one hand under my forearm. I was shaking. I couldn't stop listening to the military tap of our shoes on the smooth concrete floor.

"—so a couple of weeks ago we confirmed the entire series of storage crates for you, sir," the warehouse supervisor was saying, "and I had my people pull everything and relocate the items near the loading dock for dispersal at your request."

"That sounds fine. Thank you," Gib responded. "Do you think you can transport everything to Tennessee before the end of the week?"

"Yes, sir. Whatever you want, sir."

Gib Cameron, one of the President and the First Lady's favorite Secret Service agents, had called on a few extremely high-level sources for help. "Well, here you go, sir," our guide said, waving a hand at several dozen crates isolated in one corner. They were cordoned off with yellow tape attached to orange cones. Some of the crates were small enough to hold only a lamp or a framed picture. Others were so large they must have contained furniture. "Per your request, sir," the supervisor said, "I had the lids removed temporarily so you could check the contents."

"Thank you."

"I'll be in my office near the front door when you're finished, sir."

"We'll try not to take too long."

"No hurry, sir. You're the only business I've got on Christmas Day."

Dimly I heard the sharp rhythm of the supervisor's footsteps as he walked away. Then there was silence—only the slight groan of a heating system keeping the air above freezing. Premium air for cherished goods. My family's goods. Stolen by our own government.

"Are you all right?" Gib asked softly.

"I don't know."

"I didn't plan to spring it on you like this. I debated whether I should tell you first, then bring you here—what would be easier."

"I thought . . . the government . . . sold everything at auction. Years ago. Like our house."

"No. I started checking just to see what'd been done—I didn't really believe everything was in storage somewhere."

"That's what you've been doing on the computer. On the Internet. Research."

"I had help. I have contacts. I have resources other people don't have. You know that."

"It doesn't matter. How you found out—doesn't matter." I lunged for the yellow tape and jerked a section between my hands. It made me think of crime scenes. When it tore I rushed past to the nearest crate, then halted, one hand thrust out tentatively, shaking. The sides reached chest level on me. One step closer and I looked down. All I could see was a jumble of shaved-wood packing material. It was as if giant birds had made a yellow, pine-scented nest in the top of every crate.

Gib was beside me. "I could look and let you know what's there, if you want me to."

"No." The packing material was soft and maddeningly thick. I stuck my hands deep into it, clawing, pushing. Finally I shoved a mound aside and touched grainy cloth over a rounded surface.

I stood on tiptoe and gazed down at the upholstery on the top of a plush armchair. "Pop's chair," I whispered. "He kept this in his bedroom. Ella and I would sit in this chair and watch him at his dresser. He'd knot his tie and brush his hair, and then he'd walk over to us with his cuff links in one hand,

and he'd bow. 'My ladies, how's about it?' he'd say. And we'd each take a cuff link. He made a big production out of letting us pin them on for him."

I shut my eyes. "I can see him," I whispered helplessly. "He loved us and he loved that routine." I looked over at Gib.

"I never realized how devoted he was to you and Ella," he said slowly. "Or how you remember him."

I went to another crate, flinging the curlicues of wood fiber aside. And then another crate, and another. I was panting and half crying and nearly blind with a strange mixture of grief and relief and fury. The living-room chairs, the dining-room table, the Dresden ballet-dancer lamp that had been Mom's favorite, remnants of her fine china, knickknacks and books and linens, pots and pans—it was all there, breaking my heart. I ran to the last large crate and hoisted myself over the top of it.

"Easy, now, easy," Gib ordered, clasping me around the waist. I crawled forward, sinking.

"They stole everything from my family!" I beat the soft padding with my fist. "Don't tell me to take it easy! My heart is in here! My memories. How dare they take all this and keep it and lock it away in boxes! How could they? *How could they?*"

I bowed my head, sobbing. I was crouched in the top of the open crate, huddled in the wood-curlicue nest like an Easter egg in a basket, but I was beyond humiliation. I felt Gib's hand on my hair, stroking. "I don't know," he admitted hoarsely. "I'm ashamed it happened to you." I turned my face to his palm and kissed his hand.

There was a broad, flat surface deep beneath my knees. I dug down frantically. My fingertips scraped over black, glossy, glass-smooth wood. Shoving the packing material aside, I saw the dear and familiar sight of the piano I'd played from the time I was old enough to sit in Pop's lap and reach the ivories.

I thrust my hand down and played a single, simple chord. The sound was distorted, muffled, and out of tune. But by God it was strong enough to echo off the walls of the cold steel warehouse.

We survived. We would not live in silence.

Tearful but victorious, I raised my head and met Gib's gaze. I had a real part of my family's heritage and my childhood back. I had spent so many years at this piano, I had grown up there, talking to Gib, my boy in the photograph that had sat on top of this piano with far more grace than I now demonstrated.

"The music," I said. "I can't leave it. Can't leave it here. Can't leave anything. I have to take care of my family's—"

"The supervisor is shipping everything to Tennessee right away." Gib held out his arms. "*This week.* No doubt about it. No tricks, no lies, no manipulation. I can't change what happened in the past, but in this instance the *government* is made up of people who want to do the right thing, people you can trust."

I shook my head wildly. "I'll never believe any so-called 'official' decision or any promise—"

"You only have to believe *me.* You have my word." He emphasized every syllable. "*You have my word.*"

I gazed at him, growing calmer. He was right. I didn't need to dissect the circumstances, the motives, the outcome. I trusted him. I had always believed in him; he had always been, whether he knew it or not, the one true and unbroken man in my life.

I nodded finally. I had Gib Cameron's word.

By the time we left the warehouse the snow had already made a white frost on the pastures and the cattle. Winter twilight settled in. I couldn't leave without something to show Ella, so we took the only crate small enough for us to put in the jeep's backseat. I nonchalantly wound one arm between Gib's car seat and mine, so I could rest a hand tenderly on the crate. I would have liked to touch him with the same possessiveness.

"It's too late to drive to Tennessee tonight," he said, "and the roads may be bad once we get back into the mountains. I'm going to stop at that motel we passed when we got off the interstate. See if we can get a couple of rooms."

"Fine." I was limp with exhaustion and emotionally drained.

We had no trouble booking two rooms, since it was Christmas and the motel was empty except for us and a bored clerk at the front desk. Gib placed the crate on the floor of my room then left me there while he went in search of dinner. I sat on one of my room's double beds with my shoulders slumped. My body ached as if I'd pulled every nerve, muscle, and vein. My *mind* hurt. I looked at the crate with painful anticipation.

A quick peek inside showed that it contained a jumble of scrapbooks and loose photos, plus stacks of greeting cards bound with ribbon. Ella and I had hoarded every card our family received when we were children. Those and other miscellaneous items had been dumped together when everything was seized.

I heard a knock on the door and ran to open it gratefully. Gib scowled when I did. He held a large pizza box and a six-pack of beer. "I could have been a mugger," he accused. "Are you losing your street smarts, Nellie?"

"Sorry. I guess I feel safe when you're around."

Awkward silence closed over us. "Interested in Christmas dinner?" he asked gruffly.

"Turkey-and-dressing pizza?"

"I have no idea. The guy said there were two choices today: pizza or pizza."

"My *favorite.* Come in."

We sat on separate beds and ate while we pretended to

watch the weather forecast on TV. I kept looking at Gib, and then at the crate. The room was warm and pleasant enough. Through a part in the window curtains we watched large snowflakes sift through a streetlamp. "Are you going to look through the crate tonight?" Gib asked.

"Yes. Do you want to help?"

"If you don't feel it's too personal."

I touched the crate. "I'm not sure I'm ready to look through what's in there."

"It's up to you. You know as well as I do that living with fear is worse than confronting the reality behind the fear." He hesitated, giving me a slight, sardonic smile. "Godawmighty, now you've got me offering philosophy like a dime-store horoscope book."

"Yes, Great Mystical One, but any soothsayer who brings pizza must be obeyed." Taking a deep breath, I moved the lid off the crate.

We piled scrapbooks and assorted stacks of cards, loose photos, and keepsake boxes on one of the beds. I looked at it all with grieving recognition and couldn't bear to pick anything up. "What's wrong?" Gib asked quietly.

"I'm happy to have it all back. But it hurts to remember."

"I'll start. Let's look at this." By some absolute quirk of fate Gib picked up a small wooden box decoupaged with flowers and pictures of musical instruments cut from magazines. I saw the box at the moment he reached for it, and I tried to subtly snatch it before he could, but he sat down on the opposite bed and opened it.

"Oh, that old thing," I said anxiously. "That's nothing important. Don't bother."

"If it's not important then why did you make a grab for it?" He flipped the box open and took out a yellowed stack of cards and envelopes. "Aha," he said drolly. He pointed to the words decoupaged on the inside of the box lid. *The boy I love*. "The secret boyfriend card box."

"When I decorated that box I hadn't learned to be evasive and coy yet," I said in a small voice. "To twist men around my little finger and never let them know I cared."

Gib flipped a card open. "Let's see who the poor, manipulated slobs *were*." He read the inscription. He frowned and grew very still. I moved over and sat down, slowly, beside him. "This is a card I sent you when we were kids," he said.

"I know." He looked through the others. I felt heat creeping up my face. All of the cards were from him. "This was my special Gib Cameron collection," I said. "I was only in the first grade but already single-minded and methodical."

He slowly pulled a slender swath of black hair from the box. It was tied with a white ribbon. He looked at me for an explanation. "Voodoo," I admitted. "I was told to put a piece of my hair in the box. As a charm to make you mine." Flustered and depressed, I reached for the box. "It seems silly now, but at the time it was—"

"It worked," he said. "The hair worked."

I kissed him. Just on the jaw, first, near the corner of his mouth, so we could both pretend it meant nothing but sentimental sweetness, if need be. "Where are you going?" he asked in a gruff tone as I pulled back.

I hesitated. Then, "Just switching sides." I kissed the other side of his jaw.

"That's getting there," he said. Both of us understood we were playing with fire, but didn't stop what was happening. Gratitude mingled with lust, admiration, respect, and affection. With love, I hoped.

"Here?" I kissed his lower lip.

"Closer."

Slowly, I kissed him fully on the mouth. The taste of him was reinforced by his skilled yet careful response; if he had moved too fast or surprised me in other ways I might have pulled back. But he nuzzled me gently with his jaw against my cheek, and he put his arms around me in a deep hug. He wasn't in a hurry, even though we were sharing a finely tuned vibration that made my breath short. Calm relief slipped through my body. I knew him so well now.

"I've wanted you all my life," I admitted. Those were hard words to speak, and I feared he didn't want that much honesty. He drew his head back and studied me. I searched his expression anxiously but saw only pleasure in his face. "You've always had me," he answered.

That night with him was the purest experience I'd ever known. Wing-walking, blind, obsessive, playing by heart, glorious. We were both fierce, hungry, tender, not aggressive so much as desperate, feeding and being fed a banquet after starving for so long.

"Look at me," he ordered as he moved inside me. His tone was both urgent and pleading. The context of the order made it exciting—a surge went through me. Both of us were in tune with every nuanced whisper of our bodies; we were caught by each slightest touch, barely able to look at each other, we were so ready.

Afterward I felt wounded but also restored. We needed each other. We understood each other. I'd never felt addicted to a man before. It was as if I had to have more of Gib or I'd die. As if I'd throw everything away to stay with him.

I knew from the moment I met him that Gib was the kind of man I would meet only once in my life—unlike anyone before or anyone yet to come along. It was visceral; I was nearly speechless, reverent, like looking at a fine painting or listening to Chopin.

Life had always seemed chaotic to me. That was why I liked music. The precision, the order, the logic of it. It was the same with a well-oiled machine, a fine meal, a freshly polished floor, a perfect sunset. A moment of pure order, where the world is safe and absolutely right, and just by being there to appreciate the moment, to observe, to listen, to perform, to learn, you're the center of the universe.

The snow was beautiful at midnight, and later, too, and just before dawn. We watched it from the dark, warm cave of the room through the space between the window curtains. I lay with my head on Gib's shoulder and one arm curled over him. He stroked his left hand up and down my bare arm, and I gently tapped my fingers on his chest.

"You're playing a song on me," he said.

"Something by Schubert. It's a long, beautiful piece with a lot of energy, and the main theme repeats with amazing variations."

He laughed soundlessly; I pressed closer to feel the vibrations. He took my hand, silhouetted it to the shaft of light from the streetlamp outside, and we fitted our fingers together. "I think it's time to admit this is a lost cause," Gib said.

A chill went through me. I lifted my head quickly and studied him. "If you're about to get up and leave this bed and tell me what we've done wasn't a smart idea—well, maybe I agree, but I think you owe me—"

"It's a lost cause to go on pretending we don't love each other." He watched me. I went very still, trying to recover my dignity. "It's interesting," he went on with gruff amusement, "to watch your hackles go up and down every time you have to reevaluate me. Are you going to disagree with what I just said?"

"No, but I don't have any intention of turning silly and reckless either. I mean, we're not kids. I'm twenty-nine, you're thirty-five, we're experienced—"

"Are we?" His voice was low, serious. "You've never told me anything about your *experience* with men. You know what kind of experience I mean. I don't want the details, Nellie, but I've given you an idea of where I've hung my hat in the past, so to say, and I'd like you to at least give me a clue what my competition has been."

"No one compares to you."

"Well, hell, of course not," he said dryly. "My superiority is a given. Now drop the flattery and talk turkey to me."

Searching for distractions and other diplomatic diversions, I hesitated. Then, "First, tell me. How do I rate among the women you've known?"

He sat up enough to look at me. "I wouldn't even know where to list you if I had a rating system. I'd have to come up with a new category."

"Why? Have I done something unique and kinky that I'm not aware of?"

Gib studied me, frowning. "Apparently." He continued to search my face.

I grew agitated, cornered under his intense scrutiny. "I'm discreet, choosy, and nobody's fool." I sat up abruptly. "It's almost dawn. Let's get dressed and dig a path to that diner up the road. I want scrambled eggs—"

"Coward." He snaked an arm around me from behind, gently pinning my back against his chest. "It's not going to be that easy to avoid me from now on."

I looked down at my bare breasts couched atop his forearm. "You don't own me. We don't own each other. We are adults who agree that we shouldn't be dewy-eyed, sentimental, and *nosy about each other*—"

"Look at me. Stop it. Look at me." Gib took me by the shoulders and turned me to face him. "Were you raped?"

The words froze me. I sat there stiffly in his embrace. Suddenly I understood how Olivia lost her voice. Some words are impossible to speak. He placed both hands around my face and looked into my eyes. "After your father died and you were being harassed—you already told me some of it was sexual—now tell me how far it really went. *Were you raped?*"

I couldn't force a sound. I'd never discussed it with anyone, not even Ella. "I'll take no answer as a yes," Gib said gruffly.

"No." I shivered then took a deep breath. "Almost," I managed finally. My shoulders sagged. *"Almost."*

He exhaled. "Keep talking."

"One of the FBI men cornered me in my bedroom. He didn't strong-arm me, he . . . was intimidating, insinuating . . . I can't describe it, and it's always made me feel so ashamed of myself because it wasn't as if he forced me—I don't know. I just, I ended up half-dressed and shaking and . . . he stopped because some of his fellow agents drove up. He heard the car. So he didn't go all the way. And I made sure I was never alone with him again after that."

Gib rested his forehead against mine for a moment, then simply pulled me closer and held me. I finally gave up the pretense of pride and burrowed my head in the crook of his neck. "Hell, yes, he forced you," Gib said, his tone hard. "Let's be clear on that. He didn't have to throw you against the wall or threaten to hit you for it to be force. You've got nothing to be ashamed of. If you'll tell me his name I promise that when I find him I won't kill the bastard."

"Thank you. But it's a moot point. He died a few years ago. I kept track of him. Ella doesn't know any of this story. Please don't ever tell her."

Gib drew his head back. "Of course I won't tell her."

I reached up and rubbed my knuckle under each of his eyes. There were tears beneath them. "Don't cry, John Wayne," I ordered in a broken whisper. "I'll fall apart if you do."

He placed several slow, careful kisses on my face before looking at me again. "Give me your word that you're all right."

"I swear. I'm telling you the truth. He didn't rape me. But he would have."

"Trust is the first rule of sharing a bed. You give me your word. I trust you. That's how it works."

"Okay," I said in a shaky voice. "Then I have to explain something else. It's not bad, but it's embarrassing."

"Oh, I like embarrassing confessions," he said with a trace of jaunty effort. He cleared his throat. "Go ahead. Make me blush."

"Not you. Me."

"Wait. I'll turn on the light."

"I'm a—" I stopped.

"For God's sake, Nellie. It's all right. Whatever it is."

"I'm—" I stopped again, and took a deep breath.

"You're a . . . what? A secret Junior Leaguer?" His voice hoarse, he tried to soothe me with teasing. He looked at me from under his brows, with very solemn concern. "You wear white gloves and bake cookies and host charity balls? No, let me think. You're an operative for the United Nations' top-secret New World Order movement. Your goal is to implant innocent Americans with computer tracking chips so that the men in the black helicopters can scan us like canned tomatoes at the grocery store. You know, Ebb and Flo do believe that's going to happen. They swear there's a secret invasion code on all of the interstate highway signs. Of course, they also swear they've seen UFOs over Grandmother Mountain and a big furry Sasquatch walking Hodger's Ridge."

"I bet they've never seen a twenty-nine-year-old virgin," I said flatly.

It was Gib's turn to be speechless. "What did you say?" he asked, finally.

"I'm a virgin. I mean I *was,* until tonight."

He sat there, stunned.

There is no stronger woman than a dedicated nun, and I was disciplined by the best. I grew up practical and unyielding because of Sister Mary Catherine. She didn't need men, sex, or marriage; she was filled with steely dignity that allowed no excuses. So many times I've thought of her. How she could look at me with quiet, disappointed, soulful eyes and shame me that way without ever lifting a hand.

As Ella and I got older the subject of my virginity humiliated us both. I was too embarrassed to discuss it with her. It had become part idealism, part albatross, and because of what I went through with the government, a large part pride and self-defense.

I had so little left that was private and innocent. The

ultimate intimacy was a treasure I didn't intend to bestow lightly. I was too stubborn to have sex.

"If modern society weren't so afraid to set standards," I said between gritted teeth, "I would be considered a *role model*. And if the idea of me being a role model strikes you as funny or outrageous—"

"Shhh." He simply pulled me against him and held me again, stroking my bare back with long, slow, soothing caresses. "See what I'm able to do because of you?" he whispered. He stroked my skin with his damaged hand. "You wouldn't let me avoid touching you with both hands. We don't have to hide anything from each other."

"Then you don't mind?"

He made a strangled sound that was part laughter and part sympathy. "I noticed that you . . . there were times when you had a look of absolute wonder on your face," he said in a low, gentle tone. "Discovery. Surprise. Amazement. However I try to describe it. And every time—it was the most exciting thing, to provoke that look—well, I started telling myself, *damn, I'm good*."

His wry emphasis jolted a teary smile from me. He kissed me and then we held each other desperately. "You *are* good," I murmured.

"All that matters to me is that gleam in your eyes. I want to keep it there."

"Don't be so *experienced*," I said. "Not right now. I want to pretend you've never touched anyone before me."

"That's easy. There's never been anyone like you," he whispered.

We didn't leave the room until noon that day.

The valley was covered in moonlit snow when we arrived at the Hall that night. "Magic," I said. I studied Gib pensively as he drove up the main road. The Christmas lights were on outside the Hall, casting beautiful crystalline pools on the snow.

"For a lot of months I looked at my own home but didn't see it," Gib replied. "Since you've been here I remember how pretty it is."

He carried the crate into the kitchen. "Well, well, the adventurers return," Ruth said. She had stayed to help prepare for the opening weekend, now only ten days away. "We swore y'all had gone skiing or been hijacked by aliens."

"I seen some black helicopters a week ago," Ebb added darkly.

I looked at Gib's shuttered eyes and nearly choked. "We were snowed in," he said. "Two days of bad take-out pizza and bad stay-in cable TV."

"I see." Ruth looked unconvinced. Isabel and Min gazed at us curiously.

"Vee!" Ella hurried into the kitchen, brushing snow from the hem of her coat and long wool skirt. Carter was beside her. She was rosy and glowing, pink cheeks, green eyes, and black hair combining to make a stunningly vibrant impression. She halted and stared at the small wooden crate sitting on the kitchen table. "That's from the warehouse? Is it ours? Oh, Vee."

I went over and put my arms around her, then whispered "yes" in her ear. I held her because she did exactly what I expected: she trembled and began to cry. She got herself under control and listened joyfully as I told her what I'd seen. She insisted I tell her every detail about the furniture. She called Gib over, hugged him, and cupped his hands in hers. "You've honored us so much. You've given us back something intangible—not just heirlooms or sentimental belongings."

"It was my pleasure," he said with courtly grace.

I took a small book, its old cover frayed and faded, from my purse. I held it out to Ella. "Our grandmother Akiko's poetry collection," I said.

She took the book with tearful awe and opened it. " 'They tell me I have no place next to you,' " she read slowly, " 'but the feather follows the spirit of the wind.' " She shut her eyes, then pressed the book to her heart.

•   •   •

Just as Gib promised, a moving van showed up a few days later containing the contents of Ella's and my childhood home—the only real home we'd known until we came to Cameron Hall. She and I spent hours prowling over the belongings, talking and touching and occasionally crying about it all. "You'll have your choice of furniture for your house," I told Ella. "Our own furniture, things from our family."

"Oh, Vee! I can't take all of it."

"I only want the piano."

"When you decide what else you'd like you can pick pieces to take to the cottage."

"All right." There were times when I actually allowed myself to imagine the best. I wanted to believe Carter and Ella were a permanent couple.

And I wanted to believe I could stay with Gib, no matter what.

Gib sent everything but the piano to a rented storage warehouse in Hightower. "I want to put my piano in the front room of the cottage," I told him. "I know I'll be cramped, but I have to have it there. Please."

He turned to Carter and Jasper. "Get your back braces and your hernia belts," he said. I watched happily as they helped Gib ease the old baby grand through the cottage's door.

That night, when I played my own piano for the first time in ten years, Gib pulled a chair close by and listened for hours, unmoving. Memories were a sweet addiction I had to hear to survive. The piano had suffered. Its legs were scratched, it was woefully out of tune, and the middle-C key stuck sometimes. But that didn't matter.

I played until I was damp with perspiration and my hands ached. Then I bowed my head against the backstop and slumped in relief and sorrow.

Gib helped me up, then picked me up and carried me into the bathroom. He filled the big whirlpool tub and helped me

undress, then guided me into the tub and sat on the wide rim,
rubbing my shoulders. "I owe you a favor," I whispered.

"Play the piano naked for me on New Year's Eve," he said.

I laughed. He simplified the emotional issues, the sexual
issues, everything. I loved him for that.

"It's a deal," I told him.

Twenty-eight

Opening day arrived. The sky was full of low-hanging, lead-gray clouds, and the weather forecast threatened snow. The temperature was just above freezing at early afternoon. "Oh, this is a bad sign," Isabel fretted, looking out the window at the sky as she carried fresh flowers to a desk in a corner of the main hall.

"No one's called to cancel," Gib said sternly. He double-checked the dial tone on the desk's large console phone, as if he couldn't trust it. Min sat down and spread her hands atop the small wooden box that was used as a file for the guest registry. It was stuffed with alphabetized index cards clipped to credit-card invoices. "I wish they'd all cancel," she said.

I walked into the music room, adjusting lamps, then fiddling with the cut flowers in a ceramic bowl atop the piano. Olivia and Bea were huddled on a worn leather couch. A large scrapbook lay on Bea's broad lap. She turned the pages slowly, while Olivia gazed at them. Olivia raised her head and beckoned me with a small, queenly gesture. "Take yourself away from your nervous piddling," Bea ordered, "and come see what's important."

Biting my tongue, I sat down on the couch at Bea's other side. Olivia planted a fingertip on a scrapbook page filled with snapshots. I caught my breath.

The pictures were of Mom and Pop at the opening of Cameron Hall. The page contained a gallery of images from the stories Gib had told me about that special weekend—Pop seated at the piano, with Mom standing beside him, smiling as she sang some song I wished I could hear. I stared at a photo of Mom in her yellow sun-hat, breezy polka-dot blouse, and pedal pushers, posing in the Hall's sunny courtyard with five-year-old Gib standing straight and stoic beside her. Ruth pouted from her seat in a toy wagon Gib pulled. Mom cradled Isabel—a brown-haired baby—in her arms.

"Nice," I managed to say around the knot in my throat.

Olivia wrote on a notepad:

Your parents are here again, hopeful and happy, in spirit and form, because of you and Ella. I'm sure you'll make them proud, and us as well.

"I intend to," I said stiffly. She had even enlisted my dead parents in her determined efforts to preserve her family, her home. I'd never admit it openly, but maybe my service to her and my devotion to Gib were the only way Mom and Pop could rest in peace.

"Pray, Venus de Milo," Ruth ordered. "We need all the help we can get. Even yours." Everyone was gathered for a benediction in the library, with Hoss and Sophia officiating. It was noon; there wouldn't be time for any more family meetings after guests began arriving.

I leaned close to Ruth and whispered, "I'll pray for you to stop bellyaching and predicting this weekend will be a failure. Are you sure you're not Emory's secret daughter? You sound just like him." I leered at her melodramatically. "That's it, isn't it? You're Emory's secret love child and Joey is your *twin*."

Ruth glared at me. "Why, look who's suddenly become the Cameron cheerleader. Now *there's* a phony transformation if I ever heard one. You should take a lesson from your sister. If you're going to pretend to care about this family, at least be consistent about it."

I opened my mouth to barbecue her with a few choice words, but Sophia waved her ring-decked hands for attention. She pointed to Hoss. He cleared his throat. "Let us bow our heads," he intoned. But as Hoss recited the benediction I peeked across the room at Gib, who also gazed at me while everyone else's eyes were shut.

He gave me a look that made me want to find some private place with him and pull the window shades. Even as Hoss somberly invoked divine support for the inn and the family, Gib and I traded the silent, reckless music of our alliance. We were wild, besotted with each other, and during the past week we'd used that obsession to avoid worrying about the future. "I can either concentrate on the inn or on you," he'd said one night after we'd dragged ourselves to the cottage following a brutal day of last-minute chores. "But not both, thank God. Right now all I want to do is lock the door and get us both naked."

"I'll lock the door," I said. "I'll take your clothes off. Then you can undress me. Voilà."

Now, while replaying the explicit details of that night and others we'd shared, I glanced at my sister's angelic face. She clasped Carter's hand. Her lips moved along with the prayer. Carter had his eyes closed dutifully, but he circled the tip of his forefinger atop Ella's hand with sensual intent.

I frowned at him and Ella but fought a tide of guilt, all too aware that I was a hypocrite for condemning their impulses when I'd given in to my own.

.   .   .

At two o'clock, we were all spruced and polished, waiting for the imminent arrival of the first guest. I wore a gold blouse and black slacks, the most demure outfit I'd owned in years. Gib had put on a pin-striped shirt and gray trousers. He had gained some weight back and no longer needed the leather suspenders he wore, but he knew I liked them.

Min paced the front hall. Gib and I waited with her. She was trembling. "I'm not ready," she said. I patted her hand and didn't admit my own stomach was full of butterflies.

Gib put his arm around her, though he didn't seem relaxed, himself. "Minnie, did I ever tell you about the time the President's teeth fell out?"

"No. I'm sure I'd remember *that*." We both gazed at Gib with wan curiosity.

"We were in Moscow. We'd left the President's hotel, we were in a motorcade headed to the Kremlin. The President was about to go on Russian television with Yeltsin and give a major speech. His partial plate popped out. All four of his upper front teeth. He couldn't get the partial back in. The leader of the free world was about to make a major television appearance in Russia, and he looked like an old boxer who could spit watermelon seeds."

"What did you do?"

"I said, 'Sir, I can find ways to stall this motorcade for thirty minutes while we get some dental cement.' He said, 'No, son, give me your glue.' Because he knew I always carried a little tube of heavy-duty household glue. To make a long story short, I glued his false teeth back in place and the Russians never knew the difference. Now *that's* grace under pressure, Minnie."

She smiled gently. "So you're saying if the President can meet Russians with his false teeth glued in, we can greet a few harmless guests for the weekend?"

"You got it. I'll be right here next to you. I know I'm not Simon, but I'll do my best."

She hugged him, then reached out to me. "Thank you for being here, too." I nodded awkwardly and squeezed her hand. She sighed, brushed the front of her brown dress, and straightened her shoulders. "Ready," she said.

We heard shrieks and strange running noises outside on the cobblestones. Gib bolted to the front doors and flung them open. "Goddamn," he said softly. The entire herd of British pigs scrambled past and headed for the front lawn. "They rooted a hole under their fence," Isabel called as she darted after them. Ella followed her gamely, waving to me with the end of a fringed plaid scarf she wore with a plaid jumper.

Carter galloped into the yard on his gray gelding. He slid the horse to a stop inches from the pigs. "The Manchesters are here! They drove by the barns to visit! They ought to be here any minute!"

Our first guests, of course. They had perfect timing and formidable credentials. Sissy Manchester was a travel correspondent for a dozen major southern newspapers; her husband, Casper, wrote a column titled "Inn-Side View" for a prominent regional-history magazine. "I'm trying to think what Simon would do," Min said quietly. "He'd laugh. But I can't."

Gib swung into calm crisis-command mode, calling to Carter, "Wait here and help me with the Manchesters' luggage!" He gestured brusquely for me to follow him. Then, to Min, "Minnie, you stay here at the doors and smile as if we chase pigs every day."

"It's beginning to feel that way," she answered.

We hurried into the courtyard. Gib pointed. "You flank the pigs that way; I'll take the other side. We'll help Isabel and Ella corner the herd out there by the box shrubs."

I made a wide arc to the right, waving my arms. "FeeMolly was right about the little bastards," I called. "I wish I had her meat cleaver at the moment."

Gib strode to the left. "I can see *that* headline on the first-weekend reviews. *Entertainment at Cameron Hall Now Includes Pig Massacres.*"

Carter leaped off his horse and blew a kiss at Ella, who had scooped up one of the miniature pigs in her arms. "Why, ma'am, your baby is my spittin' image," Carter teased. She laughed. I scowled past him at the point where the main drive curled out of the forest. We had no time for Carter's flirtations. I wanted everything to go well.

Gib and I assisted as Ella and Isabel started gently coaxing pigs into a corner hemmed by shrubs. But then Shag and several other dogs loped around a corner of the Hall and happily dived into the pig population. Pigs scattered in all directions.

Ella held her hapless porker against her chest as a hound reared on his hind legs and nosed the pig in the fanny, at the same time raking Ella's hands with his paws. "Get down, dog, get down," she ordered with no effect. The already hysterical pig squealed like mad. Gib and I ran to Ella. He pulled the dog away and I grabbed the pig out of her arms.

As if on cue the small, squirming, offended pig squirted watery brown pig shit. The pungent stream arced across the front of my gold blouse and down the right sleeve of Gib's dress shirt. We stared at each other. A smell like a thousand acres of rotting Louisiana swamp rose from us both. We heard the distant sound of a car. "Oh, dear," Ella said, and covered her nose.

It was hopeless. The Manchesters, the first and most influential guests of the grand reopening, the symbolic embodiment of the approvals that would honor Simon but also gently push him into the past, arrived in their big blue Mercedes as Gib and I stood there doused in pig excrement. They were neatly clad in matching ski jackets, plaid shirts, brown slacks, and loafers with fringed tongues. They had the look of well-fed gourmands, but more than anything they resembled Phyllis Diller and Bob Hope about to set out on a hike along the back nine of a Palm Springs golf course. They gaped at Gib and me.

Min went to them, a smile pasted on her ashen face, her hands extended. "Sissy. Casper," she began. "How nice to see you again—"

One of the loose pigs bolted out of the shrubbery and nearly knocked Sissy Manchester down. She staggered against her Mercedes, then plucked a miniature tape recorder from her purse. "I was attacked by a pig," she said into it.

Casper pulled a large professional camera from a bag and began snapping pictures of us.

"Next week we're having miniature pork chops," Gib said.

By evening the Hall had a full quota of paying guests. Their luggage had been carried to their rooms, and a shaky but warm welcome had been offered by Min to the guests who came after the Manchesters—whom we greased with champagne and pastries as quickly as possible. There were tears and kind words from many of the longtime guests, but ultimately they made it clear they'd come to survey the inn's new management with professional thoroughness. They soon sprawled out over the house and the back decks, into the woods on the hiking trails and off to the stable to select horses for weekend riding jaunts.

I showered and scrubbed myself, then, with no time to go back to the cottage for clean clothes, I donned a pink-silk pantsuit outfit Ella loaned me. It was two sizes too large. I looked like I was wearing pajamas. I hid behind the piano and played Chopin while high tea was served in the library that afternoon.

Gib disappeared then returned looking fresh-scrubbed, dressed in clean clothes and smelling of excess cologne. I switched to Broadway show tunes for the cocktail hour, during which I drank four cups of coffee and massaged my tired hands. The guests filled the tables in the elegant main dining room and a second, more intimate room that Simon and Min had converted to an additional dining space over the years. I was glad for the long dinner break.

Meals at the Hall were served family style in huge bowls and platters. The feast would take a good two hours. "Still the best nouvelle southern cuisine in the region," I heard one guest sigh as I passed the dining-room door. FeeMolly's famous reputation remained intact and glowing after a year's hiatus. Outsiders didn't know she was a homicidal maniac, or that FeeMolly probably thought *nouvelle* was a liberal word meaning *expensive*. She might be right.

As dinner progressed I washed highball glasses and straightened the self-serve bar in the music room. Ella and Isabel had been pressed into service as wine stewards.

Gib had disappeared into the inner mazes of the Hall—those dim, claustrophobic service alleys some old mansions harbor between the main rooms. Several guests complained that their room thermostats weren't working. Wearing a bulky toolbelt, he emerged from a narrow service door in the back hall as I went past with a tray of freshly dried wineglasses for the music room's bar.

"Hello, gorgeous, when did a looker like you start waitressing in this hallway?" he quipped, just as his belt snagged the corner of my tray. We collided, toppling four glasses onto the floor. One bounced safely on the rug, one smacked the leg of a sideboard, cracking off its glass stem, and the other two shattered.

"At least we're not cleaning up pig crap," I said wearily as we squatted together, picking pieces of broken glass out of a dignified old Turkish rug. Gib pulled me to him for a kiss.

"I swear I still stink," he said. "But I put on a gallon of Carter's Old Spice." I wound my arms around his neck and kissed him back.

"Oink," I answered. "It's your imagination."

"I don't think so. The woman who produces the *Travel South* cable-channel show sidles away from me every time I go past her." He hesitated. "But maybe she's repulsed by this." He nodded toward his maimed hand.

"She's gagging on the pig aroma," I assured him solemnly. "Without a doubt."

He feigned a sniffing gesture at my floppy pink suit. "Either that's pig, too—or really *bad* Chanel Number Five."

"Hey, buddy, I bought this Chanel Number Five from a guy on a street corner in Chicago. And it cost me *five* whole dollars. So don't you go insulting pig shit with any comparisons. Not while you're wearing a cologne appreciated by Carter and old men whose sense of smell is gone."

"Is this weekend going to be a total fiasco?"

"Behind the scenes? Yes. But all we have to do is look calm *on*stage while we run like rats on caffeine *back*stage. That's all that matters. That's show biz."

"The system worked smoothly when my brother was in charge."

"No, it didn't. He and Min just knew how to make it *look* easy. It's all about gluing your teeth in and smiling like a Cheshire cat. You said so yourself."

We stood. He cupped some of the glass shards in his hands, and a few fine specks glittered with eerie decoration on the scarred area where the other half of his hand had been. Carter had whispered to Ella that Gib avoided shaking hands with any of the guests. "It'll get easier," I said gently. He shook his head.

Saturday was another unending sequence of fumbles. Isabel dropped a platter of French toast she was carrying to the buffet table at breakfast. At noon Ebb and Flo walked into a guest room intending to make up the bed and instead surprised a naked couple in the throes of a less-than-dignified activity involving one of the complimentary apple muffins from the baskets Ella had arranged in each room. The couple was irate. Ebb and Flo retreated quickly. "I ain't sayin' we haven't walked in on a few dillydallies over the years," Ebb reported, then Flo finished hotly, "But we ain't *never* walked in on anybody using a baked good that way."

As we all tried to appear nonchalant Ella interjected hopefully, "See? I told you a gift basket would be appreciated."

"You can't hide down there. What are you doing?" Gib asked. I was seated on the floor behind the music room's elegant carved-oak bar. Until Min rang the Saturday lunch bell I'd had a good twenty people in the music room, well-dressed outdoorsy folk playing cards, reading, chatting, or listening to me play the piano. I astonished them—if I do say so myself—by playing every song from *West Side Story*. I was exhausted.

Ella had gone upstairs with Carter. I suspected they were in bed together in a spare room. I raised a glass to Gib from my cozy enclave behind the bar. "I'm drinking a lovely vintage of crisp seltzer water. With two aspirins in it. I have a headache."

"Must be catching." He poured seltzer water in a glass, popped in three aspirin from the bottle I'd left on the bar, and downed the mixture in two gulps. "Mrs. Echlestine fell off Primrose this morning. Carter says she's got a sore back."

"Who has a sore back? Primrose?" Primrose was the horse Carter had taught Ella to ride. She was a fat, placid old mare, a sofa with hooves.

"Very funny. Mrs. Echlestine is upstairs soaking in a tubful of Isabel's wildflower bath oil."

"She'll be all right, but she may sprout blooms."

Gib sighed. "I think it's safe to say she's not having a great experience under the inn's new management." He pulled out a low footstool and sat down facing me, behind the bar. I smoothed a hand up his thigh. I wished we could sneak upstairs, too. "Let's hide," I said. "Even if we're only hiding behind this bar. I'll go get some sandwiches. We'll have a picnic."

He nodded. "We could call out for pizza. It'd only take two hours' delivery from Knoxville. But I wouldn't mind soggy pepperoni and a cold crust if I could stay here with you." He considered his hand as if it were the key to the inn's future. "One of the guests asked me about the accident. I didn't know what to say."

"Give me your paw," I ordered. I held it in both of mine. "Shake. There. It doesn't feel so odd. People won't notice if you act like there's no reason for them to notice."

He said gruffly, "I imagine my own fingers. It's called phantom finger syndrome. The doctors say it's common in amputees. I wake up sometimes, or I reach for something, and I could swear my fingers are still there. They tingle, they itch, they hurt. Is that crazy?"

"No. I believe you."

"Why?"

"You're the most bluntly *sane* man I've ever seen."

"I think that's a compliment."

"Pshaw. I'm drunk from the seltzer water."

"Good." He turned one of my hands over and gazed solemnly at my palm. "How interesting. You've got a new love line."

"Do you see any predictions about us using food in shocking ways?"

"Oh, yeah."

"Let's go upstairs, then. I'll get the muffins."

"But what I really see is a woman who's been afraid to re-lax since her mother died and her father turned his back on the whole damned world. I wonder what that woman would say if I told her I can't imagine the place without her?"

"She'd say she's not planning to go anywhere."

His hand, the damaged one, was warm and careful as he lifted my palm to his lips. He could hold a damaged piece of my heart as gently as a whisper. But like all Camerons, when he held on he rarely let go.

Twenty-nine

Before Gib and I became the stuff of drama that Saturday night, dinner was going about as well as anything had so far.

"I'm bored. I need a chore to do," I said. I stood at the kitchen's back door halfway through the elaborate meal. I knew better than to enter the kitchen with FeeMolly there.

She was arranging vegetable casseroles in large bowls on the big trestle worktable in the kitchen's center. Ebb, Flo, and Isabel tromped through a swinging service door, carrying the bowls and returning empty ones. Every time the door swung I heard voices, laughter, and the musical chime of silverware and china being played by contented diners. At least they were well fed.

"It's going fine tonight," I said when no one responded to my first request. Gib was back in the innards of the house, working on thermostats. Min was in her room trying to recuperate from a nervous stomach and a stress headache, Carter was in a cellar behind Simon's office, hunting for specific bottles of wine the guests had requested, and Ella was playing some godawful fiddle tune she'd learned to please Carter. She strolled about in a soft, romantic blue dress, wafting the scent of vanilla potpourri from a small Victorian sachet Isabel had pinned to her shoulder, and her violin was just off-key enough to set my teeth on edge if I listened too long.

But the guests adored Ella. She was comfortable in the role of hostess. Carter looked as if he'd burst with pride at the compliments she received.

I continued to stand at the screen door to the cluttered kitchen porch, being ignored. Finally Isabel noticed me and slid to a stop. "Mr. Rubins, the publisher of the retired-teachers' travel magazine, found a hair in the fried chicken. Thank goodness he mentioned it just as Ebb set the platter down. So we're scrambling to serve something else. FeeMolly won't tolerate a hair. Not even one."

I wasn't going to brave FeeMolly's bad mood. "*Hasta la vista,* ladies. I'm going back to the music room and crouch behind the bar."

Dylan suddenly wailed from a corner. He was cornered in his stroller. Isabel ran over and picked him up. "Here's what you can do! Take Dylan for a walk. He's so fussy! Here."

Before I could protest my lack of maternal skills she slid the chubby, sweater-suited baby into a coat, mittens, and a knitted cap, then set him in a cloth sling and brought him out on the porch. I grudgingly donned Gib's quilted jacket, which hung on a peg along the porch wall. Isabel held out Dylan cheerfully, "Now you put your arms through the sling there, and there; turn around—that's it—I'll latch this clasp across your back, and voilà! You're wearing a baby on your chest! It's the latest fashion trend."

I looked down at Dylan. He looked up at me. We were both too amazed to make a sound. He drummed his heels into my rib cage on both sides. "Ouch."

"Take him for a walk around the yards," Isabel urged. "He *loves* to walk, and you've got a good thirty minutes before dark."

"Terrific," I said with no enthusiasm. I lumbered down the porch steps. I felt as if I'd suddenly gained thirty pounds, all in my breasts. Doing what came naturally, Dylan sank one of his tiny, strong hands into my sweater and grabbed the nearest soft spot.

"I bet you learned *that* technique from your cousin Carter." I pried his fingers off and trudged onward. Shag and about six other dogs trotted after me, then veered off to chase a rabbit that raced through the apple orchard. The cold evening air felt damp; the sky was lower and grayer than the day before. I ambled awkwardly toward a cluster of old wooden sheds on the far side of the yards, where the hills were lined with rows of wire trellises covered in the naked, spidery vines of cultivated muscadine, blueberry, and blackberry.

One of the sheds was no more than a peaked tin roof supported on either side by thick peeled-log posts. The shed sat off by itself, with a large truck partially parked under it, so that the truck's sun-faded red cab protruded from one end. Its scraped and dented metal bed had a high wooden tailgate and head-high wooden sides screened with fine-mesh hardware wire to keep out foraging critters.

This was the Hall's low-tech garbage-processing system. Cans and bottles went into separate boxes for transportation to a recycling center in Knoxville. Paper went into a burn pile beyond the horse barn.

The kitchen's meatier food scraps were fed to the dogs and cats, but the rest of the leftovers went into large plastic garbage cans that one of Ebb's ex-husbands, Elmer—who ran a sporting goods shop in Hightower—carted off to spread on his bait-worm beds.

As I walked along a path behind the fruit-vine trellises, I glanced toward the garbage truck. Two thirty-gallon galvanized-steel garbage cans were locked inside the bed. As I squinted into the shadows I thought I saw movement in the back of the truck. Suddenly one of the trash-can lids clattered to the metal floor.

"I bet one of the cats got in there," I muttered. "Come on,

Dylan, my little nipple-twister, let's go chase the kitty out of the trash cans. The last thing we need is ripe garbage spread from here to yon for the guests to smell."

I marched up to the tailgate, peered through the screen in the dim light, and banged on the wire. "Shoo, cat! You want to end up in Fee-Molly's stew?"

A chubby black form darted from behind the cans. It was several times taller than any cat, too wide to be a dog, and too upset to be a tame farm animal of any known variety. My nose curled at its odor, a stink like rancid lard. Two beady eyes met mine. The small, black, nasty-smelling *thing* took one look at me and began trying to climb the walls of the truck bed. Falling back down repeatedly, it began bawling with piteous, growling wails.

My heart stopped. "You're a baby—"

Dylan waved his hands at something behind us. I whirled around. A large, full-grown black bear galloped toward Dylan and me. I assumed she was the cub's mother. She opened a mouth full of pointed teeth, and roared.

I ran toward the front of the truck. Dylan bounced merrily in his sling. I grabbed the handle on the passenger door and jerked it open. The window was rolled down. I scooted onto the seat and reached for the window crank.

A babyish growl came from behind me. I pivoted wildly and looked down. A cub about half the size of the other one huddled on the floorboard under the steering wheel. It looked up at me with a wad of greasy waxed paper in its mouth. The shredded remnants of a lunch bag were strewn around it.

I had no idea whether a cub that small would attack or not. I shoved the door open and bounded outside again. I began screaming steadily and at the top of my lungs, like a female gibbon alerting the other monkeys to danger.

My four-hundred-pound Mama Bear nemesis was less than a dozen strides away, and gaining on me. Still screaming, I launched myself at the truck's hood and scrambled clumsily. I made my way on hands and knees to the windshield, staggered to my feet, and climbed up on the cab's roof, and then—a foot higher—onto the roof of the shed.

The bear circled, growling. I squatted on the peak of the slippery tin roof, my arms curled around Dylan. He chortled and waved his hands. The dogs returned, adding their high-pitched yelps to the chaos. Most weren't brave enough to close in on the bear, but at least Shag and his blue-eyed brethren began nipping at her hind end.

She couldn't have cared less. She uttered one gut-twisting bellow after another as she rose on her back legs and shoved the truck with her front paws. She snarled and paced, swinging her head and sniffing the air, while her cubs scrambled to get out—a feat that obviously proved harder than getting in. Suddenly the mother bear bit the truck's front bumper. Then she used it like a footstool and started climbing. She got up on the hood and bit the windshield wipers. I had horrifying visions of her coming right up on the shed's roof. She roared at me and started climbing.

A shot rang out. The bear slipped and tumbled off the truck's hood like a huge black marshmallow. Once she righted herself she swung her head toward the Hall. I'm sure the average, unmotivated bear would have run for the hills long before dogs and guns became an issue, but with both of her cubs trapped in the truck, dogs and gunshots only made her pause.

I peered frantically down the path beyond the vineyard, yelling, "It's a bear, it's a bear!" to be helpful. Gib ran into sight. He tucked a large, wicked automatic pistol into his belt. In his left hand he held the antique, ceremonial Scottish claymore that hung by the Hall's front doors.

He threw back his head then gave a ferocious shout that made the bear bristle. She bounded forward as he reached her, swatting the tip of the sword with her front paw. Gib parried then thrust, nicking the tip of her nose enough to draw blood. She shook her head then turned around and defiantly bit the truck's right front tire. Gib jabbed the sword's tip into her rump.

With that prodding she galloped around to the truck's opposite side. Gib climbed nimbly atop the truck and handed me the pistol, butt-end first. The gun was heavy enough to make my arm sag when I took it.

"Use both hands," he lectured calmly. "The gun's cocked and ready. Aim for her eyes and pull the trigger if she gets up here again. If you have to kill her, do it."

"I will," I said just as calmly. Screaming had weaned me from nervous confusion. I absorbed his confidence and felt strong. I had a baby to protect. How primitive we are when life and death are that simple.

Gib crawled down into the bed of the truck. The half-grown bear cub pounced at him and caught his left arm with its claws. His shirtsleeve ripped. He lightly smacked the cub with the flat side of the sword, and when it backed off he reached over the tailgate, jerked the bolt on the latch, and the tailgate fell open.

The cub scrambled to the edge and tumbled off. Gib swung the tailgate up again, and locked it. Then he climbed back up beside me on the roof. Knotting both hands around the claymore's engraved silver handle, he frowned as he tracked the mother bear's continued, ferocious pacing beneath us. "She ought to leave now," he said. "There's no reason for her to hang around after her cub's free."

"There's another cub in the cab," I explained.

He looked at me askance. Then he sighed. "I *hate* it when that happens."

He climbed down, again. When he landed beside the truck the mother bear roared and came at him on her hind legs. Gib jousted with her, keeping her at bay, but she wouldn't give in. When she slapped the sword hard and knocked it out of his hand I panicked. I didn't want to kill anything's mother, but this was, after all, a battle between females to protect their own. She had her cubs. I had Dylan and Gib.

I wrapped one arm around Dylan's ears, thrust the heavy

pistol out with adrenaline-inspired strength, and aimed at the bear's broad forehead. "I'm going to shoot," I yelled.

"No, wait." Gib grabbed blindly for the latch on the driver's-side door. His stiff, scarred fingers performed their simple service like an unyielding hook. The door swung open. The other bear cub rolled out like a balled-up mealybug and hit the ground running. It bolted in the direction its older sibling had taken, straight for the safety of the woods.

The mother bear pivoted and galloped after it. The dogs chased her for a few seconds, then, panting, lay down in the grass under the muscadine vines.

In the newly restored silence, my own breath sounded like a tidal wave.

Gib picked up the sword, then looked at me. I had the gun trained on the woods where the bear had disappeared. "Easy now," he said. "I know that gun isn't as lethal as pepper spray, but it's a helluva lot louder." A thin trickle of blood slipped from under his torn shirtsleeve and dripped from his left hand. I stared at it. My stomach churned. "I think I'll stay right here for a few months," I said.

Dylan, meanwhile, had started to yawn.

Gib climbed up patiently and took the pistol from my frozen grip. "Come on down, Goldilocks. The three bears are off in the woods settling the profound question of whether their hearing's gone. You scream like a banshee."

Gib tucked the pistol in the back of his trousers, then held out his hands. I clambered down with enough grace, but my knees shook when I reached the ground. We turned and saw a crowd running our way—most of the guests and all of the family. Isabel, crying, unlatched the baby harness and cuddled Dylan to her chest. I sagged gratefully. Gib put his arm around me. "I think this weekend is doomed," he said, "but all that matters is you and Dylan are safe. And I'm proud of you."

"I'll love you forever," I answered, just low enough that only I could hear it.

.   .   .

Right after dinner it began to snow. An hour later, the electricity went out and the gas furnace broke down.

We parceled out quilts, brought in extra wood for all the fireplaces, moved mattresses downstairs so that people could gather in the lower rooms, and patrolled two dozen kerosene lamps that were lit throughout. Ruth showed up in her four-wheel-drive truck with extra wood and propane tanks for emergency space-heaters. "We should have known better than to open in the winter," Ruth complained to Isabel. "Simon had the good sense to shut down when the weather was about to turn bad."

"But he never turned people away," she replied. "And some of the best weekends were snowy."

"This isn't snow. This is a *blizzard*. Guests will be broiling each other's gizzards for snacks before it's over."

When Isabel tearfully reported this conversation to Bea, Bea snorted. She consulted with Olivia, then told Gib, "It's time to call on Bacchus, the god of wine! Go tell the guests. Free liquor for all!"

The situation turned into a giant adult pajama party, and the Hall took on a different, ghostly nature as the lamplight and firelight turned back time. I played dance tunes and Broadway ballads in the music room; people danced and drank hot-rum ciders and feasted on platters of Fee-Molly's cheese straws and pastries.

"People eat so *much* when they're drinking in the dark," Ella joked weakly as she traipsed back to the kitchen for another plate. Carter caught her by one arm. "You've done enough. I'll haul these groceries."

"Sit," I agreed. "You're so tired you're wobbling." Ella immediately snuggled down in a chair by the fireplace in the family den. I brought her a glass of brandy. She refused it, smiled at me, and in a few minutes fell asleep. I pulled a knitted throw higher over her shoulder.

"Is she okay?" Gib asked from the den doorway.

"She's just tired. When she gets nervous she loses steam in a hurry."

Sometime after midnight the guests burrowed into their makeshift beds on the floor. Isabel, Gib, and I slumped at the kitchen table with exhausted relief. "Ruth's going to staff the front desk for the rest of the night," Gib noted. "Ebb's back on duty at dawn."

Min walked in. "I checked on the guests. I just hope nobody got on the wrong mattress. I haven't got the energy to break up a fight."

"Or an orgy," I added. "I hope rumors don't get around about that apple-muffin technique."

Gib rubbed his forehead. "The snoring reminds me of the Marine barracks after a long night on leave."

Min groaned. "Pigs, bears, broken furnaces, snow, no electricity—this is a disaster."

Isabel shook her head. "I may be wrong, but I think the guests are having fun."

"They're being polite."

"They're having a unique experience," Gib countered. "We know that much for sure."

He and I disappeared discreetly to his lodge at about three in the morning. The jeep's tires were bolstered by tire chains; we rolled through a foot of sleet-crusted snow. A limb snapped off a pine tree and dropped with a loud crash on the jeep's hood. Allegra yowled from inside my coat, where I'd tucked her.

"Just a twig!" Gib said tensely, around the butt of a cigar.

I opened my coat and said to Allegra, "Just a twig, the man says. Just an ice cube, the captain of the *Titanic* said." Allegra looked up at me with green-eyed fury, and yowled again in terror.

The waterfall was beautiful in wintertime. It froze at its edges and the rocks shimmered as if covered in a diamond-like sheen. Inside the lodge, the logs of the walls in the big main room were dark with smoke and carved with initials, including the names of Gib's parents inside a heart. Every married couple in the family had a tradition of cutting their names into that wall. The wall was covered.

"One more name," I'd said the first time I went inside, "and this wall turns into kindling." The fireplace was massive, the chairs and couches heavily cushioned and so deep and worn they were like fat leather marshmallows on carved oak feet. There were water rings on the heavy tables and cigarette burns on the rugs. The smell of woodsmoke and stone and leather and *man* was in the air.

I built a fire in the fireplace while Gib got an oil lamp from a storage room and lit it. I went outside and used a hatchet to chop icicles into a bucket, because we feared the lodge's creaky plumbing might freeze. A raccoon waddled across the yard and I tossed him food scraps from a pot on the kitchen's scarred wooden countertop. A fox scurried across the edge of the porch and headed for the leftovers, too. He and the raccoon made noises at each other.

As I lugged my bucket of ice indoors, stomping snow from knee-high rubber boots and looking eagerly toward the warm light of the fire in the main room, Gib offered me a slice of cold grilled venison stuffed into a cold biscuit. I'd cooked the Bambi and made the biscuit with my own two hands. I sat down and chewed wearily as Gib took my coat and pulled my boots off. "I fed our pet raccoon. Spotted a fox, too. If they fight over the food scraps I'll bet money on the raccoon. He's huge."

Gib rubbed his jaw and looked at me with such affection that I stopped eating and said, "What?"

"You're turning into a mountain woman."

"I doubt it."

"But you've got one more test to pass. You've got to get in my bed with me and make love wearing a nightgown, wool socks, and a scarf, under five heavy quilts and six inches of goose-down comforter, and *you've got to make me forget how this damned weekend is going.*" He stood before the fire, his shoulders slumping as he gazed into the flames. "Maybe I can't manage the inn," he added. "Maybe I can't replace Simon as the leader of this family. Maybe Emory's right."

I went to him, wound my hands into his shirt, and stared up at him belligerently. *"I believe in you."*

He took me in his arms. "I wish I did."

"Where's Ella?" I asked at daybreak, when Carter met us at the Hall's kitchen. Gib and I were sitting at the table with bleary-eyed Min, Isabel, and Ruth, all desperately drinking coffee. Carter scrubbed snow from his black hair and laughed hoarsely. "She's asleep at the houseboat. Safe in bed, *this* time."

I leaped to my feet. "What do you mean?"

"Whoa, whoa, Vee Nellie. She's fine. I woke up about an hour ago and she was gone. I ran outside and tracked her footprints in the snow."

"In the snow?" I sank down on the edge of my chair.

He chuckled. "She was sound asleep in the cab of my truck. Curled up like a kid with my coat around her shoulders. I woke her up and she said, 'How'd I get out here?' I swear, she looks so cute when she's surprised at herself."

Gib frowned. "She was sleepwalking?"

"Yep."

I propped my head on my hands. "She does it occasionally when she's under stress. But it's been a long time since the last episode."

Carter poured himself a cup of coffee. "She warned me she sleepwalks sometimes, but I never thought she'd traipse out in a snowstorm without batting an eyelash."

I felt Min's, Isabel's, Ruth's, and Gib's gazes on me, and knew Ruth in particular was gauging this strange behavior of Ella's. "But she's all right?" I asked. "You're sure?"

"I tucked her in and gave her a kiss right before I came back over here. I braced a chair under the outside doorknob for insurance."

After Carter left Ruth stared at me and snorted. "How often does your nutty sister take nighttime hikes? Is this another peculiar Arinelli trait?"

Gib stood before I could say a word. The condemning stare he gave Ruth brought a tense hush to the group. "I've listened to you make remarks like that since Vee and Ella came here last fall. I've talked to you in private about your attitude, but you won't listen. Vee shrugs it off, so I tried to let the two of you handle the problem yourselves, but not anymore. I'm ashamed of you. I expect you to apologize to Vee."

"I don't want Ruth to—" I began, but Gib held up a hand.

"I want her to," he said.

Ruth gazed up at him with obvious chagrin that quickly became red-faced defensiveness. "Lately you're oversensitive on the subject of Arinellis, big brother. I don't appreciate being lectured to. Haven't we got enough problems, trying to start up the inn without Simon's help?" She got up and stomped out.

"I'll go talk to her," Isabel said. "She's just worried about the way things are going with the guests." She hurried after Ruth. Gib scowled as he sat back down.

Min looked at me somberly. "I apologize for Ruth. She doesn't mean what she says. This horrible weekend seems to be getting to us all."

I nodded vaguely, but I couldn't care less about Ruth's sarcasm. I was thinking of Ella's sleepwalking episodes. They usually occurred when she had migraines.

Or when she was hiding something from me.

The snow began melting by noon on Sunday, but the sky threatened more. All of the guests packed quickly, paid their bills, told us they'd had a lovely experience, then left as fast as their Mercedes and Beemers and Lexuses could travel without sliding.

The opening weekend was over. It was special and memorable only in the sense that no one had frozen in the storm, been eaten by a bear, or trampled by their fellow guests in the mad rush to leave. "We have the most hideous hangovers," Sissy and Casper Manchester wrote in the guest ledger.

Gloom settled on us all when the last car disappeared from sight. "Debriefing. In the main dining room. Right now, please," Gib announced.

We sat stiffly around the big table. Olivia wrote on her notepad:

> *I see no reason for such misery on your faces. Thirty years ago we had two guests. Only two. But they changed everything for us. That's all we need this time. Two who looked beyond the small indignities and saw the spirit of hospitality shining brightly.*

I barely paid attention; I was busy scrutinizing Ella as she sat across from me. She'd laughed when I questioned her about her sleepwalking; she swore she'd never felt better, but she looked flushed and tired to me.

"Emory called this morning," Min said. "He wants to meet with us all on Friday. We promised, remember? We said we'd meet with him the week after the opening. We have to vote on his proposal."

"Stall him," Gib said. "Everybody needs more time to analyze what went wrong, how we could have made the problems work out more smoothly, and then we'll talk about what went *right*. Vee and Ella's music, for one thing. I think that kept the guests' mood a few notches higher than it would have been."

"Oh, hell, Gib, the guests weren't in a good mood. They were freezing and *drunk* most of Saturday night," Ruth retorted.

Min steepled her hands to her chin. "Gib, I'm not trying to insult you. I'm just not sure there's been enough time for you to realize the kind of responsibility you're taking on."

I looked away, my eyes burning. Gib exhaled wearily. "We're getting off the subject."

Min shook her head. "I can't pretend I feel good about the weekend. I'm so sorry, Gib. We can't risk the future of the Hall on wishful thinking. We nearly worked ourselves sick. I'm afraid it will always be like that without Simon in charge. We've run out of time."

"I can't promise you everything'll go smoothly next time," Gib admitted in a low, hoarse voice. "But I'm not going to give up just because we hit a few snags—"

"That isn't what matters," Ruth interjected. She looked neither happy nor victorious; in fact every word seemed to hang heavily on her tongue. "What matters is the publicity. We're going to get mediocre reviews, Gib. There's no use pretending otherwise. And those reviews are going to translate into lost bookings. We can't wait and hope for the best. The inn could go bankrupt. We could lose the Hall and this valley."

"What will we have if we turn over control of the valley to Emory?"

Isabel offered wistfully, "We'll still have our home. Our heritage."

"It won't be a real home. And we won't deserve to claim our heritage if we aren't willing to fight for it."

"I'm tired of fighting, Gib."

Ella stood. "May I speak?" Surprised, everyone grew quiet and stared at her. I studied her closely. A stab of alarm went through me. She had the glazed look she got when she was on the verge of a headache.

"Of course you can speak," Gib told her.

Carter looked up at her with mild puzzlement, but grasped one of her hands when she fluttered it in his direction. "You say whatever you feel like saying, darlin'."

She rubbed her forehead. "Was I wrong to believe in the

safety Vee and I found here? The *sanctuary*? Are you all willing to let go of your dreams so easily?"

"We're not going to lose anything you really care about," Ruth snapped. "Money, for instance."

Olivia slapped her hand on the table. She pointed to Ella then nodded vigorously. Bea interpreted. "Herself couldn't agree more with dear Ella."

Ella faltered. "I'm so . . . afraid it was all an illusion." Slowly, her head lolled back and she collapsed. Carter caught her in his arms and lowered her to the floor. I ran to her side. Gib and the rest of the family crowded around us. "Ellie, Ellie?" Carter said frantically.

As I rubbed her ice-cold hands I crooned, "Come on, honey." She moved weakly, gasped, then clutched her stomach.

"My baby," she moaned.

I stared at her in horror.

She was pregnant again.

Thirty

That afternoon, in a hospital in Knoxville, my sister lost her second child.

The small, new life that would have been my niece or nephew seeped away just as before. Ella was two months pregnant but hadn't told anyone, not even Carter. I understood why she'd hidden the pregnancy in its early weeks, but he didn't. Now her happy dreams of surprising us all were destroyed. Knowing how the first miscarriage had devastated her, I feared she couldn't survive another one.

Quietly terrified, I sat on the edge of Ella's hospital bed, holding her right hand. Carter sat on the opposite side, holding her left hand. We balanced her between us as if she might sink out of sight if we let her go. Carter watched her with his dark, hooded eyes filled with misery and shock. "Why didn't you tell me about the baby?" he kept asking her.

"I wanted everything to be perfect this time," she mumbled in a drugged daze. "I was only going to wait a little longer."

"Sweetie, what do you mean, 'this time'?"

I shook my head. "She doesn't know what she's saying."

Ella's secret weighed on me along with my fears about her health. Her face was swollen from crying. Her fingers squeezed spasmodically against mine. Her eyes were glazed.

"Everything was so perfect," she repeated in a small, breathy voice, blinking slowly. "I thought we were finally safe." Her gaze shifted to me. "But you're right not to believe in fairy tales, Sis. You tried to warn me."

"Don't make judgments right now. You can't think straight. Try to sleep."

"Why did this happen to *my* baby? Why me again?"

My eyes burned. I glanced at Carter's bewildered expression and swallowed hard. "Listen to me. You'll be all right. You'll grieve and then you'll go on with your life."

"It will never be the same. What did I do to deserve this punishment again?"

"Don't go Catholic on me. This isn't a punishment."

Carter's subdued emotions surfaced in a low, frantically soothing murmur. He hunched over her, massaging her hand as he clasped it against his chest. "You didn't do anything wrong, darlin'." His voice shook. "Nothing. Whatever you think you did before—I don't understand. Why couldn't you tell me we were going to have a baby? I'd have been so happy. I wouldn't have let you work so hard. I'd have taken care of you even more than I did. Maybe you wouldn't have lost the baby."

Her eyes widened. She opened her mouth and uttered a low shriek of agony. "I'm to blame," she moaned. "It's all my fault. I killed my baby. I'm not meant to be a mother. God doesn't want to give me children."

"*You didn't do a thing.* Don't talk like that. I promise you we'll make us another baby as soon as you're ready to try. It'll be easy."

She stared at him. "I wanted *this* baby. I loved this baby. Didn't you?" Her voice was slurred.

"Of course I did! Shhh. Shhh."

"Ella," I said in a strong, demanding tone. She looked at me groggily. "Stop it. Carter is grieving, too. Be fair to him. Shut your eyes and relax. You'll be asleep in less than a minute. You and Carter can talk more when you wake up."

"That's right, darlin'," Carter went on urgently. "I'm just tryin' to make you feel better. This baby wasn't meant to be." He stroked her hand. I shook my head at him to stop talking. He didn't understand how Ella's mind worked. She did not want to hear practical assessments. She'd spent her entire life seeing beyond the practical. "The poor little thing," Carter said hoarsely, "had something wrong with it. Nature takes care of mistakes like that. We have to try to be glad."

"Glad? Glad?" Her voice shook. She pulled her hand away from his and knotted it over her stomach. "We had a girl. My daughter. Your daughter. *How can you be glad she died?*"

"There's no way you could know at two months that the baby was a daughter," I said carefully.

"I dreamed about her. I know she was there."

Carter struggled to speak. "Darlin', I—"

"You didn't want her."

"Ellie! That's not true. Is that why you didn't tell me? You thought I'd be mad? You hurt me by *not* telling me, Ellie. That's why I'm upset now."

"Leave me alone," she cried. "You didn't want her. You blame me for killing her. Maybe you don't want me either."

"Ellie."

She sobbed, then turned her back to him and hugged her pillow. He sat there dumbfounded, his eyes glistening with tears of disbelief. He reached out, his hand trembling, and he stroked her hair.

I got up and went around the bed to him, shaking my head and putting a finger to my lips. We watched her until she quieted and fell asleep. I took him by one arm. After a few seconds he stood and let me guide him into the hall. I was trembling. This was how Ella had been right after her miscarriage in Detroit. Unreasonable, full of guilt and anger and incoherent grief. It would get worse.

Gib met us outside her room. I could see Min, Isabel, and Ruth in a waiting area at the end of the hospital corridor. They started our way. I closed the room's door. "Don't believe a word she says," I told Carter, looking hard into his eyes. "She doesn't mean it."

Tears slid down his face. "How could she think that way about me?"

"Tomorrow she'll cry and apologize." *I hoped.*

"What's the problem?" Gib asked. His eyes were troubled and knowing as he looked at me.

"She hates me," Carter concluded desperately. "Maybe she blames me for not wantin' a baby so quick. I told her we should wait a year or so, but I wasn't all that serious about waiting, and we sure weren't careful——"

"You risked getting her pregnant when you weren't ready to be a father," I said between gritted teeth.

"No!"

"That's not what he said," Gib interjected patiently. "It's bad enough that Ella's hysterical. Don't add to the problem by making irrational accusations yourself."

I stared at him. He had the good grace to regret what he'd said. I could see that in his face. But when he put a hand on my arm I flinched. I began to feel my old superprotective, me-against-the-world defensiveness returning. "My sister lost a baby," I said with grim emphasis. "Any woman who's lost a baby would be hard to reason with right now."

"You're right. But Carter deserves some sympathy, too."

Min, Isabel, and Ruth hurried up to us. Ruth's flinty expression gave me chills. Carter began to pace. He looked so upset I couldn't help feeling sorry for him. When he halted in front of me I almost backed away. I knew he was about to ask questions I didn't want to answer. "Why did she talk the way she did?" he asked. "Like this wasn't the first time she'd lost a baby?"

I glanced at Gib, who confirmed his opinion with a stone-faced nod. I should tell Carter her history. But I wasn't certain that would help at the moment.

"Listen," I said companionably, as I latched my arm through Carter's. "Don't worry about the kind of nonsense she mumbles tonight. And don't be mad at her for hiding the pregnancy from you. If you really love her you'll give her time. You'll be sweet and gentle, and just listen. She'll talk to you. Maybe that'll make all the difference. You're her husband. Let her know you're not going anywhere. She's never had that kind of security before."

"Well, sure, of course, I'll treat her like she's made of eggshells, but why'd she do things this way? I feel like I'll lose my mind if I don't understand—"

"You're not the one whose mind's in trouble," Ruth interjected. Min and Isabel, flanking her, looked puzzled. My stomach twisted as Ruth went on quickly, "*I'll* tell you the truth. I did some checking on her medical records. Ella was pregnant a couple of years ago up in Detroit. She lost the baby and had a breakdown. Spent a month in a mental hospital. It wasn't the first time she'd been put away either. The men in the white coats locked her up after her daddy died, too."

Ruth smiled at me with unyielding victory. I swung around and looked up at Gib incredulously. He shook his head. "No. I didn't tell her."

"But you knew she'd found out on her own."

"Yes."

"How could you not warn me?"

"I gave him my word I wouldn't let the cat out of the bag," Ruth explained.

I pivoted to look at her again. "I see how little your *word* is worth, then."

"This situation changes everything. All bets are off." She faced Carter. "You're not going to like hearing this, but I'm counseling you the way I'd want to be counseled. When you married Ella she deceived you about her true condition—

physically and mentally. I believe you have grounds for an annulment."

I lunged at Ruth, both hands balled into fists. Gib caught me around the shoulders. Min stepped between Ruth and me, and Isabel stared at us all in horror, her hands pressed to her mouth.

"She lost a baby —she was pregnant with another man's baby?" Carter said in a low, stunned voice. I shivered. *Another man's baby.*

"Did you hear anything beyond the fact that she was pregnant before?" I asked him bitterly. "Did you notice the part about her being hospitalized for depression? I don't think so. I think all you care about is that another stallion got to your personal *broodmare* before you had the chance."

He rammed both hands through his inky, tangled hair. *"She should've been honest with me!"*

"You seduced her and you married her three days after you met her! Your big conquest! You made yourself look good for the glorious Cameron gallery of quaint stories about family romances!"

"I—I need to hear Ellie's side of this—" He started for the door of her room. I broke from Gib's grasp and blocked his way. "She's asleep. Leave her alone. Don't you think you've done enough damage for now?"

"I'm not going to hurt her, but that was my baby she lost today! Not some other guy's! Mine! And she's my wife! I'm going to wake her up. We've gotta talk."

"*No.* I'm not letting you harass and upset her by prying into the past. She's fragile. I'm not going to let her end up like last time."

"Get out of my way, Vee."

Gib stepped between us. "Carter, you won't do Ella any good in the mood you're in. Take a walk. Come back when you've calmed down. Let her sleep."

"Cousin, I don't want to punch you, but I will—"

"If you try that you'll need a hospital bed, too."

Min and Isabel grasped Carter's arms. "Gib's right," Isabel begged. "Come and walk with us. Please."

"Walk, Carter," Min ordered.

His shoulders sagged. He moved leadenly down the hall between Min and Isabel. Gib faced me. "He's her husband, and he loves her. You've got no right to keep him away from her or talk to him the way you did."

"Now that he's heard the truth he doesn't want to be responsible for her. She's not *pure* enough anymore."

"You don't know how he really feels. You didn't give him a chance to say much or even think about it."

"Just like you didn't give me a chance to prepare for Ruth's viciousness." I stared past him.

Ruth had watched the entire chaotic scene without saying another word. She had a look that said she might not be altogether pleased with the mess she'd caused. But then she shrugged. "Gib refused to tell Carter about his wife's history. I begged him to do it. You wouldn't tell Carter. Ella wouldn't. Carter has a moral and legal right to know. Now he's got to deal with it. The miscarriage isn't his fault. Ella should have had enough sense to tell him she was pregnant and warn him she might crack up if she lost the baby."

"Get your sister out of here," I said to Gib, "or I'm going to find a new use for the nearest broom handle."

"Go," Gib said to her. His tone was flat, cold. "You gave me your word and you broke it. I've got nothing else to say to you. I can't even look at you right now."

"Gib!" She gazed at him with the raw recognition that she'd crossed a line she might always regret. "I thought you believed in laying out the facts, no matter how hard it is. You and I have always—"

"You didn't give a damn about anything but hurting Vee and Ella. You've done that now." She walked away, her mouth set.

Gib took me by the shoulders. "Let's go sit with Ella. You calm down. She'll be all right."

"I'll sit with my sister *alone* "

Silence. After a brittle moment in which he studied me with growing disbelief, he said softly, "You're shutting me out?"

"I don't need your help. Obviously, I can't trust you. You took care of your family. Now I'll take care of mine."

He dropped his hands. "I'll be nearby."

I went into Ella's room and shut the door.

She slept through the night. Carter and I sat in her room, not speaking. Min and Isabel went home with Ruth. Gib sat in the waiting area. It was excruciating.

"If you tell her you know the truth she'll be worse than yesterday," I warned Carter when she began to stir. He nodded curtly. "I know when to talk to my own wife," he said. "The question we got to settle is why she doesn't think she can talk to *me*."

To my dismay, Ella didn't cry or apologize for anything she had said to Carter. She gazed at him dully when he tried to comfort her. "You blame me for losing our baby," she repeated in a small voice. "You think you've married a woman who'll never have children. You may be right."

Gib and I drove them home in one of the Hall's vans, and she sat on the opposite side of the backseat from Carter, wrapped in a heavy coat and hugging a pillow as she gazed out the window at the frosty mountains.

When we arrived at the entrance to the valley she announced, "Take me to the cottage, please." I turned around and eyed her steadily. She began to cry. "I need to be with you, Sis. You're the only one who understands how I feel. I want to stay with you at the cottage."

Carter looked stunned. "You can't do that to me."

Ella moaned, "You don't want me."

"This isn't how a wife treats her husband."

"You blame me."

"Goddammit, Ellie, quit lying to me! I know what's eating you! I know you lost a baby before! And I know you nearly lost your mind over it, too! I don't blame you for anything but lying to me by not telling me any of that! And I'm mad as hell that you didn't even do me the courtesy of telling me you were knocked up with *my* baby!"

She turned white. She opened the van's door and staggered out. I jumped out behind her and caught her by one arm. I had to hold her up. Gib and Carter rushed to us. Carter tried to take her in his arms but she shoved him away. One look at Carter's stricken face told me he wished he could cut his tongue out. "I only meant—" he began, holding out his hands to her.

She backed away wildly. "You . . . you know about Detroit! Vee, did *you* tell him?"

"No, I didn't."

"Who would do that to me?"

"My sister," Gib admitted. "I wish to God I could tell you it wasn't a member of the family, but Ruth learned the truth and told Carter."

She groaned. "It was the only secret I cared about! Now everyone knows what a failure I am. Vee. Help me. Vee." She dissolved into sobs. I latched an arm around her. "We're going to the cottage. Shhh. I'll take care of you."

Carter turned numbly and disappeared into the woods. Gib said nothing. He drove us to the cottage, carried Ella to the bedroom, then walked out and stood, just looking at me. "You don't want me here," he said flatly.

"I don't want any Camerons around her right now," I answered.

He left.

I tried very hard not to fall back into the old mothering routines Ella welcomed easily. Carter took on the gaunt-eyed look of a lost soul. Gib looked after him with Jasper and Hoss and Bo Burton, who showed up casually with gifts of interesting gourmet foods and flowers that everyone ignored.

Over the next several days Ella became quieter and more withdrawn. Blue circles bloomed beneath her eyes. She never mentioned the baby. She spent all day huddled in bed. I played the piano for her, coaxed her to eat, and fussed over her obsessively.

"You need to stop avoiding Carter," I said. "I'll call Gib. He'll find Carter and bring him here."

"He doesn't want me."

"Okay. Then you need to hear him tell you that in person."

Unfortunately, Gib did find him—drunk, on the back porch of Hoss and Sophia's house, with a pair of his sympathetic ex-girlfriends and the goat on hand for comfort.

"What was he doing with the *women*?" I asked bitterly.

"Nothing. Sitting. Drinking."

"What would have happened if you hadn't found him, you think?"

Gib looked at me frankly. "He'd have ended up leaving with them. Not that he was sober enough to do much. The goat would have had a better shot at it."

"If we don't get this settled between them soon, he's going to get in trouble and Ella will never forgive him."

"Your sister is the problem."

"If Carter is so easily provoked to adultery, I'd say *he's* the problem."

We stared at each other. "Let's not do this to ourselves," Gib said. "I miss you."

He went back to the lodge. Ella was asleep—or pretending to sleep—in the cottage's bedroom. I sat on the porch in the dark and listened to the silence of the winter night, thinking of Gib, missing him in ways I couldn't allow myself to put into words.

•   •   •

The next day I found Ella curled up in the empty bathtub with her wedding ring clutched in one hand and a half-empty bottle of wine nestled in her lap. She was wearing one of Carter's flannel shirts. She looked up at me blearily. "He'll never want me again," she moaned. "We're doomed to roam the world without a home, without love, without respect. That's the only tradition we Arinellis have perfected, Vee."

"I've had enough of your morbid shit. This family is in a mess and we need to either help or get out of the way. Which is it going to be?"

"That won't work," she said. "You can't bully me with tough love. This isn't something you can understand, Sis. You've never wanted children the way I do."

"You have *no* idea what I want. You think the world revolves around you and your heartfelt emotions. I don't look for feathers and I don't talk to angels, and I don't suffer dramatically with migraines and nervous twitches, but I *do* have feelings."

"You should be happy that your dire predictions have come true. You never believed in my fantasies. You were right."

"I'm sick of your self-pity. We don't need fantasy here— the reality is pretty good. We have friends, we have, dammit, we have *family*, we have work, we have goals. *You* have a husband who's miserable over the way you're treating him. He really loves you. All right, I've admitted it. Hear me? He loves you and you can depend on him."

"I love him but I don't understand him. I'm disappointed in him. I never thought he'd be so casual about our children. To him our lost baby is only a *trial run*." She was crying by then, and gesturing wildly with both hands. "And he thinks I'm crazy."

"Ella, he's not a poet. He's a twenty-four-year-old guy whose idea of talking to women, before he met you, was limited to cheesy one-liners and quotes from country-western songs. If you don't get yourself under control you'll damage this marriage past the point of recovery. Stop looking for fantasies and appreciate what you've got. Grow up."

"You've changed. Before we came here you would never have talked to me this way."

"Maybe I should have. I'm ashamed of you."

"Oh, Vee!" She huddled over her wedding ring, sobbing.

Olivia and Bea drove up to the cottage in their golf cart. Isabel clung to the side. I walked out into the yard as if guarding the cottage's front door. Bea spoke. "Herself says a woman must grieve inside without words in the way. Leave Ella to her own means. She'll come about when she can speak without pain."

This didn't reassure me. Olivia had not overcome the loss of her children in half a century and counting. I wanted my sister to develop the Cameron strength but not the tendency to mourn destructively for a lifetime.

"You must come to the Hall," Bea ordered. "Emory's shown up a day early. He's conniving."

"I can't leave Ella."

"I'll stay with her until you get back," Isabel begged. She climbed off the golf cart and looked at me wistfully. "Please. Maybe I can talk to her."

"She's asleep."

Bea read a note Olivia held out. "Herself says what Ruth did was unforgivable, but do no' be adding to the misery yourself. Gib's taken Carter to Knoxville for the day to get his mind off Ella. He's no' here to defend our side."

"He's not at the Hall?"

"No, he's away all afternoon. Herself needs you more than ever today. I think you care for Gib"—Olivia prodded her arm with a fingertip, and Bea sighed—"All right, all right, anyone with eyes can see you and Gib are all for each other. Do it for him, eh?"

"That's not—" I stopped. Gib and I were no secret,

obviously. For a moment longer I struggled with refusal. Then, to Isabel, "If Ella wakes up tell her I'll be back as soon as I can."

Isabel nodded eagerly. "I want to talk to her about something. Min gave me permission. If you think it might help."

"What is it?"

"Min and Simon were married for over ten years before Jasper and Kelly were born. They'd almost given up on ever having children. Min miscarried five times." Knotting her hands together, Isabel waited for my reaction.

"All right. If Ella feels like talking, you can tell her that."

"And I'd like to tell her that I was in therapy last year. After my divorce, and Simon's death. I couldn't take antidepressants because I was nursing Dylan. I went to a counselor twice a week."

"I'd rather you not talk about psychological problems and babies any more than can be helped. It upsets her."

"Certainly. I'll be very careful. Vee, we really aren't rejecting her. Nobody but Ruth wants to be cruel, and Ruth realizes everyone's angry at her tactics. That's all I'm trying to tell you."

"The damage is done. It's not me you need to convince."

Bea snorted. "Come along, Venus. Leave Isabel to watch over your sister. And stop worrying. Poor Ella's no more looney than the rest of us."

Olivia nodded her agreement. Her eyes, direct and fiercely calm, said she'd been judged far more harshly.

"I decided to have a preliminary meeting with Minnie alone," Emory said smoothly. He carried a portfolio of drawings and documents he wouldn't open for anyone but her. Min, looking somber, acquiesced. They closeted themselves in the library.

"Underhanded bastard," Bea growled. She helped Olivia into a chair in the music room. When Min came out of the library she looked troubled. Emory all but glowed with satisfaction.

"I'm going to let Minnie tell you how generous the investors are willing to be," Emory said. "I'll leave the new proposal and drawings in the library for all of you to look at before our formal meeting tomorrow." He eyed me. "I'm so sorry to hear about your sister. I'm assuming, considering her emotional state, she won't be capable of participating in the vote."

"If she can't participate, there won't be a vote."

"What?"

"Olivia gave her a vote, so now she has to be included. Therefore, you'd better reschedule. I can't tell you how long it might be before Ella's well enough to make a decision."

"This is outrageous!" Emory pivoted toward Olivia. "This is some ploy of *yours,* isn't it? You'll hang on to the last hurrah! But I *will* get what's best for the Hall one way or another."

Olivia's expression grew so calm that only her eyes seemed alive, but they gleamed ferociously. She pulled a pad and a large black Magic Marker from her dress pocket. She wrote slowly, then thrust the pad at Bea.

Bea read in a loud, ringing voice, " 'I have had enough of you. I am overthrowing my own democracy and naming myself queen. Therefore the decision to sell is mine alone. I vote no. There. *No.* It is settled. This is the last time you'll torment me.' " Bea drew a deep breath, then finished grandly, pointing at Emory, " 'I banish you and your kin from the Hall forever.' "

Olivia's pronouncement was not quaint. Min reacted with profound silence. I heard gasps from Ebb and Flo, who were hiding around a corner. Emory's face turned livid. "Now, look," he said, his voice rising. "There's no need for—"

"It's about time," Bea said. "I've ne'er understood why Herself tolerated you. I've told Herself for years she should put the Word on you."

"I'm sure you have. You've never liked competition for Olivia's attention, have you? You absurd old woman. You have no idea what I could have done to you when you came here and established yourself as Olivia's personal aide-de-camp. What I can *still* do to you, if forced."

"Emory, I'll ban you from this house myself if you keep talking petty nonsense like that," Min said in a low voice.

Instantly he composed himself. "I'm sorry, Minnie. But I think it's time to clear something up. I will not be summarily dismissed. I will not be saddled with *banishment*. This is the modern world, and it's time to move away from the useless traditions that have held this ancestral property of ours in a time warp. We agreed last fall to take another vote. I intend to have it."

He pointed to Olivia. "Do you think I'd have put up with your insults and the arrogance of this family all these years when all I'm trying to do is what's best for the Hall—do you think I'd put up with that unless I was *convinced* I have a duty to this place and that my work on behalf of its future would pay off eventually? I know why you've put up with *me*, Aunt Olivia. I know what's stopped you from just closing the doors to me and mine before now. I'm sorry you've always felt a little pressured, but Aunt Olivia, I've done right by you. I really have."

She had gone as still as a bird. He dropped to one knee by her chair. "I'm going to guarantee you something," he said in a courtly tone. "A promise I have honored since I was a boy, for the sake of you and our family's good name. My father consigned that responsibility to me when he passed on, and I've protected it dearly. For your sake. But now the time has come for you to honor *me*."

This mysterious speech of Emory's brought frowns of bewilderment to Min and Bea's faces. Olivia, however, remained still, her hands clasped hard around the ends of the chair arms. She held his gaze as if some horror would leap the instant she faltered.

He bent his head next to hers and whispered something

in her ear. Then he stood and nodded to her. "I'll grant you one more week to think about it," he said, then he walked out of the Hall.

Bea lumbered over and patted Olivia's hand, but was obviously shaken. "There's ne'er been a secret between us, old doll, and you must no' sit here now with one clenched inside you," she sputtered. "What's his meanin'? It could no' be so terrible that you should sit lookin' like doom."

Olivia stood shakily, grabbed for the cane beside her chair, then swung it. She smashed a small vase on the end of a massive antique sideboard along the wall outside the library. Glass scattered everywhere. She walked through the scattered pieces, barefoot, as Min and I dashed to stop her and shove shards of glass from her path. "You'll no' do such nonsense and tell naught of the reason to me!" Bea cried, but Olivia only moved as swiftly as possible down the hall toward the kitchen.

She and Bea disappeared into the family wing and then into their suite of rooms. Min went after them but Olivia had shut herself in her own bedroom and Bea was so agitated she sat in her recliner, refusing to say much to anyone. She vowed not to move until Olivia confessed the mystery.

"Don't any of you know what that was about?" I asked as we hunted for stray pieces of the crystal vase. Min shook her head. Ebb and Flo went off to the kitchen to ask their mother. But even FeeMolly had no clue.

Min sat down limply at the library table, Emory's closed portfolio in front of her. "His new proposal doubles the size of the museum," she explained. "It includes a separate folk-art gallery for Isabel."

Min raised her eyes to mine. "And a small music pavilion for you and Ella. He says the whole complex would be like nothing else in the mountains. He suggests we call it the Simon Cameron Center for Folk History and Culture." She paused, her throat working. "And his proposal includes a permanent foundation to fund and develop the center. I don't know what to say. How can I vote against something that honors Simon and everything he believed in so much?"

"You have to have faith in Gib, now," I told her.

She looked away.

Gib walked into the Hall and was immediately confronted by the news of Emory, Olivia, and the whole chaotic mess. "We can't just dismiss this," Min said hoarsely. "We have to get Ruth and Carter and Ella—everybody concerned—we have to have a meeting and discuss this."

"You're not dragging my sister over here," I said.

"Do you want to see the Hall and the valley turned into some kind of theme park?" Gib asked Min. "There's a downside. There's a sacrifice. The more control we give up the more we risk in the long run."

"Have we proved we're ready for the 'long run,' without Emory's help?"

"I'll never be Simon, but I thought that's exactly what I'd been doing since last fall. Proving myself." Gib exhaled wearily. "We'll hold a family meeting tomorrow. I need your wholehearted support, Minnie. Either we stop this dance with Emory once and for all or we settle it and take the offer."

"I agree. We can't go on saying maybe. It isn't fair to us. It's certainly not fair to Emory."

"I don't give a damn about Emory. He's always looked after his own interests. I'm going back to Knoxville tonight and see him. By God, one way or the other he'll tell me what he said to Aunt Olivia."

I grabbed his arm. Min crowded close. "No," she and I said in unison.

"He obviously terrified her. I won't have it."

Min nodded. "But I'm sure there's a simple explanation. It's probably nothing sinister. You know how some people squabble over feuds and fights so old that no one else even re-members the point."

Gib gave her a hard look. "Aunt Olivia isn't a senile old lady who gets the vapors over petty quarrels. You know that as well as I do."

Min's expression fell. She nodded. "I'm afraid you're right."

Suddenly a buzzer sounded. Gib had installed several emergency alarms in Bea and Olivia's suite. They were part of his security innovations. We'd all shaken our heads over it, not laughing at him so much as amazed at his methodical ap-proach. He'd placed simple remote controls on Bea's and Olivia's nightstands and on the tea table of their sitting room.

Now the alarm echoed ominously through the family wing. We rushed to their rooms. Bea lay on the floor of the sitting room, half leaning against the cluttered bookcases, di-sheveled and half-conscious, her eyes dazed. Olivia was crouched beside her, clutching the remote and still pushing the alarm button.

Gib and Min knelt on either side of Bea. Gib checked her pulse. Her mouth moved sluggishly. She moaned. I gently pried the remote from Olivia's small hands. She fumbled for her notepad and looked around frantically. I snatched a pencil from the tea table.

Fainted, Olivia wrote. *Help. Help. Her pressure.*

"Her blood pressure," Min said.

"Dizzy," Bea moaned.

"Get Carter," Gib told me. "Tell him to bring one of the vans to the front." He cupped his hand along the right side of Bea's fleshy face, touching his fingertip to the corner of her eye and mouth. I saw what he was noticing. The slight, un-natural droop on that side. Min saw it, too.

"Funny-headed," Bea groaned.

"I'll call Bo," Min said quickly. "He'll send a forestry he-licopter for her. We can meet it in Hightower."

She and I leaped up and ran out of the suite. "I think she's had a stroke," Min cried softly.

I nodded.

I felt as if everything I loved was falling apart around me again.

Thirty-one

For the second time in a week we gathered at the hospital in Knoxville. It turned out that Bea was in no serious danger; she'd suffered a very mild stroke and was able to talk slowly but intelligibly the next day.

Tests were done to check the arteries in her neck for blockage, but none was found. "She's eighty years old. This kind of thing happens," the cardiovascular specialist told us. "I don't see any sign of long-term disability. The only thing that worries me now is her mental health. She seems very depressed."

She lay in bed dully gazing at soap operas on her room's television set, eating only because her regular doctor threatened to keep her hospitalized longer if she didn't, and refusing most conversation.

Olivia insisted on staying with her constantly. Gib arranged for a cot. Olivia huddled beside Bea's bed, watching her with profound sadness. There was a strange new dynamic between the two of them; something had happened before Bea collapsed, we were certain, but neither of them would answer when asked about it.

· · ·

Bea came home two days later, but retreated to her room and wouldn't get out of bed. "I've lost my heart," she said repeatedly, with no explanation. She held Olivia's hand because Olivia forced her, but she rarely looked at her. Gib and Min gently questioned Olivia, but she would only write,

It is between us. Only us.

"What did Emory whisper to you that upset you so much?" Gib persisted.

It is my business alone. Don't ask him. Don't meet with him. Don't give him any answers. Don't let him in this house again until Bea is stronger. I cannot fight so well without her beside me.

"You don't have to fight now. That's my job."

This battle is far older than you.

I returned to the cottage, brooding over the strange turn of events while Ella continued to reject help. "I brought a care package," Gib said. He set a wicker basket on the porch and lifted a checkered napkin to reveal containers filled with food.

Food was not what I needed. I wanted him to absorb me, I wanted to be naked with him, I wanted to press close to him and listen to his voice. Gib looked down at me with the same crackling intensity. "I'm taking you for a walk," he said. Then he gripped my hand and led me into the woods. The weather was freezing; the ground was hard. We didn't care. Once we were alone we were rough with urgency and need.

We walked back in the early-winter dusk. Ella had turned on the porch light but sat in the shadows, wrapped in a blanket. Gib saw her first and put a hand on my arm. We stopped at the foot of the steps. I felt guilty.

Carter drove up in his truck. He got out, looked at the odd scene—Gib and me standing in the yard, Ella hunched in a rocking chair in the shadows. "I just came to see if you were feelin' better today," he said to Ella.

She wobbled to her feet. "Can't we talk? I've been thinking—maybe we could visit a priest for some marriage counseling."

"I don't need some outsider telling me what-for, darlin'. I need for you to make up your mind. If you need somebody to tell you how to think then we got a worse problem than I thought. I *know* what I think. I *know* how I feel. I don't need a shrink to talk to."

"You're saying that I need that kind of help?"

"You've been making all the rules. Now I'm making some."

He turned to leave, jerking his truck door open. She stumbled to the edge of the porch. *"Don't go."* She tripped and Gib lunged to catch her. I leaped forward, too. He caught her by the waist. I heard Carter running toward us.

"Ellie!" Carter said. He thrust his hands under her arms and helped guide her down on the top step. We sat in a mutual huddle.

"My head," she murmured.

Carter got in front of her and dropped to one knee. He bent close to my sister and began stroking her hair. "I don't understand. Is this one of your headaches?" She nodded.

"It's a migraine, not an ordinary headache," I told him. I looked at Gib. "I need your help to get her inside." He eyed me meaningfully then nodded toward Carter. "Carter," I corrected, "I need your help."

Carter snared Ella around the waist. "I'm carryin' you, darlin'," he announced, his voice choked. "I've got you." He carried her inside.

Gib and I looked at each other. "Do you think she's faking?" he asked.

I hesitated. Then, "If it works, that's all that matters."

.   .   .

Carter was back on our doorstep the next morning. He'd spent most of the night watching Ella sleep. "I need to see my wife," he said hopefully, "if she's awake and feeling better."

I called Ella, and finally she walked outside. She was dressed in her robe, pale and hollow-eyed, her black hair disheveled. "Are you still angry at me?" she asked.

"You're my woman. If you move out on me then you never meant to stick with me forever. Enough of this hooey. You needed me last night. You need me now. Now come on with me, right this minute. I mean it."

I could have kicked him. His domineering attitude blew the fragile reconciliation to shreds. Ella reacted by sinking into a rocking chair and clutching the armrests as if no force on earth could move her. "You think I'm a possession? You think you can order me to follow you as if I'm a *dog*? I can't . . . touch you! I can't bear to touch myself! I feel empty. I can't even think. And you don't understand!"

He gaped at her. "You don't have to think. Just do what I tell you. I was trying to make it *easy* for you. Ellie, please. I don't know what to say, goddammit." Anger rose in his face. The moment of vulnerable entreaty evaporated. "I never knew my daddy, and my own mama left me with her kin. I won't put up with being walked out on again."

"I'm not good enough for you. That's what you think. That's what everyone in the family thinks. That I'm mentally defective and . . . and *barren*."

"Oh, for God's sake. I'm half-crazy myself over this, Ellie. So bad I went up to New Inverness the other night. I got stinkin' drunk and called a couple of my old friends. They came and sat with me."

"Girls?"

"That's right. But nothing happened."

"You're telling me this to hurt me. You're saying I've driven you to other women *already*."

"Goddammit, Ellie, I'm telling you because I'm ashamed of it and I don't want you to hear it from somebody else. Nothing happened."

"If you want other women, then go and sleep with them. Have babies with *them*. Everyone would approve of your choice." She fled indoors, crying. Carter turned numbly and wandered toward his truck. I stalked him across the yard.

"Don't do it," I said. "The women. Don't do it."

"I couldn't," he mumbled. Tears on his face, he leaned on the truck's hood. His long hair dangled around his jaw. He looked terrible. "I can't give up on her. But I can't hang around here tearing myself up when she won't even listen to me. I've had it. I'm leaving for Oklahoma tomorrow."

"For how long?"

"Until Ellie agrees to come back to me."

"This isn't the way to deal with her."

"It's *my* way," he said.

"Carter's gone," Gib told me.

We stood in the yard of the cottage the next afternoon. I exhaled wearily. "I have to think of some way to convince Ella he isn't deserting her just like that bastard in Detroit did."

"Do you want me to come inside and talk to her?"

"No."

"I see. Do you realize how you're making me feel? What your attitude is doing to *us*?"

"I'm taking care of my sister."

"I'd help you if you'd let me. You're as bad as she is. When the chips are down she rejects everyone but you. You're doing the same thing for her sake."

"She could end up in a hospital psych ward if this goes on much longer. I've got decisions to make."

"What's that supposed to mean?"

My heart was breaking. "It means I'll take her away from here if I have to."

Those words were like flint on stone. He looked at me as if I'd lost my mind now. "Forget it. You don't want to go and I won't let you do it." His bald-faced warning, delivered not as a threat but as a simple statement of fact, left me speechless. His blunt possessiveness didn't upset me; with alarming ease I loved him more than ever.

"I hope it doesn't come to that," I finally managed to say.

"I have enough problems already."

"I see. So keeping me here is nothing personal."

"I had to cancel all the bookings for this coming weekend."

"Gib!"

He shook his head. "Ella's sick, you can't leave her side, Bea's sick, Olivia's obsessed with her and Emory, Carter's gone, and Ruth's staying away because no one's speaking to her. I had no choice."

"I'm sorry. I didn't want this to happen. Any of it."

He dragged me into his arms and we kissed with the easy wildness I knew so well. When I finally caught my breath and, crying silently, pushed myself away from him, I glimpsed a movement and looked quickly toward the porch. Ella stood there, staring at us woozily. She squinted in the sunlight and rubbed her forehead. Gib and I traded worried looks.

"Y'all should have told me the truth about your situation," Ella complained in a soft, tired voice. "Sis, you don't have to hide your life from me. You never used to." She fumbled with her hands and her gaze dropped. "Of course I don't have any right to say that, after what I've hidden from you. And . . . and from my own husband."

Gib walked up the steps to her. "He loves you, Ella. You have to believe me. And this family is still *your* family. Nobody wants you to leave."

"I need to talk to Carter. Where is he? At the barns? I have to talk to him right away. I can't stand this. I'm so afraid of losing him. I know I'm not making much sense, but I'm so afraid."

I hurried up on the porch and put an arm around her. "He's not close by right now."

"Where is he? What do you mean—he's not *close by*?"

I took a deep breath. "He's just taken a little trip to visit Hoover Bird and Goldfish. He left this morning."

She clutched her chest. *"Is he coming back?"*

"Of course. Of course." I held on to her and looked at Gib frantically.

"When?" she mewled.

"He'll come as soon as I tell him you want to see him," Gib assured her.

"You mean he didn't say for sure if he was coming back at all. He might *never* come back!" She hunched over, gagging, sobbing. "Pop didn't care about me. A man I loved and trusted left me in Detroit. Now the man I love more than my own life has left me, too."

I held Ella by one arm. She felt too loose, a little disjointed. Alarm raced through me. She was squinting so hard her eyes were barely open. "Air," she begged. She put a hand to her head, then began to sink. "Lean this way," Gib ordered, and she eased against him as her legs folded.

I cupped my hand under her chin. She wasn't pretending, this time. "We'll get you inside and into bed, and you'll be all right. No more acting. I'll give you one of your pills."

Gib carried her to bed. She hadn't dressed in days; I pulled her robe off and helped her change her sweat-soaked flannel nightgown. "He's not coming back," she whispered. "He left me, Vee. I'll never see him again. And I love him so much. What have I done?"

I gave her a migraine pill, then pulled the bed quilt over her and smoothed her hair. I fought a lifetime of cynicism and months of doubt and said simply, "I believe he loves you. And I believe he'll be back."

As the medication took effect she slowly fell asleep.

I went into the main room. "How is she?" Gib asked.

"She's in bad shape. But the pill should give her a good twelve hours of sleep."

"Listen, Carter said he was going to head into the hills with Hoover Bird. They planned to build a sweat lodge. I won't even know where he is before tomorrow at the earliest."

"Gib, if he doesn't come back to her I'm afraid she might do something. Being deserted is her worst fear. That's why I've always worked so hard to show her that I'll *never* leave her."

"I'll fly up to Oklahoma tomorrow and find him. But I can't promise he'll come back." Gib walked to the door then halted and looked at me. "I know she swallowed a handful of sleeping pills that time in Detroit."

I didn't like to remember that, or talk about it. She'd downed the pills while in a stupor from a migraine. When she woke up at the hospital the next day she couldn't remember taking them, but I'd never forgotten. I could only look at Gib. "I wish in all your research on us you'd found a few *good* surprises."

"I did," he said. "I found you."

My travel clock read one A.M. when I woke up on the sleeper sofa in the cottage's front room, where I'd stretched out to leave Ella undisturbed in bed. I felt peculiar—that panicky sensation of waking up lost in time and place. Wandering into the bedroom to see how she was sleeping, I noticed her slippers in the middle of the floor, though I was sure I'd left them neatly by the dresser.

I moved slowly in the darkened room and brushed a hand out to smooth the covers over Ella's legs. My fingers met cool sheets and jumbled quilt. "Ella?" I shuffled my hands over the bed as if she might be hiding, then switched on a lamp and pivoted slowly, slack-jawed, searching the room. I ran to the bathroom and flung the door open. I ran back to the front room, calling her name. The door stood ajar. The cold January breeze rattled sheet music on the piano.

"Oh, my God." I raced barefoot to the car, snatched a flashlight from the glove compartment, and shone the light into the eerie wall of forest surrounding the cottage. I circled the cottage several times, shouting for her to wake up. My voice echoed back to me. The mountains channeled sounds in startling ways, sometimes carrying a hunter's gunshot, the bawl of a hungry calf, or the giggle of a screech owl miles from the source.

Something cold and wet brushed my right hand. I jumped and whirled around. The flashlight settled on Shag's china-blue eyes. My solemn canine guardian trotted down the driveway then disappeared on the hiking path that led to the chapel. I took a chance and followed him. When I saw a faint light coming from the chapel's open doors I raced up the stairs.

My sister lay curled up on a colorful geometric rug just before the altar, her hands pillowed under her head, her bare legs drawn up gracefully. She was sound asleep, still dressed in nothing but her white flannel nightgown and her panties. She looked like one of Isabel's folk-art angels, recovering after battle.

I groaned. A fire burned in a jumble of hymn books piled against one wall. Smoke rose from the books. One burst into foot-high flames as I watched. I snatched a small rug from the center aisle and threw it over the hymnals. Acrid smoke curled from underneath as I pounded the rug with both hands. Coughing, I pulled the rug back. The fire was out.

But a dozen short, fat beeswax candles sat around Ella on the floor, flickering brightly. I knelt beside her. What part of her drugged mind had thought up this ritualistic scene, this attempt to destroy something I knew she loved?

She might have burned to death if I hadn't found her.

Shaking, I bent over each candle and blew it out. The candles were kept in a wooden box under one of the front pews. Olivia had shown the box to us when we visited the chapel with her once. She wrote that the candles had been left from Dylan's christening ceremony. Isabel had made them herself. I remembered how Ella—who loved candles of all kinds—admired them. Now the small wooden box of candles sat open near Ella on the floor. Matches were scattered around it.

One lit candle had almost burned down to a puddle of melted wax. In the back of my mind was an agonizing thought: Our father had been the money man for political fanatics who used arson as their trademark. Now Ella had set fire to a holy place. She'd tried to burn down the most beloved, shared part of Arinelli and Cameron heritage.

I piled all the burnt hymn books onto the rug I'd used to smother the fire, then carried both the rug and the books outside. I hid everything in the edge of the forest then ran back up to the chapel. Ella was still asleep. I hurried around with my flashlight, looking at the floor where the hymnals had burned, and then I shone the light on the wall. The bottom of the mural there was singed black. There was no way to hide that damage.

"Oh, no," I whispered. Everyone would see this. Everyone would know that *someone* had set a fire. Of course, no one would automatically suspect Ella.

But Ella would remember. She couldn't blank out everything about this incident—walking through the woods for a good ten minutes, barefoot and wearing no coat in the cold, setting up the hymnals and the candles, lighting the fire. Too much detail. She would remember at least bits of the night, until at last she would realize what she'd done.

She'd never forgive herself. She'd confess.

Perhaps no one else would forgive her either.

Carter might be gone forever, and now this.

My breath coming in short, fast gulps, I knelt beside her again, shining the flashlight on her face. I shook her. She moved groggily and blinked. "Where? Hmmm?" she managed, lightly brushing one limp hand over her face. "Carter?"

"Ella, Ella, we have to leave. *Get up.*" I slapped her lightly on the cheeks. "What?" she mumbled, shifting and rolling her head.

"Get up, Ella! Do what I say. Come on, Sis."

She had done what I told her for so many years that habit took over. I helped her sit up and roll over onto her hands and knees. She wobbled, her nightgown hiked up to her waist, her pale panties gleaming pristinely in a cold patch of moonlight that crept through the open doors.

I latched my arms around her waist and pulled her to her feet. I don't know how I did it, except that the thought of anyone discovering us there gave me a surge of strength. "You can make it, just walk, we'll take it slow," I begged, with me holding her up and her sagging against me.

"Have to . . . try, hmmm, where . . . are we?"

"Shhh. Concentrate on walking. Walk! It's a dance! It's music. Keep the beat! It's four-four time and it's simple!"

We shuffled precariously down the stone steps of the tall, earthen, ancient mound and into the forest. It seemed like hours before we reached the cottage. I was drenched in sweat and my back felt as if it might break. Ella's head drooped. "Hmmm?" she said occasionally.

"I'm putting you back in bed for a few minutes. That's it. A few more steps. There. We're here. Sit. That's it. There you go." She collapsed gracefully on the mattress. Before I covered her I wiped dirt and debris from her bare feet with the tail of the long sweater I wore over baggy sweatpants. She tucked her hands under her chin and fell asleep. I was staggering, exhausted.

I knew what I had to do. I began to pack. I loaded my luggage and portable keyboard into the car, then gathered the few things of Ella's we'd brought over from the houseboat. I'd get her out to the car somehow, and she'd keep sleeping while I drove.

By the time she woke up in the morning we'd be hundreds

of miles away. I decided we'd drive west, look for work in the casino lounges of Las Vegas, or even go all the way to Los Angeles.

When she began to remember what she'd done tonight I'd help her deal with it somehow, and if she wanted to come back here and face Carter and the rest of the family, I'd bring her when she was stronger.

I was fairly certain she'd never be that strong.

I sank down on the piano bench with a piece of paper and a pen. For a minute I ran my hands over the yellowed keys, fighting emotions that threatened to play out in sheer agony. But the only music I heard was the silent song of Gib's touch, his voice. Finally I wrote:

Gib—
Keep the money. Keep the piano. Take care of Allegra. I give it all to you openly and freely and with love. There's no way I can pay you and your family enough for making us feel wanted, at least for a few months. Please don't look for us. I know you can find us, but I won't come back even if you do. I have to do what's best for Ella. Whatever you think of me, don't ever doubt that I loved you even before I met you, I love you now, and I'll always love you.
I had a home here, with you.
Nellie

I left the note atop the piano then walked out onto the porch and looked up at the clear, star-filled night sky.

I was running like a thief in the night.

Like a criminal.

Like a true daughter of Max Arinelli.

I threw back my head and sought my namesake planet, glimmering low over the horizon. I thought about Gib, and all he'd expected from the baby girl he'd helped to name. That was the only time that night I cried.

As I turned to go inside, I smelled smoke.

•   •   •

Ella's candles had outwitted me. Some spark, some smoldering filament of wool deep in a dusty old rug, had caught fire again by the time I ran back to the chapel. It was the details, as Gib always said, that ruined people.

I raced up to the steps and saw the yellow glow of flames inside the building. I darted inside and halted, choking. A soft, breathable cloud of smoke swirled around me. Flames rose from a rug and had spread on the varnished wooden floor around it, curling under one of the front pews. I looked around for anything I could use to beat out the fire again, but no other small rugs remained.

I heard a human sound. Swinging my flashlight frantically, coughing, I yelled, "Who's there?" The beam of light landed on Olivia's pale, wrinkled face. She lay on the floor beyond the front pew. How she'd gotten there, and why she was there alone in the middle of the night, were questions that darted through my shocked thoughts for only a second. I ran to her and knelt down. When I shoved her long gray hair away from her face, I saw that an egg-sized knot had risen on her forehead. Her eyes flickered. She moved weakly. She was dressed only in a gown and robe.

She lifted both arms into the air but made shoving gestures at me. "Stop it! I'm not leaving you here!" I shouted. I dropped the flashlight and wound my hands under her arms then heaved with all my strength, pulling her down the center aisle and out the front doors. Tugging desperately, I pulled her down the grassy slope of the mound beside the steps.

When we reached the cool, safe ground at the bottom of the mound I bent over her. "I've got to go back up there! I can't let it burn!" Olivia waved weakly but furiously, trying to hold on to me.

I hugged her as if she were some elderly daughter of mine, but she couldn't stop me. I wouldn't let anyone be hurt or killed by a fire one of my own family had set. No Arinelli would ever be connected with death and destruction again, if I could help it.

I climbed the mound and staggered into the chapel. The fire crackled louder. I gathered an armful of hymnals and threw them outside. I went back in, got yellowed stacks of sheet music from a table beside the organ, and carried that outside, too. But when I returned the next time the heat was escalating, making me gag. I had just one chance to make any serious difference in the damage being done. *Hail Mary full of grace.* . . .

The clear crystal oil lamps on nearby wall pediments now had a sinister gleam. The bases of the lamps were filled to the brims with oil. I had to get the lamps away from the fire. I went to a pedestal, reached up, and grabbed a lamp around its delicate base, but the glass was already so hot I juggled the lamp between my palms as I ran to the door. The heavy glass globe tumbled off, along with the glass chimney, thudding on the doorsill and rolling aside. I nearly dropped the base. As I ran out into the yard warm lamp oil poured over my hands.

I dropped the lamp onto the grass, fell to my knees and scrubbed my greasy hands on the grass as best I could, then ran into the chapel. I repeated the trip with eleven more lamps.

The last time, I glimpsed myself in the globe of a lamp, just the flicker of a distorted image, my eyes wild and glowing with reflected flames.

Like father, like daughter.

No.

Pop deserved better than that memory. I would save his soul from this fire, in this holy place where he and my mother had married.

One more time. I went back in. The antique organ was small, almost delicate by modern standards. I crouched and hooked my hands around the frame on one side. I pulled. The organ creaked and slid. I got it off the raised platform behind the altar. I stood behind it then, and shoved. I was gagging, I felt as if I were burning up, I couldn't see much through the smoke. I only knew that I was moving down the side aisle on the right, that I was just a few feet from the door, and if I could somehow get the organ over the sill and out onto the porch, both it and I would survive.

Its ornately carved feet caught on a rug runner that lay under the last pew. I made some guttural, furious sound then tried to hoist the organ's front feet over the edge of the rug. They snagged. Sparks shimmered down on me. My lungs filled with smoke, suddenly, and I reeled backward, dizzy and confused. My head slammed into the wall and I turned blindly, completely disoriented.

I was going to die in this chapel.

But then I felt arms reaching around me, and I heard Gib's voice. "I've got you," Gib shouted. He began issuing orders to Jasper and Kelly in a loud, firm voice.

"The music," I moaned, and grabbed for the old organ obsessively. He fitted his hands under its side and heaved. It moved. We pulled it to the door. I heard shouts and screams outside and closer. Min and Isabel bolted into the chapel and helped us.

The organ popped through the door and onto the porch. I was aware of Gib telling Jasper and Kelly to carry it farther away, then suddenly his hands closed on my shoulders and he dragged me forward. Another shower of sparks drifted down on us, and Gib raised one arm to shield my face. He pushed me like a human bulldozer.

The residue of lamp oil on my hands ignited in a soft aura of orange-and-blue flames. I screamed as we stumbled into the smoky fresh air. Gib snatched my hands against his stomach and bent over. He smothered the flames instantly. But pain like a million lit matches blossomed.

My hands. Gib hoisted me over one shoulder then carried me down the steps to the flat, grassy area in front of the ancient ceremonial mound. The night air smelled of burning wood. I heard a siren in the distance. It made my groggy brain conjure up images of men in dark suits arresting Ella for arson.

I lay on the ground with my head in Gib's arms. My hands hurt so badly. I kept them raised in front of my eyes to reassure myself they still existed. "Put up your hand, too," I begged dizzily. "I need to know if I can feel something."

Gib slowly touched the forefinger of his maimed hand to the raw-pink forefinger of my hand. I exhaled. "Feel you there."

"I'm there. I'm here," he answered. "You're going to be okay, Nellie."

But I couldn't hope. He would find the note, and the packed car. He'd figure out everything I'd meant to do, and why. I was helpless, terrified that Ella would be accused and despised, and that we would both be forgotten by the world, hated by Gib and the family I'd come to love.

For the first time in my life, I fainted.

Thirty-two

When I was a teenager at the conservatory Dr. Andre Vander-butcn was my professor of theory and composition. He loved New Orleans's steamy, gothic culture and all things southern. He tried to drawl, but his Dutch accent was as thick as a wooden shoe. "Play faster for me, yah, Arinelli?" he'd purr. "I'll grade y'all by the extra notes y'all can dream in the space of a bird's whisper, yah? Because beautiful music sings in the silence between the notes, as well. Play the silence. Yah."

I dreamed I was playing as fast as I could, obsessed with the notion I could smoke out the lovely silences, but the smoke burned me. Then I dreamed I stood at the narrow stone bridge over Cameron River, gazing up with doelike happiness at the Hall and the mountains behind it, all brilliantly colored like a fantastic movie, a kingdom illustrated in too bright, unrealistic hues, and then I turned slowly and saw Gib.

He was dressed in the sterling-silver armor of a medieval knight, but also had a swath of red Cameron plaid buckled over his shoulder. Gib bent over me and shaded me from the heat. He set our wishing-rock, our earth-bound piece of the evening star, the white quartz rock, on my forehead and it felt like a wonderful amulet, healing and cooling. He took me by the shoulders and I reached up for him.

"Ella did it," he said. "You know she did. I'll never forgive you if you don't tell me the truth. Don't betray my trust the way your father betrayed yours."

Fear returned like the wail of a Tennessee gully-witch. The Camerons had put Ella in jail by now. Ruth had sprouted fangs and horns and claws the second she heard my sister's confession, and Ella hadn't stood a chance. She'd apologized to all the Camerons, begged forgiveness, but she'd been put in jail anyway.

I jerked my eyes open. I was trying to hold on to Gib with both hands, but they were bandaged like giant cotton swabs. His face blurred in my vision. Then I blinked and he snapped into focus. I saw the singed hair around his forehead, and the red splotches where he'd been stung by sparks. His shirt and jeans were filthy. He smelled like smoke. He smelled like the 250-year-old Cameron chapel my sister had burned.

"Easy, easy," he crooned. "You're only having bad dreams. There's nobody to fight with here. It's only me. You're in the family wing of the Hall. In the yellow guest bedroom you and Ella shared when you first came here." I struggled to speak but my throat felt raw.

Gib grasped my chin. "Slow, now," he warned. "You're only blistered, and you pulled a back muscle. Your throat's sore because you inhaled a lot of smoke. But you're going to be fine. And Aunt Olivia's doing all right, too. She's got a mild concussion and she's bruised. But she's doing fine."

I dragged one puffy, white-mitted hand over my eyes. The room was full of soft sunlight. "Ella," I moaned. My throat felt like living sandpaper.

"Ella's fine, too," he assured me. "When she woke up Isabel was with her. Izzy told her what happened. Ella got dressed and came over here. She's been hovering over you all morning. Min made her come downstairs a few minutes ago to have a cup of tea." He hesitated. "There's something you need to know about your sister. Something not even you suspected."

Terrified, I tried to sit up but I was sunk in the deep feather mattress. Gib put a hand on my shoulder and held me down, which wasn't hard to do. "Your sister," he went on patiently, "has never had to take care of *you* before. It snapped her back to reality."

"What?"

"She's a hundred percent calm, cool, and collected. You've given her a purpose. You need *her* instead of her needing *you*, for once. It's an amazing transformation. She changed overnight."

He had no idea. Stunned, I raised a bandaged hand and stroked Gib's chest. Even with bandages I felt an odd, padded texture inside his shirt. I frowned up at him. He sighed. "Don't look so worried. Are you afraid I'm wearing a corset?"

"You . . . hurt?"

"You were a hot tomato last night." He smiled wearily as he unbuttoned his shirt from the bottom up, pulling the rumpled front tail from his trousers as he worked the buttons. When the shirt was open to his chest he parted the sides then carefully tugged up a thin white undershirt.

I studied a large pink splotch at the center of his stomach, from his navel to the breastbone. He'd done this to himself when he smothered the fire on my hands. In the center was a six-inch white square of gauze and tape. Shiny ointment spread from under it, shimmering on his skin. Around the bandage was a singed stubble of dark body hair. At the top perimeter of the burned area his chest hair survived in thick glory. At the bottom was a nasty blister on his navel, exactly where the belly ring had been.

"I got a little metal burn there," he said. "You should have seen everybody's face when I took off my shirt at the emergency room. They saw my jewelry." I made a garbled sound of distress. "Don't look at me that way," he said quickly. "Don't cry."

But I did cry—with large, choking sobs—over him, and Ella, and my secret. He gently cupped my face between his hands. Blinking hard, I got out one hoarse word: "Chapel."

He hesitated, downcast. "I won't lie to you. It's bad. But chestnut and stone can stand a fire and not collapse. The roof and the walls and the new floor—" He managed a slight smile "—are still solid. The interior can be rebuilt. Isabel's already talking about restoring the murals herself. Hoover Bird called. He'll send handwoven Cherokee rugs to replace the ones that burned."

"But . . . the music? The organ!"

"The organ's fine. Just singed. Listen to me. You saved it. You saved Olivia. And you're alive and all right. Nothing else matters. *The family is all right and the chapel still stands.*"

"Can you tell how it . . . caught fire?" My voice was a raspy whisper. I felt every muscle strain in my throat.

"Not yet. I was hoping you could give *me* a clue. Aunt Olivia isn't able to write any notes. She's too sore. Bea woke up about midnight and realized she was gone. Olivia must have walked to the chapel."

"Not . . . possible. Her walking . . . that far."

"Don't underestimate her, Nellie. When she's got a mission she can astonish you."

"But why—"

"She's been odd, lately—you know that. Well, odder than usual, because of this peculiar thing between her and Bea. She decided to visit the chapel in the middle of the night. By God, there was no one around to drive her, so she *walked*."

"But—the fire?" I couldn't meet his eyes. I felt guilty and deceitful, asking for answers I already knew.

"My theory is that she managed to get one of the oil lamps down and light it. Then she fell and dropped the lamp on the rug. That's my theory right now, at least. Thank God you were awake and smelled the smoke. You saved her life." I almost choked. How could I let him praise me and put the blame on Olivia?

"Oh, God," I whispered.

"Shhh." His throat worked. He struggled for a few seconds. "We didn't lose somebody we loved, this time. Not Olivia. Not you. *I didn't lose you*."

I was nobody's inspiration. I harbored a gutless secret. I tried to push my hands against Gib's chest, but he carefully took me by the wrists and guided my gauzy mittens atop the tufted chenille bedspread. My mother's gift. "You rest now," he whispered. "I love you. I'll be right here beside you."

"Sorry. So sorry," I whispered.

"Shhh." He went very still for a moment, then he bent down and kissed my forehead. If I didn't trust him now, then nothing we'd been through together was valid.

"I'll talk," I whispered. "I'll talk to you, I promise."

"Hell, yes, you'll be able to talk," he said patiently. "Your throat's fine." He didn't understand. He trusted me too much to suspect some hidden meaning.

I drifted helplessly into another round of drugged and miserable nightmares, and more than once I felt or dreamed, when I was struggling, that Gib soothed me with his cool, scarred fingertips against my face.

Bright and cheerful in a long white skirt and print blouse, Ella was bustling around me when I woke up again a few hours later. I stared at her incredulously as she straightened boxes of gauze and tape, wiped a tube of antibiotic ointment, and freshened the ice water in my bedside water glass.

"Sis," I whispered.

"Oh!" She sprang to my side, held my head between her hands, and kissed my cheeks several times. Tears streamed down her face. "How are you?"

"Shut the door. We have to talk."

Ella frowned but glided to the door and shut it, then came back and pulled an armchair close to the bed. She sat down and gazed at me gently. "Yes," she said emphatically.

I swallowed hard. "Yes, what?"

"I've already slipped back over to the cottage and un-packed the car. No one noticed it before I did, I'm sure. Oh, Vee, I know you thought it was best for me to go elsewhere, but this really is our home."

I nearly cried. She'd unpacked the car but hadn't found my sentimental good-bye letter. That meant someone else had it. "What happened to you last night?"

"Last night?"

"The fire. Do you remember?"

"I only know what you told Gib. You smelled smoke, you went to the chapel, you saw Olivia on the floor—"

"You never woke up even *once* at the cottage? I mean, you didn't know what happened at the chapel until today?"

She nodded but looked at me with bewilderment. Slowly a thought dawned, her mouth popped open, and she clasped her chest. "Do you think I'd lie in bed and let other people take care of you when you were hurt? I don't care how sick I was, if anyone had gotten me awake during the night I'd have insisted on going wherever you were!"

"No, no, no, I'm not . . . accusing you." My head swam. "I just wanted to make sure you were being honest about feel-ing better. That you really did sleep all night."

"Why? Have I been behaving oddly in some way?"

To say the least. "Distracted."

She smiled pensively. "It's this." She held up her left hand. "I've misplaced my wedding ring."

I stared at her hand. "When?"

"I must have dropped it in the cottage last night when I was sick. I wasn't wearing it when I woke up this morning. I've lost a little weight. I think it just slipped off."

"Go look for it. Go ahead. I'm fine. Gib will be back any

minute to sit with me. You go to the cottage and hunt for that ring."

"Oh, Sis, you're so sweet."

There was a knock at the door. She hurried over and opened it. Carter stood there. He smiled at her and gazed at me solemnly. "Mind if I come in?" he asked. I was speechless. Ella took him by one hand and led him to the foot of the bed. Her eyes were glowing. "He came back," she said simply. "He came back to me."

Carter put his arm around her. "I got to Uncle's house and couldn't stand my own company. I turned around this morning and headed back to Tennessee. When I walked into the Hall and Ellie looked at me like I was covered in gold, that was all it took. I never figured that all she needed to know was that I'd stand by her no matter what."

"Vee's worried about my wedding ring," Ella whispered to him.

He shook his head. "I can buy Ellie a thousand rings. All I care about is that she trusts me with her whole heart now."

"Find the ring," I urged hoarsely.

Ella sighed. "Carter's looked for it already. I've cried and worried all I intend to. We can get another ring." She hesitated, looking at him sadly. "And we can try to have another baby, when we're ready."

He kissed her. "We'll have us a whole bunch of babies. I guarantee it."

Ella came over and fussed with my bed covers. "You rest now. I'll go to the kitchen and bring back some fresh muffins FeeMolly made just for you." She kissed my forehead again then walked out of the room. Carter gave me a thumbs-up and followed her.

I lay there in a cold sweat. For the first time in years I prayed to every saint I still believed in. *I'll pay for Pop's sins in a thousand burning hells if you'll please just not let anyone learn the truth.*

• • •

I stared at the group headed my way. Isabel, Min, and Ruth. They'd all come to visit me. Gib waved them into the bedroom and Ella smiled.

"I want to thank you," Isabel announced.

"Now look, I didn't do anything to deserve all this—" My voice faded as little fireflies of dizzy light spun in my vision. Twinges erupted in every muscle and crispy nerve ending in my body. I gasped for air. Ella urged, "Breathe, breathe," until I nodded that I was okay.

"Oh, hell, don't be so damned modest," Ruth growled. "You kept Aunt Olly from roasting and you saved the chapel from worse damage by throwing the lamps outside. We're going to bronze you and put you on a pedestal."

"Absolutely," Isabel chimed. She dropped into a chair. "I've felt awfully sorry for myself for a long time," she said. "Simon was killed, and Gib was hurt so badly, and in the middle of it all I discovered my husband was the woman-chasing loser I'd always known he was, deep down. So I left him, and here I was, a grown woman living at home again, with a little boy to raise, divorced, and—" She halted, her throat working. "It's awfully easy to think, woe is me. But you've shown me how much courage really matters. Unselfish courage. I will *not* dwell on unhappiness anymore. Thank you."

Min stood as straight as a symphony conductor with her bony, hard-worked hands clasped in front of khaki trousers. "My husband always knew better than to value buildings over people," Min said. "He loved the chapel but he'd rejoice today because no one was hurt. Vee, my husband believed we receive what we give. You gave us selfless loyalty. I intend to draw from your example. Thank you for reminding me that miracles still happen."

"Vee's got to get some rest now," Ella announced in a worried voice. "She's very pale."

"No more heroics for now, Nellic," Gib said gently.

"I love all of you," I said.

When I woke up again the light was dim and I smelled the concrete scent of winter rain. The room was shadowy except for the lemon glow from a lamp covered in a fringed, yellow-flowery shade. My hands stung like the mother of all sun-burns, and even the slightest movement of my head made a tourniquet of nerves tighten down the right side of my spine. I lay on my back, staring up at the bed's yellow canopy. I finally craned my head enough to find the clock on the room's fire-place mantel. It was late afternoon.

Even turning my head an inch made me feel as if some-one were cracking my spine. I spent several seconds blinking and taking deep breaths to get myself under control, trying to focus. From the corner of one eye I saw rain trickling down a window's wavy, oversized antique panes. I heard the sighs of the Hall—heavy oak floors creaking, odds and ends of ac-tivity, doors shutting—and then, ominously, a sound that could only be the give-and-take of many voices downstairs.

I got out of bed, a maneuver that left me sweaty, sick to my stomach, and dizzy. I crept to the room's open door and then down the long hall, wobbling, inching along, my hands twitching painfully inside the gauze mitts, my back muscles cramping. I glimpsed myself in a gilt-framed mirror over a side table cluttered with two dozen Cameron family snap-shots in a hodgepodge of picture frames.

It was as if I'd been added to the Cameron family gallery, and I wasn't a noble accessory. I was dressed in a plaid, long-sleeved, floor-length flannel gown I suspected was one of Min's. My face was speckled with red marks. My eyebrows and eyelashes were singed. I eased down the staircase and made my way to the den. The voices grew louder, and took form.

"The early evidence," someone said, "supports a clear

case of malicious arson. Mr. Nolan here is a consultant for the state fire marshal's office." The snide tone, the patronizing inflections. *Emory*. Emory was there. "I asked him to check out the chapel discreetly because he can make precisely this kind of quick analysis. And he absolutely believes the fire couldn't have been accidental."

"Aunt Olivia did *not* set the fire with any deliberate or malicious goal in mind," I heard Gib say. "She lit a lamp and dropped it. I don't know why she got the candles out. I don't know how or why she hid the burned hymn books and the rug in the woods. But there's no doubt in my mind that she didn't mean to set a fire."

"Whatever happened last night was entirely unintentional," Min added. "Aunt Olivia's been upset about Bea's condition. She's not herself."

"Not herself?" Emory's voice, again. "Are we talking about the same woman I've known all my life? The fire was an accident? Was it an *accident* when she poisoned her husband fifty years ago?"

"That's an insulting analogy," Ruth said.

"Let's consider a different scenario then. The only other person involved. Venus."

"Don't you dare!" Ella's voice was a soft shriek.

"We're not even going to discuss that," Gib said, in a cold tone.

"All right, all right," Emory conceded. "But someone started that fire—and I'm going to find out who and why and what for. I'm not saying formal charges must be brought, but I *am* saying that if we have a firebug among us she must be identified and controlled with humane but appropriate measures."

"You want to lock Aunt Olivia up?" Isabel asked in breathy shock.

"If she's suffering some kind of dementia, there are many fine nursing homes in Knoxville—"

"Forget it," Gib said, cutting Emory off.

"Gib, my only concern is protecting our heritage. I believe everyone but you and Olivia is ready to admit the opening weekend was a disaster. It is *clearly* time to turn this property over to new management. Now, Aunt Olivia is *technically* the only person who can make that decision, but if someone was to have her declared incompetent—"

"You scheming son of a bitch," Gib said, and then there were crashing sounds, and a myriad of raised voices. I clawed my way down the hallway and staggered into the den. Min, Isabel, Carter, and Ruth were pulling Gib away from Emory. Gib had his hands around Emory's throat. A well-dressed stranger—Mr. Nolan, the arson expert—stood nearby, gaping at the scene. Joey lurked beside him. Ella, who stood to my left cradling a sleeping Dylan in her arms, turned and saw me. "Vee! What are you doing out of bed!"

Gib released Emory and strode toward me. "You don't need to be part of this mess tonight," he said, but when he moved to pick me up I stopped him. I had come to Tennessee to reclaim memories of Mom and Pop's happiness—of our family's right to be happy. But happy memories couldn't survive in the silences between failures. I had brought Ella here, and together we'd destroyed what was left of our fantasies. What was left of our family's music. Sooner or later, if I didn't stop this, either Olivia would be blamed for another crime of the heart, or Ella's ring would be discovered at the chapel and she would be accused, ruined, punished.

"I did it," I announced, looking straight into Gib's eyes. "I set the fire."

Silence. I was the center of a hot universe, feeling the stares from everyone. Gib's gaze never left my face. I thought my heart would break—he would hate me, he would turn away. He searched my eyes with strange calm, an intensity that went beyond surprise, and then he said softly, "You're not capable of destroying the chapel. You almost died trying to save it."

That was the faith he had in me, not knowing that I'd lied

to him already, a sin of omission. "I set the damned fire," I in-sisted shakily. "I did it because I wanted revenge for what this family did to Ella. I was going to take Ella and leave last night. But I went back to see if the chapel was burning, and I found Olivia there. I couldn't let her be hurt. The fire wasn't her fault. It was mine."

"You're only trying to take the blame off Olivia," Ella cried, "because we owe her so much for her kindness. Don't honor her by sacrificing yourself. I'm sure she doesn't want that."

Carter rushed to Ella's side. He handed Dylan to Isabel then put his arms around Ella tightly. "Vee's a hellcat," he said, "but I don't believe she's a firebug."

"I don't believe it, either," Isabel said.

"You loved that chapel," Min added quietly. "Gib's right. You almost died trying to save it. You can't convince any of us you meant to harm it."

Stunned, I could only repeat, "None of you really know me or what I'm capable of doing."

Gib reached into his shirt pocket. "Oh? I think we do." He pulled out a folded sheet of paper. *My good-bye note*. He opened it and read slowly, " 'Keep the money. Keep the piano. I give it all to you openly and freely and with love. There's no way I can pay you and your family enough for making us feel wanted, at least for a few months.' "

He looked at me quietly. "So you gave up everything you originally came here for. You gave it to the family, with love. That's a strange kind of revenge."

"You're not taking me seriously, dammit—"

"For God's sake," Emory snapped. "She said she set the fire. There's no logical reason to doubt her." He rubbed the red-streaked skin above his shirt collar. "She's given you a confession. Be that as it may, I really don't want to see this public-relations soap opera get into the press or the legal sys-tem. Despite being attacked just now, I'm still willing to be as fair as anyone could be."

"Daddy's being reasonable," Joey said. "And he'll be fair when he's in charge, here, too."

Ruth stepped past him. "Shut up, Joey." She walked over to me, her gaze frozen on mine. "I hate to admit this, but I recognize a criminal when I see one, and you don't qualify."

"Aren't any of you listening to me? I said I did it."

Gib picked me up. "All right. The person you need to confess to is Olivia. Right now."

"I will," I said dully.

Bea looked bewildered as she ushered Gib and me into the parlor she shared with Olivia. She clucked at me as Gib set me in a chair across from the tea table. "My poor brave, over-wrought, singed dearies, you look the way Herself feels. Like ghosts have bit you on the arse. I'll fetch Herself. She can no' even write, she's so stiff and sore, but I know she's wanting to see you, Venus."

"Should I help you?" Gib asked. "I could carry her if she's still too sore to walk."

"She'll whack you if you pick her up. She's in no mood for pampering." Bea shuffled away.

My throat hurt, my back throbbed, and my hands felt raw inside the gauze mitts. I stared at my lap and felt Gib watching me. "Did you really think I'd believe you set the fire?" he asked in a low voice. I refused to answer him. What Ella had done stuck in my chest. "Who are you trying to protect?" Gib asked. "I need you to trust me with the truth, Nellie."

"Facts aren't the whole truth. The truth is harder to condemn."

"Are we arguing your father's case again?"

Olivia crept into the sitting room before I had to answer him. Gib stood. She leaned heavily on Bea's arm; every movement seemed an effort. The ruffled nightgown she wore with an equally ruffled robe stood out like a bell around her body. But she met my eyes with shrewd energy.

"Sit," Bea ordered Gib. When everyone was settled she gestured toward the tea table, which bore a small fresh flower arrangement in a basket. The room was filled with flowers. "Herself has received such a bounty from old friends and admirers already," Bea told us. " 'Tis certainly her due for trying to put out the fire."

Olivia scowled. Bea saw the look and scowled back. "I know that's what you were about doing. There's no shame in enjoying a bit of grandeur on your own behalf. I do no' care if some tongues are wagging." Bea gave a grand huff and frowned at us. "Herself knows what the rumors are. That she spilled the lamp. Caused the accident her own very self. But it's no' true. The fire is a mystery we must solve, dear Gib, you with your expert ways, but until then I'll no' have folks whispering that Herself may have been responsible. When she can work her poor sore hands again she'll do her explaining. Look at her hands! Swollen with arthritis due to the brave efforts she made!"

I met Olivia's blue eyes. "You won't have to explain to anyone," I said, "because I know what happened, and it wasn't your fault at all."

Olivia's fine white brows arched in surprise. Bea leaned forward. "What are you saying, child?"

"I set the fire before Olivia got to the chapel. I'm sure she found the rugs burning when she went there. I did it."

Olivia's expression frightened me. It slowly became more and more intense—shocked, upset, bewildered, angry. Gib looked concerned. He leaned toward Olivia, his eyes respectful but steady on hers. "I don't believe Vee did it," he said. "Whatever happened last night, I don't think it was deliberate. When you can write again you can tell me what you saw and what you did at the chapel."

Olivia's mouth moved in wordless fury. She shook her head. Moving her hands stiffly, she clawed at a pen and pad on the tea table. "Stop, you'll hurt your poor self!" Bea cried, snatching the writing tools away. "Calm yourself! Are you in such a fit you've lost your mind? Vee is asking for your mercy, I'm sure of that, and it tears at her soul to see she caused harm! I, for one, know what pain that means!"

After that odd comment Olivia gazed at Bea, her mouth working again, frustration obviously building to a steam inside her. She shoved her hands into Bea's ample bosom, punching her. Bea gasped. Gib and I stood quickly. Gib gently grabbed Olivia's wrists and kept her from pummeling Bea again.

"I don't understand," he said grimly. "You taught us all to be fair, to listen to both sides, to never judge people on their words alone. Why are you condemning Vee without a second thought?"

Olivia turned her tortured, enraged face up and stared at me. She trembled wildly. Her lips pursed. She swallowed with convulsive effort. She seemed so angry, she might spit at me.

"Gib, let her go," I whispered. I could barely speak myself. "I had no right to expect special treatment."

I struggled out of my chair and started for the door. Olivia kicked the tea table and it wobbled sideways then crashed to the floor. She struggled to rise from her chair. Bea shrieked. Gib knelt by her chair and firmly trapped his tiny, enraged great-aunt against his chest as if she were a child. Her hair dangled in disheveled gray shanks. She stared at me, her crystalline blue eye almost savage.

"Please, stop," I cried, backing away. "Please, don't hate me."

She flailed an arm at me. I continued to retreat. Her throat flexed convulsively. *"Not you,"* she said.

Silence. Shock. We all stared at her, incredulous. The frail, breathy, rusty little sound that had come out of her might have been an illusion. She writhed as if giving birth, breathing hard, trying to push more words to the surface. Finally they broke free.

"I set . . . the fire," she rasped.

Thirty-three

After fifty years of silence, Olivia Cameron had finally found her voice. Amazed she'd formed audible words, we were incapable of analyzing what she'd confessed. She seemed amazed, herself, afraid to try another sound.

Gib carried her into the den of the family wing. "Where's Emory?" he said.

"I politely kicked him out," Ruth answered. "At least for now."

"Good."

Bea sat beside Olivia on the couch, staring at her and murmuring, "It can be so, it can be so," like a chant to keep the voice muse from deserting. Deep inside me was a symphony, an entire music festival of relief. I had no idea how or why Olivia could have set fire to the chapel, I only knew she'd freed Ella from blame.

Min, Isabel, Ruth, Ella, and Carter clustered around her. "What happened?" Ruth demanded, studying Gib's and my expressions.

"She spoke," Gib said simply. "And she told us she started the fire."

Olivia absorbed everyone's shock with wide-eyed wonder of her own. "Let me get this straight," Ruth said. "Aunt Olivia *spoke*. Actually by God *spoke out loud* and formed recognizable words. And on top of that she said she deliberately tried to burn the chapel down?"

Gib nodded toward their great-aunt as if her solemn presence were proof enough. Ruth pulled a small footstool close to Olivia and perched on it. She laid one hand on Olivia's arm. "Aunt Olly," she began with patronizing concern, "with all my heart I want to believe you can speak again. But I *cannot* believe you started that fire on purpose."

Olivia frowned fiercely. Her throat worked. We all held our breath while she struggled. Then she said quite plainly, "You doubt my *word*?"

Min and Isabel gasped. Ella clapped her hands to her mouth. Carter whooped. Ebb and Flo, listening from a doorway as usual, screamed and ran to tell FeeMolly. Bea cried gently and silently, curling her thick, fleshy hand around one of Olivia's thin ones. Gib and I traded new incredulous looks. Ruth sat back, gaping at her annoyed great-aunt.

Olivia tasted her own lips with the tip of her tongue. She raised a hand and touched just her fingertips to her mouth, and then touched them over her heart. She looked at me, her eyes gleaming. I nodded.

The connection had been restored.

Gib questioned Olivia gently. She explained about the chapel in short, halting sentences. The explanation made no sense at that point. We were all so caught up in the miracle of hearing her voice. Each word came hard, with stilted pronunciation. Slowly a new, even more bewildering scenario of the fire emerged.

"I walked through the woods. It took a long time."

"Weren't you too tired? How did you walk that far?"

"I rested every few minutes. I know how to be patient."

"Why didn't you ask one of us to drive you?"

"I did not want an audience. I had plans."

"What kind of plans?"

"To set a fire, of course."

This stopped the progress for a second, as we looked at one another in shock. Gib shook his head slowly, frowning. He cleared his throat. "We'll come back to that point in a minute."

"I will only repeat it. Don't be so shocked."

"Let's talk about *how* you set the fire."

"I poured lamp oil on the rug. I set candles in the oil."

"All right. Then you decided you could light the candles and leave? That you'd have time to walk back to the Hall before the candles burned down and set the oil on fire?"

"No. I planned to sit outside and watch the fire. I intended to tell everyone that I did it. That was the point."

So far, her rationale had been impossible to fathom. Gib scrubbed a hand over his face and looked at her askance as each new answer was more astonishing than the last. "What happened next?"

"I lit one candle. Then I had second thoughts. I felt a presence around me. I sat down to consider it."

"A presence? You mean Vee found you, then?"

"No. She came later."

Isabel said eagerly, "Then you mean you felt a *spiritual* presence?"

Olivia glanced at Ella then looked straight at me. My heart raced. Oh, yes, it must have been a *spiritual* dilemma, having my sleepwalking sister glide in unannounced. I could imagine Ella sitting down on the floor, dazedly admiring the flames of the candles. Olivia must have been flabbergasted when Ella curled up on the floor and went to sleep.

"Yes," Olivia said. "I believe an angel visited me."

Gib rubbed his jaw and sighed. "What did you do after you sat down for a while?"

After I found Ella and hustled her away, I added silently.

Olivia looked at everyone calmly. "I started to light more candles. But I dropped the match and the oil caught on fire. It startled me. I moved away too fast. I slipped on the oil and fell. I hit my head."

"Did you black out?"

"Yes. When I woke up, Venus was there." She wheezed a little. Tears glistened in her eyes. "I was afraid we would both die. She wouldn't leave me."

"I guess I'm stubborn, like you," I said.

"Now wait a minute," Ruth interjected. "Aunt Olly, I'm sorry to pressure you, but we can't avoid this *slightly* important point. *Why did you want to burn the chapel?*"

Olivia hesitated. Until then she'd been firm and sure. But now her eyes clouded and she seemed lost in troubled thought. "Emory's investors," she said slowly, "might not spend their money where a crazy old woman would start more fires."

"Aunt Olly," Min said in a low voice, "no matter what I considered doing before, let me tell you something now. I would *never* agree to Emory's proposal now. Simon wouldn't want a museum built in his name that way. It wouldn't honor him at all."

Olivia looked at Min tenderly. "I was only afraid we'd all forget what is important, the way we did after Simon died. We are no saints. But we are not victims, either." She looked at Bea when she said that.

Bea gasped softly. She understood some implication that evaded the rest of us. Her face convulsed with tenderness and sorrow. "Were you trying to gather shame about yourself so I'd stop grieving over my own shame?"

"I love you," Olivia said. "And if you are evil, then I will be evil, too. Now I am notorious again. Let Emory do what he likes with our letters. The world has changed. We shouldn't be ashamed anymore."

Letters. This was new information. Everyone leaned closer. Bea and Olivia gazed at us stoically. Gib said carefully, "Are these mysterious *letters* what upset you two? Is

that what Emory whispered about the last time he was here?"
Gib's mouth tightened. "Is that what upset Bea so much that
she had a stroke?"

Olivia looked at Bea. Their silent, poignant communication held a lifetime of shared joy and pain. A lifetime of
shared strength. "Let me speak for us," Bea said quietly. "It's
such a dear old habit."

Olivia nodded wearily. Bea faced everyone. "When we
were young, Herself's husband—I will no' call that monster
by his name—Herself's husband stole our letters. Letters I
wrote to Herself before she married the bastard, and after,
too. I was foolish and impulsive. Herself was so unhappy. She
could no' stay with me in Scotland—it just wasn't done. She
had to make a proper marriage. But she never meant to marry
a *beast*. I wanted so much for her to run away from him. But
she would no' do it. She'd made vows, she said. She had her
bairns to think of."

"You wrote . . . indiscreet letters to her?" Isabel asked
gently.

"I wrote *my love* to her," Bea corrected firmly. She
sighed. "Her husband found the letters and stole them to torment her. He used them to bully Herself."

"You mean he threatened to tell the family about her rela-
tionship with you?" Ruth asked.

"Aye. What a shame it would have been. People had no
sense. Herself worried that her children would be tormented
if others knew about us."

Min touched her shoulder. "How did Emory get the
letters?"

"Old Raymond Cameron, Emory's father, he was tight
with Herself's husband, up in Knoxville. They were thick as
thieves. Did business together. Kept rooms at the Greenbriar
gentlemen's club. But they were no gentlemen."

"I know about that place," Min told us. "The Greenbriar
Town Club. One of my grandfathers was a member. Bankers,

judges, politicians—you know, every man who was prominent in Knoxville society back then. The club bought the old
Marker mansion. It was very elegant and very private. Some
of the members kept apartments or offices there. I grew up
hearing rumors that my grandfather went there to drink and
gamble."

"Aye," Bea said, nodding. "Herself's husband kept the
letters locked up at that bloody club. And when the murdering
bastard went to his bloody demise"—Olivia stared grimly at
the floor when Bea said that, but Bea's eyes glinted with
sarcasm—"Raymond, Emory's father, being a *dear* bloody
friend and relative by marriage—Emory's father went to the
club and took our letters. Emory came into them later, by inheritance. We knew this, Herself and I, we've suspected for
years he had them. But he ne'er quite had the bloody *balls* to
admit it, before. Or to threaten Herself with them."

Silence. The implications and innuendo needed very little time to sink in. I'd often watched Bea and Olivia together,
and wondered. What I'd wondered about them was no secret
to Gib, his sisters, or Min. I could see years of quiet acceptance on their faces.

Agony began to seep into Bea's eyes. "I blame myself for
provoking Herself's husband to the worst of his mean nature." Bea paused. "And so, when the jealous moods were on
him, *he shook her wee bairns to death.*" She broke down then,
and cried.

"There was no one to blame but *him*," Olivia said. "And
me. I stayed with him out of shame and vanity and fear. How
silly I was! He hurt our children because he was a cruel man
straight to his soul. If it hadn't been about your letters it
would have been something else. *I will not be afraid again.* I
will not allow shame to condemn anyone else I love. *I will
speak and be heard.*"

"I love you so dearly," Bea said.

Olivia leaned close to Bea, kissed her cheek, then sang a

low, crooning sound to her. Such an odd, sweet, dovelike noise, the soft melody of old heartaches and redemption.

I knew it well.

While Gib and Bea helped Olivia back to bed, the rest of us looked at one another in quiet amazement. Ella sank onto the couch. "Lesbians," she said gently. "We've certainly come full circle, haven't we? There's a symmetry in it. From playing a lesbian nightclub in Chicago to being taken underwing by two wonderful old ladies who love each other in that way."

"Hon, it took you this long to figure it out?" Carter teased gently. "I thought you knew."

"Yes, but all these years, Emory's been trying to scare Aunt Olly into accepting his plan?" Isabel asked. "Isn't that extortion?"

Ruth's eyes narrowed to predatory slits. "That's blackmail," she said softly. "All this time I thought he was greedy but honest."

"You've been known to be pathetically *wrong* about people," I said.

"Is there any doubt that we're finished with him?" Min asked. "I could never sanction any deal with him now."

"We're more than finished with him," Ruth confirmed. She gazed at me. "And by the way, regarding that remark you just made, *kiss my ass*. Who are you to tell me I'm no judge of human nature? You've got so little sense you intended to take the rap for Aunt Olly. You're supposed to hate us but you *love us*. You were going to run off into the night with Ella in tow, and donate all your inheritance to us. You're a great one to lecture me about my judgment. Hell, there'll even come a day when you'll decide you like *me*."

"Anything's possible," I said. "When pigs fly."

. . .

Gib carried me down the hallway. "You tote well," he said.

"You're sure she wants to see me again tonight?" I fretted.

"Her voice is so hoarse she can barely talk, but she keeps drawing a V on her notepad."

"Maybe she wants a vodka martini."

He smiled. When he carried me into Olivia's bedroom I gazed down into her somber blue eyes. She lay in her bed like a queenly elf in a pale ivory robe, revealing a nightgown collar of ivory lace and ribbons at her throat. Her gray hair streamed down her shoulders in frizzled waves. A fringe around her face stuck up in singed tufts, like a halo, and red burn splotches peppered her dough-soft complexion.

Bea sat in a chair at the foot of the bed. She patted my foot as I dangled in Gib's arms. "Thank you for coming back, dearie. Seeing you is a comfort to Herself." She gestured to Gib. "Just set Venus on the bed beside the old doll."

Gib lowered me carefully.

"Hello," Olivia said in a tired whisper.

"Hello," I answered.

She began inching toward me. I watched speechlessly as she moved with painful determination, hunching down beside me until, finally, she laid her head on my shoulder. "Thank you," she said.

"There's nothing to thank me for."

"The heart's silence is a terrible burden," she whispered. "Not a shield."

I laid one of my bandaged hands on her head, stroking her hair. "I know," I whispered back.

Allegra was curled like a black fur hat atop the delicate old lemon-colored chenille bedspread. It was so late the night felt ancient, and the room was shadowy. Outside the window there were no streetlights, no cars on any public road, no pinpoints of airplanes moving high across the night sky. Darkness in the mountains of Tennessee whispered that wild, dangerous animals still lurked close by. That only the good spirits inside a house could fight off the evil spirits hiding outside in that blackness. I drew a tight breath until I heard Gib moving around the room. He switched on a lamp.

I was cocooned in pillows and swaddled in my mother's gift. "You could lie down beside me," I said to Gib.

"You're a mind reader now?" He sat down then gently traced my lips with the tip of his finger. He looked so good in a soft blue shirt, open at the throat, with leather suspenders and faded jeans.

"I see all, I know all," I whispered. "I am elevated to a high spiritual plane on narcotics and thousands of goose feathers."

With him close above me, looking down at me while I looked up, we were suddenly just simply studying each other. He kissed me. "I've been answering E-mail from people who heard about the chapel. Media requests for information. Historical societies wanting to know how they can help. Ruth's working on that part of it, too. The reaction is a helluva thing. It confirms how many people prize this valley just the way it is."

"I could have told you that. The chapel didn't have to burn to prove it. I'm so sorry."

He tilted his head and eyed me curiously. "Why do you keep saying you're sorry?"

"It seems a long time since you accused me of anything. I miss being a troublemaker."

"I can honestly accuse you of changing my life for the better. Of making me happy. Of making yourself such a special part of this family that I don't know what we'd do without you. What *I'd* do without you. If you want to talk about something, then let's talk about this." He cupped my face in his hands. "On the day we finish restoring the chapel, you marry me. Marry me in the chapel, that same day. That's the best luck we can bring to it."

"You may not want me, after I tell you the truth."

He drew back, frowning. "What?"

I took a deep breath. In a slow, halting voice I told him about the fire, and Ella. What I'd seen, what I'd done, what I'd meant to run from. How I'd feared my own sister had set the fire that nearly killed Olivia and damaged the most cherished symbol of his family heritage. He watched me with no outward reaction. I was beyond tears. I wanted to touch him but felt I didn't have the right to ask for or give simple sympathy.

When I finished speaking he reached into his pants pocket. "I meant to give this back to her tonight," he said, "but in all the commotion, I forgot."

He held up Ella's wedding band.

I stared at the gleaming diamond-and-gold ring. I was afraid to ask, but finally forced the words. "Where did you find it?"

"I dug it out of a melted candle at the chapel."

I shut my eyes. "You knew all along. You knew she'd been there. That she must be the one I was trying to protect."

"Yes. I was afraid that was the case."

I looked at him tearfully. "Why didn't you say something, at least to me?"

"Because I hoped you'd tell me yourself. That you'd trust me. It took a helluva effort to keep quiet tonight when you started taking the blame." He bent over me. There were tears in his eyes. "Did you really want to leave me?"

"No. Never."

"I just needed to hear you say so." He pulled my letter from his pocket again, and read the rest of it aloud. " 'I loved you even before I met you, I love you now, and I'll always love you.' " He folded the letter and laid it on the nightstand. Then he carefully gathered me in his arms and stretched out on the bed beside me. "Every time I think of all the reasons I love you," he said, "what you did tonight will be at the top of the list."

Thirty-four

I think Ruth saw the face of her parents' murderers, the Irish terrorists who set the bomb, in every person she prosecuted, and Gib had seen them in every face in every crowd he worked as an agent. Isabel submerged the tragedy in her fantasy art. Only Simon had invited it into his life, by inviting strangers to Cameron Hall and making them friends, as if in some way he could transform the hatred and lunacy in the world by bringing it to the heart of the family.

All four of the siblings had searched for sense and justice, but then Simon left them, refueling all that bewilderment and free-floating anger at fate and circumstance. I think I was welcome at first because I put a face on survival. But I was also the hard-eyed outside world personified. How does a person fight fate? Simon's death and Gib's injury, Isabel's ill-chosen husband and Ella's headlong romantic impulses, were evidence that fate chooses first.

I was pondering all that when Ruth drove over to the Waterfall Lodge a few days after the fire. I rocked on the front porch, dressed in a sweater and jeans, warm enough for a mild winter afternoon. I was testing my newly unbandaged hands on my keyboard, which was set up in front of me.

When I saw Ruth the hairs rose on the back of my neck. She was still an uncertain force of nature, Rubenesque in her combination of heft and delicacy, fashionably suited, with bright red power scarves peeking from the necklines or pockets of her deep blue pin-striped dress suits, and her brunette hair twisted up in elaborate knots. She always made me think of Wagner's Valkyries. All she needed to complete the image was a pair of fat blond braids and a horned Viking helmet. She marched up the cottage walkway, a sleek alligator-skin purse bouncing on one hip. "Howdy, *kin*," she drawled, scowling.

"Howdy. What's shaking in the Matlock business today?"

She snorted. "You are *some* piece of work. Here I come to be nice and neighborly, and you bite me on the proverbial ass. Remember, my cousin sleeps with your sister. You're sleeping with my brother. You're going to be my sister-in-law."

"Go ahead. Ruin my day."

"Yep." She pulled two corncob pipes from her purse. Real corncobs, with stems made from river cane. "Let's smoke to a truce," Ruth said. "I make these pipes myself. They're the best smokin' around. Sweet. I rub honey into the bowls and the stems. And the tobacco is local. Good Tennessee-mountain top-grade homegrown *tobaccy*. I've already packed the cobs for us. You up for the Tennessee equivalent of a peace pipe?"

I stared at the pipes, took the one she thrust toward me, and nodded. "Will this give me any urges to slap my legs and yell hee-haw?"

"Only if you're lucky."

I was going to be sick as a dog. She handed me a sleek gold lighter. "Flick the flame and suck the stem," Ruth ordered. "You've heard that before, I bet."

"Shut up." Pop had smoked a pipe. Usually filled with marijuana, but a pipe nonetheless. So I knew the technique. I got my pipe lit then put on a good show of rocking and puffing while Ruth lit her pipe.

"Here's to treaties between the sisterhood," she announced. She puffed on her pipe, then held it out to me. "Trade."

We traded. "Here's to treaties," I echoed, eyeing her warily.

"Now, here's the thing," Ruth said contemplatively. "When you and Ella came here I said, They want that money. That's all. When Ella married Carter I said, She wants more money." Ruth hesitated. "Well, I'm here to say, *Case closed*. I was wrong."

"That's a given," I said coldly.

"Oh, hell," she went on blithely, "and about your daddy? We may all seem ready for sainthood around here, but the fact is we've got enough skeletons in our closet to keep us from being too judgmental. You already know about Aunt Olivia murderin' her own husband—a morally justified killing, of course, but let me tell you, there are a lot of other bones in the closet that don't rattle so kindly. There were Camerons who helped the government kick the Cherokees out—Camerons who turned their backs on our own MacIntosh kin. There were Camerons in the Klan. There was a Cameron out in Texas who burned down a courthouse in the nineteen thirties and shot the county judge and five jurors as they ran out the front door. My point is, whatever your daddy did or didn't do, it's clear you and Ella aren't going around burning any flags." She paused. "Or chapels."

"But you won't catch me saluting any flags, either."

She sighed. "If you stick around, and I do get elected president some year, will you say 'No comment' when reporters come to interview you and the rest of my colorful kin?"

"Can't make any promises."

"How's about I let you visit the White House and scribble old hell-raising Joan Baez songs on the bathroom walls?"

I couldn't help laughing. "All right." I nodded. My head

buzzed with the smoke. "If that's an apology, I accept it." I just wanted her to leave so I could stagger indoors and throw up.

Ruth clicked her pipe to mine. "Here's to smoke and mirrors," she said. I nodded sickly.

Pipe dreams and conversations with Camerons were hard on the stomach.

· · ·

Imagine this scene, gentle readers. We witnessed it firsthand: Beautiful classical pianist Vee Arinelli—the newest addition to Cameron Hall's fine entertainments— was trapped atop a picturesque farm shed with a terrified baby in her arms. Below her, a savage bear threatened to attack. To the rescue came Gib Cameron, brandishing an heirloom Scottish claymore, the proud sword of his Cameron Highland kinsmen.

Risking his own life and limb, Gib refused to slay the giant, furious bear, but instead gallantly and gracefully thwarted the creature's every vicious move, until finally— as both the man and the violent beast dripped blood from honorable wounds—the bear retreated.

And then, his bloody sword propped proudly on his shoulder, and the rescued damsel in distress embracing him in gratitude, Gib Cameron walked humbly—as expected of a true gentleman warrior and former Secret Service agent—amid his cheering guests.

Picture that, gentle readers, because that is what we guests at Cameron Hall experienced this winter. We cheered a modern battle as wild and exciting as any storyteller's tale of the glorious Tennessee frontier.

Cameron Hall, dear readers, is better than ever.

When the Manchesters' travel column began to circulate, Min took another hundred calls for reservations in one day's time.

"This is embarrassing," Gib said as we all read the article. "Distorted, melodramatic, and way over the top. I poked an aggravated mother bear with the claymore, and she ran once her babies were free. It's not as if she fenced with me for points."

"At least they didn't call you a damsel in distress," I said.

Min shushed us. "You created a fantasy. You made people remember how it felt to be part of something special here." She paused. "You made me remember, too. Now I'm sure we'll be all right. What happened to Simon is hard on guests who've been coming here for years, people who liked Simon. I was afraid this would never be thought of again as a happy place to spend time. But people want to see what's new. They want to see Gib. They want to see you, Venus."

"You're kidding."

"You're new and fresh. Someone interesting. They won't have to pretend nothing's changed."

I didn't know what to say. My whole life had changed.

Olivia studied the Manchesters' article. "As I told you once before," she said calmly, "all we needed were one or two wise souls who looked beyond the insignificant." She then resorted to her old silent habit, which seemed appropriate for the task. She scrawled across the top of the article:

They saw bravery and loyalty. Hospitality and hard work.
Everything they saw was true.

Gib had already begun the restoration work on the chapel, with Bo Burton's help. Bo opted for early retirement from his state forestry commission position. He came to Gib and Min with ideas for the valley's preservation. He and Isabel and Ella had cooked up some plans for placing a few handsome, cozy log cabins in the lower hills, out of sight from us and each other. These wouldn't be new structures; Isabel had been in contact with various Cameron kin throughout the south who had old cabins they'd donate.

Bo and I were talking about a small music pavilion, nothing fancy, maybe just a covered outdoor stage at first. He had drawn up some modest plans for a small museum.

The Simon Cameron Center. Not the elaborate, expensive operation Emory had promised us, but a good start. It could grow. Gib planned to use chestnut logs in the building. Simon's museum would be birthed from the earth of the valley, built by his own loved ones, nurtured and promoted and cherished. Min had lovingly approved the plans.

This would all take time—years, decades even. But time was a slow song in a place where the memories of more than two centuries still whispered in our ears.

Min was appointed to invite Emory back. He immediately assumed the family had decided to accept his proposal. We went to the chapel to wait for him. We set up a celebration in its charred interior, spread fresh rugs on the floor, brought in folding chairs and picnic tables covered in antique Cameron linens, the best china and silver, bottles of champagne, and a feast of FeeMolly's food.

And we waited.

When Emory arrived he brought a slender leather folder containing what he called "just a simple two-page agreement to agree" that he expected everyone to sign. And he brought corpulent, smugly smiling Joseph, and an even beefier stranger whom Emory introduced as a security expert he had already hired to begin overseeing the property. "Since no one except myself considers Aunt Olivia a serious threat to our lives or property," Emory said, "my first priority will be installing an alarm system and sprinklers. My security man advises placing locks on the chapel door once the renovation is underway. Also encasing the stained-glass windows in Plexiglas shields."

Emory snapped his fingers. Joseph handed him a small wooden box with a gold latch on it. "A gift for you," he said to Olivia, who sat in one of the chapel's heavy, ornate, smoke-damaged armchairs. Bea stood beside her. Emory bowed slightly and put the box on her lap.

"My own letters cannot be a *gift*," she said. "You've merely returned stolen property."

Emory snapped upright. He gaped at her. His gaze darted to the rest of us. "When did she start talking again?"

"When the truth needed a voice," Olivia said evenly. "And the truth is, Emory, we've brought you here to make it official. You're banished."

"What? Again? Now really, this is ludicrous. We had an understanding."

"Blackmail is no understanding, you bloody bastard," Bea intoned.

She stepped forward and cuffed the side of his head so hard he lurched into Joseph, who caught him. Mouths open, stunned, both men stared at us. "You can't back out now," Joseph said. "There's a clear agreement."

"No one agreed to anything," Gib said. "You made your own assumptions and they were wrong."

"Perversion," Emory rasped, clasping the side of his head and staring at Bea and Olivia. "You've lived your lives in perversion and have always been a goddamned embarrassment to my family and to all of our relatives who are decent-minded—"

"You're banished," Gib said. He took Emory by one arm. Carter bounded forward and planted a hand on Joseph's arm. Gib jerked his head toward the chapel door. "Take your father out of here and get him out of this valley before I forget he's kin and hit him myself."

"I can't allow this—" the security man said, stepping in-between.

"I think you better keep out of it," I said to the man.

"Sir, remove your hands from Mr. Emory." The security expert pointed to Carter. "You, too."

"I think you better stay out of this," Gib agreed calmly. "This is a family argument. It could get more violent."

The security man thrust an arm around Gib's chest. The next moment the security expert was lying on the floor with his nose broken, courtesy of Gib's right fist, which had the compact effect of a punch with the end of a thick stick. Gib helped him up. The man clasped a hand to his bleeding face. "I don't want to work for Camerons," he said grimly, and walked out.

With much sputtering of obscenities and righteous indignation, Emory and Joseph were escorted by the whole group of us down the chapel steps and to their car. "You can't do this!" Emory shouted. "None of you! And you—" he pointed a finger in Gib's face, "you'll come to me in a year or two begging for help. You have no authority! You have no business trying to manage the Hall or this valley or be the head of a family! You're disabled! You're pathetic!"

"You're banished," Gib repeated. "It's permanent."

"You have no right to make these ridiculous pronouncements! Who do you think you are?"

Gib turned his back, walked to our group, nodded to Min, who nodded back, and to Olivia, who stood with Bea at the top of the chapel mound. She inclined her head. Gib pivoted and looked at Emory quietly.

"I'm The Cameron," he said.

We celebrated. Gib and Carter went outside the chapel and returned, carrying the organ. Jasper lugged its stool in behind them. They set both carefully on the smoke-blackened chestnut floor, which proved itself by not giving so much as a single sigh of protest.

Ella and I smiled at each other. We went to the organ. I sat down and played "Evening Star," while she sang the lyrics. When we finished, Min slipped out the door and walked down to the cemetery. "Should we leave her alone?" Isabel asked softly.

"Give her a minute," Ruth suggested. "Then we'll all go down there."

Eventually we followed her, all of us in a quiet procession.

Bo Burton brought up the rear. Before I realized it, he had stopped. He stayed back at the edge of the woods.

Min stood at the foot of Simon's grave, which was marked by a simple gray stone. When she looked at us there were tears on her face, but she smiled. "I think he knows," she said. "We're all going to be fine, now. And he's so proud."

"I swear to you, Min," Gib said, "we'll build the history center. We'll set up a foundation and work from there. It won't be funded by moneymen using Simon's legacy for window dressing; it'll be built and paid for and managed by people who loved him."

She nodded. "I know we'll do it. This family is his legacy, and it won't let him down." She looked tenderly at each of us, and finally at Kelly and Jasper, who came forward and put their arms around her. "He's already been honored," Min whispered.

"Bo's hitting the trail," Ruth announced bluntly. She pointed. He was walking toward his car, which was parked in the chapel drive along the woods.

"He's just trying to be formal," Min said uneasily. "He doesn't butt into family events that are this intimate."

"Yeah," Ruth grunted, "but if you keep treating him this way the day will come when he drives off and doesn't come back. Is that what you want, Minnie? You think Simon wants you to be alone for the rest of your life?"

"Mama, go tell Bo to come back," Kelly whispered.

"It's okay," Jasper added. "Dad always liked him. We like him, too."

Min whipped around and gazed tearfully at Simon's grave. "Minnie, look," Ella said in soft awe. She bent near the tombstone and picked a small white feather from the grass.

Isabel uttered a soft *oh* of delight. "A feather," she said. "Minnie, it's a sign."

Minnie pivoted and hurried after Bo, calling his name. He stopped. His head came up. He gazed at her with amazement as she walked up to him. She spoke to him for a moment, then took his arm. A stunned smile lit his face.

The two of them walked back together.

I wandered over to my sister and eyed her with flinty suspicion. "Did you plant that feather?"

She gazed at me innocently. "No. It fell out of my hand."

After a moment, I hugged her. A sign is a sign, and people find their wings in the strangest places.

Gib and I sat by the spring with our bare feet dangling in the warm water. It was almost dark. The day had dissolved into soft tones. From where we sat the sky was a deep cobalt-blue above a rim of gold along the mountaintops. The bare winter trees around the spring opened our view to a wide panorama of the heavens.

"Look," he said in a hushed voice. He pointed to the spring's mirror-surface. At almost the center of the pool we saw the white pinpoint reflection of the evening star.

"It can't be," I whispered. I scanned the sky, what we could see of it. "I can't find the new moon, much less Venus."

"Over there," Gib said, gesturing through the lacework of treetops. "Just now rising."

We gazed from the sky to the water's glimmering reflection. "It's true," he said. "I always wanted to believe it could happen. Now I know."

I held his hand tightly. "When the stars are right, we have to believe in them."

"That's not hard to do anymore."

He kissed me. We slid our hands together, just under the surface of the water, mingling with the reflection. The namesake my mother had given me, and my father had preserved, when Gib was a hopeful child and I was no larger than a star's shadow, now lay like a diamond in our palms.

About the Author

A former newspaper editor and multiple award winner for her novels and contemporary romances, DEBORAH SMITH lives in the mountains of Georgia.